Raymond Carver was born in 1939. He was a Guggenheim Fellow in 1979 and has twice been awarded grants by the National Endowment for the Arts. He has taught at the University of Iowa, the University of Texas, and the University of California. As well as these books of short fiction, he has published three collections of poetry. Raymond Carver died in 1988.

The Stories of Raymond Carver

Will You Please Be Quiet, Please?
What We Talk About When We Talk About Love
Cathedral

**published by Pan Books
in association with Collins**

Will You Please Be Quiet, Please? first published in the
United States of America 1976 by Alfred A. Knopf Inc.
© Raymond Carver 1963, 1964, 1965, 1966, 1967, 1968, 1969, 1970, 1971, 1972,
1973, 1974, 1975, 1976
What We Talk About When We Talk About Love first published in the
United States of America 1981 by Alfred A. Knopf Inc.
© Raymond Carver 1974, 1976, 1978, 1980, 1981
Cathedral first published in the United States of America 1983 by
Alfred A. Knopf Inc.
© Raymond Carver 1981, 1982, 1983

This collected Picador edition published 1985 by Pan Books Ltd,
Cavaye Place, London SW10 9PG
in association with Collins
19 18 17 16 15 14 13 12 11 10
ISBN 0 330 28552 1

Some of the stories in this collection have appeared, sometimes in somewhat
different form and under different titles in the following publications:
*The Antioch Review, Antaeus, The Atlantic, Carolina Quarterly,
Chicago Review, Colorado State Review, December, Discourse, Esquire, Fiction,
Grand Street, Harper's Bazaar, Kansas Quarterly, The Missouri Review,
New England Review, North American Review, The Northwest Review, The Paris Review,
Perspective, Ploughshares, Quarterly West, Seneca Review, Sou'wester,
Tri-Quarterly, Western Humanities Review.*

'So Much Water Close To Home', 'Everything Stuck to Him'
(originally 'Distance'), and 'The Third Thing That Killed My Father Off'
(originally 'Dummy'), are from *Furious Seasons* © Raymond Carver 1977.
Reprinted by permission of Capra Pree, Santa Barbara.

'The Bridle', 'Chef's House', and 'Where I'm Calling From'
originally appeared in the *New Yorker*.

Printed and bound in Great Britain by
Richard Clay Ltd, Bungay, Suffolk

Contents

Will You Please Be Quiet, Please?

This book is for Maryann

Fat

I am sitting over coffee and cigarets at my friend Rita's and I am telling her about it.

Here is what I tell her.

It is late of a slow Wednesday when Herb seats the fat man at my station.

This fat man is the fattest person I have ever seen, though he is neat-appearing and well dressed enough. Everything about him is big. But it is the fingers I remember best. When I stop at the table near his to see to the old couple, I first notice the fingers. They look three times the size of a normal person's fingers – long, thick, creamy fingers.

I see to my other tables, a party of four businessmen, very demanding, another party of four, three men and a woman, and this old couple. Leander has poured the fat man's water, and I give the fat man plenty of time to make up his mind before going over.

Good evening, I say. May I serve you? I say.

Rita, he was big, I mean big.

Good evening, he says. Hello. Yes, he says. I think we're ready to order now, he says.

He has this way of speaking – strange, don't you know. And he makes a little puffing sound every so often.

I think we will begin with a Caesar salad, he says. And then a bowl of soup with some extra bread and butter, if you please. The lamb chops, I believe, he says. And baked potato with sour cream. We'll see about dessert later. Thank you very much, he says, and hands me the menu.

God, Rita, but those were fingers.

I hurry away to the kitchen and turn in the order to Rudy, who takes it with a face. You know Rudy. Rudy is that way when he works.

As I come out of the kitchen, Margo – I've told you about Margo? The one who chases Rudy? Margo says to me, Who's your fat friend? He's really a fatty.

Now that's part of it. I think that is really part of it.

I make the Caesar salad there at his table, him watching my every move, meanwhile buttering pieces of bread and laying them off to one side, all the time making this puffing noise. Anyway, I am so keyed up or something, I knock over his glass of water.

I'm so sorry, I say. It always happens when you get into a hurry. I'm very sorry, I say. Are you all right? I say. I'll get the boy to clean up right away, I say.

It's nothing, he says. It's all right, he says, and he puffs. Don't worry about it, we don't mind, he says. He smiles and waves as I go off to get Leander, and when I come back to serve the salad, I see the fat man has eaten all his bread and butter.

A little later, when I bring him more bread, he has finished his salad. You know the size of those Caesar salads?

You're very kind, he says. This bread is marvelous, he says.

Thank you, I say.

Well, it is very good, he says, and we mean that. We don't often enjoy bread like this, he says.

Where are you from? I ask him. I don't believe I've seen you before, I say.

He's not the kind of person you'd forget, Rita puts in with a snicker.

Denver, he says.

I don't say anything more on the subject, though I am curious.

Your soup will be along in a few minutes, sir, I say, and I go off to put the finishing touches to my party of four businessmen, very demanding.

When I serve his soup, I see the bread has disappeared again. He is just putting the last piece of bread into his mouth.

Believe me, he says, we don't eat like this all the time, he says. And puffs. You'll have to excuse us, he says.

Don't think a thing about it, please, I say. I like to see a man eat and enjoy himself, I say.

I don't know, he says. I guess that's what you'd call it. And puffs. He arranges the napkin. Then he picks up his spoon.

God, he's fat! says Leander.

He can't help it, I say, so shut up.

I put down another basket of bread and more butter. How was the soup? I say.

Thank you. Good, he says. Very good, he says. He wipes his lips and dabs his chin. Do you think it's warm in here, or is it just me? he says.

No, it is warm in here, I say.

Maybe we'll take off our coat, he says.

Go right ahead, I say. A person has to be comfortable, I say.

That's true, he says, that is very, very true, he says.

But I see a little later that he is still wearing his coat.

My large parties are gone now and also the old couple. The place is emptying out. By the time I serve the fat man his chops and baked potato, along with more bread and butter, he is the only one left.

I drop lots of sour cream onto his potato. I sprinkle bacon and chives over his sour cream. I bring him more bread and butter.

Is everything all right? I say.

Fine, he says, and he puffs. Excellent, thank you, he says, and puffs again.

Enjoy your dinner, I say. I raise the lid of his sugar bowl and look in. He nods and keeps looking at me until I move away.

I know now I was after something. But I don't know what.

How is old tub-of-guts doing? He's going to run your legs off, says Harriet. You know Harriet.

For dessert, I say to the fat man, there is the Green Lantern Special, which is a pudding cake with sauce, or there is a cheesecake or vanilla ice cream or pineapple sherbet.

We're not making you late, are we? he says, puffing and looking concerned.

Not at all, I say. Of course not, I say. Take your time, I say. I'll bring you more coffee while you make up your mind.

We'll be honest with you, he says. And he moves in the seat. We would like the Special, but we may have a dish of vanilla ice cream as well. With just a drop of chocolate syrup, if you please. We told you we were hungry, he says.

I go off to the kitchen to see after his dessert myself, and Rudy says, Harriet says you got a fat man from the circus out there. That true?

Rudy has his apron and hat off now, if you see what I mean.

Rudy, he is fat, I say, but that is not the whole story.

Rudy just laughs.

Sounds to me like she's sweet on fat-stuff, he says.

Better watch out, Rudy, says Joanne, who just that minute comes into the kitchen.

I'm getting jealous, Rudy says to Joanne.

I put the Special in front of the fat man and a big bowl of vanilla ice cream with chocolate syrup to the side.

Thank you, he says.

You are very welcome, I say – and a feeling comes over me.

Believe it or not, he says, we have not always eaten like this.

Me, I eat and I eat and I can't gain, I say. I'd like to gain, I say.

No, he says. If we had our choice, no. But there is no choice.

Then he picks up his spoon and eats.

What else? Rita says, lighting one of my cigarets and pulling her chair closer to the table. This story's getting interesting now, Rita says.

That's it. Nothing else. He eats his desserts, and then he leaves and then we go home, Rudy and me.

Some fatty, Rudy says, stretching like he does when he's tired. Then he just laughs and goes back to watching the T.V.

I put the water on to boil for tea and take a shower. I put my hand on my middle and wonder what would happen if I had children and one of them turned out to look like that, so fat.

I pour the water in the pot, arrange the cups, the sugar bowl, carton of half and half, and take the tray in to Rudy. As if he's been thinking about it, Rudy says, I knew a fat guy once, a couple of fat guys, really fat guys, when I was a kid. They were tubbies, my God. I don't remember their names. Fat, that's the only name this one kid had. We called him Fat, the kid who lived next door to me. He was a neighbor. The other kid came along later. His name was Wobbly. Everybody called him Wobbly except the teachers. Wobbly and Fat. Wish I had their pictures, Rudy says.

I can't think of anything to say, so we drink our tea and pretty soon I get up to go to bed. Rudy gets up too, turns off the TV, locks the front door, and begins his unbuttoning.

I get into bed and move clear over to the edge and lie there on my stomach. But right away, as soon as he turns off the light and gets into bed, Rudy begins. I turn on my back and relax some, though it is against my will. But here is the thing. When he gets on me, I suddenly feel I am fat. I feel terrifically fat, so fat that Rudy is a tiny thing and hardly there at all.

That's a funny story, Rita says, but I can see she doesn't know what to make of it.

I feel depressed. But I won't go into it with her. I've already told her too much.

She sits there waiting, her dainty fingers poking her hair.

Waiting for what? I'd like to know.

It is August.

My life is going to change. I feel it.

Neighbors

Bill and Arlene Miller were a happy couple. But now and then they felt they alone among their circle had been passed somehow, leaving Bill to attend to his bookkeeping duties and Arlene occupied with secretarial chores. They talked about it sometimes, mostly in comparison with the lives of their neighbors, Harriet and Jim Stone. It seemed to the Millers that the Stones lived a fuller and brighter life. The Stones were always going out for dinner, or entertaining at home, or traveling about the country somewhere in connection with Jim's work.

The Stones lived across the hall from the Millers. Jim was a salesman for a machine-parts firm and often managed to combine business with pleasure trips, and on this occasion the Stones would be away for ten days, first to Cheyenne, then on to St. Louis to visit relatives. In their absence, the Millers would look after the Stone's apartment, feed Kitty, and water the plants.

Bill and Jim shook hands beside the car. Harriet and Arlene held each other by the elbows and kissed lightly on the lips.

'Have fun,' Bill said to Harriet.

'We will,' said Harriet. 'You kids have fun too.'

Arlene nodded.

Jim winked at her. 'Bye, Arlene. Take good care of the old man.'

'I will,' Arlene said.

'Have fun,' Bill said.

'You bet,' Jim said, clipping Bill lightly on the arm. 'And thanks again, you guys.'

The Stones waved as they drove away, and the Millers waved too.

'Well, I wish it was us,' Bill said.

'God knows, we could use a vacation,' Arlene said. She took his arm and put it around her waist as they climbed the stairs to their apartment.

After dinner Arlene said, 'Don't forget. Kitty gets liver flavor the first night.' She stood in the kitchen doorway folding the handmade tablecloth that Harriet had bought for her last year in Santa Fe.

Bill took a deep breath as he entered the Stone's apartment. The air was already heavy and it was vaguely sweet. The sunburst clock over the television said half past eight. He remembered when Harriet had come home with the clock, how she had crossed the hall to show it to Arlene, cradling the brass case in her arms and talking to it through the tissue paper as if it were an infant.

Kitty rubbed her face against his slippers and then turned onto her side, but jumped up quickly as Bill moved to the kitchen and selected one of the stacked cans from the gleaming drainboard. Leaving the cat to pick at her food, he headed for the bathroom. He looked at himself in the mirror and then closed his eyes and then looked again. He opened the medicine chest. He found a container of pills and read the label – *Harriet Stone. One each day as directed* – and slipped it into his pocket. He went back to the kitchen, drew a pitcher of water, and returned to the living room. He finished watering, set the pitcher on the rug, and opened the liquor cabinet. He reached in the back for the bottle of Chives Regal. He took two drinks from the bottle, wiped his lips on his sleeve, and replaced the bottle in the cabinet.

Kitty was on the couch sleeping. He switched off the lights, slowly closing and checking the door. He had the feeling he had left something.

'What kept you?' Arlene said. She sat with her legs turned under her, watching television.

'Nothing. Playing with Kitty,' he said, and went over to her and touched her breasts.

'Let's go to bed, honey,' he said.

The next day Bill took only ten minutes of the twenty-minute break allotted for the afternoon and left at fifteen minutes before five. He parked the car in the lot just as Arlene hopped down from the bus. He waited until she entered the building, then ran up the stairs to catch her as she stepped out of the elevator.

'Bill! God, you scared me. You're early,' she said.

He shrugged. 'Nothing to do at work,' he said.

She let him use her key to open the door. He looked at the door across the hall before following her inside.

'Let's go to bed,' he said.

'Now?' She laughed. 'What's gotten into you?'

'Nothing. Take your dress off.' He grabbed for her awkwardly, and she said, 'Good God, Bill.'

He unfastened his belt.

Later they sent out for Chinese food, and when it arrived they ate hungrily, without speaking, and listened to records.

'Let's not forget to feed Kitty,' she said.

'I was just thinking about that,' he said. 'I'll go right over.'

He selected a can of fish flavor for the cat, then filled the pitcher and went to water. When he returned to the kitchen, the cat was scratching in her box. She looked at him steadily before she turned back to the litter. He opened all the cupboards and examined the canned goods, the cereals, the packaged foods, the cocktail and wine glasses, the china, the pots and pans. He opened the refrigerator. He sniffed some celery, took two bites of cheddar cheese, and chewed on an apple as he walked into the bedroom. The bed seemed enormous, with a fluffy white bedspread draped to the floor. He pulled out a nightstand drawer, found a half-empty package of cigarets and stuffed them into his pocket. Then he stepped to the closet and was opening it when the knock sounded at the front door.

He stopped by the bathroom and flushed the toilet on his way.

'What's been keeping you?' Arlene said. 'You've been over here more than an hour.'

'Have I really?' he said.

'Yes, you have,' she said.

'I had to go to the toilet,' he said.

'You have your own toilet,' she said.

'I couldn't wait,' he said.

That night they made love again.

In the morning he had Arlene call in for him. He showered, dressed, and made a light breakfast. He tried to start a book. He went out for a walk and felt better. But after a while, hands still in his pockets, he returned to the apartment. He stopped at the Stone's door on the chance he might hear the cat moving about. Then he let himself in at his own door and went to the kitchen for the key.

Inside it seemed cooler than his apartment, and darker too. He wondered if the plants had something to do with the temperature of the air. He looked out the window, and then he moved slowly through each room considering everything that fell under his gaze, carefully, one object at a time. He saw ashtrays, items of furniture, kitchen utensils, the clock. He saw everything. At last he entered the bedroom, and the cat appeared at his feet. He stroked her once, carried her into the bathroom, and shut the door.

He lay down on the bed and stared at the ceiling. He lay for a while with his eyes closed, and then he moved his hand under his belt. He tried to recall what day it was. He tried to remember when the Stones were due back, and then he wondered if they would ever return. He could not remember their faces or the way they talked and dressed. He sighed and with effort rolled off the bed to lean over the dresser and look at himself in the mirror.

He opened the closet and selected a Hawaiian shirt. He looked until he found Bermudas, neatly pressed and hanging over a pair of brown twill slacks. He shed his own clothes and slipped into the shorts and the shirt. He looked in the mirror again. He went to the living room and poured himself a drink and sipped it on his way back to the bedroom. He put on a blue shirt, a dark suit, a blue and white tie, black wing-tip shoes. The glass was empty and he went for another drink.

In the bedroom again, he sat on a chair, crossed his legs, and smiled, observing himself in the mirror. The telephone rang twice and fell silent. He finished the drink and took off the suit. He rummaged through the top drawers until he found a pair of panties and a brassiere. He stepped into the panties and fastened the brassiere, then looked through the closet for an outfit. He put on a black and white checkered skirt and tried to zip it up. He put on a burgundy blouse that buttoned up the front. He considered her shoes, but understood they would not fit. For a long time he looked out the living-room window from behind the curtain. Then he returned to the bedroom and put everything away.

He was not hungry. She did not eat much, either. They looked at each other shyly and smiled. She got up from the table and checked that the key was on the shelf and then she quickly cleared the dishes.

He stood in the kitchen doorway and smoked a cigaret and watched her pick up the key.

'Make yourself comfortable while I go across the hall,' she said. 'Read the paper or something.' She closed her fingers over the key. He was, she said, looking tired.

He tried to concentrate on the news. He read the paper and turned on the television. Finally he went across the hall. The door was locked.

'It's me. Are you still there, honey?' he called.

After a time the lock released and Arlene stepped outside and shut the door. 'Was I gone so long?' she said.

'Well, you were,' he said.

'Was I?' she said. 'I guess I must have been playing with Kitty.'

He studied her, and she looked away, her hand still resting on the doorknob.

'It's funny,' she said. 'You know – to go in someone's place like that.'

He nodded, took her hand from the knob, and guided her toward their own door. He let them into their apartment.

'It *is* funny,' he said.

He noticed white lint clinging to the back of her sweater, and the color was high in her cheeks. He began kissing her on the neck and hair and she turned and kissed him back.

'Oh, damn,' she said. 'Damn, damn,' she sang, girlishly clapping her hands. 'I just remembered. I really and truly forgot to do what I went over there to do. I didn't feed Kitty or do any watering.' She looked at him. 'Isn't that stupid?'

'I don't think so,' he said. 'Just a minute. I'll get my cigarets and go back with you.'

She waited until he had closed and locked their door, and then she took his arm at the muscle and said, 'I guess I should tell you. I found some pictures.'

He stopped in the middle of the hall. 'What kind of pictures?'

'You can see for yourself,' she said, and she watched him.

'No kidding.' He grinned. 'Where?'

'In a drawer,' she said.

'No kidding,' he said.

And then she said, 'Maybe they won't come back,' and was at once astonished at her words.

'It could happen,' he said. 'Anything could happen.'

'Or maybe they'll come back and . . . ' but she did not finish.

They held hands for the short walk across the hall, and when he spoke she could barely hear his voice.

'The key,' he said. 'Give it to me.'

'What?' she said. She gazed at the door.

'The key,' he said. 'You have the key.'

'My God,' she said, 'I left the key inside.'

He tried the knob. It was locked. Then she tried the knob. It would not turn. Her lips were parted, and her breathing was hard, expectant. He opened his arms and she moved into them.

'Don't worry,' he said into her ear. 'For God's sake, don't worry.'

They stayed there. They held each other. They leaned into the door as if against a wind, and braced themselves.

The idea

We'd finished supper and I'd been at the kitchen table with the light out for the last hour, watching. If he was going to do it tonight, it was time, past time. I hadn't seen him in three nights. But tonight the bedroom shade was up over there and the light burning.

I had a feeling tonight.

Then I saw him. He opened the screen and walked out onto his back porch wearing a T-shirt and something like Bermuda shorts or a swimsuit. He looked around once and hopped off the porch into the shadows and began to move along the side of the house. He was fast. If I hadn't been watching, I wouldn't have seen him. He stopped in front of the lighted window and looked in.

'Vern,' I called. 'Vern, hurry up! He's out there. You'd better hurry!'

Vern was in the living room reading his paper with the TV going. I heard him throw down the paper.

'Don't let him see you!' Vern said. 'Don't get up too close to the window!'

Vern always says that: Don't get up too close. Vern's a little embarrassed about watching, I think. But I know he enjoys it. He's said so.

'He can't see us with the light out.' It's what I always say. This has been going on for three months. Since September 3, to be exact. Anyway that's the first night I saw him over there. I don't know how long it was going on before that.

I almost got on the phone to the sheriff that night, until I recognized who it was out there. It took Vern to explain it to me. Even then it took a while for it to penetrate. But since that night I've watched, and I can tell you he averages one out of every two or three nights, sometimes more. I've seen him out there when it's been raining too. In fact, if it *is* raining, you can bet on seeing him. But tonight it was clear and windy. There was a moon.

We got down on our knees behind the window and Vern cleared his throat.

'Look at him,' Vern said. Vern was smoking, knocking the ash into his hand when he needed. He held the cigaret away from the window when he puffed. Vern smokes all the time; there's no stopping him. He even sleeps with an ashtray three inches from his head. At night I'm awake and he wakes up and smokes.

'By God,' Vern said.

'What does she have that other women don't have?' I said to Vern after a minute. We were hunkered on the floor with just our heads showing over the windowsill and were looking at a man who was standing and looking into his own bedroom window.

'That's just it,' Vern said. He cleared his throat right next to my ear.

We kept watching.

I could make out someone behind the curtain now. It must have been her undressing. But I couldn't see any detail. I strained my eyes. Vern was wearing his reading glasses, so he could see everything better than I could. Suddenly the curtain was drawn aside and the woman turned her back to the window.

'What's she doing now?' I said, knowing full well.

'By God,' Vern said.

'What's she doing, Vern?' I said.

'She's taking off her clothes,' Vern said. 'What do you think she's doing?'

Then the bedroom light went out and the man started back along the side of his house. He opened the screen door and slipped inside, and a little later the rest of the lights went out.

Vern coughed, coughed again, and shook his head. I turned on the light. Vern just sat there on his knees. Then he got to his feet and lighted a cigaret.

'Someday I'm going to tell that trash what I think of her,' I said and looked at Vern.

Vern laughed sort of.

'I mean it,' I said. 'I'll see her in the market someday and I'll tell her to her face.'

'I wouldn't do that. What the hell would you do that for?' Vern said.

But I could tell he didn't think I was serious. He frowned and looked at his nails. He rolled his tongue in his mouth and narrowed his eyes like he does when he's concentrating. Then his expression changed and he scratched his chin. 'You wouldn't do anything like that,' he said.

'You'll see,' I said.

'Shit,' Vern said.

I followed him into the living room. We were jumpy. It gets us like that.

'You wait,' I said.

Vern ground his cigaret out in the big ashtray. He stood beside his leather chair and looked at the TV a minute.

'There's never anything on,' he said. Then he said something else. He said, 'Maybe he *has* something there.' Vern lighted another cigaret. 'You don't know.'

'Anybody comes looking in my window,' I said, 'they'll have the cops on them. Except maybe Cary Grant,' I said.

Vern shrugged. 'You don't know,' he said.

I had an appetite. I went to the kitchen cupboard and looked, and then I opened the fridge.

'Vern, you want something to eat?' I called.

He didn't answer. I could hear water running in the bathroom. But I thought he might want something. We get hungry this time of night. I put bread and lunch-meat on the table and I opened a can of soup. I got out crackers and peanut butter, cold meat loaf, pickles, olives, potato chips. I put everything on the table. Then I thought of the apple pie.

Vern came out in his robe and flannel pajamas. His hair was wet and slicked down over the back of his head, and he smelled of toilet water. He looked at the things on the table. He said, 'What about a bowl of corn flakes with brown sugar?' Then he sat down and spread his paper out to the side of his plate.

We ate our snack. The ashtray filled up with olive pits and his butts.

When he'd finished, Vern grinned and said, 'What's that good smell?'

I went to the oven and took out the two pieces of apple pie topped with melted cheese.

'That looks fine,' Vern said.

In a little while, he said, 'I can't eat any more. I'm going to bed.'

'I'm coming too,' I said. 'I'll clear this table.'

I was scraping plates into the garbage can when I saw the ants. I looked closer. They came from somewhere beneath the pipes under the sink, a steady stream of them, up one side of the can and down the other, coming and going. I found the spray in one of the drawers and sprayed the outside and the inside of the garbage can, and I sprayed as far back under the sink as I could reach. Then I washed my hands and took a last look around the kitchen.

Vern was asleep. He was snoring. He'd wake up in a few hours, go to the bathroom, and smoke. The little TV at the foot of the bed was on, but the picture was rolling.

I'd wanted to tell Vern about the ants.

I took my own time getting ready for bed, fixed the picture, and crawled in. Vern made the noises he does in his sleep.

I watched for a while, but it was a talk show and I don't like talk shows. I started thinking about the ants again.

Pretty soon I imagined them all over the house. I wondered if I should wake Vern and tell him I was having a bad dream. Instead, I got up and went for the can of spray. I looked under the sink again. But there was no ants left. I turned on every light in the house until I had the house blazing.

I kept spraying.

Finally I raised the shade in the kitchen and looked out. It was late. The wind blew and I heard branches snap.

'That trash,' I said. 'The idea!'

I used even worse language, things I can't repeat.

They're not your husband

Earl Ober was between jobs as a salesman. But Doreen, his wife, had gone to work nights as a waitress at a twenty-four-hour coffee shop at the edge of town. One night, when he was drinking, Earl decided to stop by the coffee shop and have something to eat. He wanted to see where Doreen worked, and he wanted to see if he could order something on the house.

He sat at the counter and studied the menu.

'What are you doing here?' Doreen said when she saw him sitting there.

She handed over an order to the cook. 'What are you going to order, Earl?' she said. 'The kids okay?'

'They're fine,' Earl said. 'I'll have coffee and one of those Number Two sandwiches.'

Doreen wrote it down.

'Any chance of, you know?' he said to her and winked.

'No' she said. 'Don't talk to me now. I'm busy.'

Earl drank his coffee and waited for the sandwich. Two men in business suits, their ties undone, their collars open, sat down next to him and asked for coffee. As Doreen walked away with the coffeepot, one of the men said to the other, 'Look at the ass on that. I don't believe it.'

The other man laughed. 'I've seen better,' he said.

'That's what I mean,' the first man said. 'But some jokers like their quim fat.'

'Not me,' the other man said.

'Not me, neither,' the first man said. 'That's what I was saying.'

Doreen put the sandwich in front of Earl. Around the sandwich there were French fries, coleslaw, dill pickle.

'Anything else?' she said. 'A glass of milk?'

He didn't say anything. He shook his head when she kept standing there.

'I'll get you more coffee,' she said.

She came back with the pot and poured coffee for him and for the two men. Then she picked up a dish and turned to get some ice cream. She reached down into the container and with the dipper began to scoop up the ice cream. The white skirt yanked against her hips and crawled up her legs. What showed was girdle, and it was pink, thighs that were rumpled and gray and a little hairy, and veins that spread in a berserk display.

The two men sitting beside Earl exchanged looks. One of them raised his eyebrows. The other man grinned and kept looking at Doreen over his cup as she spooned chocolate syrup over the ice cream. When she began shaking the can of whipped cream, Earl got up, leaving his food, and headed for the door. He heard her call his name, but he kept going.

He checked on the children and then went to the other bedroom and took off his clothes. He pulled the covers up, closed his eyes, and allowed himself to think. The feeling started in his face and worked down into his stomach and legs. He opened his eyes and rolled his head back and forth on the pillow. Then he turned on his side and fell asleep.

In the morning, after she had sent the children off to school, Doreen came into the bedroom and raised the shade. Earl was already awake.

'Look at yourself in the mirror,' he said.

'What?' she said. 'What are you talking about?'

'Just look at yourself in the mirror,' he said.

'What am I supposed to see?' she said. But she looked in the mirror over the dresser and pushed the hair away from her shoulders.

'Well?' he said.

'Well, what?' she said.

'I hate to say anything,' Earl said, 'but I think you better give a diet some thought. I mean it. I'm serious. I think you could lose a few pounds. Don't get mad.'

'What are you saying?' she said.

'Just what I said. I think you could lose a few pounds. A few pounds, anyway,' he said.

'You never said anything before,' she said. She raised her nightgown over her hips and turned to look at her stomach in the mirror.

'I never felt it was a problem before,' he said. He tried to pick his words.

The nightgown still gathered around her waist, Doreen turned her back to the mirror and looked over her shoulder. She raised one buttock in her hand and let it drop.

Earl closed his eyes. 'Maybe I'm all wet,' he said.

'I guess I could afford to lose. But it'd be hard,' she said.

'You're right, it won't be easy,' he said. 'But I'll help.'

'Maybe you're right,' she said. She dropped her nightgown and looked at him and then she took her nightgown off.

They talked about diets. They talked about the protein diets, the vegetable-only diets, the grapefruit-juice diets. But they decided they didn't have the money to buy the steaks the protein diet called for. And Doreen said she didn't care for all that many vegetables. And since she didn't like grapefruit juice that much, she didn't see how she could do that one, either.

'Okay, forget it,' he said.

'No, you're right,' she said. 'I'll do something.'

'What about exercises?' he said.

'I'm getting all the exercise I need down there,' she said.

'Just quit eating,' Earl said. 'For a few days, anyway.'

'All right,' she said. 'I'll try. For a few days I'll give it a try. You've convinced me.'

'I'm a closer,' Earl said.

He figured up the balance in their checking account, then drove to the discount store and bought a bathroom scale. He looked the clerk over as she rang up the sale.

At home he had Doreen take off all her clothes and get on the scale. He frowned when he saw the veins. He ran his finger the length of one that sprouted up her thigh.

'What are you doing?' she asked.

'Nothing,' he said.

He looked at the scale and wrote the figure down on a piece of paper.

'All right,' Earl said. 'All right.'

The next day he was gone for most of the afternoon on an interview. The employer, a heavyset man who limped as he showed Earl around the plumbing fixtures in the warehouse, asked if Earl were free to travel.

'You bet I'm free,' Earl said.

The man nodded.

Earl smiled.

He could hear the television before he opened the door to the house. The children did not look up as he walked through the living room. In the kitchen, Doreen, dressed for work, was eating scrambled eggs and bacon.

'What are you doing?' Earl said.

She continued to chew the food, cheeks puffed. But then she spit everything into a napkin.

'I couldn't help myself,' she said.

'Slob,' Earl said. *'Go ahead, eat! Go on!'* He went to the bedroom, closed the door, and lay on the covers. He could still hear the television. He put his hands behind his head and stared at the ceiling.

She opened the door.

'I'm going to try again,' Doreen said.

'Okay,' he said.

Two mornings later she called him into the bathroom. 'Look,' she said.

He read the scale. He opened a drawer and took out the paper and read the scale again while she grinned.

'Three-quarters of a pound,' she said.

'It's something,' he said and patted her hip.

He read the classifieds. He went to the state employment office. Every three or four days he drove some-place for an interview, and at night he counted her tips. He smoothed out the dollar bills on the table and stacked the nickels, dimes, and quarters in piles of one dollar. Each morning he put her on the scale.

In two weeks she had lost three and a half pounds.

'I pick,' she said. 'I starve myself all day, and then I pick at work. It adds up.'

But a week later she had lost five pounds. The week after that, nine and a half pounds. Her clothes were loose on her. She had to cut into the rent money to buy a new uniform.

'People are saying things at work,' she said.

'What kind of things?' Earl said.

'That I'm too pale, for one thing,' she said. 'That I don't look like myself. They're afraid I'm losing too much weight.'

'What is wrong with losing?' he said. 'Don't you pay any attention to them. Tell them to mind their own business. They're not your husband. You don't have to live with them.'

'I have to work with them,' Doreen said.

'That's right,' Earl said. 'But they're not your husband.'

Each morning he followed her into the bathroom and waited while she stepped onto the scale. He got down on his knees with a pencil and the piece of paper. The paper was covered with dates, days of the week, numbers. He read the number on the scale, consulted the paper, and either nodded his head or pursed his lips.

Doreen spent more time in bed now. She went back to bed after the children had left for school, and she napped in the afternoons before going to work. Earl helped around the house, watched television, and let her sleep. He did all the shopping, and once in a while he went on an interview.

One night he put the children to bed, turned off the television, and decided to go for a few drinks. When the bar closed, he drove to the coffee shop.

He sat at the counter and waited. When she saw him, she said, 'Kids okay?'

Earl nodded.

He took his time ordering. He kept looking at her as she moved up and down behind the counter. He finally ordered a cheeseburger. She gave the order to the cook and went to wait on someone else.

Another waitress came by with a coffeepot and filled Earl's cup.

'Who's your friend?' he said and nodded at his wife.

'Her name's Doreen,' the waitress said.

'She looks a lot different than the last time I was in here,' he said.

'I wouldn't know,' the waitress said.

He ate the cheeseburger and drank the coffee. People kept sitting down and getting up at the counter. Doreen waited on most of the people at the counter, though now and then the other waitress came along to take an order. Earl watched his wife and listened carefully. Twice he had to leave his place to go to the bathroom. Each time he wondered if he might have missed hearing something. When he came back the second time, he found his cup gone and someone in his place. He took a stool at the end of the counter next to an older man in a striped shirt.

'What do you want?' Doreen said to Earl when she saw him again. 'Shouldn't you be home?'

'Give me some coffee,' he said.

The man next to Earl was reading a newspaper. He looked up and watched Doreen pour Earl a cup of coffee. He glanced at Doreen as she walked away. Then he went back to his newspaper.

Earl sipped his coffee and waited for the man to say something. He watched the man out of the corner of his eye. The man had finished eating and his plate was pushed to the side. The man lit a cigaret, folded the newspaper in front of him, and continued to read.

Doreen came by and removed the dirty plate and poured the man more coffee.

'What do you think of that?' Earl said to the man, nodding at Doreen as she moved down the counter. 'Don't you think that's something special?'

The man looked up. He looked at Doreen and then at Earl, and then went back to his newspaper.

'Well, what do you think?' Earl said. 'I'm asking. Does it look good or not? Tell me.'

The man rattled the newspaper.

When Doreen started down the counter again, Earl nudged the man's shoulder and said, 'I'm telling you something. Listen. Look at the ass on her. Now you watch this now. Could I have a chocolate sundae?' Earl called to Doreen.

She stopped in front of him and let out her breath. Then she turned and picked up a dish and the ice-cream dipper. She leaned over the freezer, reached down, and began to press the dipper into the ice cream. Earl looked at the man and winked as Doreen's skirt traveled up her thighs. But the man's eyes caught the eyes of the other waitress. And then the man put the newspaper under his arm and reached into his pocket.

The other waitress came straight to Doreen. 'Who is this character?' she said.

'Who?' Doreen said and looked around with the ice-cream dish in her hand.

'Him,' the other waitress said and nodded at Earl. 'Who is this joker, anyway?'

Earl put on his best smile. He held it. He held it until he felt his face pulling out of shape.

But the other waitress just studied him, and Doreen began to shake her head slowly. The man had put some change beside his cup and stood up, but he too waited to hear the answer. They all stared at Earl.

'He's a salesman. He's my husband,' Doreen said at last, shrugging. Then she put the unfinished chocolate sundae in front of him and went to total up his check.

Are you a doctor?

In slippers, pajamas, and robe, he hurried out of the study when the telephone began to ring. Since it was past ten, the call would be his wife. She phoned – late like this, after a few drinks – each night when she was out of town. She was a buyer, and all this week she had been away on business.

'Hello, dear,' he said. 'Hello,' he said again.

'Who is this?' a woman asked.

'Well, who is *this*?' he said. 'What number do you want?'

'Just a minute,' the woman said. 'It's 273-8063.'

'That's my number,' he said. 'How did you get it?'

'I don't know. It was written down on a piece of paper when I got in from work,' the woman said.

'Who wrote it down?'

'I don't know,' the woman said. 'The sitter, I guess. It must be her.'

'Well, I don't know how she got it,' he said, 'but it's my telephone number, and it's unlisted. I'd appreciate it if you'd just toss it away. Hello? Did you hear me?'

'Yes, I heard,' the woman said.

'Is there anything else?' he said. 'It's late and I'm busy.' He hadn't meant to be curt, but one couldn't take chances. He sat down on the chair by the telephone and said, 'I hadn't meant to be curt. I only meant that it's late, and I'm concerned how you happen to have my number.' He pulled off his slipper and began massaging his foot, waiting.

'I don't know either,' she said. 'I told you I just found the number written down, no note or anything. I'll ask Annette – that's the sitter – when I see her tomorrow. I didn't mean to disturb you. I only just now found the note. I've been in the kitchen ever since I came in from work.'

'It's all right,' he said. 'Forget it. Just throw it away or something and forget it. There's no problem, so don't worry.' He moved the receiver from one ear to the other.

'You sound like a nice man,' the woman said.

'Do I? Well, that's nice of you to say.' He knew he should hang up now, but it was good to hear a voice, even his own, in the quiet room.

'Oh, yes,' she said. 'I can tell.'

He let go his foot.

'What's your name, if you don't mind my asking?' she said.

'My name is Arnold,' he said.

'And what's your first name?' she said.

'Arnold is my first name,' he said.

'Oh, forgive me,' she said. 'Arnold is your *first* name. And your second name, Arnold? What's your second name?'

'I really must hang up,' he said.

'Arnold, for goodness sake, I'm Clara Holt. Now *your* name is Mr. Arnold what?'

'Arnold Breit,' he said and then quickly added, 'Clara Holt. That's nice. But I really think I should hang up now, Miss Holt. I'm expecting a call.'

'I'm sorry, Arnold. I didn't mean to take up your time,' she said.

'That's all right,' he said. 'It's been nice talking with you.'

'You're kind to say that, Arnold.'

'Will you hold the phone a minute?' he said. 'I have to check on something.' He went into the study for a cigar, took a minute lighting it up with the desk lighter, then removed his glasses and looked at himself in the mirror over the fireplace. When he returned to the telephone, he was half afraid she might be off the line.

'Hello?'

'Hello, Arnold,' she said.

'I thought you might have hung up.'

'Oh no,' she said.

'About your having my number,' he said. 'Nothing to worry about, I don't suppose. Just throw it away, I suppose.'

'I will, Arnold,' she said.

'Well, I must say goodbye, then.'

'Yes, of course,' she said. 'I'll say good night now.'

He heard her draw her breath.

'I know I'm imposing, Arnold, but do you think we could meet somewhere we could talk? Just for a few minutes?'

'I'm afraid that's impossible,' he said.

'Just for a minute, Arnold. My finding your number and everything. I feel strongly about this, Arnold.'

'I'm an old man,' he said.

'Oh, you're not,' she said.

'Really, I'm old,' he said.

'Could we meet somewhere, Arnold? You see, I haven't told you everything. There's something else,' the woman said.

'What do you mean?' he said. 'What is this exactly? Hello?'

She had hung up.

When he was preparing for bed, his wife called, somewhat intoxicated, he could tell, and they chatted for a while, but he said nothing about the other call. Later, as he was turning the covers down, the telephone rang again.

He picked up the receiver. 'Hello. Arnold Breit speaking.'

'Arnold, I'm sorry we got cut off. As I was saying, I think it's important we meet.'

The next afternoon as he put the key into the lock, he could hear the telephone ringing. He dropped his brief-case and, still in hat, coat, and gloves, hurried over to the table and picked up the receiver.

'Arnold, I'm sorry to bother you again,' the woman said. 'But you must come to my house tonight around nine or nine-thirty. Can you do that for me, Arnold?'

His heart moved when he heard her use his name. 'I couldn't do that,' he said.

'Please, Arnold,' she said. 'It's important or I wouldn't be asking. I can't leave the house tonight because Cheryl is sick with a cold and now I'm afraid for the boy.'

'And your husband?' He waited.

'I'm not married,' she said. 'You will come, won't you?'

'I can't promise,' he said.

'I implore you to come,' she said and then quickly gave him the address and hung up.

'*I implore you to come*,' he repeated, still holding the receiver. He slowly took off his gloves and then his coat. He felt he had to be careful. He went to wash up. When he looked in the bathroom mirror, he discovered the hat. It was then that he made the decision to see her, and he took off his hat and glasses and soaped his face. He checked his nails.

'You're sure this is the right street?' he asked the driver.

'This is the street and there's the building,' the driver said.

'Keep going,' he said. 'Let me out at the end of the block.'

He paid the driver. Lights from the upper windows illuminated the balconies. He could see planters on the balustrades and here and there a piece of lawn furniture. At one balcony a large man in a sweatshirt leaned over the railing and watched him walk toward the door.

He pushed the button under C. HOLT. The buzzer sounded, and he stepped back to the door and entered. He climbed the stairs slowly, stopping to rest briefly at each landing. He remembered the hotel in Luxembourg, the five flights he and his wife had climbed so many years ago. He felt a sudden pain in his side, imagined his heart, imagined his legs folding under him, imagined a loud fall to the bottom of the stairs. He took out his handkerchief and wiped his forehead. Then he removed his glasses and wiped the lenses, waiting for his heart to quiet.

He looked down the hall. The apartment house was very quiet. He stopped at her door, removed his hat, and knocked lightly. The door opened a crack to reveal a plump little girl in pajamas.

'Are you Arnold Breit?' she said.

'Yes, I am,' he said. 'Is your mother home?'

'She said for you to come in. She said to tell you she went to the drugstore for some cough syrup and aspirin.'

He shut the door behind him. 'What is your name? Your mother told me, but I forgot.'

When the girl said nothing, he tried again.

'What is your name? Isn't your name Shirley?'

'Cheryl,' she said. 'C-h-e-r-y-l.'

'Yes, now I remember. Well, I was close, you must admit.'

She sat on a hassock across the room and looked at him.

'So you're sick, are you?' he said.

She shook her head.

'Not sick?'

'No,' she said.

He looked around. The room was lighted by a gold floor lamp that had a large ashtray and a magazine rack affixed to the pole. A television set stood against the far wall, the picture on, the volume low. A narrow hallway led to the back of the apartment. The furnace was turned up, the air close with a medicinal smell. Hairpins and rollers lay on the coffee table, a pink bathrobe lay on the couch.

He looked at the child again, then raised his eyes toward the kitchen and the glass doors that gave off the kitchen onto the balcony. The doors stood slightly ajar, and a little chill went through him as he recalled the large man in the sweatshirt.

'Mama went out for a minute,' the child said, as if suddenly waking up.

He leaned forward on his toes, hat in hand, and stared at her. 'I think I'd better go,' he said.

A key turned in the lock, the door swung open, and a small, pale, freckled woman entered carrying a paper sack.

'Arnold! I'm glad to see you!' She glanced at him quickly, uneasily, and shook her head strangely from side to side as she walked to the kitchen with the sack. He heard a cupboard door shut. The child sat on the hassock and watched him. He leaned his weight first on one leg and then the other, then placed the hat on his head and removed it in the same motion as the woman reappeared.

'Are you a doctor?' she asked.

'No,' he said, startled. 'No, I am not.'

'Cheryl is sick, you see. I've been out buying things. Why didn't you take the man's coat?' she said, turning to the child. 'Please forgive her. We're not used to company.'

'I can't stay,' he said. 'I really shouldn't have come.'

'Please sit down,' she said. 'We can't talk like this. Let me give her some medicine first. Then we can talk.'

'I really must go,' he said. 'From the tone of your voice, I thought there was something urgent. But I really must go.' He looked down at his hands and was aware he had been gesturing feebly.

'I'll put on tea water,' he heard her say, as if she hadn't been listening. 'Then I'll give Cheryl her medicine, and then we can talk.'

She took the child by the shoulders and steered her into the kitchen. He saw the woman pick up a spoon, open a bottle of something after scanning the label, and pour out two doses.

'Now, you say good night to Mr. Breit, sweetness, and go to your room.'

He nodded to the child and then followed the woman to the kitchen. He did not take the chair she indicated, but instead one that let him face the balcony, the hallway, and the small living room. 'Do you mind if I smoke a cigar?' he asked.

'I don't mind,' she said. 'I don't think it will bother me, Arnold. Please do.'

He decided against it. He put his hands on his knees and gave his face a serious expression.

'This is still very much of a mystery to me,' he said. 'It's quite out of the ordinary, I assure you.'

'I understand, Arnold,' she said. 'You'd probably like to hear the story of how I got your number?'

'I would indeed,' he said.

They sat across from each other waiting for the water to boil. He could hear the television. He looked around the kitchen and then out toward the balcony again. The water began to bubble.

'You were going to tell me about the number,' he said.

'What, Arnold? I'm sorry,' she said.

He cleared his throat. 'Tell me how you acquired my number,' he said.

'I checked with Annette. The sitter – but of course you know that. Anyway, she told me the phone rang while she was here and it was somebody wanting me. They left a number to call, and it was your number she took down. That's all I know.' She moved a cup around in front of her. 'I'm sorry I can't tell you any more.'

'Your water is boiling,' he said.

She put out spoons, milk, sugar and poured the steaming water over the tea bags.

He added sugar and stirred his tea. 'You said it was urgent that I come.'

'Oh, *that*, Arnold,' she said, turning away. 'I don't know what made me say that. I can't imagine what I was thinking.'

'Then there's nothing?' he said.

'No. I mean *yes*.' She shook her head. 'What you said, I mean. Nothing.'

'I see,' he said. He went on stirring his tea. 'It's unusual,' he said after a time, almost to himself. 'Quite unusual.' He smiled weakly, then moved the cup to one side and touched his lips with the napkin.

'You aren't leaving?' she said.

'I must,' he said. 'I'm expecting a call at home.'

'Not yet, Arnold.'

She scraped her chair back and stood up. Her eyes were a pale green, set deep in her pale face and surrounded by what he had at first thought was dark makeup. Appalled at himself, knowing he would despise himself for it, he stood and put his arms clumsily around her waist. She let herself be kissed, fluttering and closing her eyelids briefly.

'It's late,' he said, letting go, turning away unsteadily. 'You've been very gracious. But I must be leaving, Mrs. Holt. Thank you for the tea.'

'You will come again, won't you, Arnold?' she said.

He shook his head.

She followed him to the door, where he held out his hand. He could hear the television. He was sure the volume had been turned up. He remembered the other child then – the *boy*. Where was he?

She took his hand, raised it quickly to her lips.

'You mustn't forget me, Arnold.'

'I won't,' he said. 'Clara. Clara Holt,' he said.

'We had a good talk,' she said. She picked at something, a hair, a thread, on his suit collar. 'I'm very glad you came, and I feel certain you'll come again.' He looked at her carefully, but she was staring past him now as if she were trying to remember something. 'Now – good night, Arnold,' she said, and with that she shut the door, almost catching his overcoat.

'Strange,' he said as he started down the stairs. He took a long breath when he reached the sidewalk and paused a moment to look back at the building. But he was unable to determine which balcony was hers. The large man in the sweatshirt moved slightly against the railing and continued looking down at him.

He began walking, hands deep in his coat pockets. When he reached home, the telephone was ringing. He stood very quietly in the middle of the room, holding the key between his fingers until the ringing stopped. Then, tenderly, he put a hand against his chest and felt, through the layers of clothes, his beating heart. After a time he made his way into the bedroom.

Almost immediately the telephone came alive again, and this time he answered it. 'Arnold. Arnold Breit speaking,' he said.

'Arnold? My, aren't we formal tonight!' his wife said, her voice strong, teasing. 'I've been calling since nine. Out living it up, Arnold?'

He remained silent and considered her voice.

'Are you there, Arnold?' she said. 'You don't sound like yourself.'

The father

The baby lay in a basket beside the bed, dressed in a white bonnet and sleeper. The basket had been newly painted and tied with ice blue ribbons and padded with blue quilts. The three little sisters and the mother, who had just gotten out of bed and was still not herself, and the grandmother all stood around the baby, watching it stare and sometimes raise its fist to its mouth. He did not smile or laugh, but now and then he blinked his eyes and flicked his tongue back and forth through his lips when one of the girls rubbed his chin.

The father was in the kitchen and could hear them playing with the baby.

'Who do you love, baby?' Phyllis said and tickled his chin.

'He loves us all,' Phyllis said, 'but he really loves Daddy because Daddy's a boy too!'

The grandmother sat down on the edge of the bed and said, 'Look at its little arm! So fat. And those little fingers! Just like its mother.'

'Isn't he sweet?' the mother said. 'So healthy, my little baby.' And bending over, she kissed the baby on its forehead and touched the cover over its arm. 'We love him too.'

'But who does he look like, who does he look like?' Alice cried, and they all moved up closer around the basket to see who the baby looked like.

'He has pretty eyes,' Carol said.

'*All* babies have pretty eyes,' Phyllis said.

'He has his grandfather's lips,' the grandmother said. 'Look at those lips.'

'I don't know . . .' the mother said. 'I wouldn't say.'

'The nose! The nose!' Alice cried.

'What about his nose?' the mother asked.

'It looks like somebody's nose,' the girl answered.

'No, I don't know,' the mother said. 'I don't think so.'

'Those lips . . .' the grandmother murmured. 'Those little fingers . . .' she said, uncovering the baby's hand and spreding out its fingers.

'Who does the baby look like?'

'He doesn't look like anybody,' Phyllis said. And they moved even closer.

'*I* know! *I* know!' Carol said. 'He looks like *Daddy!*' Then they looked closer at the baby.

'But who does Daddy *look* like?' Phyllis asked.

'Who does Daddy *look* like?' Alice repeated, and they all at once looked through to the kitchen where the father was sitting at the table with his back to them.

'Why, nobody!' Phyllis said and began to cry a little.

'Hush,' the grandmother said and looked away and then back at the baby.

'Daddy doesn't look like *anybody!*' Alice said.

'But he has to look like *somebody*,' Phyllis said, wiping her eyes with one of the ribbons. And all of them except the grandmother looked at the father, sitting at the table.

He had turned around in his chair and his face was white and without expression.

Nobody said anything

I could hear them out in the kitchen. I couldn't hear what they were saying, but they were arguing. Then it got quiet and she started to cry. I elbowed George. I thought he would wake up and say something to them so they would feel guilty and stop. But George is such an asshole. He started kicking and hollering.

'Stop gouging me, you bastard,' he said. 'I'm going to tell!'

'You dumb chickenshit,' I said. 'Can't you wise up for once? They're fighting and Mom's crying. Listen.'

He listened with his head off the pillow. 'I don't care,' he said and turned over toward the wall and went back to sleep. George is a royal asshole.

Later I heard Dad leave to catch his bus. He slammed the front door. She had told me before he wanted to tear up the family. I didn't want to listen.

After a while she came to call us for school. Her voice sounded funny — I don't know. I said I felt sick at my stomach. It was the first week in October and I hadn't missed any school yet, so what could she say? She looked at me, but it was like she was thinking of something else. George was awake and listening. I could tell he was awake by the way he moved in the bed. He was waiting to see how it turned out so he could make his move.

'All right.' She shook her head. 'I just don't know. Stay home, then. But no TV, remember that.'

George reared up. 'I'm sick too,' he said to her. 'I have a headache. He gouged me and kicked me all night. I didn't get to sleep at all.'

'That's enough!' she said. 'You are going to school, George! You're not going to stay here and fight with your brother all day. Now get up and get dressed. I mean it. I don't feel like another battle this morning.'

George waited until she left the room. Then he climbed out over the foot of the bed. 'You bastard,' he said and yanked all the covers off me. He dodged into the bathroom.

'I'll kill you,' I said but not so loud that she could hear.

I stayed in bed until George left for school. When she started to get ready for work, I asked if she would make a bed for me on the couch. I said I wanted to study. On the coffee table I had the Edgar Rice Burroughs books I had gotten for my birthday and my Social Studies book. But I didn't feel like reading. I wanted her to leave so I could watch TV.

She flushed the toilet.

I couldn't wait any longer. I turned the picture on without the volume. I went out to the kitchen where she had left her pack of weeds and shook out three. I put them in the cupboard and went back to the couch and started reading *The Princess of Mars*. She came out and glanced at the TV but didn't say anything. I had the book open. She poked at her hair in front of the mirror and then went into the kitchen. I looked back at the book when she came out.

'I'm late. Goodbye, sweetheart.' She wasn't going to bring up the TV. Last night she'd said she wouldn't know what it meant any more to go to work without being 'stirred up.'

'Don't cook anything. You don't need to turn the burners on for a thing. There's tuna fish in the icebox if you feel hungry.' She looked at me. 'But if your stomach is sick, I don't think you should put anything on it. Anyway, you don't need to turn the burners on. Do you hear? You take that medicine, sweetheart, and I hope your stomach feels better by tonight. Maybe we'll all feel better by tonight.'

She stood in the doorway and turned the knob. She looked as if she wanted to say something else. She wore the white blouse, the wide black belt, and the black skirt. Sometimes she called it her outfit, sometimes her uniform. For as long as I could remember, it was always hanging in the closet or hanging on the clothesline or getting washed out by hand at night or being ironed in the kitchen.

She worked Wednesdays through Sundays.

'Bye, Mom.'

I waited until she had started the car and had it warm. I listened as she pulled away from the curb. Then I got up and turned the sound on loud and went for the weeds. I smoked one and beat off while I watched a show about doctors and nurses. Then I turned to the other channel. Then I turned off the TV. I didn't feel like watching.

I finished the chapter where Tars Tarkas falls for a green woman, only to see her get her head chopped off the next morning by this jealous brother-in-law. It was about the fifth time I had read it. Then I went to their bedroom and looked around. I wasn't after anything in particular unless it was rubbers again and though I had looked all over I had never found any. Once I found a jar of Vaseline at the back of a drawer. I knew it must have something to do with it, but I didn't know what. I studied the label and hoped it would reveal something, a description of what people did, or else about how you applied the Vaseline, that sort of thing. But it didn't. *Pure Petroleum Jelly*, that was all it said on the front label. But just reading that was enough to give you a boner. *An Excellent Aid in the Nursery*, it said on the back. I tried to make the connection between *Nursery* – the swings and slides, the sandboxes, monkeybars – and what went on in bed between them. I had opened the jar lots of times and smelled inside and looked to see how much had been used since last time. This time I passed up the *Pure Petroleum Jelly*. I mean, all I did was look to see the jar was still there. I went through a few drawers, not really expecting to find anything. I looked under the bed. Nothing anywhere. I looked in the jar in the closet where they kept the grocery money. There was no change, only a five and a one. They would miss that. Then I thought I would get dressed and walk to Birch Creek. Trout season was open for another week or so, but almost everybody had quit fishing. Everybody was just sitting around now waiting for deer and pheasant to open.

I got out my old clothes. I put wool socks over my regular socks and took my time lacing up the boots. I made a couple of tuna sandwiches and some double-decked peanut-butter crackers. I filled my canteen and attached the hunting knife and the canteen to my belt. As I was going out the door, I decided to leave a note. So I wrote: 'Feeling better and going to Birch Creek. Back soon. R. 3:15.' That was about four hours from now. And about fifteen minutes before George would come in from school. Before I left, I ate one of the sandwiches and had a glass of milk with it.

It was nice out. It was fall. But it wasn't cold yet except at night. At night they would light the smudgepots in the orchards and you would wake up in the morning with a black ring of stuff in your nose. But nobody said anything. They said the smudging kept the young pears from freezing, so it was all right.

To get to Birch Creek, you go to the end of our street where you hit Sixteenth Avenue. You turn left on Sixteenth and go up the hill past the cemetery and down to Lennox, where there is a Chinese restaurant. From the crossroads there, you can see the airport, and

Birch Creek is below the airport. Sixteenth changes to View Road at the crossroads. You follow View for a little way until you come to the bridge. There are orchards on both sides of the road. Sometimes when you go by the orchards you see pheasants running down the rows, but you can't hunt there because you might get shot by a Greek named Matsos. I guess it is about a forty-minute walk all in all.

I was halfway down Sixteenth when a woman in a red car pulled onto the shoulder ahead of me. She rolled down the window on the passenger's side and asked if I wanted a lift. She was thin and had little pimples around her mouth. Her hair was up in curlers. But she was sharp enough. She had a brown sweater with nice boobs inside.

'Playing hooky?'

'Guess so.'

'Want a ride?'

I nodded.

'Get in. I'm kind of in a hurry.'

I put the fly rod and the creel on the back seat. There were a lot of grocery sacks from Mel's on the floorboards and back seat. I tried to think of something to say.

'I'm going fishing,' I said. I took off my cap, hitched the canteen around so I could sit, and parked myself next to the window.

'Well, I never would have guessed.' She laughed. She pulled back onto the road. 'Where are you going? Birch Creek?'

I nodded again. I looked at my cap. My uncle had bought it for me in Seattle when he had gone to watch a hockey game. I couldn't think of anything more to say. I looked out the window and sucked my cheeks. You always see yourself getting picked up by this woman. You know you'll fall for each other and that she'll take you home with her and let you screw her all over the house. I began to get a boner thinking about it. I moved the cap over my lap and closed my eyes and tried to think about baseball.

'I keep saying that one of these days I'll take up fishing,' she said. 'They say it's very relaxing. I'm a nervous person.'

I opened my eyes. We were stopped at the crossroads. I wanted to say, *Are you real busy? Would you like to start this morning?* But I was afraid to look at her.

'Will this help you? I have to turn here. I'm sorry I'm in a hurry this morning,' she said.

'That's okay. This is fine.' I took my stuff out. Then I put my cap on and took it off again while I talked. 'Goodbye. Thanks. Maybe next summer,' but I couldn't finish.

'You mean fishing? Sure thing.' She waved with a couple of fingers the way women do.

I started walking, going over what I should have said. I could think of a lot of things. What was wrong with me? I cut the air with the fly rod and hollered two or three times. What I should have done to start things off was ask if we could have lunch together. No one was home at my house. Suddenly we are in my bedroom under the covers. She asks me if she can keep her sweater on and I say it's okay with me. She keeps her pants on too. That's all right, I say. I don't mind.

A Piper Cub dipped low over my head as it came in for a landing. I was a few feet from the bridge. I could hear the water running. I hurried down the embankment, unzipped, and shot off five feet over the creek. It must have been a record. I took a while eating the other sandwich and the peanut-butter crackers. I drank up half the water in the canteen. Then I was ready to fish.

I tried to think where to start. I had fished here for three years, ever since we had moved. Dad used to bring George and me in the car and wait for us, smoking, baiting our hooks, tying up new rigs for us if we snagged. We always started at the bridge and moved down, and we always caught a few. Once in a while, at the first of the season, we caught the limit. I rigged up and tried a few casts under the bridge first.

Now and then I cast under a bank or else in behind a big rock. But nothing happened. One place where the water was still and the bottom full of yellow leaves, I looked over and saw a few crawdads crawling there with their big ugly pinchers raised. Some quail flushed out of a brush pile. When I threw a stick, a rooster pheasant jumped up cackling about ten feet away and I almost dropped the rod.

The creek was slow and not very wide. I could walk across almost anywhere without it going over my boots. I crossed a pasture full of cow pads and came to where the water flowed out of a big pipe. I knew there was a little hole below the pipe, so I was careful. I got down on my knees when I was close enough to drop the line. It had just touched the water when I got a strike, but I missed him. I felt him roll with it. Then he was gone and the line flew back. I put another salmon egg on and tried a few more casts. But I knew I had jinxed it.

I went up the embankment and climbed under a fence that had a KEEP OUT sign on the post. One of the airport runways started here. I stopped to look at some flowers growing in the cracks in the pavement. You could see where the tires had smacked down on the pavement and left oily skid marks all around the flowers. I hit the creek again on the other side and fished along for a little way until I came to the hole. I thought this was as far as I would go. When I had first been up here three years ago, the water was roaring right up to the top of the banks. It was so swift then that I couldn't fish. Now the creek was about six feet below the bank. It bubbled and hopped through this little run at the head of the pool where you could hardly see bottom. A little farther down, the bottom sloped up and got shallow again as if nothing had happened. The last time I was up here I caught two fish about ten inches long and turned one that looked twice as big—a summer steelhead, Dad said when I told him about it. He said they come up during the high water in early spring but that most of them return to the river before the water gets low.

I put two more shot on the line and closed them with my teeth. Then I put a fresh salmon egg on and cast out where the water dropped over a shelf into the pool. I let the current take it down. I could feel the sinkers tap-tapping on rocks, a different kind of tapping than when you are getting a bite. Then the end tightened and the current carried the egg into sight at the end of the pool.

I felt lousy to have come this far up for nothing. I pulled out all kinds of line this time and made another cast. I laid the fly rod over a limb and lit the next to last weed. I looked up the valley and began to think about the woman. We were going to her house because she wanted help carrying in the groceries. Her husband was overseas. I touched her and she started shaking. We were French-kissing on the couch when she excused herself to go to the bathroom. I followed her. I watched as she pulled down her pants and sat on the toilet. I had a big boner and she waved me over with her hand. Just as I was going to unzip, I heard a plop in the creek. I looked and saw the tip of my fly rod jiggling.

He wasn't very big and didn't fight much. But I played him as long as I could. He turned on his side and lay in the current down below. I didn't know what he was. He looked strange. I tightened the line and lifted him over the bank into the grass, where he stared wiggling. He was a trout. But he was green. I never saw one like him before. He had green sides with black trout spots, a greenish head, and like a green stomach. He was the color of moss, that color green. It was as if he had been wrapped up in moss a long time, and the color had come off all over him. He was fat, and I wondered why he hadn't put up more of a fight. I wondered if he was all right. I looked at him for a time longer, then I put him out of his pain.

I pulled some grass and put it in the creel and laid him in there on the grass.

I made some more casts, and then I guessed it must be two or three o'clock. I thought I had better move down to the bridge. I thought I would fish below the bridge awhile before I started home. And I decided I would wait until night before I thought about the woman again. But right away I got a boner thinking about the boner I would get that night. Then I thought I had better stop doing it so much. About a month back, a Saturday when they were all gone, I had picked up the Bible right after and promised and swore I wouldn't do it again. But I got jism on the Bible, and the promising and swearing lasted only a day or two, until I was by myself again.

I didn't fish on the way down. When I got to the bridge, I saw a bicycle in the grass. I looked and saw a kid about George's size running down the bank. I started in his direction. Then he turned and started toward me, looking in the water.

'Hey, what is it!' I hollered. 'What's wrong?' I guessed he didn't hear me. I saw his pole and fishing bag on the bank, and I dropped my stuff. I ran over to where he was. He looked like a rat or something. I mean, he had buck teeth and skinny arms and this ragged longsleeved shirt that was too small for him.

'God, I swear there's the biggest fish here I ever saw!' he called. 'Hurry! Look! Look here! Here he is!'

I looked where he pointed and my heart jumped.

It was as long as my arm.

'God, oh God, will you look at him!' the boy said.

I kept looking. I was resting in a shadow under a limb that hung over the water. 'God almighty,' I said to the fish, 'where did you come from?'

'What'll we do?' the boy said. 'I wish I had my gun.'

'We're going to get him,' I said. 'God, look at him! Let's get him into the riffle.'

'You want to help me, then? We'll work it together!' the kid said.

The big fish had drifted a few feet downstream and lay there finning slowly in the clear water.

'Okay, what do we do?' the kid said.

'I can go up and walk down the creek and start him moving,' I said. 'You stand in the riffle, and when he tries to come through, you kick the living shit out of him. Get him onto the bank someway, I don't care how. Then get a good hold of him and hang on.'

'Okay. Oh shit, look at him! Look, he's going! Where's he going?' the boy screamed.

I watched the fish move up the creek again and stop close to the bank. 'He's not going anyplace. There's no place for him to go. See him? He's scared shitless. He knows we're here. He's just cruising around now looking for someplace to go. See, he stopped again. He can't go anyplace. He knows that. He knows we're going to nail him. He knows it's tough shit. I'll go up and scare him down. You get him when he comes through.'

'I wish I had my gun,' the boy said. 'That would take care of him,' the boy said.

I went up a little way, then started wading down the creek. I watched ahead of me as I went. Suddenly the fish darted away from the bank, turned right in front of me in a big cloudy swirl, and barrel-assed downstream.

'Here he comes!' I hollered. 'Hey, hey, here he comes!' But the fish spun around before it reached the riffle and headed back. I splashed and hollered, and it turned again. 'He's coming! Get him, get him! Here he comes!'

But the dumb idiot had himself a club, the asshole, and when the fish hit the riffle, the boy drove at him with the club instead of trying to kick the sonofabitch out like he should have. The fish veered off, going crazy, shooting on his side through the shallow water. He made it. The asshole idiot kid lunged for him and fell flat.

He dragged up onto the bank sopping wet. 'I hit him!' the boy hollered. 'I think he's hurt, too. I had my hands on him, but I couldn't hold him.'

'You didn't have anything!' I was out of breath. I was glad the kid fell in. 'You didn't even come close, asshole. What were you doing with that club? You should have kicked him. He's probably a mile away by now.' I tried to spit. I shook my head. 'I don't know. We haven't got him yet. We just may not get him,' I said.

'Goddam it, I hit him!' the boy screamed. 'Didn't you see? I hit him!', and I had my hands on him too. How close did you get? Besides, whose fish is it?' He looked at me. Water ran down his trousers over his shoes.

I didn't say anything else, but I wondered about that myself. I shrugged. 'Well, okay. I thought it was both ours. Let's get him this time. No goof-ups, either one of us,' I said.

We waded downstream. I had water in my boots, but the kid was wet up to his collar. He closed his buck teeth over his lip to keep his teeth from chattering.

The fish wasn't in the run below the riffle, and we couldn't see him in the next stretch, either. We looked at each other and began to worry that the fish really had gone far enough downstream to reach one of the deep holes. But then the goddamn thing rolled near the bank, actually knocking dirt into the water with his tail, and took off again. He went through another riffle, his big tail sticking out of the water. I saw him cruise over near the bank and stop, his tail half out of the water, finning just enough to hold against the current.

'Do you see him?' I said. The boy looked. I took his arm and pointed his finger. 'Right *there*. Okay now, listen. I'll go down to that little run between those banks. See where I mean? You wait here until I give you a signal. Then you start down. Okay? And this time don't let him get by you if he heads back.'

'Yeah,' the boy said and worked his lip with those teeth. 'Let's get him this time,' the boy said, a terrible look of cold in his face.

I got up on the bank and walked down, making sure I moved quiet. I slid off the bank and waded in again. But I couldn't see the great big sonofabitch and my heart turned. I thought it might have taken off already. A little farther downstream and it would get to one of the holes. We would never get him then.

'He still there?' I hollered. I held my breath.

The kid waved.

'Ready!' I hollered again.

'Here goes!' the kid hollered back.

My hands shook. The creek was about three feet wide and ran between dirt banks. The water was low but fast. The kid was moving down the creek now, water up to his knees, throwing rocks ahead of him, splashing and shouting.

'Here he comes!' The kid waved his arms. I saw the fish now; it was coming right at me. He tried to turn when he saw me, but it was too late. I went down on my knees, grasping in the cold water. I scooped him with my hands and arms, up, up, raising him, throwing him out of the water, both of us falling onto the bank. I held him against my shirt, him flopping and twisting, until I could get my hands up his slippery sides to his gills. I ran one hand in and clawed through to his mouth and locked around his jaw. I knew I had him. He was still flopping and hard to hold, but I had him and I wasn't going to let go.

'We got him!' the boy hollered as he splashed up. 'We got him, by God! Ain't he something! Look at him! Oh God, let me hold him,' the boy hollered.

'We got to kill him first,' I said. I ran my other hand down the throat. I pulled back on the head as hard as I could, trying to watch out for the teeth, and felt the heavy crunching. He gave a long slow tremble and was still. I laid him on the bank and we looked at him. He was at least two feet long, queerly skinny, but bigger than anything I had ever caught. I took hold of his jaw again.

'Hey,' the kid said but didn't say any more when he saw what I was going to do. I washed off the blood and laid the fish back on the bank.

'I want to show him to my dad so bad,' the kid said.

We were wet and shivering. We looked at him, kept touching him. We pried open his big mouth and felt his rows of teeth. His sides were scarred, whitish welts as big as quarters and kind of puffy. There were nicks out of his head around his eyes and on his snout where I guess he had banged into the rocks and been in fights. But he was so skinny, too skinny for how long he was, and you could hardly see the pink stripe down his sides, and his belly was gray and slack instead of white and solid like it should have been. But I thought he was something.

'I guess I'd better go pretty soon,' I said. I looked at the clouds over the hills where the sun was going down. 'I better get home.'

'I guess so. Me too. I'm freezing,' the kid said. 'Hey, I want to carry him,' the kid said.

'Let's get a stick. We'll put it through his mouth and both carry him,' I said.

The kid found a stick. We put it through the gills and pushed until the fish was in the middle of the stick. Then we each took an end and started back, watching the fish as he swung on the stick.

'What are we going to do with him?' the kid said.

'I don't know,' I said. 'I guess I caught him,' I said.

'We both did. Besides, I saw him first.'

'That's true,' I said. 'Well, you want to flip for him or what?' I felt with my free hand, but I didn't have any money. And what would I have done if I had lost?

Anyway, the kid said, 'No, let's not flip.'

I said, 'All right. It's okay with me.' I looked at that boy, his hair standing up, his lips gray. I could have taken him if it came to that. But I didn't want to fight.

We got to where we had left our things and picked up our stuff with one hand, neither of us letting go of his end of the stick. Then we walked up to where his bicycle was. I got a good hold on the stick in case the kid tried something.

Then I had an idea. 'We could half him,' I said.

'What do you mean?' the boy said, his teeth chattering again. I could feel him tighten his hold on the stick.

'Half him. I got a knife. We cut him in two and each take half. I don't know, but I guess we could do that.'

He pulled at a piece of his hair and looked at the fish. 'You going to use that knife?'

'You got one?' I said.

The boy shook his head.

'Okay,' I said.

I pulled the stick out and laid the fish in the grass beside the kid's bicycle. I took out the knife. A plane taxied down the runway as I measured a line. 'Right here?' I said. The kid nodded. The plane roared down the runway and lifted up right over our heads. I started cutting down into him. I came to his guts and turned him over and stripped everything out. I kept cutting until there was only a flap of skin on his belly holding him together. I took the halves and worked them in my hands and I tore him in two.

I handed the kid the tail part.

'No,' he said, shaking his head. 'I want that half.'

I said, 'They're both the same! Now goddamn, watch it, I'm going to get mad in a minute.'

'I don't care,' the boy said. 'If they're both the same, I'll take that one. They're both the same, right?'

'They're both the same,' I said. 'But I think I'm keeping this half here. I did the cutting.'

'I want it,' the kid said. 'I saw him first.'

'Whose knife did we use?' I said.

'I don't want the tail,' the kid said.

I looked around. There were no cars on the road and nobody else fishing. There was an airplane droning, and the sun was going down.

I was cold all the way through. The kid was shivering hard, waiting.

'I got an idea,' I said. I opened the creel and showed him the trout. 'See? It's a green one. It's the only green one I ever saw. So whoever takes the head, the other guy gets the green trout and the tail part. Is that fair?'

The kid looked at the green trout and took it out of the creel and held it. He studied the halves of the fish.

'I guess so,' he said. 'Okay, I guess so. You take that half. I got more meat on mine.'

'I don't care,' I said. 'I'm going to wash him off. Which way do you live?' I said.

'Down on Arthur Avenue.' He put the green trout and his half of the fish into a dirty canvas bag. 'Why?'

'Where's that? Is that down by the ball park?' I said.

'Yeah, but why, I said.' That kid looked scared.

'I live close to there,' I said. 'So I guess I could ride on the handlebars. We could take turns pumping. I got a weed we could smoke, if it didn't get wet on me.'

But the kid only said, 'I'm freezing.'

I washed my half in the creek. I held his big head under water and opened his mouth. The stream poured into his mouth and out the other end of what was left of him.

'I'm freezing,' the kid said.

I saw George riding his bicycle at the other end of the street. He didn't see me. I went around to the back to take off my boots. I unslung the creel so I could raise the lid and get set to march into the house, grinning.

I heard their voices and looked through the window. They were sitting at the table. Smoke was all over the kitchen. I saw it was coming from a pan on the burner. But neither of them paid any attention.

'What I'm telling you is the gospel truth,' he said. 'What do kids know? You'll see.'

She said, 'I'll see nothing. If I thought that, I'd rather see them dead first.'

He said, 'What's the matter with you? You better be careful what you say!'

She started to cry. He smashed out a cigaret in the ashtray and stood up.

'Edna, do you know this pan is burning up?' he said.

She looked at the pan. She pushed her chair back and grabbed the pan by its handle and threw it against the wall over the sink.

He said, 'Have you lost your mind? Look what you've done!' He took a dish cloth and began to wipe up stuff from the pan.

I opened the back door. I started grinning. I said, 'You won't believe what I caught at Birch Creek. Just look. Look here. Look at this. Look what I caught.'

My legs shook. I could hardly stand. I held the creel out to her, and she finally looked in. 'Oh, oh, my God! What is it? A snake! What is it? Please, please take it out before I throw up.'

'Take it out!' he screamed. 'Didn't you hear what she said? Take it out of here!' he screamed.

I said, 'But look, Dad. Look what it is.'

He said, 'I don't want to look.'

I said, 'It's a gigantic summer steelhead from Birch Creek. Look! Isn't he something? It's a monster! I chased him up and down the creek like a madman!' My voice was crazy. But I could not stop. 'There was another one, too,' I hurried on. 'A green one. I swear! It was green! Have you ever seen a green one?'

He looked into the creel and his mouth fell open.

He screamed, 'Take that goddamn thing out of here! What in the hell is the matter with you? Take it the hell out of the kitchen and throw it in the goddamn garbage!'

I went back outside. I looked into the creel. What was there looked silver under the porch light. What was there filled the creel.

I lifted him out. I held him. I held that half of him.

Sixty acres

The call had come an hour ago, when they were eating. Two men were shooting on Lee Waite's part of Toppenish Creek, down below the bridge on the Cowiche Road. It was the third or fourth time this winter someone had been in there, Joseph Eagle reminded Lee Waite. Joseph Eagle was an old Indian who lived on his government allotment in a little place off the Cowiche Road, with a radio he listened to day and night and a telephone in case he got sick. Lee Waite wished the old Indian would let him be about that land, that Joseph Eagle would do something else about it, if he wanted, besides call.

Out on the porch, Lee Waite leaned on one leg and picked at a string of meat between his teeth. He was a small thin man with a thin face and long black hair. If it had not been for the phone call, he would have slept awhile this afternoon. He frowned and took his time pulling into his coat; they would be gone anyway when he got there. That was usually the way. The hunters from Toppenish or Yakima could drive the reservation roads like anyone else; they just weren't allowed to hunt. But they would cruise by that untenanted and irresistible sixty acres of his, two, maybe three times, then, if they were feeling reckless, park down off the road in the trees and hurry through the knee-deep barley and wild oats, down to the creek – maybe getting some ducks, maybe not, but always doing a lot of shooting in the little time before they cleared out. Joseph Eagle sat crippled in his house and watched them plenty of times. Or so he told Lee Waite.

He cleaned his teeth with his tongue and squinted in the late-afternoon winter half-light. He wasn't afraid; it wasn't that, he told himself. He just didn't want trouble.

The porch, small and built on just before the war, was almost dark. The one window glass had been knocked out years before, and Waite had nailed a beet sack over the opening. It hung there next to the cabinet, matted-thick and frozen, moving slightly as the cold air from outside came in around the edges. The walls were crowded with old yokes and harnesses, and up on one side, above the window, was a row of rusted hand tools. He made a last sweep with his tongue, tightened the light bulb into the overhead socket, and opened the cabinet. He took out the old double-barrel from in back and reached into the box on the top shelf for a handful of shells. The brass ends of the shells felt cold, and he rolled them in his hand before dropping them into a pocket of the old coat he was wearing.

'Aren't you going to load it, Papa?' the boy Benny asked from behind.

Waite turned, saw Benny and little Jack standing in the kitchen doorway. Ever since the call they had been after him – had wanted to know if this time he was going to shoot somebody. It bothered him, kids talking like that, like they would enjoy it, and now they stood at the door, letting all the cold air in the house and looking at the large gun up under his arm.

'Get back in that house where the hell you belong,' he said.

They left the door open and ran back in where his mother and Nina were and on through to the bedroom. He could see Nina at the table trying to coax bites of squash into the baby, who was pulling back and shaking her head. Nina looked up, tried to smile.

Waite stepped into the kitchen and shut the door, leaned against it. She was plenty tired, he could tell. A beaded line of moisture glistened over her lip, and, as he watched, she stopped to move the hair away from her forehead. She looked up at him again, then back at the baby. It had never bothered her like this when she was carrying before. The other times she could hardly sit still and used to jump up and walk around, even if there wasn't much to do except cook a meal or sew. He fingered the loose skin around his neck and glanced covertly at his mother, dozing since the meal in a chair by the stove. She squinted her eyes at him and nodded. She was seventy and shriveled, but her hair was still crow-black and hung down in front over her shoulders in two long tight braids. Lee Waite was sure she had something wrong with her because sometimes she went two days without saying something, just sitting in the other room by the window and staring off up the valley. It made him shiver when she did that, and he didn't know any more what her little signs and signals, her silences, were supposed to mean.

'Why don't you say something?' he asked, shaking his head. 'How do I know what you mean, Mama, if you don't say?' Waite looked at her for a minute and watched her tug at the ends of her braids, waited for her to say something. Then he grunted and crossed by in front of her, took his hat off a nail, and went out.

It was cold. An inch or two of grainy snow from three days past covered everything, made the ground lumpy, and gave a foolish look to the stripped rows of beanpoles in front of the house. The dog came scrabbling out from under the house when it heard the door, started off for the truck without looking back. 'Come here!' Waite called sharply, his voice looping in the thin air.

Leaning over, he took the dog's cold, dry muzzle in his hand. 'You better stay here this time. Yes, yes.' He flapped the dog's ear back and forth and looked around. He could not see the satus Hills across the valley because of the heavy overcast, just the wavy flatness of sugar-beet fields – white, except for black places here and there where the snow had not gotten. One place in sight – Charley Treadwell's, a long way off – but no lights lit that he could tell. Not a sound anywhere, just the low ceiling of heavy clouds pressing down on everything. He'd thought there was a wind, but it was still.

'Stay here now. You hear?'

He started for the truck, wishing again he did not have to go. He had dreamed last night, again – about what he could not remember – but he'd had an uneasy feeling ever since he woke up. He drove in low gear down to the gate, got out and unhooked it, drove past, got out again and hooked it. He did not keep horses any more – but it was a habit he had gotten into, keeping the gate shut.

Down the road, the grader was scraping toward him, the blade shrieking fiercely every time the metal hit the frozen gravel. He was in no hurry, and he waited the long minutes it took the grader to come up. One of the men in the cab leaned out with a cigaret in his hand and waved as they went by. But Waite looked off. He pulled out onto the road after they passed. He looked over at Charley Treadwell's when he went by, but there were still no lights, and the car was gone. He remembered what Charley had told him a few days ago, about a fight Charley had had last Sunday with some kid who came over his fence in the afternoon and shot into a pond of ducks, right down by the barn. The ducks came in there every afternoon, Charley said. They *trusted* him, he said, as if that mattered. He'd run down from the barn where he was milking, waving his arms and shouting, and the kid had pointed the gun at him. If I could've just got that gun away from him, Charley had said, staring hard at Waite with his one good eye and nodding slowly. Waite hitched a little in the seat. He did not want any trouble like that. He hoped whoever it was would be gone when he got there, like the other times.

*

Out to the left he passed Fort Simcoe, the white-painted tops of the old buildings standing behind the reconstructed palisade. The gates of the place were open, and Lee Waite could see cars parked around inside and a few people in coats, walking. He never bothered to stop. Once the teacher had brought all the kids out here – a field trip, she called it – but Waite had stayed home from school that day. He rolled down the window and cleared his throat, hawked it at the gate as he passed.

He turned onto Lateral B and then came to Joseph Eagle's place – all the lights on, even the porch light. Waite drove past, down to where the Cowiche Road came in, and got out of the truck and listened. He had begun to think they might be gone and he could turn around and go on back when he heard a grouping of dull far-off shots come across the fields. He waited awhile, then took a rag and went around the truck and tried to wipe off some of the snow and ice in the window edges. He kicked the snow off his shoes before getting in, drove a little farther until he could see the bridge, then looked for the tracks that turned off into the trees, where he knew he would find their car. He pulled in behind the gray sedan and switched the ignition off.

He sat in the truck and waited, squeaking his foot back and forth on the brake and hearing them shoot every now and then. After a few minutes he couldn't sit still any longer and got out, walked slowly around to the front. He had not been down there to do anything in four or five years. He leaned against the fender and looked out over the land. He could not understand where all the time had gone.

He remembered when he was little, wanting to grow up. He used to come down here often then and trap this part of the creek for muskrat and set night-lines for German brown. Waite looked around, moved his feet inside his shoes. All that was a long time ago. Growing up, he had heard his father say he intended this land for the three boys. But both brothers had been killed. Lee Waite was the one it came down to, all of it.

He remembered: deaths. Jimmy first. He remembered waking to the tremendous pounding on the door – dark, the smell of wood pitch from the stove, an automobile outside with the lights on and the motor running, and a crackling voice coming from a speaker inside. His father throws open the door, and the enormous figure of a man in a cowboy hat and wearing a gun – the deputy sheriff – fills the doorway. *Waite? Your boy Jimmy been stabbed at a dance in Wapato.* Everyone had gone away in the truck and Lee was left by himself. He had crouched, alone the rest of the night, in front of the wood stove, watching the shadows jump across the wall. Later, when he was twelve, another one came, a different sheriff, and only said they'd better come along.

He pushed off from the truck and walked the few feet over to the edge of the field. Things were different now, that's all there was to it. He was thirty-two, and Benny and little Jack were growing up. And there was the baby. Waite shook his head. He closed his hand around one of the tall stalks of milkweed. He snapped its neck and looked up when he heard the soft chuckling of ducks overhead. He wiped his hand on his pants and followed them for a moment, watched them set their wings at the same instant and circle once over the creek. Then they flared. He saw three ducks fall before he heard the shots.

He turned abruptly and started back for the truck.

He took out his gun, careful not to slam the door. He moved into the trees. It was almost dark. He coughed once and then stood with his lips pressed together.

They came thrashing through the brush, two of them. Then, jiggling and squeaking the fence, they climbed over into the field and crunched through the snow. They were breathing hard by the time they got up close to the car.

'My God, there's a truck there!' one of them said and dropped the ducks he was carrying.

It was a boy's voice. He had on a heavy hunting coat, and in the game pockets Waite could dimly make out the enormous padding of ducks.

'Take it easy, will you!' The other boy stood craning his head around, trying to see. 'Hurry up! There's nobody inside. Get the hell in the car!'

Not moving, trying to keep his voice steady, Waite said, 'Stand there. Put your guns right there on the ground.' He edged out of the trees and faced them, raised and lowered his gun barrels. 'Take off them coats now and empty them out.'

'O God! *God* almighty!' one of them said.

The other did not say anything but took off his coat and began pulling out the ducks, still looking around.

Waite opened the door of their car, fumbled an arm around inside until he found the headlights. The boys put a hand up to shield their eyes, then turned their backs to the light.

'Whose land do you think this is?' Waite said. 'What do you mean, shooting ducks on my land!'

One boy turned around cautiously, his hand still in front of his eyes. 'What are you going to do?'

'What do you think I'm going to do?' Waite said. His voice sounded strange to him, light, insubstantial. He could hear the ducks settling on the creek, chattering to other ducks still in the air. 'What do you think I'm going to do with you?' he said. 'What would you do if you caught boys trespassing on your land?'

'If they said they was sorry and it was the first time, I'd let them go,' the boy answered.

'I would too, sir, if they said they was sorry,' the other boy said.

'You would? You really think that's what you'd do?' Waite knew he was stalling for time.

They did not answer. They stood in the glare of the headlights and then turned their backs again.

'How do I know you wasn't here before?' Waite said. 'The other times I had to come down here?'

'Word of honor, sir, we never been here before. We just drove by. For godsake,' the boy sobbed.

'That's the whole truth,' the other boy said. 'Anybody can make a mistake once in his life.'

It was dark now, and a thin drizzle was coming down in front of the lights. Waite turned up his collar and stared at the boys. From down on the creek the strident quacking of a drake carried up to him. He glanced around at the awful shapes of the trees, then back at the boys again.

'Maybe so,' he said and moved his feet. He knew he would let them go in a minute. There wasn't much else he could do. He was putting them off the land; that was what mattered. 'What's your names, anyway? What's yours? You. Is this here your car or not? What's your name?'

'Bob Roberts,' the one boy answered quickly and looked sideways at the other.

'Williams, sir,' the other boy said. 'Bob Williams, sir.'

Waite was willing to understand that they were kids, that they were lying to him because they were afraid. They stood with their backs to him, and Waite stood looking at them.

'You're lying!' he said, shocking himself. 'Why you lying to me? You come onto my land and shoot my ducks and then you lie like hell to me!' He laid the gun over the car door to steady the barrels. He could hear branches rubbing in the treetops. He thought of Joseph Eagle sitting up there in his lighted house, his feet on a box, listening to the radio.

'All right, all right,' Waite said. 'Liars! Just stand there, liars.' He walked stiffly around to his truck and got out an old beet sack, shook it open, had them put all the ducks in that. When he stood still, waiting, his knees unaccountably began to shake.

'Go ahead and go. Go on!'

He stepped back as they came up to the car. 'I'll back up to the road. You back up along with me.'

'Yes, sir,' the one boy said as he slid in behind the wheel. 'But what if I can't get this thing started now? The battery might be dead, you know. It wasn't very strong to begin with.'

'I don't know,' Waite said. He looked around. 'I guess I'd have to push you out.'

The boy shut off the lights, stamped on the accelerator, and hit the starter. The engine turned over slowly but caught, and the boy held his foot down on the pedal and raced the engine before firing up the lights again. Waite studied their pale cold faces staring out at him, looking for a sign from him.

He slung the bag of ducks into his truck and slid the double-barrel across the seat. He got in and backed out carefully onto the road. He waited until they were out, then followed them down to Lateral B and stopped with his motor running, watching their taillights disappear toward Toppenish. He had put them off the land. That was all that mattered. Yet he could not understand why he felt something crucial had happened, a failure.

But nothing had happened.

Patches of fog had blown in from down the valley. He couldn't see much over toward Charley's when he stopped to open the gate, only a faint light burning out on the porch that Waite did not remember seeing that afternoon. The dog waited on its belly by the barn, jumped up and began snuffling the ducks as Waite swung them over his shoulder and started up to the house. He stopped on the porch long enough to put the gun away. The ducks he left on the floor beside the cabinet. He would clean them tomorrow or the next day.

'Lee?' Nina called.

Waite took off his hat, loosened the light bulb, and before opening the door he paused a moment in the quiet dark.

Nina was at the kitchen table, the little box with her sewing things beside her on another chair. She held a piece of denim in her hand. Two or three of his shirts were on the table, along with a pair of scissors. He pumped a cup of water and picked up from a shelf over the sink some of the colored rocks the kids were always bringing home. There was a dry pine cone there too and a few big papery maple leaves from the summer. He glanced in the pantry. But he was not hungry. Then he walked over to the doorway and leaned against the jamb.

It was a small house. There was no place to go.

In the back, in one room, all of the children slept, and in the room off from this, Waite and Nina and his mother slept, though sometimes, in the summer, Waite and Nina slept outside. There was never a place to go. His mother was still sitting beside the stove, a blanket over her legs now and her tiny eyes open, watching him.

'The boys wanted to stay up until you came back,' Nina said, 'but I told them you said they had to go to bed.'

'Yes, that's right,' he said. 'They had to go to bed, all right.'

'I was afraid,' she said.

'Afraid?' He tried to make it sound as if this surprised him. 'Were you afraid too, Mama?'

The old woman did not answer. Her fingers fiddled around the sides of the blanket, tucking and pulling, covering against draft.

'How do you feel, Nina? Feel any better tonight?' He pulled out a chair and sat down by the table.

His wife nodded. He said nothing more, only looked down and began scoring his thumbnail into the table.

'Did you catch who it was?' she said.

'It was two kids,' he said. 'I let them go.'

He got up and walked to the other side of the stove, spat into the woodbox, and stood with his fingers hooked into his back pockets. Behind the stove the wood was black and peeling, and overhead he could see, sticking out from a shelf, the brown mesh of a gill net wrapped around the prongs of a salmon spear. But what was it? He squinted at it.

'I let them go,' he said. 'Maybe I was easy on them.'

'You did what was right,' Nina said.

He glanced over the stove at his mother. But there was no sign from her, only the black eyes staring at him.

'I don't know,' he said. He tried to think about it, but already it seemed as if it had happened, whatever it was, long ago. 'I should've given them more of a scare, I guess.' He looked at Nina. 'My land,' he added. 'I could've killed them.'

'Kill who?' his mother said.

'Them kids down on the Cowiche Road land. What Joseph Eagle called about.'

From where he stood he could see his mother's fingers working in her lap, tracing the raised design in the blanket. He leaned over the stove, wanting to say something else. But he did not know what.

He wandered to the table and sat down again. Then he realized he still had on his coat, and he got up, took a while unfastening it, and then laid it across the table. He pulled up the chair close to his wife's knees, crossed his arms limply, and took his shirt sleeves between his fingers.

'I was thinking maybe I'll lease out that land down there to the hunting clubs. No good to us down there like that. Is it? Our house was down there or it was our land right out here in front would be something different, right?'

In the silence he could hear only the wood snapping in the stove. He laid his hands flat on the table and could feel the pulse jumping in his arms. 'I can lease it out to one of the duck clubs from Toppenish. Or Yakima. Any of them would be glad to get hold of land like that, right on the flyway. That's some of the best hunting land in the valley. . . . If I could put it to some use someway, it would be different then.' His voice trailed off.

She moved in the chair. She said, 'If you think we should do it. It's whatever you think. I don't know.'

'I don't know, either,' he said. His eyes crossed the floor, raised past his mother, and again came to rest on the salmon spear. He got up, shaking his head. As he moved across the little room, the old woman crooked her head and laid her cheek on the chairback, eyes narrowed and following him. He reached up, worked the spear and the mass of netting off the splintery shelf, and turned around behind her chair. He looked at the tiny dark head, at the brown woolen shawl shaped smooth over the hunched shoulders. He turned the spear in his hands and began to unwrap the netting.

'How much would you get?' Nina said.

He knew he didn't know. It even confused him a little. He plucked at the netting, then placed the spear back on the shelf. Outside, a branch scraped roughly against the house.

'Lee?'

He was not sure. He would have to ask around. Mike Chuck leased out thirty acres last fall for five hundred dollars. Jerome Shinpa leased some of his land every year, but Waite had never asked how much he got.

'Maybe a thousand dollars,' he said.

'A thousand dollars?' she said.

He nodded, felt relief at her amazement. 'Maybe so. Maybe more. I will have to see. I will have to ask somebody how much.' It was a lot of money. He tried to think about having a thousand dollars. He closed his eyes and tried to think.

'That wouldn't be selling it, would it?' Nina asked. 'If you lease it to them, that means it's still your land?'

'Yes, yes, it's still my land!' He went over to her and leaned across the table. 'Don't you know the difference, Nina? They can't *buy* land on the reservation. Don't you know that? I will lease it to them for them to use.'

'I see,' she said. She looked down and picked at the sleeve of one of his shirts. 'They will have to give it back? It will still belong to you?'

'Don't you understand?' he said. He gripped the table edge. 'It is a lease!'

'What will Mama say?' Nina asked. 'Will it be all right?'

They both looked over at the old woman. But her eyes were closed and she seemed to be sleeping.

'A thousand dollars,' Nina said and shook her head.

A thousand dollars. Maybe more. He didn't know. But even a thousand dollars! He wondered how he would go about it, letting people know he had land to lease. It was too late now for this year – but he could start asking around in the spring. He crossed his arms and tried to think. His legs began to tremble, and he leaned against the wall. He rested there and then let his weight slide gently down the wall until he was squatting.

'It's just a lease,' he said.

He stared at the floor. It seemed to slant in his direction; it seemed to move. He shut his eyes and brought his hands against his ears to steady himself. And then he thought to cup his palms, so that there would come that roaring, like the wind howling up from a seashell.

What's in Alaska?

Carl got off work at three. He left the station and drove to a shoe store near his apartment. He put his foot up on the stool and let the clerk unlace his work boot.

'Something comfortable,' Carl said. 'For casual wear.'

'I have something,' the clerk said.

The clerk brought out three pairs of shoes and Carl said he would take the soft beige-colored shoes that made his feet feel free and springy. He paid the clerk and put the box with his boots under his arm. He looked down at his new shoes as he walked. Driving home, he felt that his foot moved freely from pedal to pedal.

'You bought some new shoes,' Mary said. 'Let me see.'

'Do you like them?' Carl said.

'I don't like the color, but I'll bet they're comfortable. You needed new shoes.'

He looked at the shoes again. 'I've got to take a bath,' he said.

'We'll have an early dinner,' she said. 'Helen and Jack asked us over tonight. Helen got Jack a water pipe for his birthday and they're anxious to try it out.' Mary looked at him. 'Is it all right with you?'

'What time?'

'Around seven.'

'It's all right,' he said.

She looked at his shoes again and sucked her cheeks. 'Take your bath,' she said.

Carl ran the water and took off his shoes and clothes. He lay in the tub for a while and then used a brush to get at the lube grease under his nails. He dropped his hands and then raised them to his eyes.

She opened the bathroom door. 'I brought you a beer,' she said. Steam drifted around her and out into the living room.

'I'll be out in a minute,' he said. He drank some of the beer.

She sat on the edge of the tub and put her hand on his thigh. 'Home from the wars,' she said.

'Home from the wars,' he said.

She moved her hand through the wet hair on his thigh. Then she clapped her hands. 'Hey, I have something to tell you! I had an interview today, and I think they're going to offer me a job – in *Fairbanks*.'

'Alaska?' he said.

She nodded. 'What do you think of that?'

'I've always wanted to go to Alaska. Does it look pretty definite?'

She nodded again. 'They liked me. They said I'd hear next week.'

'That's great. Hand me a towel, will you? I'm getting out.'

'I'll go and set the table,' she said.

His fingertips and toes were pale and wrinkled. He dried slowly and put on clean clothes and the new shoes. He combed his hair and went out to the kitchen. He drank another beer while she put dinner on the table.

'We're supposed to bring some cream soda and something to munch on,' she said. 'We'll have to go by the store.'

'Cream soda and munchies. Okay,' he said.

When they had eaten, he helped her clear the table. Then they drove to the market and bought cream soda and potato chips and corn chips and onion-flavored snack crackers. At the checkout counter he added a handful of U-No bars to the order.

'Hey, yeah,' she said when she saw them.

They drove home again and parked, and then they walked the block to Helen and Jack's.

Helen opened the door. Carl put the sack on the dining-room table. Mary sat down in the rocking chair and sniffed.

'We're late,' she said. 'They started without us, Carl.'

Helen laughed. 'We had one when Jack came in. We haven't lighted the water pipe yet. We were waiting until you got here.' She stood in the middle of the room, looking at them and grinning. 'Let's see what's in the sack,' she said. 'Oh, wow! Say, I think I'll have one of these corn chips right now. You guys want some?'

'We just ate dinner,' Carl said. 'We'll have some pretty soon.' Water had stopped running and Carl could hear Jack whistling in the bathroom.

'We have some Popsicles and some M and M's,' Helen said. She stood beside the table and dug into the potato-chip bag. 'If Jack ever gets out of the shower, he'll get the water pipe going.' She opened the box of snack crackers and put one in her mouth. 'Say, these are really good,' she said.

'I don't know what Emily Post would say about you,' Mary said.

Helen laughed. She shook her head.

Jack came out of the bathroom. 'Hi, everybody. Hi, Carl. What's so funny?' he said, grinning. 'I could hear you laughing.'

'We were laughing at Helen,' Mary said.

'Helen was just laughing,' Carl said.

'She's funny,' Jack said. 'Look at the goodies! Hey, you guys ready for a glass of cream soda? I'll get the pipe going.'

'I'll have a glass,' Mary said. 'What about you, Carl?'

'I'll have some,' Carl said.

'Carl's on a little bummer tonight,' Mary said.

'Why do you say that?' Carl asked. He looked at her. 'That's a good way to put me on one.'

'I was just teasing,' Mary said. She came over and sat beside him on the sofa. 'I was just teasing, honey.'

'Hey, Carl, don't get on a bummer,' Jack said. 'Let me show you what I got for my birthday. Helen, open one of those bottles of cream soda while I get the pipe going. I'm real dry.'

Helen carried the chips and crackers to the coffee table. Then she produced a bottle of cream soda and four glasses.

'Looks like we're going to have a party,' Mary said.

'If I didn't starve myself all day, I'd put on ten pounds a week,' Helen said.

'I know what you mean,' Mary said.

Jack came out of the bedroom with the water pipe. 'What do you think of this?' he said to Carl. He put the water pipe on the coffee table.

'That's really something,' Carl said. He picked it up and looked at it.

'It's called a hookah,' Helen said. 'That's what they called it where I bought it. It's just a little one, but it does the job.' She laughed.

'Where did you get it?' Mary said.

'What? That little place on Fourth Street. You know,' Helen said.

'Sure. I know,' Mary said. She folded her hands and watched Jack.

'How does it work?' Carl said.

'You put the stuff here,' Jack said. 'And you light this. Then you inhale through this here and the smoke is filtered through the water. It has a good taste to it and it really hits you.'

'I'd like to get Carl one for Christmas,' Mary said. She looked at Carl and grinned and touched his arm.

'I'd like to have one,' Carl said. He stretched his legs and looked at his shoes under the light.

'Here, try this.' Jack said, letting out a thin stream of smoke and passing the tube to Carl. 'See if this isn't okay.'

Carl drew on the tube, held the smoke, and passed the tube to Helen.

'Mary first,' Helen said. 'I'll go after Mary. You guys have to catch up.'

'I won't argue,' Mary said. She slipped the tube in her mouth and drew rapidly, twice, and Carl watched the bubbles she made.

'That's really okay,' Mary said. She passed the tube to Helen.

'We broke it in last night.' Helen said, and laughed loudly.

'She was still stoned when she got up with the kids this morning,' Jack said, and he laughed. He watched Helen pull on the tube.

'How are the kids?' Mary asked.

'They're fine,' Jack said and put the tube in his mouth.

Carl sipped the cream soda and watched the bubbles in the pipe. They reminded him of bubbles rising from a diving helmet. He imagined a lagoon and schools of remarkable fish.

Jack passed the tube.

Carl stood up and stretched.

'Where are you going, honey?' Mary asked.

'No place,' Carl said. He sat down and shook his head and grinned. 'Jesus.'

Helen laughed.

'What's funny?' Carl said after a long, long time.

'God, I don't know,' Helen said. She wiped her eyes and laughed again, and Mary and Jack laughed.

After a time Jack unscrewed the top of the water pipe and blew through one of the tubes. 'It gets plugged sometimes.'

'What did you mean when you said I was on a bummer?' Carl said to Mary.

'What? Mary said.

Carl stared at her and blinked. 'You said something about me being on a bummer. What made you say that?'

'I don't remember now, but I can tell when you are,' she said. 'But please don't bring up anything negative, okay?'

'Okay,' Carl said. 'All I'm saying is I don't know why you said that. If I wasn't on a bummer before you said it, it's enough when you say it to put me on one.'

'If the shoe fits,' Mary said. She leaned on the arm of the sofa and laughed until tears came.

'What was that?' Jack said. He looked at Carl and then at Mary. 'I missed that one,' Jack said.

'I should have made some dip for these chips,' Helen said.

'Wasn't there another bottle of that cream soda?' Jack said.

'We bought two bottles,' Carl said.

'Did we drink them both?' Jack said.

'Did we drink any?' Helen said and laughed. 'No, I only opened one. I think I only opened one. I don't remember opening more than one,' Helen said and laughed.

Carl passed the tube to Mary. She took his hand and guided the tube into her mouth. He watched the smoke flow over her lips a long time later.

'What about some cream soda?' Jack said.

Mary and Helen laughed.

'What about it?' Mary said.

'Well, I thought we were going to have us a glass,' Jack said. He looked at Mary and grinned.

Mary and Helen laughed.

'What's funny?' Jack said. He looked at Helen and then at Mary. He shook his head. 'I don't know about you guys,' he said.

'We might go to Alaska,' Carl said.

'Alaska?' Jack said. 'What's in Alaska? What would you do up there?'

'I wish we could go someplace,' Helen said.

'What's wrong with here?' Jack said. 'What would you guys do in Alaska? I'm serious. I'd like to know.'

Carl put a potato chip in his mouth and sipped his cream soda. 'I don't know. What did you say?'

After a while Jack said. 'What's in Alaska?'

'I don't know,' Carl said. 'Ask Mary. Mary knows. Mary, what am I going to do up there? Maybe I'll grow those giant cabbages you read about.'

'Or pumpkins,' Helen said. 'Grow pumpkins.'

'You'd clean up,' Jack said. 'Ship the pumpkins down here for Halloween. I'll be your distributor.'

'Jack will be your distributor,' Helen said.

'That's right,' Jack said. 'We'll clean up.'

'Get rich,' Mary said.

In a while Jack stood up. 'I know what would taste good and that's some cream soda,' Jack said.

Mary and Helen laughed.

'Go ahead and laugh,' Jack said, grinning. 'Who wants some cream soda?'

'Some what?' Mary said.

'Some cream soda,' Jack said.

'You stood up like you were going to make a speech,' Mary said.

'I hadn't thought of that,' Jack said. He shook his head and laughed. He sat down, 'That's good stuff,' he said.

'We should have got more,' Helen said.

'More what?' Mary said.

'More money,' Jack said.

'No money,' Carl said.

'Did I see some U-No bars in that sack?' Helen said.

'I bought some,' Carl said. 'I spotted them the last minute.'

'U-no bars are good,' Jack said.

'They're creamy,' Mary said. 'They melt in your mouth.'

'We have some M and M's and Popsicles if anybody wants any,' Jack said.

Mary said, 'I'll have a Popsicle. Are you going to the kitchen?'

'Yeah, and I'm going to get the cream soda, too,' Jack said. 'I just remembered. You guys want a glass?'

'Just bring it all in and we'll decide,' Helen said. 'The M and M's too.'

'Might be easier to move the kitchen out here,' Jack said.

'When we lived in the city,' Mary said, 'people said you could see who'd turned on the night before by looking at their kitchen in the morning. We had a tiny kitchen when we lived in the city,' she said.

'We had a tiny kitchen too,' Carl said.

'I'm going out to see what I can find,' Jack said.

'I'll come with you,' Mary said.

Carl watched them walk to the kitchen. He settled back against the cushion and watched them walk. Then he leaned forward very slowly. He squinted. He saw Jack reach up to a shelf in the cupboard. He saw Mary move against Jack from behind and put her arms around his waist.

'Are you guys serious?' Helen said.

'Very serious,' Carl said.

'About Alaska,' Helen said.

He stared at her.

'I thought you said something,' Helen said.

Jack and Mary came back. Jack carried a large bag of M and M's and a bottle of cream soda. Mary sucked on an orange Popsicle.

'Anybody want a sandwich?' Helen said. 'We have sandwich stuff.'

'Isn't it funny,' Mary said. 'You start with the desserts first and then you move on to the main course.'

'It's funny,' Carl said.

'Are you being sarcastic, honey?' Mary said.

'Who wants cream soda?' Jack said. 'A round of cream soda coming up.'

Carl held his glass out and Jack poured it full. Carl set the glass on the coffee table, but the coffee table smacked it off and the soda poured onto his shoe.

'Goddamn it,' Carl said. 'How do you like that? I spilled it on my shoe.'

'Helen, do we have a towel? Get Carl a towel,' Jack said.

'Those were new shoes,' Mary said. 'He just got them.'

'They look comfortable,' Helen said a long time later and handed Carl a towel.

'That's what I told him,' Mary said.

Carl took the shoe off and rubbed the leather with the towel.

'It's done for,' he said. 'That cream soda will never come out.'

Mary and Jack and Helen laughed.

'That reminds me, I read something in the paper,' Helen said. She pushed on the tip of her nose with a finger and narrowed her eyes. 'I can't remember what it was now,' she said.

Carl worked the shoe back on. He put both feet under the lamp and looked at the shoes together.

'What did you read?' Jack said.

'What? Helen said.

'You said you read something in the paper,' Jack said.

Helen laughed. 'I was just thinking about Alaska, and I remembered them finding a prehistoric man in a block of ice. Something reminded me.'

'That wasn't in Alaska,' Jack said.

'Maybe it wasn't, but it reminded me of it,' Helen said.

'What *about* Alaska, you guys?' Jack said.

'There's nothing in Alaska,' Carl said.

'He's on a bummer,' Mary said.

'What'll you guys *do* in Alaska?' Jack said.

'There's nothing to do in Alaska,' Carl said. He put his feet under the coffee table. Then he moved them out under the light once more. 'Who wants a new pair of shoes?' Carl said.

'What's that noise?' Helen said.

They listened. Something scratched at the door.

'It sounds like Cindy,' Jack said. 'I'd better let her in.'

'While you're up, get me a Popsicle,' Helen said. She put her head back and laughed.

'I'll have another one too, honey,' Mary said. 'What did I say? I mean *Jack*,' Mary said. 'Excuse me. I thought I was talking to Carl.'

'Popsicles all around,' Jack said. 'You want a Popsicle, Carl?'

'What?'

'You want an orange Popsicle?'

'An orange one,' Carl said.

'Four Popsicles coming up,' Jack said.

In a while he came back with the Popsicles and handed them around. He sat down and they heard the scratching again.

'I knew I was forgetting something,' Jack said. He got up and opened the front door.

'Good Christ,' he said, 'if this isn't something. I guess Cindy went out for dinner tonight. Hey, you guys, look at this.'

The cat carried a mouse into the living room, stopped to look at them, then carried the mouse down the hall.

'Did you see what I just saw?' Mary said. 'Talk about a bummer.'

Jack turned the hall light on. The cat carried the mouse out of the hall and into the bathroom.

'She's eating this mouse,' Jack said.

'I don't think I want her eating a mouse in my bathroom,' Helen said. 'Make her get out of there. Some of the children's things are in there.'

'She's not going to get out of here,' Jack said.

'What about the mouse?' Mary said.

'What the hell,' Jack said. 'Cindy's got to learn to hunt if we're going to Alaska.'

'Alaska?' Helen said. 'What's all this about Alaska?'

'Don't ask me,' Jack said. He stood near the bathroom door and watched the cat. 'Mary and Carl said they're going to Alaska. Cindy's got to learn to hunt.'

Mary put her chin in her hands and stared into the hall.

'She's eating the mouse,' Jack said.

Helen finished the last of the corn chips. 'I told him I didn't want Cindy eating a mouse in the bathroom. Jack?' Helen said.

'What?'

'Make her get out of the bathroom, I said,' Helen said.

'For Christ's sake,' Jack said.

'Look,' Mary said. 'Ugh,' Mary said. 'The goddamn cat is coming in here,' Mary said.

'What's she doing?' Carl said.

The cat dragged the mouse under the coffee table. She lay down under the table and licked the mouse. She held the mouse in her paws and licked slowly, from head to tail.

'The cat's high,' Jack said.

'It gives you the shivers,' Mary said.

'It's just nature,' Jack said.

'Look at her eyes,' Mary said. 'Look at the way she looks at us. She's high, all right.'

Jack came over to the sofa and sat beside Mary. Mary inched toward Carl to give Jack room. She rested her hand on Carl's knee.

They watched the cat eat the mouse.

'Don't you ever feed that cat?' Mary said to Helen.

Helen laughed.

'You guys ready for another smoke?' Jack said.

'We have to go,' Carl said.

'What's your hurry?' Jack said.

'Stay a little longer,' Helen said. 'You don't have to go yet.'

Carl stared at Mary, who was staring at Jack. Jack stared at something on the rug near his feet.

Helen picked through the M and M's in her hand.

'I like the green ones best,' Helen said.

'I have to work in the morning,' Carl said.

'What a bummer he's on,' Mary said. 'You want to hear a bummer, folks? *There's* a bummer.'

'Are you coming?' Carl said.

'Anybody want a glass of milk?' Jack said. 'We've got some milk out there.'

'I'm too full of cream soda,' Mary said.

'There's no more cream soda,' Jack said.

Helen laughed. She closed her eyes and then opened them and then laughed again.

'We have to go home,' Carl said. In a while he stood up and said, 'Did we have coats? I don't think we had coats.'

'What? I don't think we had coats,' Mary said. She stayed seated.

'We'd better go,' Carl said.

'They have to go,' Helen said.

Carl put his hands under Mary's shoulders and pulled her up.

'Goodbye, you guys,' Mary said. She embraced Carl. 'I'm so full I can hardly move,' Mary said.

Helen laughed.

'Helen's always finding something to laugh at,' Jack said, and Jack grinned. 'What are you laughing at, Helen?'

'I don't know. Something Mary said,' Helen said.

'What did I say?' Mary said.

'I can't remember,' Helen said.

'We have to go,' Carl said.

'So long,' Jack said. 'Take it easy.'

Mary tried to laugh.

'Let's go,' Carl said.

'Night, everybody,' Jack said. 'Night, Carl,' Carl heard Jack say very, very slowly.

Outside, Mary held Carl's arm and walked with her head down. They moved slowly on the sidewalk. He listened to the scuffing sounds her shoes made. He heard the sharp and separate sound of a dog barking and above that a murmuring of a very distant traffic.

She raised her head. 'When we get home, Carl, I want to be fucked, talked to, diverted. Divert me, Carl. I need to be diverted tonight.' She tightened her hold on his arm.

He could feel the dampness in that shoe. He unlocked the door and flipped the light.

'Come to bed,' she said.

'I'm coming,' he said.

He went to the kitchen and drank two glasses of water. He turned off the living-room light and felt his way along the wall into the bedroom.

'Carl!' she yelled. 'Carl!'

'Jesus Christ, it's me!' he said. 'I'm trying to get the light on.'

He found the lamp, and she sat up in bed. Her eyes were bright. He pulled the stem on the alarm and began taking off his clothes. His knees trembled.

'Is there anything else to smoke?' she said.

'We don't have anything,' he said.

'Then fix me a drink. We have something to drink. Don't tell me we don't have something to drink,' she said.

'Just some beer.'

They stared at each other.

'I'll have a beer,' she said.

'You really want a beer?'

She nodded slowly and chewed her lip.

He came back with the beer. She was sitting with his pillow on her lap. He gave her the can of beer and then crawled into bed and pulled the covers up.

'I forgot to take my pill,' she said.

'What?'

'I forgot my pill.'

He got out of bed and brought her the pill. She opened her eyes and he dropped the pill onto her out-stretched tongue. She swallowed some beer with the pill and he got back in bed.

'Take this. I can't keep my eyes open,' she said.

He set the can on the floor and then stayed on his side and stared into the dark hallway. She put her arm over his ribs and her fingers crept across his chest.

'What's in Alaska?' she said.

He turned on his stomach and eased all the way to his side of the bed. In a moment she was snoring.

Just as he started to turn off the lamp, he thought he saw something in the hall. He kept staring and thought he saw it again, a pair of small eyes. His heart turned. He blinked and kept staring. He leaned over to look for something to throw. He picked up one of this shoes. He sat up straight and held the shoe with both hands. He heard her snoring and set his teeth. He waited. He waited for it to move once more, to make the slightest noise.

Night school

My marriage had just fallen apart. I couldn't find a job. I had another girl. But she wasn't in town. So I was at a bar having a glass of beer, and two women were sitting a few stools down, and one of them began to talk to me.

'You have a car?'

'I do, but it's not here,' I said.

My wife had the car. I was staying at my parents' place. I used their car sometimes. But tonight I was walking.

The other woman looked at me. They were both about forty, maybe older.

'What'd you ask him?' the other woman said to the first woman.

'I said did he have a car.'

'So do you have a car?' the second woman said to me.

'I was telling her. I have a car. But I don't have it with me,' I said.

'That doesn't do us much good, does it?' she said.

The first woman laughed. 'We had a brainstorm and we need a car to go through with it. Too bad.' She turned to the bartender and asked for two more beers.

I'd been nursing my beer along, and now I drank it off and thought they might buy me a round. They didn't.

'What do you do?' the first woman asked me.

'Right now, nothing,' I said. 'Sometimes, when I can, I go to school.'

'He goes to school,' she said to the other woman. 'He's a student. Where do you go to school?'

'Around,' I said.

'I told you,' the woman said. 'Doesn't he look like a student?'

'What are they teaching you?' the second woman said.

'Everything,' I said.

'I mean,' she said, 'what do you plan to do? What's your big goal in life? Everybody has a big goal in life.'

I raised my empty glass to the bartender. He took it and drew me another beer. I counted out some change, which left me with thirty cents from the two dollars I'd started out with a couple of hours ago. She was waiting.

'Teach. Teach school,' I said.

'He wants to be a teacher,' she said.

I sipped my beer. Someone put a coin in the jukebox and a song that my wife liked began to play. I looked around. Two men near the front were at the shuffleboard. The door was open and it was dark outside.

'We're students too, you know,' the first woman said. 'We go to school.'

'We take a night class,' the other one said. 'We take this reading class on Monday nights.'

The first woman said, 'Why don't you move down here, teacher, so we don't have to yell?'

I picked up my beer and my cigarets and moved down two stools.

'That's better,' she said. 'Now, did you say you were a student?'

Sometimes, yes, but not now,' I said.

'Where?'

'State College.'

'That's right,' she said. 'I remember now.' She looked at the other woman. 'You ever hear of a teacher over there name of Patterson? He teaches adult-education classes. He teaches this class we take on Monday nights. You remind me a lot of Patterson.'

They looked at each other and laughed.

'Don't bother about us,' the first woman said. 'It's a private joke. Shall we tell him what we thought about doing, Edith? *Shall* we?'

Edith didn't answer. She took a drink of beer and she narrowed her eyes as she looked at herself, at the three of us, in the mirror behind the bar.

'We were thinking,' the first woman went on, 'if we had a car tonight we'd go over and see him. Patterson, Right, Edith?'

Edith laughed to herself. She finished her beer and asked for a round, one for me included. She paid for the beers with a five-dollar bill.

'Patterson likes to take a drink,' Edith said.

'You can say that again,' the other woman said. She turned to me. 'We talked about it in class one night. Patterson says he always has wine with his meals and a highball or two before dinner.'

'What class is this?' I said.

'This reading class Patterson teaches. Patterson likes to talk about different things.'

'We're learning to read,' Edith said. 'Can you believe it?'

'I'd like to read Hemingway and things like that,' the other woman said. 'But Patterson has us reading stories like in *Reader's Digest*.'

'We take a test every Monday night,' Edith said. 'But Patterson's okay. He wouldn't care if we came over for a highball. Wouldn't be much he could do, anyway. We have something on him. On Patterson,' she said.

'We're on the loose tonight,' the other woman said. 'But Edith's car is in the garage.'

'If you had a car now, we'd go over and see him.' Edith said. She looked at me. 'You could tell Patterson you wanted to be a teacher. You'd have something in common.'

I finished my beer. I hadn't eaten anything all day except some peanuts. It was hard to keep listening and talking.

'Let's have three more, please, Jerry,' the first woman said to the bartender.

'Thank you,' I said.

'You'd get along with Patterson,' Edith said.

'So call him,' I said. I thought it was just talk.

'I wouldn't do that,' she said. 'He could make an excuse. We just show up on his porch, he'll have to let us in.' She sipped her beer.

'So let's go!' the first woman said. 'What're we waiting for? Where'd you say the car is?'

'There's a car a few blocks from here,' I said. 'But I don't know.'

'Do you want to go or don't you?' Edith said.

'He said he does,' the first woman said. 'We'll get a six-pack to take with us.'

'I only have thirty cents,' I said.

'Who needs your goddamn money?' Edith said. 'We need your goddamn car. Jerry, let's have three more. And a six-pack to go.'

'Here's to Patterson,' the first woman said when the beer came. 'To Patterson and his highballs.'

'He'll drop his cookies,' Edith said.

'Drink up,' the first woman said.

On the sidewalk we headed south, away from town. I walked between the two women. It was about ten o'clock.

'I could drink one of those beers now,' I said.

'Help yourself,' Edith said.

She opened the sack and I reached in and tore a can loose.

'We think he's home,' Edith said.

'Patterson,' the other woman said. 'We don't know for sure. But we think so.'

'How much farther?' Edith said.

I stopped, raised the beer, and drained half the can. 'The next block,' I said. 'I'm staying with my parents. It's their place.'

'I guess there's nothing wrong with it,' Edith said. 'But I'd say you're kind of old for that.'

'That's not polite, Edith,' the other woman said.

'Well, that's the way I am,' Edith said. 'He'll have to get used to it, that's all. That's the way I am.'

'That's the way she is,' the other woman said.

I finished the beer and tossed the can into some weeds.

'Now how far?' Edith said.

'This is it. Right here. I'll try and get the car key,' I said.

'Well, hurry up,' Edith said.

'We'll wait outside,' the other woman said.

'Jesus!' Edith said.

I unlocked the door and went downstairs. My father was in his pajamas, watching television. It was warm in the apartment and I leaned against the jamb for a minute and ran a hand over my eyes.

'I had a couple of beers,' I said. 'What are you watching?'

'John Wayne,' he said. 'It's pretty good. Sit down and watch it. Your mother hasn't come in yet.'

My mother worked the swing shift at Paul's, a *hofbrau* restaurant. My father didn't have a job. He used to work in the woods, and then he got hurt. He'd had a settlement, but most of that was gone now. I asked him for a loan of two hundred dollars when my wife left me, but he refused. He had tears in his eyes when he said no and said he hoped I wouldn't hold it against him. I'd said it was all right, I wouldn't hold it against him.

I knew he was going to say no this time too. But I sat down on the other end of the couch and said, 'I met a couple of women who asked me if I'd give them a ride home.'

'What'd you tell them?' he said.

'They're waiting for me upstairs,' I said.

'Just let them wait,' he said. 'Somebody'll come along. You don't want to get mixed up with that.' He shook his head. 'You really didn't show them where we live, did you? They're not really upstairs?' He moved on the couch and looked again at the television. 'Anyway, your mother took the keys with her.' He nodded slowly, still looking at the television.

'That's okay,' I said. 'I don't need the car. I'm not going any-where.'

I got up and looked into the hallway, where I slept on a cot. There was an ashtray, a Lux clock, and a few old paperbacks on a table beside the cot. I usually went to bed at midnight and read until the lines of print went fuzzy and I fell asleep with the light on and the book in my hands. In one of the paperbacks I was reading there was something I remembered telling my wife. It made a terrific impression on me. There's a man who has a nightmare and in the nightmare he dreams he's dreaming and wakes to see a man standing at his bedroom window. The dreamer is so terrified he can't move, can hardly breathe. The man at the window stares into the room and then begins to pry off the screen. The dreamer can't move. He'd like to scream, but he can't get his breath. But the moon appears from behind a cloud, and the dreamer in the nightmare recognizes the man outside. It is his best friend, the best friend of the dreamer but no one the man having the nightmare knows.

Telling it to my wife, I'd felt the blood come to my face and my scalp prickle. But she wasn't interested.

'That's only writing,' she said. 'Being betrayed by somebody in your own family, *there's* a real nightmare for you.'

I could hear them shaking the outside door. I could hear footsteps on the sidewalk over my window.

'Goddamn that bastard!' I heard Edith say.

I went into the bathroom for a long time and then I went upstairs and let myself out. It was cooler, and I did up the zipper on my jacket. I started walking to Paul's. If I got there before my mother went off duty, I could have a turkey sandwich. After that I could go to Kirby's newsstand and look through the magazines. Then I could go to the apartment to bed and read the books until I read enough and I slept.

The women, they weren't there when I left, and they wouldn't be there when I got back.

Collectors

I was out of work. But any day I expected to hear from up north. I lay on the sofa and listened to the rain. Now and then I'd lift up and look through the curtain for the mailman.

There was no one on the street, nothing.

I hadn't been down again five minutes when I heard someone walk onto the porch, wait, and then knock. I lay still. I knew it wasn't the mailman. I knew his steps. You can't be too careful if you're out of work and you get notices in the mail or else pushed under your door. They come around wanting to talk, too, especially if you don't have a telephone.

The knock sounded again, louder, a bad sign. I eased up and tried to see onto the porch. But whoever was there was standing against the door, another bad sign. I knew the floor creaked, so there was no chance of slipping into the other room and looking out that window.

Another knock, and I said, Who's there?

This is Aubrey Bell, a man said. Are you Mr Slater?

What is it you want? I called from the sofa.

I have something for Mrs Slater. She's won something. Is Mrs Slater home?

Mrs Slater doesn't live here, I said.

Well, then, are you Mr Slater? the man said. Mr Slater . . . and the man sneezed.

I got off the sofa. I unlocked the door and opened it a little. He was an old guy, fat and bulky under his raincoat. Water ran off the coat and dripped onto the big suitcase contraption thing he carried.

He grinned and set down the big case. He put out his hand.

Aubrey Bell, he said.

I don't know you, I said.

Mrs Slater, he began. Mrs Slater filled out a card. He took cards from an inside pocket and shuffled them a minute. Mrs Slater, he read. Two-fifty-five South Sixth East? Mrs Slater is a winner.

He took off his hat and nodded solemnly, slapped the hat against his coat as if that were it, everything had been settled, the drive finished, the railhead reached.

He waited.

Mrs Slater doesn't live here, I said. What'd she win?

I have to show you, he said. May I come in?

I don't know. If it won't take long, I said. I'm pretty busy.

Fine, he said. I'll just slide out of this coat first. And the galoshes. Wouldn't want to track up your carpet. I see you do have a carpet, Mr . . . .

His eyes had lighted and then dimmed at the sight of the carpet. He shuddered. Then he took off his coat. He shook it out and hung it by the collar over the doorknob. That's a good place for it, he said. Damn weather, anyway. He bent over and unfastened his galoshes. He set his case inside the room. He stepped out of the galoshes and into the room in a pair of slippers.

I closed the door, He saw me staring at the slippers and said, W.H. Auden wore slippers all through China on his first visit there. Never took them off. Corns.

I shrugged. I took one more look down the street for the mailman and shut the door again.

Aubrey Bell stared at the carpet. He pulled his lips. Then he laughed. He laughed and shook his head.

What's so funny? I said.

Nothing. Lord, he said. He laughed again. I think I'm losing my mind. I think I have a fever. He reached a hand to his forehead. His hair was matted and there was a ring around his scalp where the hat had been.

Do I feel hot to you? he said. I don't know, I think I might have a fever. He was still staring at the carpet. You have any aspirin?

What's the matter with you? I said. I hope you're not getting sick on me. I got things I have to do.

He shook his head. He sat down on the sofa. He stirred at the carpet with his slippered foot.

I went to the kitchen, rinsed a cup, shook two aspirin out of a bottle.

Here, I said. Then I think you ought to leave.

Are you speaking for Mrs Slater? he hissed. No, no, forget I said that, forget I said that. He wiped his face. He swallowed the aspirin. His eyes skipped around the bare room. Then he leaned forward with some effort and unsnapped the buckles on his case. The case flopped open, revealing compartments filled with an array of hoses, brushes, shiny pipes, and some kind of heavy-looking blue thing mounted on little wheels. He stared at these things as if surprised. Quietly, in a churchly voice, he said, Do you know what this is?

I moved closer. I'd say it was a vacuum cleaner. I'm not in the market, I said. No way am I in the market for a vacuum cleaner.

I want to show you something, he said. He took a card out of his jacket pocket. Look at this, he said. He handed me the card. Nobody said you were in the market. But look at the signature. Is that Mrs Slater's signature or not?

I looked at the card. I held it up to the light. I turned it over, but the other side was blank. So what? I said.

Mrs Slater's card was pulled at random out of a basket of cards. Hundreds of cards just like this little card. She has won a free vacuuming and carpet shampoo. Mrs Slater is a winner. No strings. I am here even to do your mattress, Mr . . . . You'll be surprised to see what can collect in a mattress over the months, over the years. Every day, every night of our lives, we're leaving little bits of ourselves, flakes of this and that, behind. Where do they go, these bits and pieces of ourselves? Right through the sheets and into the mattress, *that's* where! Pillows, too. It's all the same.

He had been removing lengths of the shiny pipe and joining the parts together. Now he inserted the fitted pipes into the hose. He was on his knees, grunting. He attached some sort of scoop to the hose and lifted out the blue thing with wheels.

He let me examine the filter he intended to use.

Do you have a car? he asked.

No car, I said. I don't have a car. If I had a car I would drive you someplace.

Too bad, he said. This little vacuum comes equipped with a sixty-foot extension cord. If you had a car, you could wheel this little vacuum right up to your car door and vacuum the plush carpeting and the luxurious reclining seats as well. You would be surprised how much of us gets lost, how much of us gathers, in those fine seats over the years.

Mr Bell, I said, I think you better pack up your things and go. I say this without any malice whatsoever.

But he was looking around the room for a plug-in. He found one at the end of the sofa. The machine rattled as if there were a marble inside, anyway something loose inside, then settled to a hum.

Rilke lived in one castle after another, all of his adult life. Benefactors, he said loudly over the hum of the vacuum. He seldom rode in motorcars; he preferred trains. Then look at Voltaire at Cirey with

Madame Châtelet. His death mask. Such serenity. He raised his right hand as if I were about to disagree. No, no, it isn't right, is it? Don't say it. But who knows? With that he turned and began to pull the vacuum into the other room.

There was a bed, a window. The covers were heaped on the floor. One pillow, one sheet over the mattress. He slipped the case from the pillow and then quickly stripped the sheet from the mattress. He stared at the mattress and gave me a look out of the corner of his eye. I went to the kitchen and got the chair. I sat down in the doorway and watched. First he tested the suction by putting the scoop against the palm of his hand. He bent and turned a dial on the vacuum. You have to turn it up full strength for a job like this one, he said. He checked the suction again, then extended the hose to the head of the bed and began to move the scoop down the mattress. The scoop tugged at the mattress. The vacuum whirred louder. He made three passes over the mattress, then switched off the machine. He pressed a lever and the lid popped open. He took out the filter. This filter is just for demonstration purposes. In normal use, all of this, this *material*, would to into your bag, here, he said. He pinched some of the dusty stuff between his fingers. There must have been a cup of it.

He had this look to his face.

It's not my mattress, I said. I leaned forward in the chair and tried to show an interest.

Now the pillow, he said. He put the used filter on the sill and looked out the window for a minute. He turned. I want you to hold onto this end of the pillow, he said.

I got up and took hold of two corners of the pillow. I felt I was holding something by the ears.

Like this? I said.

He nodded. He went into the other room and came back with another filter.

How much do those things cost? I said.

Next to nothing, he said. They're only made out of paper and a little bit of plastic. Couldn't cost much.

He kicked on the vacuum and I held tight as the scoop sank into the pillow and moved down its length — once, twice, three times. He switched off the vacuum, removed the filter, and held it up without a word. He put it on the sill beside the other filter. Then he opened the closet door. He looked inside, but there was only a box of Mouse-Be-Gone.

I heard steps on the porch, the mail slot opened and clinked shut. We looked at each other.

He pulled on the vacuum and I followed him into the other room. We looked at the letter lying face down on the carpet near the front door.

I started toward the letter, turned and said, What else? It's getting late. This carpet's not worth fooling with. It's only a twelve-by-fifteen cotton carpet with no-skin backing from Rug City. It's not worth fooling with.

Do you have a full ashtray? he said. Or a potted plant or something like that? A handful of dirt would be fine.

I found the ashtray. He took it, dumped the contents onto the carpet, ground the ashes and cigarets under his slipper. He got down on his knees again and inserted a new filter. He took off his jacket and threw it onto the sofa. He was sweating under the arms. Fat hung over his belt. He twisted off the scoop and attached another device to the hose. He adjusted his dial. He kicked on the machine and began to move back and forth, back and forth over the worn carpet. Twice I started for the letter. But he seemed to anticipate me, cut me off, so to speak, with his hose and his pipes and his sweeping and his sweeping. . . .

I took the chair back to the kitchen and sat there and watched him work. After a time he shut off the machine, opened the lid, and silently brought me the filter, alive with dust, hair, small grainy things. I looked at the filter, and then I got up and put it in the garbage.

He worked steadily now. No more explanations. He came out to the kitchen with a bottle that held a few ounces of green liquid. He put the bottle under the tap and filled it.

You know I can't pay anything, I said. I couldn't pay you a dollar if my life depended on it. You're going to have to write me off as a dead loss, that's all. You're wasting your time on me, I said.

I wanted it out in the open, no misunderstanding.

He went about his business. He put another attachment on the hose, in some complicated way hooked his bottle to the new attachment. He moved slowly over the carpet, now and then releasing little streams of emerald, moving the brush back and forth over the carpet, working up patches of foam.

I had said all that was on my mind. I sat on the chair in the kitchen, relaxed now, and watched him work. Once in a while I looked out the

window at the rain. It had begun to get dark. He switched off the
vacuum. He was in a corner near the front door.

You want coffee? I said.

He was breathing hard. He wiped his face.

I put on water and by the time it had boiled and I'd fixed up two
cups he had everything dismantled and back in the case. Then he
picked up the letter. He read the name on the letter and looked closely
at the return address. He folded the letter in half and put it in his hip
pocket. I kept watching him. That's all I did. The coffee began to cool.

It's for a Mr Slater, he said. I'll see to it. He said, Maybe I will skip
the coffee. I better not walk across this carpet. I just shampooed it.

That's true, I said. Then I said, You're sure that's who the letter's
for?

He reached to the sofa for his jacket, put it on, and opened the front
door. It was still raining. He stepped into his galoshes, fastened them,
and then pulled on the raincoat and looked back inside.

You want to see it? he said. You don't believe me?

It just seems strange, I said.

Well, I'd better be off, he said. But he kept standing there. You
want the vacuum or not?

I looked at the big case, closed now and ready to move on.

No, I said, I guess not. I'm going to be leaving here soon. It would
just be in the way.

All right, he said, and he shut the door.

What do you do
in San Francisco?

This has nothing to do with me. It's about a young couple with three children who moved into a house on my route the first of last summer. I got to thinking about them again when I picked up last Sunday's newspaper and found a picture of a young man who'd been arrested down in San Francisco for killing his wife and her boyfriend with a baseball bat. It wasn't the same man, of course, though there was a likeness because of the beard. But the situation was close enough to get me thinking.

Henry Robinson is the name. I'm a postman, a federal civil servant, and have been since 1947. I've lived in the West all my life, except for a three-year stint in the Army during the war. I've been divorced twenty years, have two children I haven't seen in almost that long. I'm not a frivolous man, nor am I, in my opinion, a serious man. It's my belief a man has to be a little of both these days. I believe, too, in the value of work — the harder the better. A man who isn't working has got too much time on his hands, too much time to dwell on himself and his problems.

I'm convinced that was partly the trouble with the young man who lived here — his not working. But I'd lay that at her doorstep, too. The woman. She encouraged it.

Beatniks, I guess you'd have called them if you'd seen them. The man wore a pointed brown beard on his chin and looked like he needed to sit down to a good dinner and a cigar afterwards. The woman was attractive, with her long dark hair and her fair complexion, there's no getting around that. But put me down for saying she wasn't a good wife and mother. She was a painter. The young man, I don't know what he did — probably something along the same line. Neither of them worked. But they paid their rent and got by somehow — at least for the summer.

The first time I saw them it was around eleven, eleven-fifteen, a Saturday morning. I was about two-thirds through my route when I turned onto their block and noticed a '56 Ford sedan pulled up in the yard with a big open U-Haul behind. There are only three houses on Pine, and theirs was the last house, the others being the Murchisons, who'd been in Arcata a little less than a year, and the Grants, who'd been here about two years. Murchison worked at Simpson Redwood, and Gene Grant was a cook on the morning shift at Denny's. Those two, then a vacant lot, then the house on the end that used to belong to the Coles.

The young man was out in the yard behind the trailer and she was just coming out the front door with a cigaret in her mouth, wearing a tight pair of white jeans and a man's white undershirt. She stopped when she saw me and she stood watching me come down the walk. I slowed up when I came even with their box and nodded in her direction.

'Getting settled all right?' I asked.

'It'll be a little while,' she said and moved a handful of hair away from her forehead while she continued to smoke.

'That's good,' I said. 'Welcome to Arcata.'

I felt a little awkward after saying it. I don't know why, but I always found myself feeling awkward the few times I was around this woman. It was one of the things helped turn me against her from the first.

She gave me a thin smile and I started to move on when the young man – Marston was his name – came around from behind the trailer carrying a big carton of toys. Now, Arcata is not a small town and it's not a big town, though I guess you'd have to say it's more on the small side. It's not the end of the world, Arcata, by any means, but most of the people who live here work either in the lumber mills or have something to do with the fishing industry, or else work in one of the downtown stores. People here aren't used to seeing men wear beards – or men who don't work, for that matter.

'Hello,' I said. I put out my hand when he set the carton down on the front fender. 'The name's Henry Robinson. You folks just arrive?'

'Yesterday afternoon,' he said.

'Some trip! It took us fourteen hours just to come from San Francisco,' the woman spoke up from the porch. 'Pulling that damn trailer.'

'My, my,' I said and shook my head. 'San Francisco? I was just down in San Francisco, let me see, last April or March.'

'You were, were you?' she said. 'What did you do in San Francisco?'

'Oh, nothing, really. I go down about once or twice a year. Out to Fisherman's Wharf and to see the Giants play. That's about all.'

There was a little pause and Marston examined something in the grass with his toe. I started to move on. The kids picked that moment to come flying out the front door, yelling and tearing for the end of the porch. When that screen door banged open, I thought Marston was going to jump out of his skin. But she just stood there with her arms crossed, cool as a cucumber, and never batted an eye. He didn't look good at all. Quick, jerky little movements every time he made to do something. And his eyes – they'd land on you and then slip off somewhere else, then land on you again.

There were three kids, two little curly-headed girls about four or five, and a little bit of a boy tagging after.

'Cute kids,' I said. 'Well, I got to get under way. You might want to change the name on the box.'

'Sure,' he said. 'Sure. I'll see about it in a day or two. But we don't expect to get any mail for a while yet, in any case.'

'You never know,' I said. 'You never know what'll turn up in this old mail pouch. Wouldn't hurt to be prepared.' I started to go. 'By the way, if you're looking for a job in the mills, I can tell you who to see at Simpson Redwood. A friend of mine's a foreman there. He'd probably have something . . .' I tapered off, seeing how they didn't look interested.

'No thanks,' he said.

'He's not looking for a job,' she put in.

'Well, goodbye, then.'

'So long,' Marston said.

Not another word from her.

That was on a Saturday, as I said, the day before Memorial Day. We took Monday as a holiday and I wasn't by there again until Tuesday. I can't say I was surprised to see the U-Haul still there in the front yard. But it did surprise me to see he still hadn't unloaded it. I'd say about a quarter of the stuff had made its way to the front porch – a covered chair and a chrome kitchen chair and a big carton of clothes that had the flaps pulled off the top. Another quarter must have gotten inside the house, and the rest of the stuff was still in the trailer. The kids were carrying little sticks and hammering on the sides of the trailer as they climbed in and out over the tailgate. Their mama and daddy were nowheres to be seen.

On Thursday I saw him out in the yard again and reminded him about changing the name on the box.

'That's something I've got to get around to doing,' he said.

'Takes time,' I said. 'There's lots of things to take care of when you're moving into a new place. People that lived here, the Coles, just moved out two days before you came. He was going to work in Eureka. With the Fish and Game Department.'

Marston stroked his beard and looked off as if thinking of something else.

'I'll be seeing you,' I said.

'So long,' he said.

Well, the long and the short of it was he never did change the name on the box. I'd come along a bit later with a piece of mail for that address and he'd say something like, 'Marston? Yes, that's for us, Marston . . . . I'll have to change the name on that box one of these days. I'll get myself a can of paint and just paint over that other name . . . Cole,' all the time his eyes drifting here and there. Then he'd look at me kind of out the corners and bob his chin once or twice. But he never did change the name on the box, and after a time I shrugged and forgot about it.

You hear rumors. At different times I heard that he was an ex-con on parole who come to Arcata to get out of the unhealthy San Francisco environment. According to this story, the woman was his wife, but none of the kids belonged to him. Another story was that he had committed a crime and was hiding out here. But not many people subscribed to that. He just didn't look the sort who'd do something really *criminal*. The story most folks seemed to believe, at least the one that got around most, was the most horrible. The woman was a dope addict, so this story went, and the husband had brought her up here to help her get rid of the habit. As evidence, the fact of Sallie Wilson's visit was always brought up – Sallie Wilson from the Welcome Wagon. She dropped in on them one afternoon and said later that, no lie, there was something funny about them – the woman, particular. One minute the woman would be sitting and listening to Sallie run on – all ears, it seemed – and the next she'd get up while Sallie was still talking and start to work on her painting as if Sallie wasn't there. Also the way she'd be fondling and kissing the kids, then suddenly start screeching at them for no apparent reason. Well, just the way her *eyes* looked if you came up close to her, Sallie said. But Sallie Wilson has been snooping and prying for years under cover of the Welcome Wagon.

'You don't know,' I'd say when someone would bring it up. 'Who can say? If he'd just go to work now.'

All the same, the way it looked to me was that they had their fair share of trouble down there in San Francisco, whatever was the nature of the trouble, and they decided to get clear away from it. Though why they ever picked Arcata to settle in, it's hard to say, since they surely didn't come looking for work.

The first few weeks there was no mail to speak of, just a few circulars, from Sears and Western Auto and the like. Then a few letters began to come in, maybe one or two a week. Sometimes I'd see one or the other of them out around the house when I came by and sometimes not. But the kids were always there, running in and out of the house or playing in the vacant lot next door. Of course, it wasn't a model home to begin with, but after they'd been there a while the weeds sprouted up and what grass there was yellowed and died. You hate to see something like that. I understand Old Man Jessup came out once or twice to get them to turn the water on, but they claimed they couldn't buy hose. So he left them a hose. Then I noticed the kids playing with it over in the field, and that was the end of that. Twice I saw a little white sports car in front, a car that hadn't come from around here.

One time only I had anything to do with the woman direct. There was a letter with five cents postage due, and I went up to the door with it. One of the little girls let me in and ran off to fetch her mama. The place was cluttered with odds and ends of old furniture and with clothing tossed just anywhere. But it wasn't what you'd call dirty. Not tidy maybe, but not dirty either. An old couch and chair stood along one wall in the living toom. Under the window was a bookcase made out of bricks and boards, crammed full of little paperback books. In the corner there was a stack of paintings with their faces turned away, and to one side another painting stood on an easel covered over with a sheet.

I shifted my mail pouch and stood my ground, but starting to wish I'd paid the nickel myself. I eyed the easel as I waited, about to sidle over and raise the sheet when I heard steps.

'What can I do for you?' she said, appearing in the hallway and not at all friendly.

I touched the brim of my cap and said, 'A letter here with five cents postage due, if you don't mind.'

'Let me see. Who's it from? Why it's from Jer! That kook. Sending us a letter without a stamp. Lee!' she called out. 'Here's a letter from

Jerry.' Marston came in, but he didn't look too happy. I leaned on first one leg, then the other, waiting.

'Five cents,' she said. 'I'll pay it, seeing as it's from old Jerry. Here. Now goodbye.'

Things went on in this fashion – which is to say no fashion at all. I won't say the people hereabouts got used to them – they weren't the sort you'd ever really get used to. But after a bit no one seemed to pay them much mind any more. People might stare at his beard if they met him pushing the grocery cart in Safeway, but that's about all. You didn't hear any more stories.

Then one day they disappeared. In two different directions. I found out later she'd taken off the week before with somebody – a man – and that after a few days he'd taken the kids to his mother's over to Redding. For six days running, from one Thursday to the following Wednesday, their mail stayed in the box. The shades were all pulled and nobody knew for certain whether or not they'd lit out for good. But that Wednesday I noticed the Ford parked in the yard again, all the shades still down but the mail gone.

Beginning the next day he was out there at the box every day waiting for me to hand over the mail, or else he was sitting on the porch steps smoking a cigaret, waiting, it was plain to see. When he saw me coming, he'd stand up, brush the seat of his trousers, and walk over by the box. If it happened that I had any mail for him, I'd see him start scanning the return addresses even before I could get it handed over. We seldom exchanged a word, just nodded at each other if our eyes happened to meet, which wasn't often. He was suffering, though – anybody could see that – and I wanted to help the boy somehow, if I could. But I didn't know what to say exactly.

It was one morning a week or so after his return that I saw him walking up and down in front of the box with his hands in his back pockets, and I made up my mind to say something. What, I didn't know yet, but I was going to say something, sure. His back was to me as I came up the walk. When I got to him, he suddenly turned on me and there was such a look on his face it froze the words in my mouth. I stopped in my tracks with his article of mail. He took a couple of steps toward me and I handed it over without a peep. He stared at it as if dumbfounded.

'Occupant,' he said.

It was a circular from L.A. advertising a hospital-insurance plan. I'd dropped off at least seventy-five that morning. He folded it in two and went back to the house.

Next day he was out there same as always. He had his old look to his face, seemed more in control of himself than the day before. This time I had a hunch I had what it was he'd been waiting for. I'd looked at it down at the station that morning when I was arranging the mail into packets. It was a plain white envelope addressed in a woman's curlicue handwriting that took up most of the space. It had a Portland postmark, and the return address showed the initials JD and a Portland street address.

'Morning,' I said, offering the letter.

He took it from me without a word and went absolutely pale. He tottered a minute and then started back for the house, holding the letter up to the light.

I called out, 'She's no good, boy. I could tell that the minute I saw her. Why don't you forget her? Why don't you go to work and forget her? What have you got against work? It was work, day and night, work that gave me oblivion when I was in your shoes and there was a war on where I was . . . .'

After that he didn't wait outside for me any more, and he was only there another five days. I'd catch a glimpse of him, though, each day, waiting for me just the same, but standing behind the window and looking out at me through the curtain. He wouldn't come out until I'd gone by, and then I'd hear the screen door. If I looked back, he'd seem to be in no hurry at all to reach the box.

The last time I saw him he was standing at the window and looked calm and rested. The curtains were down, all the shades were raised, and I figured at the time he was getting his things together to leave. But I could tell by the look on his face he wasn't watching for me this time. He was staring past me, over me, you might say, over the rooftops and the trees, south. He just kept staring even after I'd come even with the house and moved on down the sidewalk. I looked back. I could see him still there at the window. The feeling was so strong, I had to turn around and look for myself in the same direction he was. But, as you might guess, I didn't see anything except the same old timber, mountains, sky.

The next day he was gone. He didn't leave any forwarding. Sometimes mail of some kind or other shows up for him or his wife or for the both of them. If it's first-class, we hold it a day, then send it back to where it came from. There isn't much. And I don't mind. It's all work, one way or the other, and I'm always glad to have it.

The student's wife

He had been reading to her from Rilke, a poet he admired, when she fell asleep with her head on his pillow. He liked reading aloud, and he read well – a confident sonorous voice, now pitched low and somber, now rising, now thrilling. He never looked away from the page when he read and stopped only to reach to the nightstand for a cigaret. It was a rich voice that spilled her into a dream of caravans just setting out from walled cities and bearded men in robes. She had listened to him for a few minutes, then she had closed her eyes and drifted off.

He went on reading aloud. The children had been asleep for hours, and outside a car rubbered by now and then on the wet pavement. After a while he put down the book and turned in the bed to reach for the lamp. She opened her eyes suddenly, as if frightened, and blinked two or three times. Her eyelids looked oddly dark and fleshy to him as they flicked up and down over her fixed glassy eyes. He stared at her.

'Are you dreaming?' he asked.

She nodded and brought her hand up and touched her fingers to the plastic curlers at each side of her head. Tomorrow would be Friday, her day for all the four-to-seven-year-olds in the Woodlawn Apartments. He kept looking at her, leaning on his elbow, at the same time trying to straighten the spread with his free hand. She had a smooth-skinned face with prominent cheekbones; the cheekbones, she some-times insisted to friends, were from her father, who had been one-quarter Nez Perce.

Then:'Make me a little sandwich of something, Mike. With butter and lettuce and salt on the bread.'

He did nothing and he said nothing because he wanted to go to sleep. But when he opened his eyes she was still awake, watching him.

'Can't you go to sleep, Nan?' he said, very solemnly. 'It's late.'

'I'd like something to eat first,' she said. 'My legs and arms hurt for some reason, and I'm hungry.'

He groaned extravagantly as he rolled out of bed.

He fixed her the sandwich and brought it in on a saucer. She sat up in bed and smiled when he came into the bedroom, then slipped a pillow behind her back as she took the saucer. He thought she looked like a hospital patient in her white nightgown.

'What a funny little dream I had.'

'What were you dreaming?' he said, getting into bed and turning over onto his side away from her. He stared at the nightstand waiting. Then he closed his eyes slowly.

'Do you really want to hear it?' she said.

'Sure,' he said.

She settled back comfortably on the pillow and picked a crumb from her lip.

'Well. It seemed like a real long drawn-out kind of dream, you know, with all kinds of relationships going on, but I can't remember everything now. It was all very clear when I woke up, but it's beginning to fade now. How long have I been asleep, Mike? It doesn't really matter, I guess. Anyway, I think it was that we were staying someplace overnight. I don't know where the kids were, but it was just the two of us at some little hotel or something. It was on some lake that wasn't familiar. There was another, older, couple there and they wanted to take us for a ride in their motorboat.' She laughed, remembering, and leaned forward off the pillow. 'The next thing I recall is we were down at the boat landing. Only the way it turned out, they had just one seat in the boat, a kind of bench up in the front, and it was only big enough for three. You and I started arguing about who was going to sacrifice and sit all cooped up in the back. You said you were, and I said I was. But I finally squeezed in the back of the boat. It was so narrow it hurt my legs, and I was afraid the water was going to come in over the sides. Then I woke up.'

'That's some dream,' he managed to say and felt drowsily that he should say something more. 'You remember Bonnie Travis? Fred Travis' wife? She used to have *color* dreams, she said.'

She looked at the sandwich in her hand and took a bite. When she had swallowed, she ran her tongue in behind her lips and balanced the saucer on her lap as she reached behind and plumped up the pillow. Then she smiled and leaned back against the pillow again.

'Do you remember that time we stayed overnight on the Tilton River, Mike? When you caught that big fish the next morning?' She placed her hand on his shoulder. 'Do you remember that?' she said.

She did. After scarcely thinking about it these last years, it had begun coming back to her lately. It was a month or two after they'd married and gone away for a weekend. They had sat by a little campfire that night, a watermelon in the snow-cold river, and she'd fried Spam and eggs and canned beans for supper and pancakes and

Spam and eggs in the same blackened pan the next morning. She had burned the pan both times she cooked, and they could never get the coffee to boil, but it was one of the best times they'd ever had. She remembered he had read to her that night as well: Elizabeth Browning and a few poems from the *Rubáiyát*. They had so many covers over them that she could hardly turn her feet under all the weight. The next morning he had hooked a big trout, and people stopped their cars on the road across the river to watch him play it in.

'Well? Do you remember or not?' she said, patting him on the shoulder. 'Mike?'

'I remember,' he said. He shifted a little on his side, opened his eyes. He did not remember very well, he thought. What he did remember was very carefully combed hair and loud half-baked ideas about life and art, and he did not want to remember that.

'That was a long time ago, Nan,' he said.

'We'd just got out of high school. You hadn't started to college,' she said.

He waited, and then he raised up onto his arm and turned his head to look at her over his shoulder. 'You about finished with that sandwich, Nan?' She was still sitting up in the bed.

She nodded and gave him the saucer.

'I'll turn off the light,' he said.

'If you want,' she said.

Then he pulled down into the bed again and extended his foot until it touched against hers. He lay still for a minute and then tried to relax.

'Mike, you're not asleep, are you?'

'No,' he said. 'Nothing like that.'

'Well, don't go to sleep before me,' she said. 'I don't want to be awake by myself.'

He didn't answer, but he inched a little closer to her on his side. When she put her arm over him and planted her hand flat against his chest, he took her fingers and squeezed them lightly. But in moments his hand dropped away to the bed, and he sighed.

'Mike? Honey? I wish you'd rub my legs. My legs hurt,' she said.

'God,' he said softly. 'I was sound asleep.'

'Well, I wish you'd rub my legs and talk to me. My shoulders hurt, too. But my legs especially.'

He turned over and began rubbing her legs, then fell asleep again with his hand on her hip.

'Mike?'

'What is it, Nan? Tell me what it *is*.'

'I wish you'd rub me all over,' she said, turning onto her back. 'My legs and arms both hurt tonight,' She raised her knees to make a tower with the covers.

He opened his eyes briefly in the dark and then shut them. 'Growing pains, huh?'

'O God, yes,' she said, wiggling her toes, glad she had drawn him out. 'When I was ten or eleven years old I was as big then as I am now. You should've seen me! I grew so fast in those days my legs and arms hurt me all the time. Didn't you?'

'Didn't I what?'

'Didn't you ever feel yourself growing?'

'Not that I remember,' he said.

At last he raised up on his elbow, struck a match, and looked at the clock. He turned his pillow over to the cooler side and lay down again.

She said, 'You're asleep, Mike, I wish you'd want to talk.'

'All right,' he said, not moving.

'Just hold me and get me off to sleep. I can't go to sleep,' she said.

He turned over and put his arm over her shoulder as she turned onto her side to face the wall.

'Mike?'

He tapped his toes against her foot.

'Why don't you tell me all the things you like and the things you don't like.'

'Don't know any right now,' he said. 'Tell me if you want,' he said.

'If you promise to tell *me*. Is that a promise?

He tapped her foot again.

'Well . . .' she said and turned onto her back, pleased. 'I like good foods, steaks and hash-brown potatoes, things like that. I like good books and magazines, riding on trains at night, and those times I flew in an airplane.' She stopped. 'Of course none of this is in order of preference. I'd have to think about it if it was in the order of preference. But I like that, flying in airplanes. There's a moment as you leave the ground you feel whatever happens is all right.' She put her leg across his ankle. 'I like staying up late at night and then staying in bed the next morning. I wish we could do that all the time, not just once in a while. And I like sex. I like to be touched now and then when I'm not expecting it. I like going to movies and drinking beer with friends afterwards. I like to have friends. I like Janice Hendricks very much. I'd like to go dancing at least once a week. I'd like to have nice clothes all the time. I'd like to be able to buy the kids nice clothes every time they need it without having to wait. Laurie needs a new little outfit right now for Easter. And I'd like to get Gary a little suit or something. He's old enough. I'd like you to have a new suit, too. You really need a new suit more than he does. And I'd like us to have a place of our own. I'd like to stop moving around every year, or every other year. Most of all,' she said, 'I'd like us both just to live a good honest life without having to worry about money and bills and things like that. You're asleep,' she said.

'I'm not,' he said.

'I can't think of anything else. You go now. Tell me what you'd like.'

'I don't know. Lots of things,' he mumbled.

'Well, tell me. We're just talking, aren't we?'

'I wish you'd leave me alone, Nan.' He turned over to his side of the bed again and let his arm rest off the edge. She turned too and pressed against him.

'Mike?'

'Jesus,' he said. Then: 'All right. Let me stretch my legs a minute, then I'll wake up.'

In a while she said, 'Mike? Are you asleep?' She shook his shoulder gently, but there was no response. She lay there for a time huddled against his body, trying to sleep. She lay quietly at first, without moving, crowded against him and taking only very small, very even breaths. But she could not sleep.

She tried not to listen to his breathing, but it began to make her uncomfortable. There was a sound coming from inside his nose when he breathed. She tried to regulate her breathing so that she could breathe in and out at the same rhythm he did. It was no use. The little sound in his nose made everything no use. There was a webby squeak in his chest too. She turned again and nestled her bottom against his, stretched her arm over to the edge and cautiously put her fingertips against the cold wall. The covers had pulled up at the foot of the bed, and she could feel a draft when she moved her legs. She heard two people coming up the stairs to the apartment next door. Someone gave a throaty laugh before opening the door. Then she heard a chair drag on the floor. The toilet flushed next door, and then it flushed again. Again she turned, onto her back this time, and tried to relax. She remembered an article she'd once read in a magazine: If all the bones and muscles and joints in the body could join together in perfect relaxation, sleep would almost certainly come. She took a long breath, closed her eyes, and lay perfectly still, arms straight along her sides. She tried to relax. She tried to imagine her legs suspended, bathed in something gauze-like. She turned onto her stomach. She closed her eyes, then she opened them. She thought of the fingers of her hand lying curled on the sheet in front of her lips. She raised a finger and lowered it to the sheet. She touched the wedding band on her ring finger with her thumb. She turned onto her side and then onto her back again. And then she began to feel afraid, and in one unreasoning moment of longing she prayed to go to sleep.

Please, God, let me go to sleep.

She tried to sleep.

'Mike,' she whispered.

There was no answer.

She heard one of the children turn over in the bed and bump against the wall in the next room. She listened and listened but there was no other sound. She laid her hand under her left breast and felt the beat of her heart rising into her fingers. She turned onto her stomach and began to cry, her head off the pillow, her mouth against the sheet. She cried. And then she climbed out over the foot of the bed.

She washed her hands and face in the bathroom. She brushed her teeth. She brushed her teeth and watched her face in the mirror. In the living room she turned up the heat. Then she sat down at the kitchen table, drawing her feet up underneath the nightgown. She cried again. She lit a cigaret from the pack on the table. After a time she walked back to the bedroom and got her robe.

She looked in on the children. She pulled the covers up over her son's shoulders. She went back to the living room and sat in the big chair. She paged through a magazine and tried to read. She gazed at the photographs and then she tried to read again. Now and then a car went by on the street outside and she looked up. As each car passed she waited, listening. And then she looked down at the magazine again. There was a stack of magazines in the rack by the big chair. She paged through them all.

When it began to be light outside she got up. She walked to the window. The cloudless sky over the hills was beginning to turn white. The trees and the row of two-story apartment houses across the street were beginning to take shape as she watched. The sky grew whiter, the light expanding rapidly up from behind the hills. Except for the times she had been up with one or another of the children (which she did not count because she had never looked outside, only hurried back to bed or to the kitchen), she had seen few sunrises in her life and those when she was little. She knew that none of them had been like this. Not in pictures she had seen nor in any book she had read had she learned a sunrise was so terrible as this.

She waited and then she moved over to the door and turned the lock and stepped out onto the porch. She closed the robe at her throat. The air was wet and cold. By stages things were becoming very visible. She let her eyes see everything until they fastened on the red winking light atop the radio tower atop the opposite hill.

She went through the dim apartment, back into the bedroom. He was knotted up in the center of the bed, the covers bunched over his shoulders, his head half under the pillow. He looked desperate in his heavy sleep, his arm flung out across her side of the bed, his jaws clenched. As she looked, the room grew very light and the pale sheets whitened grossly before her eyes.

She wet her lips with a sticking sound and got down on her knees. She put her hands out on the bed.

'God,' she said. 'God, will you help us, God?' she said.

Put yourself in my shoes

The telephone rang while he was running the vacuum cleaner. He had worked his way through the apartment and was doing the living room, using the nozzle attachment to get at the cat hairs between the cushions. He stopped and listened and then switched off the vacuum. He went to answer the telephone.

'Hello,' he said. 'Myers here.'

'Myers,' she said. 'How are you? What are you doing?'

'Nothing,' he said. 'Hello, Paula.'

'There's an office party this afternoon,' she said. 'You're invited. Carl invited you.'

'I don't think I can come,' Myers said.

'Carl just this minute said get that old man of yours on the phone. Get him down here for a drink. Get him out of his ivory tower and back into the real world for a while. Carl's funny when he's drinking. Myers?'

'I heard you,' Myers said.

Myers used to work for Carl. Carl always talked of going to Paris to write a novel, and when Myers had quit to write a novel, Carl had said he would watch for Myers' name on the best-seller list.

'I can't come now,' Myers said.

'We found out some horrible news this morning,' Paula continued, as if she had not heard him. 'You remember Larry Gudinas. He was still here when you came to work. He helped out on science books for a while, and then they put him in the field, and then they canned him? We heard this morning he committed suicide. He shot himself in the mouth. Can you imagine? Myers?'

'I heard you,' Myers said. He tried to remember Larry Gudinas and recalled a tall, stooped man with wire-frame glasses, bright ties, and a receding hairline. He could imagine the jolt, the head snapping back. 'Jesus,' Myers said. 'Well, I'm sorry to hear that.'

'Come down to the office, honey, all right?' Paula said. 'Everybody is just talking and having some drinks and listening to Christmas music. Come down,' she said.

Myers could hear it all at the other end of the line. 'I don't want to come down,' he said. 'Paula?' A few snowflakes drifted past the window as he watched. He rubbed his fingers across the glass and then began to write his name on the glass as he waited.

'What? I heard,' she said. 'All right,' Paula said. 'Well, then, why don't we meet at Voyles for a drink? Myers?'

'Okay,' he said. 'Voyles. All right.'

'Everybody here will be disappointed you didn't come,' she said. 'Carl especially. Carl admires you, you know. He does. He's told me so. He admires your nerve. He said if he had your nerve he would have quit years ago. Carl said it takes nerve to do what you did. Myers?'

'I'm right here,' Myers said. 'I think I can get my car started. If I can't start it, I'll call you back.'

'All right,' she said. 'I'll see you at Voyles. I'll leave here in five minutes if I don't hear from you.'

'Say hello to Carl for me,' Myers said.

'I will,' Paula said. 'He's talking about you.'

Myers put the vacuum cleaner away. He walked down the two flights and went to his car, which was in the last stall and covered with snow. He got in, worked the pedal a number of times, and tried the starter. It turned over. He kept the pedal down.

As he drove, he looked at the people who hurried along the sidewalks with shopping bags. He glanced at the gray sky, filled with flakes, and at the tall buildings with snow in the crevices and on the window ledges. He tried to see everything, save it for later. He was between stories, and he felt despicable. He found Voyles, a small bar on a corner next to a men's clothing store. He parked in back and went inside. He sat at the bar for a time and then carried a drink over to a little table near the door.

When Paula came in she said, 'Merry Christmas,' and he got up and gave her a kiss on the cheek. He held a chair for her.

He said, 'Scotch?'

'Scotch,' she said, then 'Scotch over ice' to the girl who came for her order.

Paula picked up his drink and drained the glass.

'I'll have another one, too,' Myers said to the girl. 'I don't like this place,' he said after the girl had moved away.

'What's wrong with this place?' Paula said. 'We always come here.'

'I just don't like it,' he said. 'Let's have a drink and then go someplace else.'

'Whatever you want,' she said.

The girl arrived with the drinks. Myers paid her, and he and Paula touched glasses.

Myers stared at her.

'Carl says hello,' she said.

Myers nodded.

Paula sipped her drink. 'How was your day today?'

Myers shrugged.

'What'd you do?' she said.

'Nothing,' he said. 'I vacuumed.'

She touched his hand. 'Everybody said to tell you hi.'

They finished their drinks.

'I have an idea,' she said. 'Why don't we stop and visit the Morgans for a few minutes. We've never met them, for God's sake, and they've been back for months. We could just drop by and say hello, we're the Myerses. Besides, they sent us a card. They asked us to stop during the holidays. They *invited* us. I don't want to go home,' she finally said and fished in her purse for a cigaret.

Myers recalled setting the furnace and turning out all the lights before he had left. And then he thought of the snow drifting past the window.

'What about that insulting letter they sent telling us they heard we were keeping a cat in the house?' he said.

'They've forgotten about that by now,' she said. 'That wasn't anything serious, anyway. Oh, let's do it, Myers! Let's go by.'

'We should call first if we're going to do anything like that,' he said.

'No,' she said. 'That's part of it. Let's not call. Let's just go knock on the door and say hello, we used to live here. All right? Myers?'

'I think we should call first,' he said.

'It's the holidays,' she said, getting up from her chair. 'Come on, baby.'

She took his arm and they went out into the snow. She suggested they take her car and pick up his car later. He opened the door for her and then went around to the passenger's side.

Something took him when he saw the lighted windows, saw snow on the roof, saw the station wagon in the driveway. The curtains were open and Christmas-tree lights blinked at them from the window.

They got out of the car. He took her elbow as they stepped over a pile of snow and started up the walk to the front porch. They had gone a few steps when a large bushy dog hurtled around the corner of the garage and headed straight for Myers.

'Oh, God,' he said, hunching, stepping back, bringing his hands up. He slipped on the walk, his coat flapped, and he fell onto the frozen grass with the dread certainty that the dog would go for his throat. The dog growled once and then began to sniff Myers' coat.

Paula picked up a handful of snow and threw it at the dog. The porch light came on, the door opened, and a man called, 'Buzzy!' Myers got to his feet and brushed himself off.

'What's going on?' the man in the doorway said. 'Who is it? Buzzy, come here, fellow. Come here!'

'We're the Myerses,' Paula said. 'We came to wish you a Merry Christmas.'

'The Myerses?' the man in the doorway said. 'Get out! Get in the garage, Buzzy. Get, get! It's the Myerses,' the man said to the woman who stood behind him trying to look past his shoulder.

'The Myerses,' she said. 'Well, ask them in, ask them in, for heaven's sake.' She stepped onto the porch and said, 'Come in, please, it's freezing. I'm Hilda Morgan and this is Edgar. We're happy to meet you. Please come in.'

They all shook hands quickly on the front porch. Myers and Paula stepped inside and Edgar Morgan shut the door.

'Let me have your coats. Take off your coats,' Edgar Morgan said. 'You're all right?' he said to Myers, observing him closely, and Myers nodded. 'I knew that dog was crazy, but he's never pulled anything like this. I saw it. I was looking out the window when it happened.'

This remark seemed odd to Myers, and he looked at the man. Edgar Morgan was in his forties, nearly bald, and was dressed in slacks and a sweater and was wearing leather slippers.

'His name is Buzzy,' Hilda Morgan announced and made a face. 'It's Edgar's dog. I can't have an animal in the house myself, but Edgar bought this dog and promised to keep him outside.'

'He sleeps in the garage,' Edgar Morgan said. 'He begs to come in the house, but we can't allow it, you know.' Morgan chuckled. 'But sit down, sit down, if you can find a place with this clutter. Hilda, dear, move some of those things off the couch so Mr and Mrs Myers can sit down.'

Hilda Morgan cleared the couch of packages, wrapping paper, scissors, a box of ribbons, bows. She put everything on the floor.

Myers noticed Morgan staring at him again, not smiling now.

Paula said, 'Myers, there's something in your hair, dearest.'

Myers put a hand up to the back of his head and found a twig and put it in his pocket.

'That dog,' Morgan said and chuckled again. 'We were just having a hot drink and wrapping some last-minute gifts. Will you join us in a cup of holiday cheer? What would you like?'

'Anything is fine,' Paula said.

'Anything,' Myers said. 'We wouldn't have interrupted.'

'Nonsense,' Morgan said. 'We've been . . . very curious about the Myerses. You'll have a hot drink, sir?'

'That's fine,' Myers said.

'Mrs Myers?' Morgan said.

Paula nodded.

'Two hot drinks coming up,' Morgan said. 'Dear, I think we're ready too, aren't we?' he said to his wife. 'This is certainly an occasion.'

He took her cup and went out to the kitchen. Myers heard the cupboard door bang and heard a muffled word that sounded like a curse. Myers blinked. He looked at Hilda Morgan, who was settling herself into a chair at the end of the couch.

'Sit down over here, you two,' Hilda Morgan said. She patted the arm of the couch. 'Over here, by the fire. We'll have Mr Morgan build it up again when he returns.' They sat. Hilda Morgan clasped her hands in her lap and leaned forward slightly, examining Myers' face.

The living room was as he remembered it, except that on the wall behind Hilda Morgan's chair he saw three small framed prints. In one print a man in a vest and frock coat was tipping his hat to two ladies who held parasols. All this was happening on a broad concourse with horses and carriages.

'How was Germany?' Paula said. She sat on the edge of the cushion and held her purse on her knees.

'We loved Germany,' Edgar Morgan said, coming in from the kitchen with a tray and four large cups. Myers recognized the cups.

'Have you been to Germany, Mrs Myers?' Morgan asked.

'We want to go,' Paula said. 'Don't we, Myers? Maybe next year, next summer. Or else the year after. As soon as we can afford it. Maybe as soon as Myers sells something. Myers writes.'

'I should think a trip to Europe would be very beneficial to a writer,' Edgar Morgan said. He put the cups into coasters. 'Please help yourselves,' He sat down in a chair across from his wife and gazed at Myers. 'You said in your letter you were taking off work to write.'

'That's true,' Myers said and sipped his drink.

'He writes something almost every day,' Paula said.

'Is that a fact?' Morgan said. 'That's impressive. What did you write today, may I ask?'

'Nothing,' Myers said.

'It's the holidays,' Paula said.

'You must be proud of him, Mrs Myers,' Hilda Morgan said.

'I am,' Paula said.

'I'm happy for you,' Hilda Morgan said.

'I heard something the other day that might interest you.' Edgar Morgan said. He took out some tobacco and began to fill a pipe. Myers lighted a cigaret and looked around for an ashtray, then dropped the match behind the couch.

'It's a horrible story, really. But maybe you could use it, Mr Myers.' Morgan struck a flame and drew on the pipe. 'Grist for the mill, you know, and all that,' Morgan said and laughed and shook the match. 'This fellow was about my age or so. He was a colleague for a couple of years. We knew each other a little, and we had good friends in common. Then he moved out, accepted a position at the university down the way. Well, you know how these things go sometimes – the fellow had an affair with one of his students.'

Mrs Morgan made a disapproving noise with her tongue. She reached down for a small package that was wrapped in green paper and began to affix a red bow to the paper.

'According to all accounts, it was a torrid affair that lasted for some months,' Morgan continued. 'Right up until a short time ago, in fact. A week ago, to be exact. On that day – it was in the evening – he announced to his wife – they'd been married for twenty years – he announced to his wife that he wanted a divorce. You can imagine how the fool woman took it, coming out of the blue like that, so to speak. There was quite a row. The whole family got into it. She ordered him out of the house then and there. But just as the fellow was leaving, his son threw a can of tomato soup at him and hit him in the forehead. It caused a concussion that sent the man to the hospital. His condition is quite serious.'

Morgan drew on his pipe and gazed at Myers.

'I've never heard such a story,' Mrs Morgan said. 'Edgar, that's disgusting.'

'Horrible,' Paula said.

Myers grinned.

'Now *there's* a tale for you, Mr Myers,' Morgan said, catching the grin and narrowing his eyes. 'Think of the story you'd have if you could get inside that man's head.'

'Or her head,' Mrs Morgan said. 'The wife's. Think of *her* story. To be betrayed in such fashion after twenty years. Think how she must feel.'

'But imagine what the poor *boy* must be going through,' Paula said. 'Imagine, having almost killed his father.'

'Yes, that's all true,' Morgan said. 'But here's something I don't think any of you has thought about. Think about *this* for a moment. Mr Myers, are you listening? Tell me what you think of this. Put yourself in the shoes of that eighteen-year-old coed who fell in love with a married man. Think about *her* for a moment, and then you see the possibilities for your story.'

Morgan nodded and leaned back in the chair with a satisfied expression.

'I'm afraid I don't have any sympathy for her, Mrs Morgan said. 'I can imagine the sort she is. We all know what she's like, that kind preys on older men. I don't have any sympathy for him, either – the man, the chaser, no, I don't. I'm afraid my sympathies in this case are entirely with the wife and son.'

'It would take a Tolstoy to tell it and tell it *right*,' Morgan said. 'No less than a Tolstoy. Mr Myers, the water is still hot.'

'Time to go,' Myers said.

He stood up and threw his cigaret into the fire.

'Stay,' Mrs Morgan said. 'We haven't gotten acquainted yet. You don't know how we have . . . speculated about you. Now that we're together at last, stay a little while. It's such a pleasant surprise.'

'We appreciated the card and your note,' Paula said.

'The card?' Mrs Morgan said.

Myers sat down.

'We decided not to mail any cards this year,' Paula said. 'I didn't get around to it when I should have, and it seemed futile to do it at the last minute.'

'You'll have another one, Mrs Myers?' Morgan said, standing in front of her now with his hand on her cup. 'You'll set an example for your husband.'

'It *was* good,' Paula said. 'It warms you.'

'Right,' Morgan said. 'It warms you. That's right. Dear, did you hear Mrs Myers? It warms you. That's very good. 'Mr Myers?' Morgan said and waited. 'You'll join us?'

'All right,' Myers said and let Morgan take the cup.

The dog began to whine and scratch at the door.

'That dog. I don't know what's gotten into that dog,' Morgan said. He went to the kitchen and this time Myers distinctly heard Morgan curse as he slammed the kettle onto a burner.

Mrs Morgan began to hum. She picked up a half-wrapped package, cut a piece of tape, and began sealing the paper.

Myers lighted a cigaret. He dropped the match in his coaster. He looked at his watch.

Mrs Morgan raised her head. 'I believe I hear singing,' she said. She listened. She rose from her chair and went to the front window. 'It *is* singing. Edgar!' she called.

Myers and Paula went to the window.

'I haven't seen carolers in years,' Mrs Morgan said.

'What is it?' Morgan said. He had the tray and cups. 'What is it? What's wrong?'

'Nothing's wrong, dear. It's carolers. There they are over there, across the street,' Mrs Morgan said.

'Mrs Myers,' Morgan said, extending the tray. 'Mr Myers. Dear.'

'Thank you,' Paula said.

'Muchas gracias,' Myers said.

Morgan put the tray down and came back to the window with his cup. Young people were gathered on the walk in front of the house across the street, boys and girls with an older, taller boy who wore a muffler and a topcoat. Myers could see the faces at the window across the way – the Ardreys – and when the carolers had finished, Jack Ardrey came to the door and gave something to the older boy. The group moved on down the walk, flashlights bobbing, and stopped in front of another house.

'They won't come here,' Mrs Morgan said after a time.

'What? Why won't they come here?' Morgan said and turned to his wife. 'What a goddamned silly thing to say! Why won't they come here?'

'I just know they won't,' Mrs Morgan said.

'And I say they will,' Morgan said. 'Mrs Myers, are those carolers going to come here or not? What do you think? Will they return to bless this house? We'll leave it up to you.'

Paula pressed closer to the window. But the carolers were far down the street now. She did not answer.

'Well, now that all the excitement is over,' Morgan said and went over to his chair. He sat down, frowned, and began to fill his pipe.

Myers and Paula went back to the couch. Mrs Morgan moved away from the window at last. She sat down. She smiled and gazed into her cup. Then she put the cup down and began to weep.

Morgan gave his handkerchief to his wife. He looked at Myers. Presently Morgan began to drum on the arm of his chair. Myers moved his feet. Paula looked into her purse for a cigaret. 'See what you've caused?' Morgan said as he stared at something on the carpet near Myers' shoes.

Myers gathered himself to stand.

'Edgar, get them another drink.' Mrs Morgan said as she dabbed at her eyes. She used the handkerchief on her nose. 'I want them to hear about Mrs Attenborough. Mr Myers writes. I think he might appreciate this. We'll wait until you come back before we begin the story.'

Morgan collected the cups. He carried them into the kitchen. Myers heard dishes clatter, cupboard doors bang. Mrs Morgan looked at Myers and smiled faintly.

'We have to go,' Myers said. 'We have to go. Paula, get your coat.'

'No, no, we insist, Mr Myers,' Mrs Morgan said. 'We want you to hear about Mrs Attenborough, poor Mrs Attenborough. You might appeciate this story, too Mrs Myers, This is your chance to see how your husband's mind goes to work on raw material.'

Morgan came back and passed out the hot drinks. He sat down quickly.

'Tell them about Mrs Attenborough, dear,' Mrs Morgan said.

'That dog almost tore my leg off,' Myers said and was at once surprised at his words. He put his cup down.

'Oh, come, it wasn't that bad,' Morgan said. 'I saw it.'

'You know writers,' Mrs Morgan said to Paula. 'They like to exaggerate.'

'The power of the pen and all that,' Morgan said.

'That's it,' Mrs Morgan said. 'Bend your pen into a plowshare, Mr Myers.'

'We'll let Mrs Morgan tell the story of Mrs Attenborough,' Morgan said, ignoring Myers, who stood up at that moment. 'Mrs Morgan was intimately connected with the affair. I've already told you of the fellow who was knocked for a loop by a can of soup.' Morgan chuckled. 'We'll let Mrs Morgan tell this one.'

'You tell it, dear. And Mr Myers, you listen closely,' Mrs Morgan said.

'We have to go,' Myers said. 'Paula, let's go.'

'Talk about honesty,' Mrs Morgan said.

'Let's talk about it,' Myers said. Then he said, 'Paula, are you coming?'

'I want you to hear this story,' Morgan said, raising his voice. 'You will insult Mrs Morgan, you will insult us both, if you don't listen to this story.' Morgan clenched his pipe.

'Myers, please,' Paula said anxiously. 'I want to hear it. Then we'll go. Myers? Please, honey, sit down for another minute.'

Myers looked at her. She moved her fingers, as if signaling him. He hesitated, and then he sat next to her.

Mrs Morgan began. 'One afternoon in Munich, Edgar and I went to the Dortmunder Museum. There was *a Bauhaus* exhibit that fall, and Edgar said the heck with it, let's take a day off – he was doing his research, you see – the heck with it, let's take a day off. We caught a tram and rode across Munich to the museum. We spent several hours viewing the exhibit and revisiting some of the galleries to pay homage to a few of our favorites amongst the old masters. Just as we were to leave, I stepped into the ladies' room. I left my purse. In the purse was Edgar's monthly check from home that had come the day before and a hundred and twenty dollars cash that I was going to deposit along with the check. I also had my identification cards in the purse. I did not miss my purse until we arrived home. Edgar immediately telephoned the museum authorities. But while he was talking I saw a taxi out front. A well-dressed woman with white hair got out. She was a stout woman and she was carrying two purses. I called for Edgar and went to the door. The woman introduced herself as Mrs Attenborough, gave me my purse, and explained that she too had visited the museum that afternoon and while in the ladies' room had noticed a purse in the trash can. She of course had opened the purse in an effort to trace the owner. There were the identification cards and such giving our local address. She immediately left the museum and took a taxi in order to deliver the purse herself. Edgar's check was there, but the money, the one hundred twenty dollars, was gone. Nevertheless, I was grateful the other things were intact. It was nearly four o'clock and we asked the woman to stay for tea. She sat down, and after a little while she began to tell us about herself. She had been born and reared in Australia, had married young, had had three children, all sons, been widowed, and still lived in Australia with two of her sons. They raised sheep and had more than twenty thousand acres of land for the sheep to run in, and many drovers and shearers and such who worked for them at certain times of the year. When she came to our home in Munich, she was then on her way to Australia from England, where she had been to visit her youngest son, who was a barrister. She was returning to Australia when we met her,' Mrs Morgan said. 'She was seeing some of the world in the process. She had many places yet to visit on her itinerary.'

'Come to the point, dear,' Morgan said.

'Yes. Here is what happened, then. Mr Myers, I'll go right to the climax, as you writers say. Suddenly, after we had had a very pleasant conversation for an hour, after this woman had told about herself and her adventurous life Down Under, she stood up to go. As she started to pass me her cup, her mouth flew open, the cup dropped, and she fell across our couch and died. Died. Right in our living room. It was the most shocking moment in our lives.'

Morgan nodded solemnly.

'God,' Paula said.

'Fate sent her to die on the couch in our living room in Germany,' Mrs Morgan said.

Myers began to laugh. 'Fate . . . sent . . . her . . . to . . . die . . . in . . . your . . . living . . . room?' he said between gasps.

'Is that funny, sir?' Morgan said. 'Do you find that amusing?'

Myers nodded. He kept laughing. He wiped his eyes on his shirt sleeve. 'I'm really sorry,' he said. 'I can't help it. That line "*Fate sent her to die on the couch in our living room in Germany.*" I'm sorry. Then what happened?' he managed to say. 'I'd like to know what happened then.'

'Mr Myers, we didn't know what to do,' Mrs Morgan said. 'The shock was terrible. Edgar felt for her pulse, but there was no sign of life. And she had begun to change color. Her face and hands were turning *gray*. Edgar went to the phone to call someone. Then he said, 'Open her purse, see if you can find where she's staying.' All the time averting my eyes from the poor thing there on the couch, I took up her purse. Imagine my complete surprise and bewilderment, my utter bewilderment, when the first thing I saw inside was my hundred twenty dollars, still fastened with the paper clip. I was never so astonished.'

'And disappointed,' Morgan said. 'Don't forget that. It was a keen disappointment.'

Myers giggled.

'If you were a real writer, as you say you are, Mr Myers, you would not laugh,' Morgan said as he got to his feet. 'You would not dare laugh! You would try to understand. You would plumb the depths of that poor soul's heart and try to understand. But you are no writer, sir!'

Myers kept on giggling.

Morgan slammed his fist on the coffee table and the cups rattled in the coasters. 'The real story lies right here, in this house, this very living room, and it's time it was told! The real story is *here*, Mr Myers,' Morgan said. He walked up and down over the brilliant wrapping paper that had unrolled and now lay spread across the carpet. He stopped to glare at Myers, who was holding his forehead and shaking with laughter.

'Consider *this* for a possibility, Mr Myers!' Morgan screamed. '*Consider!* A friend – let's call him Mr X – is friends with . . . with Mr and Mrs Y, *as well as* Mr and Mrs Z. Mr and Mrs Y and Mr and Mrs Z do not know each other, unfortunately. I say *unfortunately* because if they *had* known each other this story would not exist because it would never have taken place. Now, Mr X learns that Mr and Mrs Y are going to Germany for a year and need someone to occupy their house during the time they are gone. Mr and Mrs Z are looking for suitable accommodations, and Mr X tells them he knows of just the place. But before Mr X can put Mr and Mrs Z in touch with Mr and Mrs Y, the Ys have to leave sooner than expected. Mr X, being a friend, is left to rent the house at his discretion to anyone, including Mr and Mrs Y – I mean Z. Now, Mr and Mrs . . . . Z move into the house and bring a cat with them that Mr and Mrs Y hear about later in a letter from Mr X. Mr and Mrs Z bring a cat into the house *even though* the terms of the lease have expressly forbidden cats or other animals in the house because of Mrs Y's asthma. The *real* story, Mr Myers, lies in the situation I've just described. Mr and Mrs Z – I mean Mr and Mrs Y's moving in to the Z's house, *invading* the Zs' house, if the truth is to be told. Sleeping in the Zs' bed is one thing, but unlocking the Zs' private closet and using their linen, vandalizing the things found there, that was against the spirit and letter of the lease. And this *same* couple, the

Zs, opened boxes of kitchen utensils marked 'Don't Open.' And broke dishes when it was spelled out, *spelled out* in that same lease, that they were not to use the owners', the Zs' *personal*, I emphasize *personal*, possessions.'

Morgan's lips were white. He continued to walk up and down on the paper, stopping every now and then to look at Myers and emit little puffing noises from his lips.

'And the bathroom things, dear — don't forget the bathroom things,' Mrs Morgan said. 'It's bad enough using the Zs' blankets and sheets, but when they also get into their *bathroom* things and go through the little private things stored in the *attic*, a line has to be drawn.'

'That's the *real* story, Mr Myers,' Morgan said. He tried to fill his pipe. His hands trembled and tobacco spilled onto the carpet. 'That's the real story that is waiting to be written.'

'And it doesn't need Tolstoy to tell it,' Mrs Morgan said.

'It doesn't need Tolstoy,' Morgan said.

Myers laughed. He and Paula got up from the couch at the same time and moved toward the door. 'Good night,' Myers said merrily.

Morgan was behind him. 'If you were a real writer, sir, you would put that story into words and not pussyfoot around with it, either.'

Myers just laughed. He touched the doorknob.

'One other thing,' Morgan said. 'I didn't intend to bring this up, but in light of your behavior here tonight, I want to tell you that I'm missing my two-volume set of 'Jazz at the Philharmonic.' Those records are of great sentimental value. I bought them in 1955. And now I insist you tell me what happened to them!'

'In all fairness, Edgar,' Mrs Morgan said as she helped Paula on with her coat, 'after you took inventory of the records, you admitted you couldn't recall the last time you had seen those records.'

'But I am sure of it now,' Morgan said. 'I am positive I saw those records just before we left, and now, now I'd like this *writer* to tell me exactly what he knows of their whereabouts. Mr Myers?'

But Myers was already outdoors, and, taking his wife by the hand, he hurried her down the walk to the car. They surprised Buzzy. The dog yelped in what seemed fear and then jumped to the side.

'I insist on *knowing*!' Morgan called. 'I am waiting, sir!'

Myers got Paula into the car and started the engine. He looked again at the couple on the porch. Mrs Morgan waved, and then she and Edgar Morgan went back inside and shut the door.

Myers pulled away from the curb.

'Those people are crazy,' Paula said.

Myers patted her hand.

'They were scary,' she said.

He did not answer. Her voice seemed to come to him from a great distance. He kept driving. Snow rushed at the windshield. He was silent and watched the road. He was at the very end of a story.

Jerry and Molly
and Sam

As Al saw it, there was only one solution. He had to get rid of the dog without Betty or the kids finding out about it. At night. It would have to be done at night. He would simply drive Suzy – well, someplace, later he'd decide where – open the door, push her out, drive away. The sooner the better. He felt relieved making the decision. Any action was better than no action at all, he was becoming convinced.

It was Sunday. He got up from the kitchen table where he had been eating a late breakfast by himself and stood by the sink, hands in his pockets. Nothing was going right lately. He had enough to contend with without having to worry about a stinking dog. They were laying off at Aerojet when they should be hiring. The middle of the summer, defense contracts let all over the country and Aerojet was talking of cutting back. *Was* cutting back, in fact, a little more every day. He was no safer than anyone else even though he'd been there two years going on three. He got along with the right people, all right, but seniority or friendship, either one, didn't mean a damn these days. If your number was up, that was that – and there was nothing anybody could do. They got ready to lay off, they laid off. Fifty, a hundred men at a time.

No one was safe, from the foreman and supers right on down to the man on the line. And three months ago, just before all the layoffs began, he'd let Betty talk him into moving into this cushy two-hundred-a-month place. Lease, with an option to buy. Shit!

Al hadn't really wanted to leave the other place. He had been comfortable enough. Who could know that two weeks after he'd move they'd start laying off? But who could know anything these days? For example, there was Jill. Jill worked in bookkeeping at Weinstock's. She was a nice girl, said she loved Al. She was just lonely, that's what she told him the first night. She didn't make it a habit, letting herself be picked up by married men, she also told him the first night. He'd met Jill about three months ago, when he was feeling depressed and jittery with all the talk of layoffs just beginning. He met her at the Town and Country, a bar not too far from his new place. They danced a little and he drove her home and they necked in the car in front of her apartment. He had not gone upstairs with her that night, though he was sure he could have. He went upstairs with her the next night.

Now he was having an *affair*, for Christ's sake, and he didn't know what to do about it. He did not want it to go on, and he did not want to break it off: you don't throw everything overboard in a storm. Al was drifting, and he knew he was drifting, and where it was all going to end he could not guess at. But he was beginning to feel he was losing control over everything. Everything. Recently, too, he had caught himself thinking about old age after he'd been constipated a few days – an affliction he had always associated with the elderly. Then there was the matter of the tiny bald spot and of his having just begun to wonder how he would comb his hair a different way. What was he going to do with his life? he wanted to know.

He was thirty-one.

All these things to contend with and then *Sandy*, his wife's younger sister, giving the kids, Alex and Mary, that mongrel dog about four months ago. He wished he'd never seen that dog. Or Sandy, either, for that matter. That bitch! She was always turning up with some shit or other that wound up costing him money, some little flimflam that went haywire after a day or two and *had* to be repaired, something the kids could scream over and fight over and beat the shit out of each other about. God! And then turning right around to touch him, through *Betty*, for twenty-five bucks. The mere thought of all the twenty-five- or fifty-bucks checks, and the one just a few months ago for eighty-five to make her car payment – her *car* payment, for God's sake, when he didn't even know if he was going to have a roof over his head – made him want to *kill* the goddamn dog.

Sandy! Betty and Alex and Mary! Jill! And Suzy the goddamn dog!

This was Al.

He had to start someplace – setting things in order, sorting all this out. It was time to *do* something, time for some straight thinking for a change. And he intended to start tonight.

He would coax the dog into the car undetected and, on some pretext or another, go out. Yet he hated to think of the way Betty would lower her eyes as she watched him dress, and then, later, just before he went out the door, ask him where, how long, etc., in a resigned voice that made him feel all the worse. He could never get used to the lying. Besides, he hated to use what little reserve he might have left with Betty by telling her a lie for something different from what she suspected. A wasted lie, so to speak. But he could not tell her the truth, could not say he was *not* going drinking, was *not* going calling on somebody, was instead going to do away with the goddamn dog and thus take the first step toward setting his house in order.

He ran his hand over his face, tried to put it all out of his mind for a minute. He took out a cold half quart of Lucky from the fridge and popped the aluminum top. His life had become a maze, one lie overlaid upon another until he was not sure he could untangle them if he had to.

'The goddamn dog,' he said out loud.

'She doesn't have good sense!' was how Al put it. She was a sneak, besides. The moment the back door was left open and everyone gone, she'd pry open the screen, come through to the living room, and urinate on the carpet. There were at least a half dozen map-shaped stains on it right now. But her favorite place was the utility room, where she could root in the dirty clothes, so that all of the shorts and panties now had crotch or seat chewed away. And she chewed through the antenna wires on the outside of the house, and once Al pulled into the drive and found her lying in the front yard with one of his Florsheims in her mouth.

'She's crazy,' he'd say. 'And she's driving me crazy. I can't make it fast enough to replace it. The sonofabitch, I'm going to kill her one of these days!'

Betty tolerated the dog at greater durations, would go along apparently unruffled for a time, but suddenly she would come upon it, with fists clenched, call it a bastard, a bitch, shriek at the kids about keeping it out of their room, the living room, etc. Betty was that way with the children too. She could go along with them just so far, let them get away with just so much, and then she would turn on them savagely and slap their faces, screaming, 'Stop it! Stop it! I can't stand any more of it!'

But then Betty would say, 'It's their first dog. You remember how fond you must have been of your first dog.'

'My dog had brains,' he would say. 'It was an Irish setter!'

The afternoon passed. Betty and the kids returned from someplace or another in the car, and they all had sandwiches and potato chips on the patio. He fell asleep on the grass, and when he woke it was nearly evening.

He showered, shaved, put on slacks and a clean shirt. He felt rested but sluggish. He dressed and he thought of Jill. He thought of Betty and Alex and Mary and Sandy and Suzy. He felt drugged.

'We'll have supper pretty soon,' Betty said, coming to the bathroom door and staring at him.

'That's all right. I'm not hungry. Too hot to eat,' he said fiddling with his shirt collar. 'I might drive over to Carl's, shoot a few games of pool, have a couple of beers.'

She said, 'I see.'

He said, 'Jesus!'

She said, 'Go ahead, I don't care.'

He said, 'I won't be gone long.'

She said, 'Go ahead, I said. I said I don't care.'

In the garage, he said, 'Goddamn you all!' and kicked the rake across the cement floor. Then he lit a cigaret and tried to get hold of himself. He picked up the rake and put it away where it belonged. He was muttering to himself, saying, 'Order, order,' when the dog came up to the garage, sniffed around the door, and looked in.

'Here. Come here, Suzy. Here, girl,' he called.

The dog wagged her tail but stayed where she was.

He went over to the cupboard above the lawn mower and took down one, then two, and finally three cans of food.

'All you want tonight, Suzy, old girl. All you can eat,' he coaxed, opening up both ends of the first can and sliding the mess into the dog's dish.

He drove around for nearly an hour, not able to decide on a place. If he dropped her off in just any neighborhood and the pound were called, the dog would be back at the house in a day or two. The county pound was the first place Betty would call. He remembered reading stories about lost dogs finding their way hundreds of miles back home again. He remembered crime programs where someone saw a license number, and the thought made his heart jump. Held up to public view, without all the facts being in, it'd be a shameful thing to be caught abandoning a dog. He would have to find the right place.

He drove over near the American River. The dog needed to get out more anyway, get the feel of the wind on its back, be able to swim and wade in the river when it wanted; it was a pity to keep a dog fenced in all the time. But the fields near the levee seemed too desolate, no houses around at all. After all, he did want the dog to be found and cared for. A large old two-story house was what he had in mind, with happy, well-behaved reasonable children who needed a dog, who desperately needed a dog. But there were no old two-story houses here, not a one.

He drove back onto the highway. He had not been able to look at the dog since he'd managed to get her into the car. She lay quietly on the back seat now. But when he pulled off the road and stopped the car, she sat up and whined, looking around.

He stopped at a bar, rolled all the car windows down before he went inside. He stayed nearly an hour, drinking beer and playing the shuffleboard. He kept wondering if he should have left all the doors ajar too. When he went back outside, Suzy sat up in the seat and rolled her lips back, showing her teeth.

He got in and started off again.

Then he thought of the place. The neighborhood where they used to live, swarming with kids and just across the line in Yolo County, that would be just the right place. If the dog were picked up, it would be taken to the Woodland Pound, not the pound in Sacramento. Just drive onto one of the streets in the old neighborhood, stop, throw out a handful of the shit she ate, open the door, a little assistance in the way of a push, and out she'd go while he took off. Done! It would be done.

He stepped on it getting out there.

There were porch lights on and at three or four houses he saw men and women sitting on the front steps as he drove by. He cruised along, and when he came to his old house he slowed down almost to a stop and stared at the front door, the porch, the lighted windows. He felt even more insubstantial, looking at the house. He had lived there – how long? A year, sixteen months? Before that, Chico, Red Bluff, Tacoma, Portland – where he'd met Betty – Yakima . . . Toppenish, where he was born and went to high school. Not since he was a kid, it seemed to him, had he known what it was to be free from worry and worse. He thought of summers fishing and camping in the Cascades, autumns when he'd hunt pheasants behind Sam, the setter's flashing red coat a beacon through cornfields and alfalfa meadows where the boy that he was and the dog that he had would both run like mad. He wished he could keep driving and driving tonight until he was driving onto the old bricked main street of Toppenish, turning left at the first light, then left again, stopping when he came to where his mother lived, and never, never, for any reason ever, ever leave again.

He came to the darkened end of the street. There was a large empty field straight ahead and the street turned to the right, skirting it. For almost a block there were no housees on the side nearer the field and only one house, completely dark, on the other side. He stopped the car and, without thinking any longer about what he was doing, scooped a handful of dog food up, leaned over the seat, opened the back door nearer the field, threw the stuff out, and said, 'Go on, Suzy.' He pushed her until she jumped down reluctantly. He leaned over farther, pulled the door shut, and drove off, slowly. Then he drove faster and faster.

He stopped at Dupee's, the first bar he came to on the way back to Sacramento. He was jumpy and perspiring. He didn't feel exactly unburdened or relieved, as he had thought he would feel. But he kept assuring himself it was a step in the right direction, that the good feeling would settle on him tomorrow. The thing to do was to wait it out.

After four beers a girl in a turtleneck sweater and sandals and carrying a suitcase sat down beside him. She set the suitcase between the stools. She seemed to know the bartender, and the bartender had something to say to her whenever he came by, once or twice stopping briefly to talk. She told Al her name was Molly, but she wouldn't let him buy her a beer. Instead, she offered to eat half a pizza.

He smiled at her, and she smiled back. He took out his cigarets and his lighter and put them on the bar.

'Pizza it is!' he said.

Later, he said, 'Can I give you a lift somewhere?'

'No, thanks. I'm waiting for someone,' she said.

He said, 'Where you heading for?'

She said, 'No place. Oh,' she said, touching the suitcase with her toe, 'you mean that?' laughing. 'I live here in West Sac. I'm not going anyplace. It's just a washing-machine motor inside belongs to my mother. Jerry – that's the bartender – he's good at fixing things. Jerry said he'd fix it for nothing.'

Al got up. He weaved a little as he leaned over her. He said, 'Well, goodbye, honey. I'll see you around.'

'You bet!' she said. 'And thanks for the pizza. Hadn't eaten since lunch. Been trying to take some of this off.' She raised her sweater, gathered a handful of flesh at the waist.

'Sure I can't give you a lift someplace?' he said.

The woman shook her head.

In the car again, driving, he reached for his cigarets and then, frantically, for his lighter, remembering leaving everything on the bar. The hell with it, he thought let her have it. Let her put the lighter and the cigarets in the suitcase along with the washing machine. He chalked it up against the dog, one more expense. But the last, by God! It angered him now, now that he was getting things in order, that the girl hadn't been more friendly. If he'd been in a different frame of mind, he could have picked her up. But when you're depressed, it shows all over you, even the way you light a cigaret.

He decided to go see Jill. He stopped at a liquor store and bought a pint of whiskey and climbed the stairs to her apartment and he stopped at the landing to catch his breath and to clean his teeth with his tongue. He could still taste the mushrooms from the pizza, and his mouth and throat were seared from the whiskey. He realized that what he wanted to do was to go right to Jill's bathroom and use her toothbrush.

He knocked. 'It's me, Al.' he whispered. 'Al,' he said louder. He heard her feet hit the floor. She threw the lock and then tried to undo the chain as he leaned heavily against the door.

'Just a minute, honey. Al, you'll have to quit pushing – I can't unhook it. There,' she said and opened the door, scanning his face as she took him by the hand.

They embraced clumsily, and he kissed her on the cheek.

'Sit down, honey. Here.' She switched on a lamp and helped him to the couch. Then she touched her fingers to her curlers and said, 'I'll put on some lipstick. What would you like in the meantime? Coffee? Juice? A beer? I think I have some beer. What do you have there . . . whiskey? What would you like, honey?' She stroked his hair with one hand and leaned over him, gazing into his eyes. 'Poor baby, what would you like?' she said.

'Just want you hold me,' he said. 'Here. Sit down. No lipstick,' he said, pulling her onto his lap. 'Hold. I'm falling,' he said.

She put an arm around his shoulders. She said, 'You come on over to the bed, baby, I'll give you what you like.'

'Tell you, Jill,' he said, 'skating on thin ice. Crash through any minute . . . I don't know.' He stared at her with a fixed, puffy expression that he could feel but not correct. 'Serious,' he said.

She nodded. 'Don't think about anything, baby. Just relax,' she said. She pulled his face to hers and kissed him on the forehead and then the lips. She turned slightly on his lap and said, 'No, don't move, Al,' the fingers of both hands suddenly slipping around the back of his neck and gripping his face at the same time. His eyes wobbled around the room an instant, then tried to focus on what she was doing. She held his head in place in her strong fingers. With her thumbnails she was squeezing out a blackhead to the side of his nose.

'Sit still!' she said.

'No,' he said. 'Don't! Stop! Not in the mood for that.

'I almost have it. Sit still, I said! . . . There, look at that. What do you think of that? Didn't know that was there, did you? Now just one more, a big one, baby. The last one,' she said.

'Bathroom,' he said, forcing her off, freeing his way.

At home it was all tears, confusion. Mary ran out to the car, crying, before he could get parked.

'Suzy's gone,' she sobbed. 'Suzy's gone. She's never coming back, Daddy, I know it. She's gone!'

My God, heart lurching. *What have I done?*

'Now don't worry, sweetheart. She's probably just off running around somewhere. She'll be back,' he said.

'She isn't, Daddy, I know she isn't. Mama said we may have to get another dog.'

'Wouldn't that be all right, honey?' he said. 'Another dog, if Suzy doesn't come back? We'll go to the pet store —'

'I don't want another dog!' the child cried, holding onto his leg.

'Can we have a monkey, Daddy, instead of a dog?' Alex asked. 'If we go to the pet store to look for a dog, can we have a monkey instead?'

'I don't want a monkey!' Mary cried. 'I want Suzy.'

'Everybody let go now, let Daddy in the house. Daddy has a terrible, terrible headache,' he said.

Betty lifted a casserole dish from the oven. She looked tired, irritable . . . older. She didn't look at him. The kids tell you? Suzy's gone? I've combed the neighborhood. Everywhere, I swear.'

'That dog'll turn up,' he said. 'Probably just running around somewhere. That dog'll come back,' he said.

'Seriously,' she said, turning to him with her hands on her hips, 'I think it's something else. I think she might have got hit by a car. I want you to drive around. The kids called her last night, and she was gone then. That's the last been seen of her. I called the pound and described her to them, but they said all their trucks aren't in yet. I'm supposed to call again in the morning.'

He went into the bathroom and could hear her still going on. He began to run the water in the sink, wondering, with a fluttery sensation in his stomach, how grave exactly was his mistake. When he turned off the faucets, he could still hear her. He kept staring at the sink.

'Did you hear me?' she called. 'I want you to drive around and look for her after supper. The kids can go with you and look too . . . Al?'

'Yes, yes,' he answered.

'What?' she said. 'What'd you say?'

'I said yes. Yes! All right. Anything! Just let me wash up first, will you?'

She looked through from the kitchen. 'Well, what in the hell is eating you? I didn't ask you to get drunk last night, did I? I've had enough of it, I can tell you! I've had a hell of a day, if you want to know. Alex waking me up at five this morning getting in with me, telling me his daddy was snoring so loud that . . . that you *scared* him! *I* saw you out there with your clothes on passed out and the room smelling to high heaven. I tell you, I've had enough of it!' She looked around the kitchen quickly, as if to seize something.

He kicked the door shut. Everything was going to hell. While he was shaving, he stopped once and held the razor in his hand and looked at himself in the mirror: his face doughy, characterless — immoral, that was the word. He laid the razor down. *I believe I have made the gravest mistake this time. I believe I have made the gravest mistake of all.* He brought the razor up to his throat and finished.

He did not shower, did not change clothes. 'Put my supper in the oven for me,' he said. 'Or in the refrigerator. I'm going out. Right now,' he said.

'You can wait till after supper. The kids can go with you.'

'No, the hell with that. Let the kids eat supper, look around here if they want. I'm not hungry, and it'll be dark soon.'

'Is everybody going crazy?' she said. 'I don't know what's going to happen to us. I'm ready for a nervous breakdown. I'm ready to lose my mind. What's going to happen to the kids if I lose my mind?' She slumped against the draining board, her face crumpled, tears rolling off her cheeks. 'You don't love them, anyway! You never have. It isn't the dog I'm worried about. It's us! It's us! I know you don't love me any more – goddamn you! – but you don't even love the kids!'

'Betty, Betty!' he said. 'My God!' he said. 'Everything's going to be all right. I promise you,' he said. 'Don't worry,' he said. 'I promise you, things'll be all right. I'll find the dog and then things will be all right,' he said.

He bounded out of the house, ducked into the bushes as he heard his children coming: the girl crying, saying, 'Suzy, Suzy'; the boy saying maybe a train ran over her. When they were inside the house, he made a break for the car.

He fretted at all the lights he had to wait for, bitterly resented the time lost when he stopped for gas. The sun was low and heavy, just over the squat range of hills at the far end of the valley. At best, he had an hour of daylight.

He saw his whole life a ruin from here on in. If he lived another fifty years – hardly likely – he felt he'd never get over it, abandoning the dog. He felt he was finished if he didn't find the dog. A man who would get rid of a little dog wasn't worth a damn. That kind of man would do anything, would stop at nothing.

He squirmed in the seat, kept staring into the swollen face of the sun as it moved lower into the hills. He knew the situation was all out of proportion now, but he couldn't help it. He knew he must somehow retrieve the dog, as the night before he had known he must lose it.

'I'm the one going crazy,' he said and then nodded his head in agreement.

He came in the other way this time, by the field where he had let her off, alert for the sign of movement.

'Let her be there,' he said.

He stopped the car and searched the field. Then he drove on, slowly. A station wagon with the motor idling was parked in the drive of the lone house, and he saw a well-dressed woman in heels come out the front door with a little girl. They stared at him as he passed. Farther on he turned left, his eyes taking in the street and the yards on each side as far down as he could see. Nothing. Two kids with bicycles a block away stood beside a parked car.

'Hi,' he said to the two boys as he pulled up alongside. 'You fellows see anything of a little white dog around today? A kind of white shaggy dog? I lost one.'

One boy just gazed at him. The other said, 'I saw a lot of little kids playing with a dog over there this afternoon. The street the other side of this one. I don't know what kind of dog it was. It was white maybe. There was a lot of kids.'

'Okay, good. Thanks,' Al said. 'Thank you very very much,' he said.

He turned right at the end of the street. He concentrated on the street ahead. The sun had gone down now. It was nearly dark. Houses pitched side by side, trees, lawns, telephone poles, parked cars, it struck him as serene, untroubled. He could hear a man calling his children; he saw a woman in an apron step to the lighted door of her house.

'Is there still a chance for me?' Al said. He felt tears spring to his eyes. He was amazed. He couldn't help but grin at himself and shake his head as he got out his handkerchief. Then he saw a group of children coming down the street. He waved to get their attention.

'You kids see anything of a little white dog?' Al said to them.

'Oh sure,' one boy said. 'Is it your dog?'

Al nodded.

'We were just playing with him about a minute ago, down the street. In Terry's yard.' The boy pointed. 'Down the street.'

'You got kids?' one of the little girls spoke up.

'I do,' Al said.

'Terry said he's going to keep him. He don't have a dog,' the boy said.

'I don't know,' Al said. 'I don't think my kids would like that. It belongs to them. It's just lost,' Al said.

He drove on down the street. It was dark now, hard to see, and he began to panic again, cursing silently. He swore at what a weather-vane he was, changing this way and that, one moment this, the next moment that.

He saw the dog then. He understood he had been looking at it for a time. The dog moved slowly, nosing the grass along a fence. Al got out of the car, started across the lawn, crouching forward as he walked, calling, 'Suzy, Suzy, Suzy.'

The dog stopped when she saw him. She raised her head. He sat down on his heels, reached out his arm, waiting. They looked at each other. She moved her tail in greeting. She lay down with her head between her front legs and regarded him. He waited. She got up. She went around the fence and out of sight.

He sat there. He thought he didn't feel so bad, all things considered. The world was full of dogs. There were dogs and there were dogs. Some dogs you just couldn't do anything with.

Why, honey?

Dear Sir:

I was so surprised to receive your letter asking about my son, how did you know I was here? I moved here years ago right after it started to happen. No one knows who I am here but I'm afraid all the same. Who I am afraid of is him. When I look at the paper I shake my head and wonder. I read what they write about him and I ask myself is that man really my son, is he really doing these things?

He was a good boy except for his outbursts and that he could not tell the truth. I can't give you any reasons. It started one summer over the Fourth of July, he would have been about fifteen. Our cat Trudy disappeared and was gone all night and the next day. Mrs Cooper who lives behind us came the next evening to tell me Trudy crawled into her backyard that afternoon to die. Trudy was cut up she said but she recognized Trudy. Mr Cooper buried the remains.

Cut up? I said. What do you mean cut up?

Mr Cooper saw two boys in the field putting firecrackers in Trudy's ears and in her you know what. He tried to stop them but they ran.

Who, who would do such a thing, did he see who it was?

He didn't know the other boy but one of them ran this way. Mr Cooper thought it was your son.

I shook my head. No, that's just not so, he wouldn't do a thing like that, he loved Trudy, Trudy has been in the family for years, no, it wasn't my son.

That evening I told him about Trudy and he acted surprised and shocked and said we should offer a reward. He typed something up and promised to post it at school. But just as he was going to his room that night he said don't take it too hard, mom, she was old, in cat years she was 65 or 70, she lived a long time.

He went to work afternoons and Saturdays as a stockboy at Hartley's. A friend of mine who worked there, Betty Wilks, told me about the job and said she would put in a word for him. I mentioned it to him that evening and he said good, jobs for young people are hard to find.

The night he was to draw his first check I cooked his favorite supper and had everything on the table when he walked in. Here's the man of the house, I said, hugging him. I am so proud, how much did you draw, honey? Eighty dollars, he said. I was flabbergasted. That's wonderful, honey, I just cannot believe it. I'm starved, he said, let's eat.

I was happy, but I couldn't understand it, it was more than I was making.

When I did the laundry I found the stub from Hartley's in his pocket, it was for 28 dollars, he said 80. Why didn't he just tell the truth? I couldn't understand.

I would ask him where did you go last night, honey? To the show he would answer. Then I would find out he went to the school dance or spent the evening riding around with somebody in a car. I would think what difference could it make, why doesn't he just be truthful, there is no reason to lie to his mother.

I remember once he was supposed to have gone on a field trip, so I asked him what did you see on the field trip, honey? And he shrugged and said land formations, volcanic rock, ash, they showed us where there used to be a big lake a million years ago, now it's just a desert. He looked me in the eyes and went on talking. Then I got a note from the school the next day saying they wanted permission for a field trip, could he have permission to go.

Near the end of his senior year he bought a car and was always gone. I was concerned about his grades but he only laughed. You know he was an excellent student, you know that about him if you know anything. After that he bought a shotgun and a hunting knife.

I hated to see those things in the house and I told him so. He laughed, he always had a laugh for you. He said he would keep the gun and the knife in the trunk of his car, he said they would be easier to get there anyway.

One Saturday night he did not come home. I worried myself into a terrible state. About ten o'clock the next morning he came in and asked me to cook him breakfast, he said he had worked up an appetite out hunting, he said he was sorry for being gone all night, he said they had driven a long way to get to this place. It sounded strange. He was nervous.

Where did you go?

Up to the Wenas. We got a few shots.

Who did you go with, honey?

Fred.

Fred?

He stared and I didn't say anything else.

On the Sunday right after I tiptoed into his room for his car keys. He had promised to pick up some breakfast items on his way home from work the night before and I thought he might have left the things in his car. I saw his new shoes sitting half under his bed and covered with mud and sand. He opened his eyes.

Honey, what happened to your shoes? Look at your shoes.

I ran out of gas, I had to walk for gas. He sat up. What do you care?

I am your mother.

While he was in the shower I took the keys and went out to his car. I opened the trunk. I didn't find the groceries. I saw the shotgun lying on a quilt and the knife too and I saw a shirt of his rolled in a ball and I shook it out and it was full of blood. It was wet. I dropped it. I closed the trunk and started back for the house and I saw him watching at the window and he opened the door.

I forgot to tell you, he said, I had a bad bloody nose, I don't know if that shirt can be washed, throw it away. He smiled.

A few days later I asked how he was getting along at work. Fine, he said, he said he had gotten a raise. But I met Betty Wilks on the street and she said they were all sorry at Hartley's that he had quit, he was so well liked, she said, Betty Wilks.

Two nights after that I was in bed but I couldn't sleep, I stared at the ceiling. I heard his car pull up out front and I listened as he put the key in the lock and he came through the kitchen and down the hall to his room and he shut the door after him. I got up. I could see light under his door, I knocked and pushed on the door and said would you like a hot cup of tea, honey, I can't sleep. He was bent over by the dresser and slammed a drawer and turned on me, get out he screamed, get out of here, I'm sick of you spying he screamed. I went to my room and cried myself to sleep. He broke my heart that night.

The next morning he was up and out before I could see him, but that was all right with me. From then on I was going to treat him like a lodger unless he wanted to mend his ways, I was at my limit. He would have to apologize if he wanted us to be more than just strangers living together under the same roof.

When I came in that evening he had supper ready. How are you? he said, he took my coat. How was your day?

I said I didn't sleep last night, honey. I promised myself I wouldn't bring it up and I'm not trying to make you feel guilty but I'm not used to being talked to like that by my son.

I want to show you something, he said, and he showed me this essay he was writing for his civics class. I believe it was on relations between the congress and the supreme court. (It was the paper that won a prize for him at graduation!) I tried to read it and then I decided, this was the time. Honey, I'd like to have a talk with you, it's hard to raise a child with things the way they are these days, it's especially hard for us having no father in the house, no man to turn to when we need him. You are nearly grown now but I am still responsible and I feel I am entitled to some respect and consideration and have tried to be fair and honest with you. I want the truth, honey, that's all I've ever asked from you, the truth. Honey, I took a breath, suppose you had a child who when you asked him something, anything, where he's been or where he's going, what he's doing with his time, anything, never, he never once told you the truth? Who if you asked him is it raining outside, would answer no, it is nice and sunny, and I guess laugh to himself and think you were too old or too stupid to see his clothes are wet. Why should he lie, you ask yourself, what does he gain I don't understand. I keep asking myself why but I don't have the answer. Why, honey?

He didn't say anything, he kept staring, then he moved over alongside me and said I'll show you. Kneel is what I say, kneel down is what I say, he said, that's the first reason why.

I ran to my room and locked the door. He left that night, he took his things, what he wanted, and he left. Believe it or not I never saw him again. I saw him at his graduation but that was with a lot of people around. I sat in the audience and watched him get his diploma and a prize for his essay, then I heard him give the speech and then I clapped right along with the rest.

I went home after that.

I have never seen him again. Oh sure I have seen him on the TV and I have seen his pictures in the paper.

I found out he joined the marines and then I heard from someone he was out of the marines and going to college back east and then he married that girl and got himself in politics. I began to see his name in the paper. I found out his address and wrote to him, I wrote a letter every few months, there never was an answer. He ran for governor and was elected, and was famous now. That's when I began to worry.

I built up all these fears. I became afraid, I stopped writing him of course and then I hoped he would think I was dead. I moved here. I had them give me an unlisted number. And then I had to change my name. If you are a powerful man and want to find somebody, you can find them, it wouldn't be that hard.

I should be so proud but I am afraid. Last week I saw a car on the street with a man inside I know was watching me, I came straight back and locked the door. A few days ago the phone rang and rang, I was lying down. I picked up the receiver but there was nothing there.

I am old. I am his mother. I should be the proudest mother in all the land but I am only afraid.

Thank you for writing. I wanted someone to know. I am very ashamed.

I also wanted to ask how you got my name and knew where to write, I have been praying no one knew. But you did. Why did you? Please tell me why?

Yours truly,

The ducks

A wind came up that afternoon, bringing gusts of rain and sending the ducks up off the lake in black explosions looking for the quiet potholes out in the timber. He was at the back of the house splitting firewood and saw the ducks cutting over the highway and dropping into the marsh behind the trees. He watched, groups of half a dozen, but mostly doubles, one bunch behind the other. Out over the lake it was already dark and misty and he could not see the other side, where the mill was. He worked faster, driving the iron wedge down harder into the big dry chunks, splitting them so far down that the rotten ones flew apart. On his wife's clothesline, strung up between the two sugar pines, sheets and blankets popped shotlike in the wind. He made two trips and carried all the wood onto the porch before it started to rain.

'Supper's ready!' she called from the kitchen.

He went inside and washed up. They talked a little while they ate, mostly about the trip to Reno. Three more days of work, then payday, then the weekend in Reno. After supper he went out onto the porch and began sacking up his decoys. He stopped when she came out. She stood there in the doorway watching him.

'You going hunting again in the morning?'

He looked away from her and out toward the lake. 'Look at the weather. I think it's going to be good in the morning.' Her sheets were snapping in the wind and there was a blanket down on the ground. He nodded at it. 'Your things are going to get wet.'

'They weren't dry, anyway. They've been out there two days and they're not dry yet.'

'What's the matter? Don't you feel good?' he said.

'I feel all right.' She went back into the kitchen and shut the door and looked at him through the window. 'I just hate to have you gone all the time. It seems like you're gone all the time,' she said to the window. Her breath produced itself on the glass, then went away. When he came inside, he put the decoys in the corner and went to get his lunch pail. She was leaning against the cupboard, her hands on the edge of the draining board. He touched her hip, pinched her dress.

'You wait'll we get to Reno. We're going to have some fun,' he said.

She nodded. It was hot in the kitchen and there were little drops of sweat over her eyes. 'I'll get up when you come in and fix you some breakfast.'

'You sleep. I'd rather have you sleep.' He reached around behind her for his lunch pail.

'Kiss me bye,' she said.

He hugged her. She fastened her arms around his neck and held him. 'I love you. Be careful driving.'

She went to the kitchen window and watched him running, jumping over the puddles until he got to the pickup. She waved when he looked back from inside the cab. It was almost dark and it was raining hard.

She was sitting in a chair by the living-room window listening to the radio and the rain when she saw the pickup lights turn into the drive. She got up quickly and hurried to the back door. He stood there in the doorway, and she touched his wet, rubbery coat with her fingers.

'They told everybody to go home. The mill boss had a heart attack. He fell right down on the floor up in the mill and died.'

'You scared me.' She took his lunch pail and shut the door. 'Who was it? Was it that foreman named Mel?'

'No, his name was Jack Granger. He was about fifty years old, I guess.' He walked over close to the oil stove and stood there warming his hands. 'Jesus, it's so funny! He'd come through where I work and asked me how I was doing and probably wasn't gone five minutes when Bill Bessie come through and told me Jack Granger had just died right up in the mill.' He shook his head. 'Just like that.'

'Don't think about it,' she said and took his hands between hers and rubbed his fingers.

'I'm not. Just one of them things, I guess. You never know.'

The rain rushed against the house and slashed across the windows.

'God, it's hot in here! There any beer?' he said.

'I think there's some left,' she said and followed him out to the kitchen. His hair was still wet and she ran her fingers through it when he sat down. She opened a beer for him and poured some into a cup for herself. He sat drinking it in little sips, looking out the window toward the dark woods.

He said, 'One of the guys said he had a wife and two grown kids.'

She said, 'That Granger man, that's a shame. It's nice to have you home, but I hate for something like that to happen.'

'That's what I told some of the boys. I said it's nice to get on to home, but Christ, I hate to have it like this.' He edged a little in the chair. 'You know, I think most of the men would've gone ahead and worked, but some of the boys up in the mill said they wouldn't work, him laying there like that.' He finished off the beer and got up. 'I'll tell you – I'm glad they didn't work,' he said.

She said, 'I'm glad you didn't either. I had a really funny feeling when you left tonight. I was thinking about it, the funny feeling I had, when I saw the lights.'

'He was just in the lunch room last night telling jokes. Granger was a good boy. Always laughing.'

She nodded. 'I'll fix us something to eat if you'll eat something.'

'I'm not hungry, but I'll eat something,' he said.

They sat in the living room and held hands and watched television.

'I've never seen any of these programs before,' he said.

She said, 'I don't much care about watching any more. You can hardly get anything worth watching. Saturday and Sunday it's all right. But there's nothing weeknights.'

He stretched his legs and leaned back. He said, 'I'm kind of tired. I think I'll go to bed.'

She said, 'I think I'll take a bath and go to bed, too.' She moved her fingers through his hair and dropped her hand and smoothed his neck. 'Maybe we'll have a little tonight. We never hardly get a chance to have a little.' She touched her other hand to his thigh, leaned over and kissed him. 'What do you think about that?'

'That sounds all right,' he said. He got up and walked over to the window. Against the trees outside he could see her reflection standing behind him and a little to the side. 'Hon, why don't you go ahead and take your bath and we'll turn in,' he said. He stood there for a while longer watching the rain beat against the window. He looked at his watch. If he were working, it would be the lunch hour now. He went into the bedroom and began getting undressed.

In his shorts, he walked back into the living room and picked up a book off the floor – *Best-Loved Poems of the American People*. He guessed it had come in the mail from the club she belonged to. He went through the house and turned off the lights. Then he went back into the bedroom. He got under the covers, put her pillow on top of his, and twisted the gooseneck lamp around so that the light fell on the pages. He opened the book to the middle and began to look at some of the poems. Then he laid the book on the bedstand and bent the lamp away toward the wall. He lit a cigaret. He put his arms behind his head and lay there smoking. He looked straight ahead at the wall. The lamplight picked up all of the tiny cracks and swells in the plaster. In a corner, up near the ceiling, there was a cobweb. He could hear the rain washing down off the roof.

She stood up in the tub and began drying herself. When she noticed him watching, she smiled and draped the towel over her shoulder and made a little step in the tub and posed.

'How does it look?'

'All right,' he said.

'Okay,' she said.

'I thought you were still . . . you know,' he said.

'I am.' She finished drying and dropped the towel on the floor beside the tub and stepped daintily onto it. The mirror beside her was steamy and the odor of her body carried to him. She turned around and reached up to a shelf for the box. Then she slipped into her belt and adjusted the white pad. She tried to look at him, she tried to smile. He crushed out the cigaret and picked up the book again.

'What are you reading?' she called.

'I don't know. Crap,' he said. He turned to the back of the book and began looking through the biographies.

She turned off the light and came out of the bathroom brushing her hair. 'You still going in the morning?' she said.

'Guess not,' he said.

She said, 'I'm glad. We'll sleep in late, then get up and have a big breakfast.'

He reached over and got another cigaret.

She put the brush in a drawer, opened another drawer and took out a nightgown.

'Do you remember when you got me this?' she said.

He looked at her in reply.

She came around to his side of the bed. They lay quietly for a time, smoking his cigaret until he nodded he was finished, and then she put it out. He reached over her, kissed her on the shoulder, and switched off the light. 'You know,' he said, lying back down, 'I think I want to get out of here. Go someplace else.' She moved over to him and put her leg between his. They lay on their sides facing each other, lips almost touching. He wondered if his breath smelled as clean as hers. He said, 'I just want to leave. We been here a long time, I'd like to go back home and see my folks. Or maybe go on up to Oregon. That's good country.'

'If that's what you want,' she said.

'I think so,' he said. 'There's a lot of places to go.'

She moved a little and took his hand and put it on her breast. Then she opened her mouth and kissed him, pulling his head down with her other hand. Slowly she inched up in the bed, gently moving his head down to her breast. He took the nipple and began working it in his mouth. He tried to think how much he loved her or if he loved her. He could hear her breathing but he could also hear the rain. They lay like this.

She said, 'If you don't want to, it's all right.'

'It's not that,' he said, not knowing what he meant.

He let her go when he could tell she was asleep and turned over to his own side. He tried to think of Reno. He tried to think of the slots and the way the dice clicked and how they looked turning over under the lights. He tried to hear the sound the roulette ball made as it skimmed around the gleaming wheel. He tried to concentrate on the wheel. He looked and looked and listened and listened and heard the saws and the machinery slowing down, coming to a stop.

He got out of bed and went to the window. It was black outside and he could see nothing, not even the rain. But he could hear it, cascading off the roof and into a puddle under the window. He could hear it all over the house. He ran his finger across the drool on the glass.

When he got back into bed, he moved close to her and put his hand on her hip. 'Hon, wake up,' he whispered. But she only shuddered and moved over farther to her own side. She kept on sleeping. 'Wake up,' he whispered. 'I hear something outside.'

How about this?

All the optimism that had colored his flight from the city was gone now, had vanished the evening of the first day, as they drove north through the dark stands of redwood. Now, the rolling pasture land, the cows, the isolated farmhouses of western Washington seemed to hold out nothing for him, nothing he really wanted. He had expected something different. He drove on and on with a rising sense of hopelessness and outrage.

He kept the car at fifty, all that the road allowed. Sweat stood on his forehead and over his upper lip, and there was a sharp heady odor of clover in the air all around them. The land began to change; the highway dipped suddenly, crossed a culvert, rose again, and then the asphalt ran out and he was holding the car on a country dirt road, an astonishing trail of dust rising behind them. As they passed the ancient burned-out foundation of a house set back among some maple trees, Emily removed her dark glasses and leaned forward, staring.

'That *is* the old Owens place,' she said. 'He and Dad were friends. He kept a still in his attic and had a big team of dray horses he used to enter in all the fairs. He died with a ruptured appendix when I was about ten years old. The house burned down a year later at Christmas. They moved to Bremerton after that.'

'Is that so?' he said. 'Christmas.' Then: 'Do I turn right or left here? Emily? Right or left?'

'Left,' she said. 'Left.'

She put on her glasses again, only to take them off a moment later. 'Stay on this road, Harry, until you come to another crossroad. Then right. Only a little farther then.' She smoked steadily, one cigaret after the other, was silent now as she looked out at the cleared fields, at the isolated stands of fir trees, at the occasional weathered house.

He shifted down, turned right. The road began to drop gradually into a lightly wooded valley. Far ahead – Canada, he supposed – he could see a range of mountains and behind those mountains a darker, still higher range.

'There's a little road,' she said, 'at the bottom. That's the road.'

He turned carefully and drove down the rutted track road slowly, waiting for the first sign of the house. Emily sat next to him, edgy, he could see, smoking again, also waiting for the first glimpse. He blinked his eyes as low shaggy branches slapped the windshield. She leaned forward slightly and touched her hand to his leg. 'Now,' she said. He slowed almost to a stop, drove through a tiny clear puddle of a stream that came out of the high grass on his left, then into a mass of dogwood that fingered and scraped the length of the car as the little road climbed. 'There it is,' she said, moving her hand from his leg.

After the first unsettling glance, he kept his eyes on the road. He looked at the house again after he had brought the car to a stop near the front door. Then he licked his lips, turned to her, and tried to smile.

'Well, we're here,' he said.

She was looking at him, not looking at the house at all.

Harry had always lived in cities – San Francisco for the last three years, and, before that, Los Angeles, Chicago, and New York. But for a long time he had wanted to move to the country, somewhere in the country. At first he wasn't too clear about where he wanted to go; he just knew he wanted to leave the city and try to start over again. A simpler life was what he had in mind, just the essentials, he said. He was thirty-two years old and was a writer in a way, but he was also an actor and a musician. He played the saxophone, performed occasionally with the Bay City Players, and was writing a first novel. He had been writing the novel since the time he lived in New York. One bleak Sunday afternoon in March, when he had again started talking about a change, a more honest life somewhere in the country, she'd mentioned, jokingly at first, her father's deserted place in the northwestern part of Washington.

'My God,' Harry had said, 'you wouldn't mind? Roughing it, I mean? Living in the country like that?'

'I was born there,' she said, laughing. 'Remember? I've lived in the country. It's all right. It has advantages. I could live there again. I don't know about you, though, Harry. If it'd be good for you.'

She kept looking at him, serious now. He felt lately that she was always looking at him.

'You wouldn't regret it?' he said. 'Giving up things here?'

'I wouldn't be giving up much, would I, Harry?' She shrugged. 'But I'm not going to encourage the idea, Harry.'

'Could you paint up there?' he asked.

'I can paint anywhere,' she said. 'And there's Bellingham,' she said. 'There's a college there. Or else Vancouver or Seattle.' She kept watching him. She sat on a stool in front of a shadowy half-finished portrait of a man and woman and rolled two paintbrushes back and forth in her hand.

That was three months ago. They had talked about it and talked about it and now they were here.

He rapped on the walls near the front door. 'Solid. A solid foundation. If you have a solid foundation, that's the main thing.' He avoided looking at her. She was shrewd and might have read something from his eyes.

'I told you not to expect too much,' she said.

'Yes, you did. I distinctly remember,' he said, still not looking at her. He gave the bare board another rap with his knuckles and moved over beside her. His sleeves were rolled in the damp afternoon heat, and he was wearing white jeans and sandals. 'Quiet, isn't it?'

'A lot different from the city.'

'God, yes . . . Pretty up here, too.' He tried to smile. 'Needs a little work, that's all. A little work. It'll be a good place if we want to stay. Neighbors won't bother us, anyway.'

'We had neighbors here when I was a little girl,' she said. 'You had to drive to see them, but they were neighbors.'

The door opened at an angle. The top hinge was loose: nothing much, Harry judged. They moved slowly from room to room. He tried to cover his disappointment. Twice he knocked on the walls and said, 'Solid.' Or, 'They don't make houses like this any more. You can do a lot with a house like this.'

She stopped in front of a large room and drew a long breath.

'Yours?'

She shook her head.

'And we could get the necessary furniture we need from your Aunt Elsie?'

'Yes, whatever we need,' she said. 'That is, if it's what we want, to stay here. I'm not pushing. It's not too late to go back. There's nothing lost.'

In the kitchen they found a wood stove and a mattress pushed against one wall. In the living room again, he looked around and said, 'I thought it'd have a fireplace.'

'I never said it had a fireplace.'

'I just had the impression for some reason it would have one . . . No outlets, either,' he said a moment later. Then: 'No electricity!'

'Toilet, either,' she said.

He wet his lips. 'Well,' he said, turning away to examine something in the corner, 'I guess we could fix up one of these rooms with a tub and all, and get someone to do the plumbing work. But electricity is something else, isn't it? I mean, let's face all these things when we come to them. One thing at a time, right? Don't you think? Let's . . . let's not let any of it get us down, okay?'

'I wish you'd just be quiet,' she said.

She turned and went outside.

He jumped down the steps a minute later and drew a breath of air and they both lighted cigarets. A flock of crows got up at the far end of the meadow and flew slowly and silently into the woods.

They walked toward the barn, stopping to inspect the withered apple trees. He broke off one of the small dry branches, turned it over and over in his hands while she stood beside him and smoked a cigaret. It *was* peaceful, more or less appealing country, and he thought it pleasant to feel that something permanent, really permanent, might belong to him. He was taken by a sudden affection for the little orchard.

'Get these bearing again,' he said. 'Just need water and some looking after's all.' He could see himself coming out of the house with a wicker basket and pulling down large red apples, still wet with the morning's dew, and he understood that the idea was attractive to him.

He felt a little cheered as they approached the barn. He examined briefly the old license plates nailed to the door. Green, yellow, white plates from the state of Washington, rusted now, 1922-23-24-25-26-27-28-29-34-36-37-40-41-1949; he studied the dates as if he thought their sequence might disclose a code. He threw the wooden latch and pulled and pushed at the heavy door until it swung open. The air inside smelled unused. But he believed it was not an unpleasant smell.

'It rains a lot here in the winter,' she said. 'I don't remember it ever being this hot in June.' Sunlight struck down through the splits in the roof. 'Once Dad shot a deer out of season. I was about—I don't know—eight or nine, around in there.' She turned to him as he stood stopped near the door to look at an old harness that hung from a nail. 'Dad was down here in the barn with the deer when the game warden drove into the yard. It was dark. Mother sent me down here for Dad, and the game warden, a big heavyset man with a hat, followed me. Dad was carrying a lamp, just coming down from the loft. He and the game warden talked a few minutes. The deer was hanging there, but the game warden didn't say anything. He offered Dad a chew of tobacco, but Dad refused – he never had liked it and wouldn't take any even then. Then the game warden pulled my ear and left. But I don't want to think about any of that,' she added quickly. 'I haven't thought about things like that in years. I don't want to make comparisons,' she said. 'No,' she said. She stepped back, shaking her head. 'I'm not going to cry. I know that sounds melodramatic and just plain stupid, and I'm sorry for sounding melodramatic and stupid. But the truth is, Harry . . .' She shook her head again. 'I don't know. Maybe coming back here was a mistake. I can feel your disappointment.'

'You don't know,' he said.

'No, that's right, I don't know,' she said. 'And I'm sorry, I'm really not meaning to try to influence you one way or the other. But I don't think you want to stay. Do you?'

He shrugged.

He took out a cigaret. She took it from him and held it, waiting for a match, waiting for his eyes to meet hers over the match.

'When I was little,' she went on, 'I wanted to be in a circus when I grew up. I didn't want to be a nurse or a teacher. Or a painter, I didn't want to be a painter then. I wanted to be Emily Horner, High-Wire Artist. It was a big thing with me. I used to practice down here in the barn, walking the rafters. That big rafter there, I walked that hundreds of times.' She started to say something else, but puffed her cigaret and put it out under her heel, tamping it down carefully into the dirt.

Outside the barn he could hear a bird calling, and then he heard a scurrying sound over the boards up in the loft. She walked past him, out into the light, and started slowly through the deep grass toward the house.

'What are we going to do, Emily?' he called after her.

She stopped, and he came up beside her.

'Stay alive,' she said. Then she shook her head and smiled faintly. She touched his arm. 'Jesus, I guess we are in kind of a spot, aren't we? But that's all I can say, Harry.'

'We've got to decide,' he said, not really knowing what he meant.

'You decide, Harry, if you haven't already. It's your decision. I'd just as soon go back if that makes it any easier for you. We'll stay with Aunt Elsie a day or two and then go back. All right? But give me a cigaret, will you? I'm going up to the house.'

He moved closer to her then and thought they might embrace. He wanted to. But she did not move; she only looked at him steadily, and so he touched her on the nose with his forefinger and said, 'I'll see you in a little while.'

He watched her go. He looked at his watch, turned, and walked slowly down the pasture toward the woods. The grass came up to his knees. Just before he entered the woods, as the grass began to thin out, he found a sort of path. He rubbed the bridge of his nose under his dark glasses, looked back at the house and the barn, and continued on, slowly. A cloud of mosquitoes moved with his head as he walked. He stopped to light a cigaret. He brushed at the mosquitoes. He looked back again, but now he could not see the house or barn. He stood there smoking, beginning to feel the silence that lay in the grass and in the trees and in the shadows farther back in the trees. Wasn't this what he'd longed for? He walked on, looking for a place to sit.

He lighted another cigaret and leaned against a tree. He picked up some wood chips from the soft dirt between his legs. He smoked. He remembered a volume of plays by Ghelderode lying on top of the things in the back seat of the car, and then he recalled some of the little towns they had driven through that morning – Ferndale, Lynden, Custer, Nooksack. He suddenly recalled the mattress in the kitchen. He understood that it made him afraid. He tried to imagine Emily walking the big rafter in the barn. But that made him afraid too. He smoked. He felt very calm really, all things considered. He wasn't going to stay here, he knew that, but it didn't upset him to know that now. He was pleased he knew himself so well. He would be all right, he decided. He was only thirty-two. Not so old. He was, for the moment, in a spot. He could admit that. After all, he considered, that was life, wasn't it? He put out the cigaret. In a little while he lit another one.

As he rounded a corner of the house, he saw her completing a cartwheel. She landed with a light thump, slightly crouched, and then she saw him.

'Hey!' she yelled, grinning gravely.

She raised herself onto the balls of her feet, arms out to the sides over her head, and then pitched forward. She turned two more cartwheels while he watched, and then she called, 'How about *this*!'

She dropped lightly onto her hands and, getting her balance, began a shaky hesitant movement in his direction. Face flushed, blouse hanging over her chin, legs waving insanely, she advanced on him.

'Have you decided?' she said, quite breathless.

He nodded.

'So?' she said. She let herself fall against her shoulder and rolled onto her back, covering her eyes from the sun with an arm as if to uncover her breasts.

She said, 'Harry.'

He was reaching to light a cigaret with his last match when his hands began to tremble. The match went out, and he stood there holding the empty matchbook and the cigaret, staring at the vast expanse of trees at the end of the bright meadow.

'Harry, we have to love each other,' she said. 'We'll just have to love each other,' she said.

Bicycles, muscles, cigarets

It had been two days since Evan Hamilton had stopped smoking, and it seemed to him everything he'd said and thought for the two days somehow suggested cigarets. He looked at his hands under the kitchen light. He sniffed his knuckles and his fingers.

'I can smell it,' he said.

'I know. It's as if it sweats out of you,' Ann Hamilton said. 'For three days after I stopped I could smell it on me. Even when I got out of the bath. It was disgusting.' She was putting plates on the table for dinner. 'I'm so sorry, dear. I know what you're going through. But, if it's any consolation, the second day is always the hardest. The third day is hard, too, of course, but from then on, if you can stay with it that long, you're over the hump. But I'm so happy you're serious about quitting, I can't tell you.' She touched his arm. 'Now, if you'll just call Roger, we'll eat.'

Hamilton opened the front door. It was already dark. It was early in November and the days were short and cool. An older boy he had never seen before was sitting on a small, well-equipped bicycle in the driveway. The boy leaned forward just off the seat, the toes of his shoes touching the pavement and keeping him upright.

'You Mr Hamilton?' the boy said.

'Yes, I am,' Hamilton said. 'What is it? Is it Roger?'

'I guess Roger is down at my house talking to my mother. Kip is there and this boy named Gary Berman. It is about my brother's bike. I don't know for sure.' the boy said, twisting the handle grips, 'but my mother asked me to come and get you. One of Roger's parents.'

'But he's all right?' Hamilton said. 'Yes, of course, I'll be right with you.'

He went into the house to put his shoes on.

'Did you find him?' Ann Hamilton said.

'He's in some kind of jam,' Hamilton answered. 'Over a bicycle. Some boy — I didn't catch his name — is outside. He wants one of us to go back with him to his house.'

'Is he all right?' Ann Hamilton said and took her apron off.

'Sure, he's all right.' Hamilton looked at her and shook his head. 'It sounds like it's just a childish argument, and the boy's mother is

143

getting herself involved.'

'Do you want me to go?' Ann Hamilton asked.

He thought for a minute. 'Yes, I'd rather you went, but I'll go. Just hold dinner until we're back. We shouldn't be long.'

'I don't like his being out after dark,' Ann Hamilton said. 'I don't like it.'

The boy was sitting on his bicycle and working the handbrake now.

'How far?' Hamilton said as they started down the sidewalk.

'Over in Arbuckle Court,' the boy answered, and when Hamilton looked at him, the boy added, 'Not far. About two blocks from here.'

'What seems to be the trouble?' Hamilton asked.

'I don't know for sure. I don't understand all of it. He and Kip and this Gary Berman are supposed to have used my brother's bike while we were on vacation, and I guess they wrecked it. On purpose. But I don't know. Anyway, that's what they're talking about. My brother can't find his bike and they had it last, Kip and Roger. My mom is trying to find out where it's at.'

'I know Kip,' Hamilton said. 'Who's this other boy?'

'Gary Berman. I guess he's new in the neighborhood. His dad is coming as soon as he gets home.'

They turned a corner. The boy pushed himself along, keeping just slightly ahead. Hamilton saw an orchard, and then they turned another corner onto a dead-end street. He hadn't known of the existence of this street and was sure he would not recognize any of the people who lived here. He looked around him at the unfamiliar houses and was struck with the range of his son's personal life.

The boy turned into a driveway and got off the bicycle and leaned it against the house. When the boy opened the front door, Hamilton followed him through the living room and into the kitchen, where he saw his son sitting on one side of a table along with Kip Hollister and another boy. Hamilton looked closely at Roger and then he turned to the stout, dark-haired woman at the head of the table.

'You're Roger's father?' the woman said to him.

'Yes, my name is Evan Hamilton. Good evening.'

'I'm Mrs Miller, Gilbert's mother,' she said. 'Sorry to ask you over here, but we have a problem.'

Hamilton sat down in a chair at the other end of the table and looked around. A boy of nine or ten, the boy whose bicycle was missing, Hamilton supposed, sat next to the woman. Another boy, fourteen or so, sat on the draining board, legs dangling, and watched another boy who was talking on the telephone. Grinning slyly at something that had just been said to him over the line, the boy reached over to the sink with a cigaret. Hamilton heard the sound of the cigaret sputting out in a glass of water. The boy who had brought him leaned against the refrigerator and crossed his arms.

'Did you get one of Kip's parents?' the woman said to the boy.

'His sister said they were shopping. I went to Gary Berman's and his father will be here in a few minutes. I left the address.'

'Mr Hamilton,' the woman said, 'I'll tell you what happened. We were on vacation last month and Kip wanted to borrow Gilbert's bike so that Roger could help him with Kip's paper route. I guess Roger's bike had a flat tire or something. Well, as it turns out –'

'Gary was choking me, Dad,' Roger said.

'What?' Hamilton said, looking at his son carefully.

'He was choking me. I got the marks.' His son pulled down the collar of his T-shirt to show his neck.

'They were out in the garage,' the woman continued. 'I didn't know what they were doing until Curt, my oldest, went out to see.'

'He started it!' Gary Berman said to Hamilton. 'He called me a jerk.' Gary Berman looked toward the front door.

'I think my bike cost about sixty dollars, you guys,' the boy named Gilbert said. 'You can pay me for it.'

'You keep out of this, Gilbert.' the woman said to him.

Hamilton took a breath. 'Go on,' he said.

'Well, as it turns out, Kip and Roger used Gilbert's bike to help Kip deliver his papers, and then the two of them, and Gary too, they say, took turns rolling it.'

'What do you mean "rolling it"?' Hamilton said.

'Rolling it,' the woman said. 'Sending it down the street with a push and letting it fall over. Then, mind you – and they just admitted this a few minutes ago – Kip and Roger took it up to the school and threw it against a goalpost.'

'Is that true, Roger?' Hamilton said, looking at his son again.

'Part of it's true, Dad,' Roger said, looking down and rubbing his finger over the table. 'But we only rolled it once. Kip did it, then Gary, and then I did it.'

'Once is too much,' Hamilton said. 'Once is one too many times, Roger. I'm surprised and disappointed in you. And you too, Kip,' Hamilton said.

'But you see,' the woman said, 'someone's fibbing tonight or else not telling all he knows, for the fact is the bike's still missing.'

The older boys in the kitchen laughed and kidded with the boy who still talked on the telephone.

'We don't know where the bike is, Mrs Miller,' the boy named Kip said. 'We told you already. The last time we saw it was when me and Roger took it to my house after we had it at school. I mean, that was the next to last time. The very last time was when I took it back here the next morning and parked it behind the house.' He shook his head. 'We don't know where it is,' the boy said.

'Sixty dollars,' the boy named Gilbert said to the boy named Kip. 'You can pay me off like five dollars a week.'

'Gilbert, I'm warning you,' the woman said. 'You see, *they* claim,' the woman went on, frowning now, 'it disappeared from *here*, from behind the house. But how can we believe them when they haven't been all that truthful this evening?'

'We've told the truth,' Roger said. 'Everything.'

Gilbert leaned back in his chair and shook his head at Hamilton's son.

The doorbell sounded and the boy on the draining board jumped down and went into the living room.

A stiff-shouldered man with a crew haircut and sharp gray eyes entered the kitchen without speaking. He glanced at the woman and moved over behind Gary Berman's chair.

'You must be Mr Berman?' the woman said. 'Happy to meet you. I'm Gilbert's mother, and this is Mr Hamilton, Roger's father.'

The man inclined his head at Hamilton but did not offer his hand.

'What's all this about?' Berman said to his son.

The boys at the table began to speak at once.

'Quiet down!' Berman said. 'I'm talking to Gary. You'll get your turn.'

The boy began his account of the affair. His father listened closely, now and then narrowing his eyes to study the other two boys.

When Gary Berman had finished, the woman said, 'I'd like to get to the bottom of this. I'm not accusing any one of them, you understand, Mr Hamilton, Mr Berman – I'd just like to get to the bottom of this.' She looked steadily at Roger and Kip, who were shaking their heads at Gary Berman.

'It's not true, Gary,' Roger said.

'Dad, can I talk to you in private?' Gary Berman said.

'Let's go,' the man said, and they walked into the living room.

Hamilton watched them go. He had the feeling he should stop them, this secrecy. His palms were wet, and he reached to his shirt pocket for a cigaret. Then, breathing deeply, he passed the back of his hand under his nose and said, 'Roger, do you know any more about this, other than what you've already said? Do you know where Gilbert's bike is?'

'No, I don't,' the boy said. 'I swear it.'

'When was the last time you saw the bicycle?' Hamilton said.

'When we brought it home from school and left it at Kip's house.'

'Kip,' Hamilton said, 'do you know where Gilbert's bicycle is now?'

'I swear I don't, either,' the boy answered. 'I brought it back the next morning after we had it at school and I parked it behind the garage.'

'I thought you said you left it behind the *house*,' the woman said quickly.

'I mean the house! That's what I meant,' the boy said.

'Did you come back here some other day to ride it?' she asked, leaning forward.

'No, I didn't,' Kip answered.

'Kip?' she said.

'I didn't! I don't know where it is!' the boy shouted.

The woman raised her shoulders and let them drop. 'How do you know who or what to believe?' she said to Hamilton. 'All I know is, Gilbert's missing a bicycle.'

Gary Berman and his father returned to the kitchen.

'It was Roger's idea to roll it,' Gary Berman said.

'It was yours!' Roger said, coming out of his chair. 'You wanted to! Then you wanted to take it to the orchard and strip it!'

'You shut up!' Berman said to Roger. 'You can speak when spoken to, young man, not before. Gary, I'll handle this – dragged out at night because of a couple of roughnecks! Now if either of you,' Berman said, looking first at Kip and then Roger, 'know where this kid's bicycle is, I'd advise you to start talking.'

'I think you're getting out of line,' Hamilton said.

'What?' Berman said, his forehead darkening. 'And I think you'd do better to mind your own business!'

'Let's go, Roger,' Hamilton said, standing up. 'Kip, you come now or stay.' He turned to the woman. 'I don't know what else we can do tonight. I intend to talk this over more with Roger, but if there is a question of restitution I feel since Roger did help manhandle the bike, he can pay a third if it comes to that.'

'I don't know what to say,' the woman replied, following Hamilton through the living room. 'I'll talk to Gilbert's father – he's out of town now. We'll see. It's probably one of those things finally, but I'll talk to his father.'

Hamilton moved to one side so that the boys could pass ahead of him onto the porch, and from behind him he heard Gary Berman say, 'He called me a jerk, Dad.'

'He did, did he?' Hamilton heard Berman say. 'Well, he's the jerk. He looks like a jerk.'

Hamilton turned and said, 'I think you're seriously out of line here tonight, Mr Berman. Why don't you get control of yourself?'

'And I told you I think you should keep out of it!' Berman said.

'You get home, Roger.' Hamilton said, moistening his lips. 'I mean it,' he said, 'get going!' Roger and Kip moved out to the sidewalk. Hamilton stood in the doorway and looked at Berman, who was crossing the living room with his son.

'Mr Hamilton,' the woman began nervously but did not finish.

'What do you want?' Berman said to him. 'Watch out now, get out of my way!' Berman brushed Hamilton's shoulder and Hamilton stepped off the porch into some prickly cracking bushes. He couldn't believe it was happening. He moved out of the bushes and lunged at the man where he stood on the porch. They fell heavily onto the lawn. They rolled on the lawn, Hamilton wrestling Berman onto his back and coming down hard with his knees on the man's biceps. He had Berman by the collar now and began to pound his head against the lawn while the woman cried, 'God almighty, someone stop them! For God's sake, someone call the police!'

Hamilton stopped.

Berman looked up at him and said, 'Get off me.'

'Are you all right?' the woman called to the men as they separated. 'For God's sake,' she said. She looked at the men, who stood a few feet apart, backs to each other, breathing hard. The older boys had crowded onto the porch to watch; now that it was over, they waited, watching the men, and then they began feinting and punching each other on the arms and ribs.

'You boys get back in the house,' the woman said. 'I never thought I'd see,' she said and put her hand on her breast.

Hamilton was sweating and his lungs burned when he tried to take a deep breath. There was a ball of something in his throat so that he couldn't swallow for a minute. He started walking, his son and the boy named Kip at his sides. He heard car doors slam, an engine start. Headlights swept over him as he walked.

Roger sobbed once, and Hamilton put his arm around the boy's shoulders.

'I better get home,' Kip said and began to cry. 'My dad'll be looking for me,' and the boy ran.

'I'm sorry,' Hamilton said. 'I'm sorry you had to see something like that,' Hamilton said to his son.

They kept walking and when they reached their block, Hamilton took his arm away.

'What if he'd picked up a knife, Dad? Or a club?'

'He wouldn't have done anything like that,' Hamilton said.

'But what if he had?' his son said.

'It's hard to say what people will do when they're angry,' Hamilton said.

They started up the walk to their door. His heart moved when Hamilton saw the lighted windows.

'Let me feel your muscle,' his son said.

'Not now,' Hamilton said. 'You just go in now and have your dinner and hurry up to bed. Tell your mother I'm all right and I'm going to sit on the porch for a few minutes.'

The boy rocked from one foot to the other and looked at his father, and then he dashed into the house and began calling, 'Mom! Mom!'

He sat on the porch and leaned against the garage wall and stretched his legs. The sweat had dried on his forehead. He felt clammy under his clothes.

He had once seen his father – a pale, slow-talking man with slumped shoulders – in something like this. It was a bad one, and both men had been hurt. It had happened in a café. The other man was a farmhand. Hamilton had loved his father and could recall many things about him. But now he recalled his father's one fistfight as if it were all there was to the man.

He was still sitting on the porch when his wife came out.

'Dear God,' she said and took his head in her hands. 'Come in and shower and then have something to eat and tell me about it. Everything is still warm. Roger has gone to bed.'

But he heard his son calling him.

'He's still awake,' she said.

'I'll be down in a minute,' Hamilton said. 'Then maybe we should have a drink.'

She shook her head. 'I really don't believe any of this yet.'

He went into the boy's room and sat down at the foot of the bed.

'It's pretty late and you're up, so I'll say good night,' Hamilton said.

'Good night,' the boy said, hands behind his neck, elbows jutting.

He was in his pajamas and had a warm fresh smell about him that Hamilton breathed deeply. He patted his son through the covers.

'You take it easy from now on. Stay away from that part of the neighborhood, and don't let me ever hear of you damaging a bicycle or any other personal property. Is that clear?' Hamilton said.

The boy nodded. He took his hands from behind his neck and began picking at something on the bedspread.

'Okay, then,' Hamilton said, 'I'll say good night.'

He moved to kiss his son, but the boy began talking.

'Dad, was Grandfather strong like you? When he was your age, I mean, you know, and you –'

'And I was nine years old? Is that what you mean? Yes, I guess he was,' Hamilton said.

'Sometimes I can hardly remember him,' the boy said. 'I don't want to forget him or anything, you know? You know what I mean, Dad?'

When Hamilton did not answer at once, the boy went on. 'When you were young, was it like it is with you and me? Did you love him more than me? Or just the same?' The boy said this abruptly. He moved his feet under the covers and looked away. When Hamilton still did not answer, the boy said, 'Did he smoke? I think I remember a pipe or something.'

'He started smoking a pipe before he died, that's true,' Hamilton said. 'He used to smoke cigarets a long time ago and then he'd get depressed with something or other and quit, but later he'd change brands and start in again. Let me show you something,' Hamilton said. 'Smell the back of my hand.'

The boy took the hand in his, sniffed it, and said, 'I guess I don't smell anything, Dad. What is it?'

Hamilton sniffed the hand and then the fingers. 'Now I can't smell anything, either,' he said. 'It was there before, but now it's gone.' Maybe it was scared out of me, he thought. 'I wanted to show you something. All right, it's late now. You better go to sleep,' Hamilton said.

The boy rolled onto his side and watched his father walk to the door and watched him put his hand to the switch. And then the boy said, 'Dad? You'll think I'm pretty crazy, but I wish I'd known you when you were little. I mean, about as old as I am right now. I don't know how to say it, but I'm lonesome about it. It's like – it's like I miss you already if I think about it now. That's pretty crazy, isn't it? Anyway, please leave the door open.'

Hamilton left the door open, and then he thought better of it and closed it halfway.

What is it?

Fact is the car needs to be sold in a hurry, and Leo sends Toni out to do it. Toni is smart and has personality. She used to sell children's encyclopedias door to door. She signed him up, even though he didn't have kids. Afterward, Leo asked her for a date, and the date led to this. This deal has to be cash, and it has to be done tonight. Tomorrow somebody they owe might slap a lien on the car. Monday they'll be in court, home free – but word on them went out yesterday, when their lawyer mailed the letters of intention. The hearing on Monday is nothing to worry about, the lawyer has said. They'll be asked some questions, and they'll sign some papers, and that's it. But sell the convertible, he said – today, *tonight*. They can hold onto the little car, Leo's car, no problem. But they go into court with that big convertible, the court will take it, and that's that.

Toni dresses up. It's four o'clock in the afternoon. Leo worries the lots will close. But Toni takes her time dressing. She puts on a new white blouse, wide lacy cuffs, the new two-piece suit, new heels. She transfers the stuff from her straw purse into the new patent-leather handbag. She studies the lizard makeup pouch and puts that in too. Toni has been two hours on her hair and face. Leo stands in the bedroom doorway and taps his lips with his knuckles, watching.

'You're making me nervous,' she says. 'I wish you wouldn't just stand,' she says. 'So tell me how I look.'

'You look fine,' he says. 'You look great. I'd buy a car from you anytime.'

'But you don't have money,' she says, peering into the mirror. She pats her hair, frowns. 'And your credit's lousy. You're nothing,' she says. 'Teasing,' she says and looks at him in the mirror. 'Don't be serious,' she says. 'It has to be done, so I'll do it. You take it out, you'd be lucky to get three, four hundred and we both know it. Honey, you'd be lucky if you didn't have to pay *them*.' She gives her hair a final pat, gums her lips, blots the lipstick with a tissue. She turns away from the mirror and picks up her purse. 'I'll have to have dinner or something, I told you that already, that's the way they work, I know them. But don't worry, I'll get out of it,' she says. 'I can handle it.'

'Jesus,' Leo says, 'did you have to say that?'

She looks at him steadily. 'Wish me luck,' she says.

'Luck,' he says. 'You have the pink slip?' he says.

She nods. He follows her through the house, a tall woman with a small high bust, broad hips and thighs. He scratches a pimple on his neck. 'You're sure?' he says. 'Make sure. You have to have the pink slip.'

'I have the pink slip,' she says.

'Make sure.'

She starts to say something, instead looks at herself in the front window and then shakes her head.

'At least call,' he says. 'Let me know what's going on.'

'I'll call,' she says. 'Kiss, kiss. Here,' she says and points to the corner of her mouth. 'Careful,' she says.

He holds the door for her. 'Where are you going to try first?' he says. She moves past him and onto the porch.

Ernest Williams looks from across the street. In his Bermuda shorts, stomach hanging, he looks at Leo and Toni as he directs a spray onto his begonias. Once, last winter, during the holidays, when Toni and the kids were visiting his mother's, Leo brought a woman home. Nine o'clock the next morning, a cold foggy Saturday, Leo walked the woman to the car, surprised Ernest Williams on the sidewalk with a newspaper in his hand. Fog drifted, Ernest Williams stared, then slapped the paper against his leg, hard.

Leo recalls that slap, hunches his shoulders, says, 'You have someplace in mind first?'

'I'll just go down the line,' she says. 'The first lot, then I'll just go down the line.'

'Open at nine hundred,' he says. 'Then come down. Nine hundred is low bluebook, even on a cash deal.'

'I know where to start,' she says.

Ernest Williams turns the hose in their direction. He stares at them through the spray of water. Leo has an urge to cry out a confession.

'Just making sure,' he says.

'Okay, okay,' she says. 'I'm off.'

'It's her car, they call it her car, and that makes it all the worse. They bought it new that summer three years ago. She wanted something to do after the kids started school, so she went back selling. He was working six days a week in the fiber-glass plant. For a while they didn't know how to spend the money. Then they put a thousand on the convertible and doubled and tripled the payments until in a year they had it paid. Earlier, while she was dressing, he took the jack and spare from the trunk and emptied the glove compartment of pencils, matchbooks, Blue Chip stamps. Then he washed it and vacuumed inside. The red hood and fenders shine.

'Good luck,' he says and touches her elbow.

She nods. He sees she is already gone, already negotiating.

'Things are going to be different!' he calls to her as she reaches the driveway. 'We start over Monday. I mean it.'

Ernest Williams looks at them and turns his head and spits. She gets into the car and lights a cigaret.

'This time next week!' Leo calls again. 'Ancient history!'

He waves as she backs into the street. She changes gear and starts ahead. She accelerates and the tires give a little scream.

In the kitchen Leo pours Scotch and carries the drink to the backyard. The kids are at his mother's. There was a letter three days ago, his name penciled on the outside of the dirty envelope, the only letter all summer not demanding payment in full. We are having fun, the letter said. We like Grandma. We have a new dog called Mr Six. He is nice. We love him. Goodbye.

He goes for another drink. He adds ice and sees that his hand trembles. He holds the hand over the sink. He looks at the hand for a while, sets down the glass, and holds out the other hand. Then he picks up the glass and goes back outside to sit on the steps. He recalls when he was a kid his dad pointing at a fine house, a tall white house surrounded by apple trees and a high white rail fence. 'That's Finch,' his dad said admiringly. 'He's been in bankruptcy at least twice. Look at that house.' But bankruptcy is a company collapsing utterly, executives cutting their wrists and throwing themselves from windows, thousands of men on the street.

Leo and Toni still had furniture. Leo and Toni had furniture and Toni and the kids had clothes. Those things were exempt. What else? Bicycles for the kids, but these he had sent to his mother's for safekeeping. The portable air-conditioner and the appliances, new washer and dryer, trucks came for those things weeks ago. What else did they have? This and that, nothing mainly, stuff that wore out or fell to pieces long ago. But there were some big parties back there, some fine travel. To Reno and Tahoe, at eighty with the top down and the radio playing. Food, that was one of the big items. They gorged on food. He figures thousands on luxury items alone. Toni would go to the grocery and put in everything she saw. 'I had to do without when I was a kid,' she says. 'These kids are not going to do without,' as if he'd been insisting they should. She joins all the book clubs. 'We never had books around when I was a kid,' she says as she tears open the heavy packages. They enroll in the record clubs for something to play on the new stereo. They sign up for it all. Even a pedigreed terrier named Ginger. He paid two hundred and found her run over in the street a week later. They buy what they want. If they can't pay, they charge. They sign up.

His undershirt is wet; he can feel the sweat rolling from his under-arms. He sits on the step with the empty glass in his hand and watches the shadows fill up the yard. He stretches, wipes his face. He listens to the traffic on the highway and considers whether he should go to the basement, stand on the utility sink, and hang himself with his belt. He understands he is willing to be dead.

Inside he makes a large drink and he turns the TV on and he fixes something to eat. He sits at the table with chili and crackers and watches something about a blind detective. He clears the table. He washes the pan and the bowl, dries these things and puts them away, then allows himself a look at the clock.

It's after nine. She's been gone nearly five hours.

He pours Scotch, adds water, carries the drink to the living room. He sits on the couch but finds his shoulders so stiff they won't let him lean back. He stares at the screen and sips, and soon he goes for another drink. He sits again. A news program begins — it's ten o'clock — and he says, 'God, what in God's name has gone wrong?' and goes to the kitchen to return with more Scotch. He sits, he closes his eyes, and opens them when he hears the telephone ringing.

'I wanted to call,' she says.

'Where are you?' he says. He hears piano music, and his heart moves.

'I don't know,' she says. 'Someplace. We're having a drink, then we're going someplace else for dinner. I'm with the sales manager. He's crude, but he's all right. He bought the car. I have to go now. I was on my way to the ladies and saw the phone.'

'Did somebody buy the car?' Leo says. He looks out the kitchen window to the place in the drive where she always parks.

'I told you,' she says. 'I have to go now.'

'Wait, wait a minute, for Christ's sake,' he says. 'Did somebody buy the car or not?'

'He had his checkbook out when I left,' she says. 'I have to go now. I have to go to the bathroom.'

'Wait!' he yells. The line goes dead. He listens to the dial tone. 'Jesus Christ,' he says as he stands with the receiver in his hand.

He circles the kitchen and goes back to the living room. He sits. He gets up. In the bathroom he brushes his teeth very carefully. Then he uses dental floss. He washes his face and goes back to the kitchen. He looks at the clock and takes a clean glass from a set that has a hand of playing cards painted on each glass. He fills the glass with ice. He stares for a while at the glass he left in the sink.

He sits against one end of the couch and puts his legs up at the other end. He looks at the screen, realizes he can't make out what the people are saying. He turns the empty glass in his hand and considers biting off the rim. He shivers for a time and thinks of going to bed, though he knows he will dream of a large woman with gray hair. In the dream he is always leaning over tying his shoelaces. When he straightens up, she looks at him, and he bends to tie again. He looks at his hand. It makes a fist as he watches. The telephone is ringing.

'Where are you, honey?' he says slowly, gently.

'We're at this restaurant,' she says, her voice strong, bright.

'Honey, which restaurant?' he says. He puts the heel of his hand against his eye and pushes.

'Downtown someplace,' she says. 'I think it's New Jimmy's. Excuse me,' she says to someone off the line, 'is this place New Jimmy's? This is New Jimmy's , Leo.' she says to him. 'Everything is all right, we're almost finished, then he's going to bring me home.'

'Honey?' he says. He holds the receiver against his ear and rocks back and forth, eyes closed. 'Honey?'

'I have to go,' she says. 'I wanted to call. Anyway, guess how much?'

'Honey,' he says.

'Six and a quarter,' she says. 'I have it in my purse. He said there's no market for convertibles. I guess we're born lucky,' she says and laughs. 'I told him everything. I think I had to.'

'Honey,' Leo says.

'What?' she says.

'Please, honey,' Leo says.

'He said he sympathizes,' she says. 'But he would have said anything.' She laughs again. 'He said personally he'd rather be classified a robber or a rapist than a bankrupt. He's nice enough, though,' she says.

'Come home,' Leo says. 'Take a cab and come home.'

'I can't,' she says. 'I told you, we're halfway through dinner.'

'I'll come for you,' he says.

'No,' she says. 'I said we're just finishing. I told you, it's part of the deal. They're out for all they can get. But don't worry, we're about to leave. I'll be home in a little while.' She hangs up.

In a few minutes he calls New Jimmy's. A man answers. 'New Jimmy's has closed for the evening,' the man says.

'I'd like to talk to my wife,' Leo says.

'Does she work here?' the man asks. 'Who is she?'

'She's a customer,' Leo says. 'She's with someone. A business person.'

'Would I know her?' the man says. 'What is her name?'

'I don't think you know her,' Leo says.

'That's all right,' Leo says. 'That's all right. I see her now.'

'Thank you for calling New Jimmy's,' the man says.

Leo hurries to the window. A car he doesn't recognize slows in front of the house, then picks up speed. He waits. Two, three hours later, the telephone rings again. There is no one at the other end when he picks up the receiver. There is only a dial tone.

'I'm right here!' Leo screams into the receiver.

Near dawn he hears footsteps on the porch. He gets up from the couch. The set hums, the screen glows. He opens the door. She bumps the wall coming in. She grins. Her face is puffy, as if she's been sleeping under sedation. She works her lips, ducks heavily and sways as he cocks his fist.

'Go ahead,' she says thickly. She stands there swaying. Then she makes a noise and lunges, catches his shirt, tears it down the front. 'Bankrupt!' she screams. She twists loose, grabs and tears his undershirt at the neck. 'You son of a bitch,' she says, clawing.

He squeezes her wrists, then let's go, steps back, looking for something heavy. She stumbles as she heads for the bedroom. 'Bankrupt,' she mutters. He hears her fall on the bed and groan.

He waits awhile, then splashes water on his face and goes to the bedroom. He turns the lights on, looks at her, and begins to take her clothes off. He pulls and pushes her from side to side undressing her.

She says something in her sleep and moves her hand. He takes off her underpants, looks at them closely under the light, and throws them into a corner. He turns back the covers and rolls her in, naked. Then he opens her purse. He is reading the check when he hears the car come into the drive.

He looks through the front curtain and sees the convertible in the drive, its motor running smoothly, the headlamps burning, and he closes and opens his eyes. He sees a tall man come around in front of the car and up to the front porch. The man lays something on the porch and starts back to the car. He wears a white linen suit.

Leo turns on the porch light and opens the door cautiously. Her makeup pouch lies on the top step. The man looks at Leo across the front of the car, and then gets back inside and releases the handbrake.

'Wait!' Leo calls and starts down the steps. The man brakes the car as Leo walks in front of the lights. The car creaks against the brake. Leo tries to pull the two pieces of his shirt together, tries to bunch it all into his trousers.

'What is it you want?' the man says. 'Look,' the man says, 'I have to go. No offense. I buy and sell cars, right? The lady left her makeup. She's a fine lady, very refined. What is it?'

Leo leans against the door and looks at the man. The man takes his hands off the wheel and puts them back. He drops the gear into reverse and the car moves backward a little.

'I want to tell you,' Leo says and wets his lips.

The light in Ernest Williams' bedroom goes on. The shade rolls up.

Leo shakes his head, tucks in his shirt again. He steps back from the car. 'Monday,' he says.

'Monday,' the man says and watches for sudden movement.

Leo nods slowly.

'Well, goodnight,' the man says and coughs. 'Take it easy, hear? Monday, that's right. Okay, then.' He takes his foot off the brake, puts it on again after he has rolled back two or three feet. 'Hey, one question. Between friends, are these actual miles?' The man waits, then clears his throat. 'Okay, look, it doesn't matter either way,' the man says. 'I have to go. Take it easy.' He backs into the street, pulls away quickly, and turns the corner without stopping.

Leo tucks at his shirt and goes back in the house. He locks the front door and checks it. Then he goes to the bedroom and locks that door and turns back the covers. He looks at her before he flicks the light. He takes off his clothes, folds them carefully on the floor, and gets in beside her. He lies on his back for a time and pulls the hair on his stomach, considering. He looks at the bedroom door, outlined now in the faint outside light. Presently he reaches out his hand and touches her hip. She does not move. He turns on his side and puts his hand on her hip. He runs his fingers over her hip and feels the stretch marks there. They are like roads, and he traces them in her flesh. He runs his fingers back and forth, first one, then another. They run everywhere in her flesh, dozens, perhaps hundreds of them. He remembers waking up the morning after they bought the car, seeing it, there in the drive, in the sun, gleaming.

Signals

As their first of the extravagances they had planned for that evening, Wayne and Caroline went to Aldo's, an elegant new restaurant north a good distance. They passed through a tiny walled garden with small pieces of statuary and were met by a tall graying man in a dark suit who said, 'Good evening, sir. Madam,' and who swung open the heavy door for them.

Inside, Aldo himself showed them the aviary – a peacock, a pair of Golden pheasants, a Chinese ring-necked pheasant, and a number of unannounced birds that flew around or sat perched. Aldo personally conducted them to a table, seated Caroline, and then turned to Wayne and said, 'A lovely lady,' before moving off – a dark, small, impeccable man with a soft accent.

They were pleased with his attention.

'I read in the paper,' Wayne said, 'that he has an uncle who has some kind of position in the Vatican. That's how he was able to get copies of some of these paintings.' Wayne nodded at a Velasquez reproduction on the nearest wall. 'His uncle in the Vatican,' Wayne said.

'He used to be *maître d'* at the Copacabana in Rio,' Caroline said. 'He knew Frank Sinatra, and Lana Turner was a good friend of his.'

'Is that so?' Wayne said. 'I didn't know that. I read that he was at the Victoria Hotel in Switzerland and at some big hotel in Paris. I didn't know he was at the Copacabana in Rio.'

Caroline moved her handbag slightly as the waiter set down the heavy goblets. He poured water and then moved to Wayne's side of the table.

'Did you see the suit he was wearing?' Wayne said. 'You seldom see a suit like that. That's a three-hundred-dollar suit.' He picked up his menu. In a while, he said, 'Well, what are you going to have?'

'I don't know,' she said. 'I haven't decided. What are you going to have?'

'I don't know,' he said. 'I haven't decided, either.'

'What about one of these French dishes, Wayne? Or else this? Over here on this side.' She placed her finger in instruction, and then she narrowed her eyes at him as he located the language, pursed his lips, frowned, and shook his head.

'I don't know,' he said. 'I'd kind of like to know what I'm getting. I just don't really know.'

The waiter returned with card and pencil and said something Wayne couldn't quite catch.

'We haven't decided yet,' Wayne said. He shook his head as the waiter continued to stand beside the table. 'I'll signal you when we're ready.'

'I think I'll just have a sirloin. You order what you want,' he said to Caroline when the waiter had moved off. He closed the menu and raised his goblet. Over the muted voices coming from the other tables Wayne could hear a warbling call from the aviary. He saw Aldo greet a party of four, chat with them as he smiled and nodded and led them to a table.

'We could have had a better table,' Wayne said. 'Instead of right here in the center where everyone can walk by and watch you eat. We could have had a table against the wall. Or over there by the fountain.'

'I think I'll have the beef Tournedos,' Caroline said.

She kept looking at her menu. He tapped out a cigaret, lighted it, and then glanced around at the other diners. Caroline still stared at her menu.

'Well, for God's sake, if that's what you're going to have, close your menu so he can take our order.' Wayne raised his arm for the waiter, who lingered near the back talking with another waiter.

'Nothing else to do but gas around with the other waiters,' Wayne said.

'He's coming,' Caroline said.

'Sir?' The waiter was a thin pock-faced man in a loose black suit and a black bow tie.

'. . . And we'll have a bottle of champagne, I believe. A small bottle. Something, you know, domestic,' Wayne said.

'Yes, sir,' the waiter said.

'And we'll have that right away. Before the salad or the relish plate,' Wayne said.

'Oh, bring the relish *tray*, anyway,' Caroline said. 'Please.'

'Yes, madam,' the waiter said.

'They're a slippery bunch,' Wayne said. 'Do you remember that guy named Bruno who used to work at the office during the week and wait tables on weekends? Fred caught him stealing out of the petty-cash box. We fired him.'

'Let's talk about something pleasant,' Caroline said.

'All right, sure,' Wayne said.

The waiter poured a little champagne into Wayne's glass, and Wayne took the glass, tasted, and said, 'Fine, that will do nicely.' Then he said, 'Here's to you, baby,' and raised his glass high. 'Happy birthday.'

They clinked glasses.

'I like champagne,' Caroline said.

'I like champagne,' Wayne said.

'We could have had a bottle of Lancer's,' Caroline said.

'Well, why didn't you say something, if that's what you wanted?' Wayne said.

'I don't know,' Caroline said. 'I just didn't think about it. This is fine, though.'

'I don't know too much about champagnes. I don't mind admitting I'm not much of a . . . connoisseur. I don't mind admitting I'm just a lowbrow.' He laughed and tried to catch her eye, but she was busy selecting an olive from the relish dish. 'Not like the group you've been keeping company with lately. But if you wanted Lancer's,' he went on. 'you should have ordered Lancer's.'

'Oh, shut up!' she said. 'Can't you talk about something else?' She looked up at him then and he had to look away. He moved his feet under the table.

He said, 'Would you care for some more champagne, dear?'

'Yes, thank you,' she said quietly.

'Here's to us,' he said.

'To us, my darling,' she said.

They looked steadily at each other as they drank.

'We ought to do this more often', he said.

She nodded.

'It's good to get out now and then. I'll make more of an effort, if you want me to.'

She reached for celery. 'That's up to you.'

'That's not true! It's not me who's . . . who's . . .'

'Who's what?' she said.

'I don't care what you do,' he said, dropping his eyes.

'Is that true?'

'I don't know why I said that,' he said.

The waiter brought the soup and took away the bottle and the wineglasses and refilled their goblets with water.

'Could I have a soup spoon?' Wayne asked.

'Sir?'

'A soup spoon,' Wayne repeated.

The waiter looked amazed and then perplexed. He glanced around at the other tables. Wayne made a shoveling motion over his soup. Aldo appeared beside the table.

'Is everything all right? Is there anything wrong?'

'My husband doesn't seem to have a soup spoon,' Caroline said. 'I'm sorry for the disturbance,' she said.

'Certainly. *Une cuiller, s'il vous plaît,*' Aldo said to the waiter in an even voice. He looked once at Wayne and then explained to Caroline. 'This is Paul's first night. He speaks little English, yet I trust you will agree he is an excellent waiter. The boy who set the table forgot the spoon.' Aldo smiled. 'It no doubt took Paul by surprise.'

'This is a beautiful place,' Caroline said.

'Thank you,' Aldo said. 'I'm delighted you could come tonight. Would you like to see the wine cellar and the private dining rooms?'

'Very much,' Caroline said.

'I will have someone show you around when you have finished dinner,' Aldo said.

'We'll be looking forward to it,' Caroline said.

Aldo bowed slightly and looked again at Wayne. 'I hope you enjoy your dinner,' he said to them.

'That jerk,' Wayne said.

'Who?' she said. 'Who are you talking about?' she said, laying down her spoon.

'The waiter,' Wayne said. 'The waiter. The newest and the dumbest waiter in the house, and we got him.'

'Eat your soup,' she said. 'Don't blow a gasket.'

Wayne lighted a cigaret. The waiter arrived with salads and took away the soup bowls.

When they had started on the main course, Wayne said, 'Well, what do you think? Is there a chance for us or not?' He looked down and arranged the napkin on his lap.

'Maybe so,' she said. 'There's always a chance.'

'Don't give me that kind of crap,' he said. 'Answer me straight for a change.'

'Don't snap at me,' she said.

'I'm asking you,' he said. 'Give me a straight answer,' he said.

She said, 'You want something signed in blood?'

He said, 'That wouldn't be such a bad idea.'

She said, 'You listen to me! I've given you the best years of my life. The best years of my life!'

'The best years of *your* life?' he said.

'I'm thirty-six years old,' she said. 'Thirty-seven tonight. Tonight, right now, at this minute, I just can't say what I'm going to do. I'll just have to see,' she said.

'I don't care what you do,' he said.

'Is that true?' she said.

He threw down his fork and tossed his napkin on the table.

'Are you finished?' she asked pleasantly. 'Let's have coffee and dessert. We'll have a nice dessert. Something good.'

She finished everything on her plate.

'Two coffees,' Wayne said to the waiter. He looked at her and then back to the waiter. 'What do you have for dessert?' he said.

'Sir?' the waiter said.

'Dessert!' Wayne said.

The waiter gazed at Caroline and then at Wayne.

'No dessert,' she said. 'Let's not have any dessert.'

'Chocolate mousse,' the waiter said. 'Orange sherbet,' the waiter said. He smiled, showing his bad teeth. 'Sir?'

'And I don't want any guided tour of this place,' Wayne said when the waiter had moved off.

When they rose from the table, Wayne dropped a dollar bill near his coffee cup. Caroline took two dollars from her handbag, smoothed the bills out, and placed them alongside the other dollar, the three bills lined up in a row.

She waited with Wayne while he paid the check. Out of the corner of his eye, Wayne could see Aldo standing near the door dropping grains of seed into the aviary. Aldo looked in their direction, smiled, and went on rubbing the seeds from between his fingers as birds collected in front of him. Then he briskly brushed his hands together and started moving toward Wayne, who looked away, who turned slightly but significantly as Aldo neared him. But when Wayne looked back, he saw Aldo take Caroline's waiting hand, saw Aldo draw his heels smartly together, saw Aldo kiss her wrist.

'Did madam enjoy her dinner?' Aldo said.

'It was marvelous,' Caroline said.

'You will come back from time to time?' Aldo said.

'I shall,' Caroline said. 'As often as I may. Next time, I should like to have your permission to check things out a little, but this time we simply must go.'

'Dear lady,' Aldo said. 'I have something for you. One moment, please.' He reached to a vase on a table near the door and swung gracefully back with a long-stemmed rose.

'For you, dear lady,' Aldo said. 'But caution, please. The thorns. A very lovely lady,' he said to Wayne and smiled at him and turned to welcome another couple.

Caroline stood there.

'Let's get out of here,' Wayne said.

'You can see how he could be friends with Lana Turner,' Caroline said. She held the rose and turned it between her fingers.

'Good night!' she called out to Aldo's back.

But Aldo was occupied selecting another rose.

'I don't think he ever knew her,' Wayne said.

Will you please
be quiet, please?

When he was eighteen and was leaving home for the first time, Ralph Wyman was counseled by his father, principal of Jefferson Elementary School and trumpet soloist in the Weaverville Elks Club Auxiliary Band, that life was a very serious matter, an enterprise insisting on strength and purpose in a young person just setting out, an arduous undertaking, everyone knew that, but nevertheless a rewarding one, Ralph Wyman's father believed and said.

But in college Ralph's goals were hazy. He thought he wanted to be a doctor and he thought he wanted to be a lawyer, and he took pre-medical courses and courses in the history of jurisprudence and business law before he decided he had neither the emotional detachment necessary for medicine nor the ability for sustained reading required in law, especially as such reading might concern property and inheritance. Though he continued to take classes here and there in the sciences and in business, Ralph also took some classes in philosophy and literature and felt himself on the brink of some kind of huge discovery about himself. But it never came. It was during this time – his lowest ebb, as he referred to it later – that Ralph believed he almost had a breakdown; he was in a fraternity and he got drunk every night. He drank so much that he acquired a reputation and was called 'Jackson,' after the bartender at The Keg.

Then, in his third year, Ralph came under the influence of a particularly persuasive teacher. Dr. Maxwell was his name; Ralph would never forget him. He was a handsome, graceful man in his early forties, with exquisite manners and with just the trace of the South in his voice. He had been educated at Vanderbilt, had studied in Europe, and had later had something to do with one or two literary magazines back East. Almost overnight, Ralph would later say, he decided on teaching as a career. He stopped drinking quite so much, began to bear down on his studies, and within a year was elected to Omega Psi, the national journalism fraternity; he became a member of the English Club; was invited to come with his cello, which he hadn't played in three years, and join in a student chamber-music group just forming; and he even ran successfully for secretary of the

senior class. It was then that he met Marian Ross—a handsomely pale
and slender girl who took a seat beside him in a Chaucer class.

Marian Ross wore her hair long and favored high-necked sweaters
and always went around with a leather purse on a long strap swinging
from her shoulder. Her eyes were large and seemed to take in everything at a glance. Ralph liked going out with Marian Ross. They went
to The Keg and to a few other spots where everyone went, but they
never let their going together or their subsequent engagement the
next summer interfere with their studies. They were solemn students,
and both sets of parents eventually gave approval to the match. Ralph
and Marian did their student teaching at the same high school in
Chico in the spring and went through graduation exercises together in
June. They married in St James Episcopal Church two weeks later.

They had held hands the night before their wedding and pledged to
preserve forever the excitement and the mystery of marriage.

For their honeymoon they drove to Guadalajara, and while they both
enjoyed visiting the decayed churches and the poorly lighted
museums and the afternoons they spent shopping and exploring in
the marketplace, Ralph was secretly appalled by the squalor and
open lust he saw and was anxious to return to the safety of California.
But the one vision he would always remember and which disturbed
him most of all had nothing to do with Mexico. It was late afternoon,
almost evening, and Marian was leaning motionless on her arms over
the ironwork balustrade of their rented *casita* as Ralph came up the
dusty road below. Her hair was long and hung down in front over her
shoulders, and she was looking away from him, staring at something
in the distance. She wore a white blouse with a bright red scarf at her
throat, and he could see her breasts pushing against the white cloth.
He had a bottle of dark, unlabeled wine under his arm, and the whole
incident put Ralph in mind of something from a film, an intensely
dramatic moment into which Marian could be fitted but he could not.

Before they left for their honeymoon they had accepted positions at
a high school in Eureka, a town in the lumbering region in the
northern part of the state. After a year, when they were sure the school
and the town were exactly what they wanted to settle down to, they
made a payment on a house in the Fire Hill district. Ralph felt,
without really thinking about it, that he and Marian understood each
other perfectly—as well, at least, as any two people might. Moreover,

Ralph felt he understood himself – what he could do, what he could not do, and where he was headed with the prudent measure of himself that he made.

Their two children, Dorothea and Robert, were now five and four years old. A few months after Robert was born, Marian was offered a post as a French and English instructor at the junior college at the edge of town, and Ralph had stayed on at the high school. They considered themselves a happy couple, with only a single injury to their marriage, and that was well in the past, two years ago this winter. It was something they had never talked about since. But Ralph thought about it sometimes – indeed, he was willing to admit he thought about it more and more. Increasingly, ghastly images would be projected on his eyes, certain unthinkable particularities. For he had taken it into his head that his wife had once betrayed him with a man named Mitchell Anderson.

But now it was a Sunday night in November and the children were asleep and Ralph was sleepy and he sat on the couch grading papers and could hear the radio playing softly in the kitchen, where Marian was ironing, and he felt enormously happy. He stared a while longer at the papers in front of him, then gathered them all up and turned off the lamp.

'Finished, love?' Marian said with a smile when he appeared in the doorway. She was sitting on a tall stool, and she stood the iron up on its end as if she had been waiting for him.

'Damn it, no,' he said with an exaggerated grimace, tossing the papers on the kitchen table.

She laughed – bright, pleasant – and held up her face to be kissed, and he gave her a little peck on the cheek. He pulled out a chair from the table and sat down, leaned back on the legs and looked at her. She smiled again and then lowered her eyes.

'I'm already half asleep,' he said.

'Coffee?' she said, reaching over and laying the back of her hand against the percolator.

He shook his head.

She took up the cigaret she had burning in the ashtray, smoked it while she stared at the floor, and then put it back in the ashtray. She looked at him, and a warm expression moved across her face. She was tall and limber, with a good bust, narrow hips, and wide wonderful eyes.

'Do you ever think about that party?' she asked, still looking at him.

He was stunned and shifted in the chair, and he said, 'Which party? You mean the one two or three years ago?'

She nodded.

He waited, and when she offered no further comment, he said, 'What about it? Now that you brought it up, what about it?' Then: 'He kissed you, after all, that night, didn't he? I mean, I knew he did. He did try to kiss you, or didn't he?'

'I was just thinking about it and I asked you, that's all,' she said. 'Sometimes I think about it,' she said.

'Well, he did, didn't he? Come on, Marian,' he said.

'Do you ever think about that night?' she said.

He said, 'Not really. It was a long time ago, wasn't it? Three or four years ago. You can tell me now,' he said. 'This is still old Jackson you're talking to, remember?' And they both laughed abruptly together and abruptly she said, 'Yes.' She said, 'He did kiss me a few times.' She smiled.

He knew he should try to match her smile, but he could not. He said, 'You told me before he didn't. You said he only put his arm around you while he was driving. So which is it?'

'What did you do that for?' she was saying dreamily. 'Where were you all night?' he was screaming, standing over her, legs watery, fist drawn back to hit again. Then she said, 'I didn't do anything. Why did you hit me?' she said.

'How did we ever get onto this?' she said.

'You brought it up,' he said.

She shook her head. 'I don't know what made me think of it,' She pulled in her upper lip and stared at the floor. Then she straightened her shoulders and looked up. 'If you'll move this ironing board for me, love, I'll make us a hot drink. A buttered rum. How does that sound?'

'Good,' he said.

She went into the living room and turned on the lamp and bent to pick up a magazine from the floor. He watched her hips under the plaid woolen skirt. She moved in front of the window and stood looking out at the streetlight. She smoothed her palm down over her skirt, then began tucking in her blouse. He wondered if she wondered if he were watching her.

After he stood the ironing board in its alcove on the porch, he sat down again and, when she came into the kitchen, he said, 'Well, what else went on between you and Mitchell Anderson that night?'

*

'Nothing,' she said. 'I was thinking about something else.'

'What?'

'About the children, the dress I want Dorothea to have for next Easter. And about the class I'm going to have tomorrow. I was thinking of seeing how they'd go for a little Rimbaud,' and she laughed. 'I didn't mean to rhyme – really, Ralph, and really, nothing else happened. I'm sorry I ever said anything about it.'

'Okay,' he said.

He stood up and leaned against the wall by the refrigerator and watched her as she spooned out sugar into two cups and then stirred in the rum. The water was beginning to boil.

'Look, honey, it *has* been brought up now,' he said, 'and it *was* four years ago, so there's no reason at all I can think of that we *can't* talk about it now if we *want* to. Is there?'

She said, 'There's really nothing to talk about.'

He said, 'I'd like to know.'

She said, 'Know what?'

'Whatever else he did besides kiss you. We're adults. We haven't seen the Andersons in literally years and we'll probably never see them again and it happened a *long* time ago, so what reason could there possibly be that we can't talk about it?' He was a little surprised at the reasoning quality in his voice. He sat down and looked at the tablecloth and then looked up at her again. 'Well?' he said.

'Well,' she said, with an impish grin, tilting her head to one side girlishly, remembering. 'No, Ralph, really. I'd really just rather not.'

'For Christ's sake, Marian! *Now* I mean it,' he said, and he suddenly understood that he did.

She turned off the gas under the water and put her hand out on the stool; then she sat down again, hooking her heels over the bottom step. She sat forward, resting her arms across her knees, her breasts pushing at her blouse. She picked at something on her skirt and then looked up.

'You remember Emily'd already gone home with the Beattys, and for some reason Mitchell had stayed on. He looked a little out of sorts that night, to begin with. I don't know, maybe they weren't getting along, Emily and him, but I don't know that. And there were you and I, the Franklins, and Mitchell Anderson still there. All of us a little drunk. I'm not sure how it happened, Ralph, but Mitchell and I just happened to find ourselves alone together in the kitchen for a minute, and there was no whiskey left, only a part of a bottle of that white wine we had. It must've been close to one o'clock, because Mitchell said, 'If we ride on giant wings we can make it before the liquor store closes.' You know how he could be so theatrical when he wanted? Soft-shoe stuff, facial expressions? Anyway, he was very witty about it all. At least it seemed that way at the time. And very drunk, too, I might add. So was I, for that matter. It was an impulse, Ralph. I don't know why I did it, don't ask me, but when he said let's go – I agreed. We went out the back, where his car was parked. We went just as . . . we were . . . didn't even get our coats out of the closet, thought we'd just be gone a few minutes. I don't know what we thought, *I* thought. I don't know *why* I went, Ralph. It was an impulse, that's all I can say. It was the wrong impulse.' She paused. 'It was my fault that night, Ralph, and I'm sorry. I shouldn't have done anything like that – I *know* that.'

'Christ!' The word leaped out of him. 'But you've always been that way, Marian!' And he knew at once that he had uttered a new and profound truth.

His mind filled with a swarm of accusations, and he tried to focus on one in particular. He looked down at his hands and noticed they had the same lifeless feeling they had had when he had seen her on the balcony. He picked up the red grading pencil lying on the table and then he put it down again.

'I'm listening,' he said.

'Listening to what?' she said. 'You're swearing and getting upset, Ralph. For nothing – nothing, honey! . . . there's nothing *else*,' she said.

'Go on,' he said.

She said, '*What* is the matter with us, anyway? Do you know how this started? Because I don't know how this started.'

He said. 'Go on, Marian.'

'That's *all*, Ralph,' she said. 'I've told you. We went for a ride. We talked. He kissed me. I still don't see how we could've been gone three hours – or whatever it was you said we were.'

'Tell me, Marian,' he said, and he knew there was more and knew he had always known. He felt a fluttering in his stomach, and then he said, 'No. If you don't want to tell me, that's all right. Actually, I guess I'd just as soon leave it at that,' he said. He thought fleetingly that he would be someplace else tonight doing something else, that it would be silent somewhere if he had not married.

'Ralph,' she said. 'you won't be angry, will you? Ralph? We're just talking. You won't, will you?' She had moved over to a chair at the table.

He said, 'I won't.'

She said, 'Promise?'

He said, 'Promise.'

She lit a cigaret. He had suddenly a great desire to see the children, to get them up and out of bed, heavy and turning in their sleep, and to hold each of them on a knee, to jog them until they woke up. He moved all his attention into one of the tiny black coaches in the tablecloth. Four tiny white prancing horses pulled each of the black coaches and the figure driving the horses had his arms up and wore a tall hat, and suitcases were strapped down atop the coach, and what looked like a kerosene lamp hung from the side, and if he were listening at all it was from inside the black coach.

'. . . We went straight to the liquor store, and I waited in the car until he came out. He had a sack in one hand and one of those plastic bags of ice in the other. He weaved a little getting into the car. I hadn't realized he was so drunk until we started driving again. I noticed the way he was driving. It was terribly slow. He was all hunched over the wheel. His eyes staring. We were talking about a lot of things that didn't make sense. I can't remember. We were talking about Nietzsche. Strindberg. He was directing *Miss Julie* second semester. And then something about Norman Mailer stabbing his wife in the breast. And then he stopped for a minute in the middle of the road. And we each took a drink out of the bottle. He said he'd hate to think of me being stabbed in the breast. He said he'd like to kiss my breast. He drove the car off the road. He put his head on my lap. . . .'

She hurried on, and he sat with his hands folded on the table and watched her lips. His eyes skipped around the kitchen – stove, napkin-holder, stove, cupboards, toaster, back to her lips, back to the coach in the tablecloth. He felt a peculiar desire for her flicker through his groin, and then he felt the steady rocking of the coach and he wanted to call *stop* and then he heard her say. 'He said shall we have a go at it?' And then she was saying, 'I'm to blame. I'm the one to blame. He said he'd leave it all up to me, I could do whatever I want.'

He shut his eyes. He shook his head, tried to create possibilities, other conclusions. He actually wondered if he could restore that night two years ago and imagined himself coming into the kitchen just as they were at the door, heard himself telling her in a hearty voice, oh no, no, you're not going out for anything with that Mitchell

Anderson! The fellow is drunk and he's a bad driver to boot and you have to go to bed now and get up with little Robert and Dorothea in the morning and stop! Thou shalt stop!

He opened his eyes. She had a hand up over her face and was crying noisily.

'Why did you, Marian?' he asked.

She shook her head without looking up.

Then suddenly he knew! His mind buckled. For a minute he could only stare dumbly at his hands. He knew! His mind roared with the knowing.

'Christ! No! Marian! *Jesus Christ!*' he said, springing back from the table. 'Christ! *No*, Marian!'

'No, no,' she said, throwing her head back.

'You let him!' he screamed.

'No, no,' she pleaded.

'You let him! A go at it! Didn't you? Didn't you? A *go* at it! Is that what he said? Answer me!' he screamed. 'Did he come in you? Did you let him come in you when you were having your go at it?

'Listen, listen to me, Ralph,' she whimpered, 'I swear to you he didn't. He didn't come. He didn't come in me.' She rocked from side to side in the chair.

'Oh God! God *damn* you!' he shrieked.

'God!' she said, getting up, holding out her hands, 'Are we crazy, Ralph? Have we lost our minds? Ralph? Forgive me, Ralph. Forgive—'

'Don't touch me! Get away from me!' he screamed. He was screaming.

She began to pant in her fright. She tried to head him off. But he took her by the shoulder and pushed her out of the way.

'Forgive me, Ralph! *Please*. Ralph!' she screamed.

2

He had to stop and lean against a car before going on. Two couples in evening clothes were coming down the sidewalk toward him, and one of the men was telling a story in a loud voice. The others were already laughing. Ralph pushed off from the car and crossed the street. In a few minutes he came to Blake's, where he stopped some afternoons for a beer with Dick Koenig before picking up the children from nursery school.

It was dark inside. Candles flamed in long-necked bottles at the tables along one wall. Ralph glimpsed shadowy figures of men and women talking, their heads close together. One of the couples, near the door, stopped talking and looked up at him. A boxlike fixture in the ceiling revolved overhead, throwing out pins of light. Two men sat at the end of the bar, and a dark cutout of a man leaned over the jukebox in the corner, his hands splayed on each side of the glass. That man is going to play something, Ralph thought as if making a momentous discovery, and he stood in the center of the floor, watching the man.

'Ralph! Mr Wyman, sir!'

He looked around. It was David Parks calling to him from behind the bar. Ralph walked over, leaned heavily against the bar before sliding onto a stool.

'Should I draw one, Mr Wyman?' Parks held a glass in his hand, smiling. Ralph nodded, watched Parks fill the glass, watched Parks hold the glass at an angle under the tap, smoothly straighten the glass as it filled.

'How's it going, Mr Wyman?' Parks put his foot up on a shelf under the bar. 'Who's going to win the game next week, Mr Wyman?' Ralph shook his head, brought the beer to his lips. Parks coughed faintly. 'I'll buy you one, Mr Wyman. This one's on me.' He put his leg down, nodded assurance, and reached under his apron into his pocket. 'Here. I have it right here,' Ralph said and pulled out some change, examined it in his hand. A quarter, nickel, two dimes, two pennies. He counted as if there were a code to be uncovered. He laid down the quarter and stood up, pushing the change back into his pocket. The man was still in front of the jukebox, his hands still out to its sides.

Outside, Ralph turned around, trying to decide what to do. His heart was jumping as if he'd been running. The door opened behind him and a man and woman came out. Ralph stepped out of the way and they got into a car parked at the curb and Ralph saw the woman toss her hair as she got into the car: He had never seen anything so frightening.

He walked to the end of the block, crossed the street, and walked another block before he decided to head downtown. He walked hurriedly, his hands balled into his pockets, his shoes smacking the pavement. He kept blinking his eyes and thought it incredible that this was where he lived. He shook his head. He would have liked to sit someplace for a while and think about it, but he knew he could not sit, could not think about it. He remembered a man he saw once sitting on a curb in Arcata, an old man with a growth of beard and a brown wool cap who just sat there with his arms between his legs. And then Ralph thought: Marian! Dorothea! Robert! It was impossible. He tried to imagine how all this would seem twenty years from now. But he could not imagine anything. And then he imagined snatching up a note being passed among his students and it said *Shall we have a go at it?* Then he could not think. Then he felt profoundly indifferent. Then he thought of Marian. He thought of Marian as he had seen her a little while ago, face crumpled. Then Marian on the floor, blood on her teeth: 'Why did you hit me?' Then Marian reaching under her dress to unfasten her garter belt! Then Marian lifting her dress as she arched back! Then Marian ablaze, Marian crying out, *Go! Go! Go!*

He stopped. He believed he was going to vomit. He moved to the curb. He kept swallowing, looked up as a car of yelling teenagers went by and gave him a long blast on their musical horn. Yes, there was a great evil pushing at the world, he thought, and it only needed a little slipway, a little opening.

He came to Second Street, the part of town people called 'Two Street.' It started here at Shelton, under the streetlight where the old roominghouses ended, and ran for four or five blocks on down to the pier, where fishing boats tied up. He had been down here once, six years ago, to a secondhand shop to finger through the dusty shelves of old books. There was a liquor store across the street, and he could see a man standing just inside the glass door, looking at a newspaper.

A bell over the door tinkled. Ralph almost wept from the sound of it. He bought some cigarets and went out again, continuing along the street, looking in windows, some with signs taped up: a dance, the Shrine circus that had come and gone last summer, an election – *Fred C. Walters for Councilman.* One of the windows he looked through had sinks and pipe joints scattered around on a table, and this too brought tears to his eyes. He came to a Vic Tanney gym where he could see light sneaking under the curtains pulled across a big window and could hear water splashing in the pool inside and the echo of exhilarated voices calling across water. There was more light now, coming from bars and cafés on both sides of the street, and more people, groups of three or four, but now and then a man by himself or a woman in bright slacks walking rapidly. He stopped in front of a window and watched some Negroes shooting pool, smoke drifting in the light burning above the table. One of the men, chalking his cue, hat on, cigaret in his mouth, said something to another man and both men grinned, and then the first man looked intently at the balls and lowered himself over the table.

Ralph stopped in front of Jim's Oyster House. He had never been here before, had never been to any of these places before. Above the door the name was spelled out in yellow lightbulbs: JIM'S OYSTER HOUSE. Above this, fixed to an iron grill, there was a huge neon-lighted clam shell with a man's legs sticking out. The torso was hidden in the shell and the legs flashed red, on and off, up and down, so that they seemed to be kicking. Ralph lit another cigaret from the one he had and pushed the door open.

It was crowded, people bunched on the dance floor, their arms laced around each other, waiting in positions for the band to begin again. Ralph pushed his way to the bar, and once a drunken woman took hold of his coat. There were no stools and he had to stand at the end of the bar between a Coast Guardsman and a shriveled man in denims. In the mirror he could see the men in the band getting up from the table where they had been sitting. They wore white shirts and dark slacks with little red string ties around their necks. There was a fireplace with gas flames behind a stack of metal logs, and the band platform was to the side of this. One of the musicians plucked the strings of his electric guitar, said something to the others with a knowing grin. The band began to play.

Ralph raised his glass and drained it. Down the bar he could hear a woman say angrily, 'Well, there's going to be trouble, that's all I've got to say.' The musicians came to the end of their number and started another. One of the men, the bass player, moved to the microphone and began to sing. But Ralph could not understand the words. When the band took another break, Ralph looked around for the toilet. He could make out doors opening and closing at the far end of the bar and headed in that direction. He staggered a little and knew he was drunk now. Over one of the doors was a rack of antlers. He saw a man go in and he saw another man catch the door and come out. Inside, in line behind three other men, he found himself staring at opened thighs and vulva drawn on the wall over a pocket-comb machine. Beneath was scrawled EAT ME, and lower down someone had added *Betty M. Eats It – RA 52275.* The man ahead moved up, and Ralph took a step forward, his heart squeezed in the weight of Betty. Finally, he moved to the bowl and urinated. It was a bolt of lightning cracking. He sighed, leaned forward, and let his head rest against the wall. Oh, Betty, he thought. His life had changed, he was willing to understand. Were there other men, he wondered drunkenly, who could look at one event in their lives and perceive in it the tiny makings of the catastrophe that thereafter set their lives on a different course? He stood there a while longer, and then he looked down: he had urinated on his fingers. He moved to the wash basin, ran water over his hands after deciding against the dirty bar of soap. As he was unrolling the towel, he put his face up close to the pitted mirror and looked into his eyes. A face: nothing out of the ordinary. He touched the glass, and then he moved away as a man tried to get past him to the sink.

When he came out the door, he noticed another door at the other end of the corridor. He went to it and looked through the glass panel in the door at four card players around a green felt table. It seemed to Ralph immensely still and restful inside, the silent movements of the men languorous and heavy with meaning. He leaned against the glass and watched until he felt the men watching him.

Back at the bar there was a flourish of guitars and people began whistling and clapping. A fat middle-aged woman in a white evening dress was being helped onto the platform. She kept trying to pull back but Ralph could see that it was a mock effort, and finally she accepted the mike and made a little curtsy. The people whistled and stamped their feet. Suddenly he knew that nothing could save him but to be in the same room with the card players, watching. He took out his wallet, keeping his hands up over the sides as he looked to see how much he had. Behind him the woman began to sing in a low drowsy voice.

The man dealing looked up.

'Decided to join us?' he said, sweeping Ralph with his eyes and checking the table again. The others raised their eyes for an instant and then looked back at the cards skimming around the table. The men picked up their cards, and the man sitting with his back to Ralph breathed impressively out his nose, turned around in his chair and glared.

'Benny, bring another chair!' the dealer called to an old man sweeping under a table that had chairs turned up on the top. The dealer was a large man; he wore a white shirt, open at the collar, the sleeves rolled back once to expose forearms thick with black curling hair. Ralph drew a long breath.

'Want anything to drink?' Benny asked, carrying a chair to the table.

Ralph gave the old man a dollar and pulled out of his coat. The old man took the coat and hung it up by the door as he went out. Two of the men moved their chairs and Ralph sat down across from the dealer.

'How's it going?' the dealer said to Ralph, not looking up.

'All right,' Ralph said.

The dealer said gently, still not looking up. 'Low ball or five card. Table stakes, five-dollar limit on raises.'

Ralph nodded, and when the hand was finished he bought fifteen dollars' worth of chips. He watched the cards as they flashed around the table, picked up his as he had seen his father do, sliding one card under the corner of another as each card fell in front of him. He raised his eyes once and looked at the faces of the others. He wondered if it had ever happened to any of them.

In half an hour he had won two hands, and, without counting the small pile of chips in front of him, he thought he must still have fifteen or even twenty dollars. He paid for another drink with a chip and was suddenly aware that he had come a long way that evening, a long way in his life. *Jackson*, he thought. He could be Jackson.

'You in or out?' one man asked. 'Clyde, what's the bid, for Christ's sake?' the man said to the dealer.

'Three dollars,' the dealer said.

'In,' Ralph said. 'I'm in.' He put three chips into the pot.

The dealer looked up and then back at his cards. 'You really want some action, we can go to my place when we finish here,' the dealer said.

'No, that's all right,' Ralph said. 'Enough action tonight. I just found out tonight. My wife played around with another guy two years ago. I found out tonight.' He cleared his throat.

One man laid down his cards and lit his cigar. He stared at Ralph as he puffed, then shook out the match and picked up his cards again. The dealer looked up, resting his open hands on the table, the black hair very crisp on his dark hands.

'You work here in town?' he said to Ralph.

'I live here,' Ralph said. He felt drained, splendidly empty.

'We playing or not?' a man said. 'Clyde?'

'Hold your water,' the dealer said.

'For Christ's sake,' the man said quietly.

'What did you find out tonight?' the dealer said.

'My wife,' Ralph said. 'I found out.'

In the alley, he took out his wallet again, let his fingers number the bills he had left: two dollars – and he thought there was some change in his pocket. Enough for something to eat. But he was not hungry, and he sagged against the building trying to think. A car turned into the alley, stopped, backed out again. He started walking. He went the way he'd come. He stayed close to the buildings, out of the path of the loud groups of men and women streaming up and down the sidewalk. He heard a woman in a long coat say to the man she was with, 'It isn't that way at all, Bruce. You don't understand.'

He stopped when he came to the liquor store. Inside he moved up to the counter and studied the long orderly rows of bottles. He bought a half pint of rum and some more cigarets. The palm trees on the label of the bottle, the large drooping fronds with the lagoon in the background, had caught his eye, and then he realized *rum!* And he thought he would faint. The clerk, a thin bald man wearing suspenders, put the bottle in a paper sack and rang up the sale and winked. 'Got you a little something tonight?' he said.

Outside, Ralph started toward the pier; he thought he'd like to see the water with the lights reflected on it. He thought how Dr Maxwell would handle a thing like this, and he reached into the sack as he walked, broke the seal on the little bottle and stopped in a doorway to take a long drink and thought Dr Maxwell would sit handsomely at the water's edge. He crossed some old streetcar tracks and turned onto another, darker, street. He could already hear the waves splashing under the pier, and then he heard someone move up behind him. A small Negro in a leather jacket stepped out in front of him and said, 'Just a minute there, man.' Ralph tried to move around. The man said, 'Christ, baby, that's my feet you're steppin on!' Before Ralph could run the Negro hit him hard in the stomach, and when Ralph groaned and tried to fall, the man hit him in the nose with his open hand, knocking him back against the wall, where he sat down with one leg turned under him and was learning how to raise himself up when the Negro slapped him on the cheek and knocked him sprawling onto the pavement.

3

He kept his eyes fixed in one place and saw them, dozens of them, wheeling and darting just under the overcast, seabirds, birds that came in off the ocean this time of morning. The street was black with the mist that was still falling, and he had to be careful not to step on the snails that trailed across the wet sidewalk. A car with its lights on slowed as it went past. Another car passed. Then another. He looked: mill workers, he whispered to himself. It was Monday morning. He turned a corner, walked past Blake's: blinds pulled, empty bottles standing like sentinels beside the door. It was cold. He walked as fast as he could, crossing his arms now and then and rubbing his shoulders. He came at last to his house, porch light on, windows dark. He crossed the lawn and went around to the back. He turned the knob, and the door opened quietly and the house was quiet. There was the tall stool beside the draining board. There was the table where they had sat. He had gotten up from the couch, come into the kitchen, sat down. What more had he done? He had done nothing more. He looked at the clock over the stove. He could see into the dining room, the table with the lace cloth, the heavy glass centerpiece of red flamingos, their wings opened, the draperies beyond the table open. Had she stood at that window watching for him? He stepped onto the living-room carpet. Her coat was thrown over the couch, and in the pale light he could make out a large ashtray full of her cork cigaret ends. He noticed the phone directory open on the coffee table as he went by. He stopped at the partially open door to their bedroom. Everything seemed to him open. For an instant he resisted the wish to look in at her, and then with his finger he pushed the door open a little bit more. She was sleeping, her head off the pillow, turned toward the wall, her hair black against the sheet, the covers bunched around her shoulders, covers pulled up from the foot of the bed. She was on her side, her secret body angled at the hips. He stared. What, after all, should he do? Take his things and leave? Go to a hotel? Make certain arrangements? How should a man act, given these circumstances? He understood things had been done. He did not understand what things now were to be done. The house was very quiet.

In the kitchen he let his head down onto his arms as he sat at the table. He did not know what to do. Not just now, he thought, not just in this, not just about this, today and tomorrow, but every day on earth. Then he heard the children stirring. He sat up and tried to smile as they came into the kitchen.

'Daddy, Daddy,' they said, running to him with their little bodies.

'Tell us a story, Daddy,' his son said, getting onto his lap.

'He can't tell us a story,' his daughter said. 'It's too early for a story. Isn't it, Daddy?'

'What's that on your face, Daddy?' his son said, pointing.

'Let me see!' his daughter said. 'Let me see, Daddy.'

'Poor Daddy,' his son said.

'What did you do to your face, Daddy?' his daughter said.

'It's nothing,' Ralph said. 'It's all right, sweetheart. Now get down now, Robert, I hear your mother.'

Ralph stepped quickly into the bathroom and locked the door.

'Is your father here?' he heard Marian calling. 'Where is he, in the bathroom? Ralph?'

'Mama, Mama!' his daughter cried. 'Daddy's face is hurt!'

'Ralph!' She turned the knob. 'Ralph, let me in, please, darling. Ralph? Please let me in, darling. I want to see you. Ralph? Please!'

He said, 'Go away, Marian.'

She said, 'I can't go away. Please, Ralph, open the door for a minute, darling. I just want to see you. Ralph. Ralph? The children said you were hurt. What's wrong, darling? Ralph?'

He said, 'Go away.'

She said, 'Ralph, open up, please.'

He said, 'Will you please be quiet, please?'

He heard her waiting at the door, he saw the knob turn again, and then he could hear her moving around the kitchen, getting the children breakfast, trying to answer their questions. He looked at himself in the mirror a long time. He made faces at himself, He tried many expressions. Then he gave it up. He turned away from the mirror and sat down on the edge of the bathtub, began unlacing his shoes. He sat there with a shoe in his hand and looked at the clipper ships making their way across the wide blue sea of the plastic shower curtain. He thought of the little black coaches in the tablecloth and almost cried out *Stop!* He unbuttoned his shirt, leaned over the bathtub with a sigh, and pressed the plug into the drain. He ran hot water, and presently steam rose.

He stood naked on the tiles before getting into the water. He gathered in his fingers the slack flesh over his ribs. He studied his face again in the clouded mirror. He started in fear when Marian called his name.

'Ralph. The children are in their room playing. I called Von Williams and said you wouldn't be in today, and I'm going to stay home.' Then she said, 'I have a nice breakfast on the stove for you, darling, when you're through with your bath. Ralph?'

'Just be quiet, please,' he said.

He stayed in the bathroom until he heard her in the children's room. She was dressing them, asking didn't they want to play with Warren and Roy? He went through the house and into the bedroom, where he shut the door. He looked at the bed before he crawled in. He lay on his back and stared at the ceiling. He had gotten up from the couch, had come into the kitchen, had . . . *sat* . . . *down*. He snapped shut his eyes and turned onto his side as Marian came into the room. She took off her robe and sat down on the bed. She put her hand under the covers and began stroking the lower part of his back.

'Ralph,' she said.

He tensed at her fingers, and then he let go a little. It was easier to let go a little. Her hand moved over his hip and over his stomach and she was pressing her body over his now and moving over him and back and forth over him. He held himself, he later considered, as long as he could. And then he turned to her. He turned and turned in what might have been a stupendous sleep, and he was still turning, marveling at the impossible changes he felt moving over him.

What We
Talk About
When We
Talk About Love

For Tess Gallagher

The author is pleased to acknowledge receipt of a
John Simon Guggenheim Memorial Fellowship and a
National Endowment for the Arts grant.
He also wishes to express grateful acknowledgement
and appreciation to Noel Young of Capra Press.

Why don't you dance?

In the kitchen, he poured another drink and looked at the bedroom suite in his front yard. The mattress was stripped and the candy-striped sheets lay beside two pillows on the chiffonier. Except for that, things looked much the way they had in the bedroom — nightstand and reading lamp on his side of the bed, nightstand and reading lamp on her side.

His side, her side.

He considered this as he sipped the whiskey.

The chiffonier stood a few feet from the foot of the bed. He had emptied the drawers into cartons that morning, and the cartons were in the living room. A portable heater was next to the chiffonier. A rattan chair with a decorator pillow stood at the foot of the bed. The buffed aluminum kitchen set took up a part of the driveway. A yellow muslin cloth, much too large, a gift, covered the table and hung down over the sides. A potted fern was on the table, along with a box of silverware and a record player, also gifts. A big console-model television set rested on a coffee table, and a few feet away from this stood a sofa and chair and a floor lamp. The desk was pushed against the garage door. A few utensils were on the desk, along with a wall clock and two framed prints. There was also in the driveway a carton with cups, glasses, and plates, each object wrapped in newspaper. That morning he had cleared out the closets, and except for the three cartons in the living room, all the stuff was out of the house. He had run an extension cord on out there and everything was connected. Things worked, no different from how it was when they were inside.

Now and then a car slowed and people stared. But no one stopped.

It occurred to him that he wouldn't, either.

'It must be a yard sale,' the girl said to the boy.

This girl and this boy were furnishing a little apartment.

'Let's see what they want for the bed,' the girl said.

'And for the TV,' the boy said.

The boy pulled into the driveway and stopped in front of the kitchen table.

They got out of the car and began to examine things, the girl touching the muslin cloth, the boy plugging in the blender and turning the dial to MINCE, the girl picking up a chafing dish, the boy turning on the television set and making little adjustments.

He sat down on the sofa to watch. He lit a cigaret, looked around, flipped the match in the grass.

The girl sat on the bed. She pushed off her shoes and lay back. She thought she could see a star.

'Come here, Jack. Try this bed. Bring one of those pillows,' she said.

'How is it?' he said.

'Try it,' she said.

He looked around. The house was dark.

'I feel funny, he said. 'Better see if anybody's home.'

She bounced on the bed.

'Try it first,' she said.

He lay down on the bed and put the pillow under his head.

'How does it feel?' she said.

'It feels firm,' he said.

She turned on her side and put her hand to his face.

'Kiss me,' she said.

'Let's get up.' he said.

'Kiss me,' she said.

She closed her eyes. She held him.

He said, 'I'll see if anybody's home.'

But he just sat up and stayed where he was, making believe he was watching the television.

Lights came on in houses up and down the street.

'Wouldn't it be funny if,' the girl said and grinned and didn't finish.

The boy laughed, but for no good reason. For no good reason, he switched the reading lamp on.

The girl brushed away a mosquito, whereupon the boy stood up and tucked in his shirt.

'I'll see if anybody's home,' he said. 'I don't think anybody's home. But if anybody is, I'll see what things are going for.'

'Whatever they ask, offer ten dollars less. It's always a good idea,' she said. 'And besides, they must be desperate or something.'

'It's a pretty good TV,' the boy said.

'Ask them how much,' the girl said.

The man came down the sidewalk with a sack from the market. He

had sandwiches, beer, whiskey. He saw the car in the driveway and the girl on the bed. He saw the television set going and the boy on the porch.

'Hello,' the man said to the girl. 'You found the bed. That's good.'

'Hello,' the girl said, and got up. 'I was just trying it out.' She patted the bed. 'It's a pretty good bed.'

'It's a good bed,' the man said, and put down the sack and took out the beer and the whiskey.

'We thought nobody was here,' the boy said. 'We're interested in the bed and maybe in the TV. Also maybe the desk. How much do you want for the bed?'

'I was thinking fifty dollars for the bed,' the man said.

'Would you take forty?' the girl asked.

'I'll take forty,' the man said.

He took a glass out of the carton. He took the newspaper off the glass. He broke the seal on the whiskey.

'How about the TV?' the boy said.

'Twenty-five.'

'Would you take fifteen?' the girl said.

'Fifteen's okay. I could take fifteen,' the man said.

The girl looked at the boy.

'You kids, you'll want a drink,' the man said. 'Glasses in that box. I'm going to sit down. I'm going to sit down on the sofa.'

The man sat on the sofa, leaned back. and stared at the boy and the girl.

The boy found two glasses and poured whiskey.

'That's enough', the girl said. 'I think I want water in mine.'

She pulled out a chair and sat at the kitchen table.

'There's water in that spigot over there,' the man said. 'Turn on that spigot.'

The boy came back with the watered whiskey. He cleared his throat and sat down at the kitchen table. He grinned. But he didn't drink anything from his glass.

The man gazed at the television. He finished his drink and started another. He reached to turn on the floor lamp. It was then that his cigaret dropped from his fingers and fell between the cushions.

The girl got up to help him find it.

'So what do you want?' the boy said to the girl.

The boy took out the checkbook and held it to his lips as if thinking.

'I want the desk,' the girl said. 'How much money is the desk?'

The man waved his hand at this preposterous question.

'Name a figure,' he said.

. He looked at them as they sat at the table. In the lamplight, there was something about their faces. It was nice or it was nasty. There was no telling.

'I'm going to turn off this TV and put on a record,' the man said. 'This record-player is going, too. Cheap. Make me an offer.'

He poured more whiskey and opened a beer.

'Everything goes,' said the man.

The girl held out her glass and the man poured.

'Thank you,' she said. 'You're very nice,' she said.

'It goes to your head,' the boy said. 'I'm getting it in the head.' He held up his glass and jiggled it.

The man finished his drink and poured another, and then he found the box with the records.

'Pick something,' the man said to the girl, and he held the records out to her.

The boy was writing the check.

'Here,' the girl said, picking something, picking anything, for she did not know the names on these labels. She got up from the table and sat down again. She did not want to sit still.

'I'm making it out to cash,' the boy said.

'Sure,' the man said.

They drank. They listened to the record. And then the man put on another.

Why don't you kids dance? he decided to say, and then he said it. 'Why don't you dance?'

'I don't think so,' the boy said.

'Go ahead,' the man said. 'It's my yard. You can dance if you want to.'

Arms about each other, their bodies pressed together, the boy and the girl moved up and down the driveway. They were dancing. And when the record was over, they did it again, and when that one ended, the boy said, 'I'm drunk.'

The girl said, 'You're not drunk.'

'Well, I'm drunk,' the boy said.

The man turned the record over and the boy said, 'I am.'

'Dance with me,' the girl said to the boy and then to the man, and when the man stood up, she came to him with her arms wide open.

'Those people over there, they're watching,' she said.
   'It's okay,' the man said. 'It's my place,' he said.
   'Let them watch,' the girl said.
   'That's right,' the man said. 'They thought they'd seen everything over here. But they haven't seen this, have they?' he said.
   He felt her breath on his neck.
   'I hope you like your bed,' he said.
   The girl closed and then opened her eyes. She pushed her face into the man's shoulder. She pulled the man closer.
   'You must be desperate or something,' she said.

Weeks later, she said: 'The guy was about middle-aged. All his things right there in his yard. No lie. We got real pissed and danced. In the driveway. Oh, my God. Don't laugh. He played us these records. Look at this record-player. The old guy gave it to us. And all these crappy records. Will you look at this shit?'
   She kept talking. She told everyone. There was more to it, and she was trying to get it talked out. After a time, she quit trying.

Viewfinder

A man without hands came to the door to sell me a photograph of my house. Except for the chrome hooks, he was an ordinary-looking man of fifty or so.

'How did you lose your hands?' I asked after he'd said what he wanted.

'That's another story,' he said. 'You want this picture or not?'

'Come in,' I said. 'I just made coffee.'

I'd just made some Jell-O, too. But I didn't tell the man I did.

'I might use your toilet,' the man with no hands said.

I wanted to see how he would hold a cup.

I knew how he held the camera. It was an old Polaroid, big and black. He had it fastened to leather straps that looped over his shoulders and went around his back, and it was this that secured the camera to his chest. He would stand on the sidewalk in front of your house, locate your house in the viewfinder, push down the lever with one of his hooks, and out would pop your picture.

I'd been watching from the window, you see.

'Where did you say the toilet was?'

'Down there, turn right.'

Bending, hunching, he let himself out of the straps. He put the camera on the sofa and straightened his jacket.

'You can look at this while I'm gone.'

I took the picture from him.

There was a little rectangle of lawn, the driveway. the carport, front steps, bay window, and the window I'd been watching from in the kitchen.

So why would I want a photograph of this tragedy?

I looked a little closer and saw my head, *my head*, in there inside the kitchen window.

It made me think, seeing myself like that. I can tell you. it makes a man think.

I heard the toilet flush. He came down the hall, zipping and smiling, one hook holding his belt, the other tucking in his shirt.

'What do you think?' he said. 'All right? Personally, I think it turned out fine. Don't I know what I'm doing? Let's face it, it takes a professional.'

He plucked at his crotch.

'Here's coffee,' I said.

He said, 'You're alone, right?'

He looked at the living room. He shook his head.

'Hard, hard,' he said.

He sat next to the camera, leaned back with a sigh, and smiled as if he knew something he wasn't going to tell me.

'Drink your coffee,' I said.

I was trying to think of something to say.

'Three kids were by here wanting to paint my address on the curb. They wanted a dollar to do it. You wouldn't know anything about that, would you?'

It was a long shot. But I watched him just the same.

He leaned forward importantly, the cup balanced between his hooks. He set it down on the table.

'I work alone,' he said. 'Always have, always will. What are you saying?' he said.

'I was trying to make a connection,' I said.

I had a headache. I know coffee's no good for it, but sometimes Jell-O helps. I picked up the picture.

'I was in the kitchen,' I said. 'Usually I'm in the back.'

'Happens all the time,' he said. 'So they just up and left you, right? Now you take me, I work alone. So what do you say? You want the picture?'

'I'll take it,' I said.

I stood up and picked up the cups.

'Sure you will,' he said. 'Me, I keep a room downtown. It's okay. I take a bus out, and after I've worked the neighborhoods, I go to another downtown. You see what I'm saying? Hey, I had kids once. Just like you,' he said.

I waited with the cups and watched him struggle up from the sofa.

He said, 'They're what gave me this.'

I took a good look at those hooks.

'Thanks for the coffee and the use of the toilet. I sympathize.'

He raised and lowered his hooks.

'Show me,' I said. 'Show me how much. Take more pictures of me and my house.'

'It won't work,' the man said. 'They're not coming back.'

But I helped him get into his straps.

'I can give you a rate,' he said. 'Three for a dollar.' He said, 'If I go any lower, I don't come out.'

We went outside. He adjusted the shutter. He told me where to stand, and we got down to it.

We moved around the house. Systematic. Sometimes I'd look sideways. Sometimes I'd look straight ahead.

'Good,' he'd say. 'That's good,' he'd say, until we'd circled the house and were back in the front again. 'That's twenty. That's enough.'

'No,' I said. 'On the roof,' I said.

'Jesus,' he said. He checked up and down the block. 'Sure,' he said. 'Now you're talking.'

I said, 'The whole kit and kaboodle. They cleared right out.'

'Look at this!' the man said, and again he held up his hooks.

I went inside and got a chair. I put it up under the carport. But it didn't reach. So I got a crate and put the crate on top of the chair.

It was okay up there on the roof.

I stood up and looked around. I waved, and the man with no hands waved back with his hooks.

It was then I saw them, the rocks. It was like a little rock nest on the screen over the chimney hole. You know kids. You know how they lob them up, thinking to sink one down your chimney.

'Ready?' I called, and I got a rock, and I waited until he had me in his viewfinder.

'Okay!' he called.

I laid back my arm and I hollered, 'Now!' I threw that son of a bitch as far as I could throw it.

'I don't know,' I heard him shout. 'I don't do motion shots.'

'Again!' I screamed, and took up another rock.

Mr Coffee and
Mr Fixit

I've seen some things. I was going over to my mother's to stay a few nights. But just as I got to the top of the stairs, I looked and she was on the sofa kissing a man. It was summer. The door was open. The TV was going. That's one of the things I've seen.

My mother is sixty-five. She belongs to a singles club. Even so, it was hard. I stood with my hand on the railing and watched as the man kissed her. She was kissing him back, and the TV was going.

Things are better now. But back in those days, when my mother was putting out, I was out of work. My kids were crazy, and my wife was crazy. She was putting out too. The guy that was getting it was an unemployed aerospace engineer she'd met at AA. He was also crazy.

His name was Ross and he had six kids. He walked with a limp from a gunshot wound his first wife gave him.

I don't know what we were thinking of in those days.

This guy's second wife had come and gone, but it was his first wife who had shot him for not meeting his payments. I wish him well now. Ross. What a name! But it was different then. In those days I mentioned weapons. I'd say to my wife, 'I think I'll get a Smith and Wesson.' But I never did it.

Ross was a little guy. But not too little. He had a moustache and always wore a button-up sweater.

His one wife jailed him once. The second one did. I found out from my daughter that my wife went bail. My daughter Melody didn't like it any better than I did. About the bail. It wasn't that Melody was looking out for me. She wasn't looking out for either one of us, her mother or me neither. It was just that there was a serious cash thing and if some of it went to Ross, there'd be that much less for Melody. So Ross was on Melody's list. Also, she didn't like his kids, and his having so many of them. But in general Melody said Ross was all right.

He'd even told her fortune once.

This Ross guy spent his time repairing things, now that he had no regular job. But I'd seen his house from the outside. It was a mess. Junk all around. Two busted Plymouths in the yard.

In the first stages of the thing they had going, my wife claimed the guy collected antique cars. Those were her words, 'antique cars.' But they were just clunkers.

I had his number. Mr Fixit.

But we had things in common, Ross and me, which was more than just the same woman. For example, he couldn't fix the TV when it went crazy and we lost the picture. I couldn't fix it either. We had volume, but no picture. If we wanted the news, we had to sit around the screen and listen.

Ross and Myrna met when Myrna was trying to stay sober. She was going to meetings, I'd say, three or four times a week. I had been in and out myself. But when Myrna met Ross, I was out and drinking a fifth a day. Myrna went to the meetings, and then she went over to Mr Fixit's house to cook for him and clean up. His kids were no help in this regard. Nobody lifted a hand around Mr Fixit's house, except my wife when she was there.

All this happened not too long ago, three years about. It was something in those days.

I left my mother with the man on her sofa and drove around for a while. When I got home, Myrna made me a coffee.

She went out to the kitchen to do it while I waited until I heard her running water. Then I reached under a cushion for the bottle.

I think maybe Myrna really loved the man. But he also had a little something on the side – a twenty-two-year-old named Beverly. Mr Fixit did okay for a little guy who wore a button-up sweater.

He was in his mid-thirties when he went under. Lost his job and took up the bottle. I used to make fun of him when I had the chance. But I don't make fun of him anymore.

God bless and keep you, Mr Fixit.

He told Melody he'd worked on the moon shots. He told my daughter he was close friends with the astronauts. He told her he was going to introduce her to the astronauts as soon as they came to town.

It's a modern operation out there, the aerospace place where Mr Fixit used to work. I've seen it. Cafeteria lines, executive dining rooms, and the like. Mr Coffees in every office.

Mr Coffee and Mr Fixit.

Myrna says he was interested in astrology, auras, I Ching – that business. I don't doubt that this Ross was bright enough and interesting, like most of our ex-friends. I told Myrna I was sure she wouldn't have cared for him if he wasn't.

My dad died in his sleep, drunk, eight years ago. It was a Friday noon and he was fifty-four. He came home from work at the sawmill, took some sausage out of the freezer for his breakfast, and popped a quart of Four Roses.

My mother was there at the same kitchen table. She was trying to write a letter to her sister in Little Rock. Finally, my dad got up and went to bed. My mother said he never said good night. But it was morning, of course.

'Honey,' I said to Myrna the night she came home. 'Let's hug awhile and then you fix us a real nice supper.'

Myrna said, 'Wash your hands.'

Gazebo

That morning she pours Teacher's over my belly and licks it off. That afternoon she tries to jump out the window.

I go, 'Holly, this can't continue. This has got to stop.'

We are sitting on the sofa in one of the upstairs suites. There were any number of vacancies to choose from. But we needed a suite, a place to move around in and be able to talk. So we'd locked up the motel office that morning and gone upstairs to a suite.

She goes, 'Duane, this is killing me.'

We are drinking Teacher's with ice and water. We'd slept awhile between morning and afternoon. Then she was out of bed and threatening to climb out the window in her undergarments. I had to get her in a hold. We were only two floors up. But even so.

'I've had it,' she goes. 'I can't take it anymore.'

She puts her hand to her cheek and closes her eyes. She turns her head back and forth and makes this humming noise.

I could die seeing her like this.

'Take what?' I go, though of course I know.

'I don't have to spell it out for you again,' she goes. 'I've lost control. I've lost pride. I used to be a proud woman.'

She's an attractive woman just past thirty. She is tall and has long black hair and green eyes, the only green-eyed woman I've ever known. In the old days I used to say things about her green eyes, and she'd tell me it was because of them she knew she was meant for something special.

And didn't I know it!

I feel so awful from one thing and the other.

I can hear the telephone ringing downstairs in the office. It has been ringing off and on all day. Even when I was dozing I could hear it. I'd open my eyes and look at the ceiling and listen to it ring and wonder at what was happening to us.

But maybe I should be looking at the floor.

'My heart is broken,' she goes. 'It's turned to a piece of stone. I'm no good. That's what's as bad as anything, that I'm no good anymore.'

'Holly,' I go.

When we'd first moved down here and taken over as managers, we thought we were out of the woods. Free rent and free utilities plus three hundred a month. You couldn't beat it with a stick.

Holly took care of the books. She was good with figures, and she did most of the renting of the units. She liked people, and people liked her back. I saw to the grounds, mowed the grass and cut weeds, kept the swimming pool clean, did the small repairs.

Everything was fine for the first year. I was holding down another job nights, and we were getting ahead. We had plans. Then one morning, I don't know. I'd just laid some bathroom tile in one of the units when this little Mexican maid comes in to clean. It was Holly had hired her. I can't really say I'd noticed the little thing before, though we spoke when we saw each other. She called me, I remember, Mister.

Anyway, one thing and the other.

So after that morning I started paying attention. She was a neat little thing with fine white teeth. I used to watch her mouth.

She started calling me by my name.

One morning I was doing a washer for one of the bathroom faucets, and she comes in and turns on the TV as maids are like to do. While they clean, that is. I stopped what I was doing and stepped outside the bathroom. She was surprised to see me. She smiles and says my name.

It was right after she said it that we got down on the bed.

'Holly, you're still a proud woman,' I go. 'You're still number one. Come on, Holly.'

She shakes her head.

'Something's died in me,' she goes. 'It took a long time for it to do it, but it's dead. You've killed something, just like you'd took an axe to it. Everything is dirt now.'

She finishes her drink. Then she begins to cry. I make to hug her. But it's no good.

I freshen our drinks and look out the window.

Two cars with out-of-state plates are parked in front of the office, and the drivers are standing at the door, talking. One of them finishes saying something to the other, and looks around at the units and pulls his chin. There's a woman there too, and she has her face up to the glass, hand shielding her eyes, peering inside. She tries the door.

The phone downstairs begins to ring.

'Even a while ago when we were doing it, you were thinking of her,'

Holly goes. 'Duane, this is hurtful.'

She takes the drink I give her.

'Holly,' I go.

'It's true, Duane,' she goes. 'Just don't argue with me,' she goes.

She walks up and down the room in her underpants and her brassiere, her drink in her hand.

Holly goes, 'You've gone outside the marriage. It's trust that you killed.'

I get down on my knees and I start to beg. But I am thinking of Juanita. This is awful. I don't know what's going to happen to me or to anyone else in the world.

I go, 'Holly, honey, I love you.'

In the lot someone leans on a horn, stops, and then leans again.

Holly wipes her eyes. She goes, 'Fix me a drink. This one's too watery. Let them blow their stinking horns. I don't care. I'm moving to Nevada.'

'Don't move to Nevada,' I go. 'You're talking crazy,' I go.

'I'm not talking crazy,' she goes. 'Nothing's crazy about Nevada. You can stay here with your cleaning woman. I'm moving to Nevada. Either there or kill myself.'

'Holly!' I go.

'Holly *nothing*!' she goes.

She sits on the sofa and draws her knees up to under her chin.

'Fix me another pop, you son of a bitch,' she goes. She goes, 'Fuck those horn-blowers. Let them do their dirt in the Travelodge. Is that where your cleaning woman cleans now? Fix me another, you son of a bitch!'

She sets her lips and gives me her special look.

Drinking's funny. When I look back on it, all of our important decisions have been figured out when we were drinking. Even when we talked about having to cut back on our drinking, we'd be sitting at the kitchen table or out at the picnic table with a six-pack or whiskey. When we made up our minds to move down here and take this job as managers, we sat up a couple of nights drinking while we weighed the pros and the cons.

I pour the last of the Teacher's into our glasses and add cubes and a spill of water.

Holly gets off the sofa and stretches on out across the bed.

She goes, 'Did you do it to her in this bed?'

I don't have anything to say. I feel all out of words inside. I give her the glass and sit down in the chair. I drink my drink and think it's not ever going to be the same.

'Duane?' she goes.

'Holly?'

My heart has slowed. I wait.

Holly was my own true love.

The thing with Juanita was five days a week between the hours of ten and eleven. It was in whatever unit she was in when she was making her cleaning rounds. I'd just walk in where she was working and shut the door behind me.

But mostly it was in 11. It was 11 that was our lucky room.

We were sweet with each other, but swift. It was fine.

I think Holly could maybe have weathered it out. I think the thing she had to do was really give it a try.

Me, I held on to the night job. A monkey could do that work. But things here were going downhill fast. We just didn't have the heart for it anymore.

I stopped cleaning the pool. It filled up with green gick so that the guests wouldn't use it anymore. I didn't fix any more faucets or lay any more tile or do any of the touch-up painting. Well, the truth is we were both hitting it pretty hard. Booze takes a lot of time and effort if you're going to do a good job with it.

Holly wasn't registering the guests right, either. She was charging too much or else not collecting what she should. Sometimes she'd put three people to a room with only one bed in it, or else she'd put a single in where the bed was a king-size. I tell you, there were complaints, and sometimes there were words. Folks would load up and go somewhere else.

The next thing, there's a letter from the management people. Then there's another, certified.

There's telephone calls. There's someone coming down from the city.

But we had stopped caring, and that's a fact. We knew our days were numbered. We had fouled our lives and we were getting ready for a shake-up.

Holly's a smart woman. She knew it first.

Then that Saturday morning we woke up after a night of rehashing the situation. We opened our eyes and turned in bed to take a good look at each other. We both knew it then. We'd reached the end of something, and the thing was to find out where new to start.

We got up and got dressed, had coffee, and decided on this talk. Without nothing interrupting. No calls. No guests.

That's when I got the Teacher's. We locked up and came upstairs here with ice, glasses, bottles. First off, we watched the color TV and frolicked some and let the phone ring away downstairs. For food, we went out and got cheese crisps from the machine.

There was this funny thing of anything could happen now that we realized everything had.

'When we were just kids before we married?' Holly goes. 'When we had big plans and hopes? You remember?' She was sitting on the bed, holding her knees and her drink.

'I remember, Holly.'

'You weren't my first, you know. My first was Wyatt. Imagine. Wyatt. And your name's Duane. Wyatt and Duane. Who knows what I was missing all those years? You were my everything, just like the song.'

I go, 'You're a wonderful woman, Holly. I know you've had the opportunities.'

'But I didn't take them up on it!' she goes. 'I couldn't go outside the marriage.'

'Holly, please,' I go. 'No more now, honey. Let's not torture ourselves. What is it we should do?'

'Listen,' she goes. 'You remember the time we drove out to that old farm place outside of Yakima, out past Terrace Heights? We were just driving around? We were on this little dirt road and it was hot and dusty? We kept going and came to that old house, and you asked if could we have a drink of water? Can you imagine us doing that now? Going up to a house and asking for a drink of water?

'Those old people must be dead now,' she goes, 'side by side out there in some cemetery. You remember they asked us in for cake? And later on they showed us around? And there was this gazebo there out back? It was out back under some trees? It had a little peaked roof and the paint was gone and there were these weeds growing up over the steps. And the woman said that years before, I mean a real long time ago, men used to come around and play music out there on a Sunday, and the people would sit and listen. I thought we'd be like that too when we got old enough. Dignified. And in a place. And people would come to our door.'

I can't say anything just yet. Then I go, 'Holly, these things, we'll look back on them too. We'll go, "Remember the motel with all the crud in the pool?" ' I go, 'You see what I'm saying, Holly?'

But Holly just sits there on the bed with her glass.

I can see she doesn't know.

I move over to the window and look out from behind the curtain. Someone says something below and rattles the door to the office. I stay there. I pray for a sign from Holly. I pray for Holly to show me.

I hear a car start. Then another. They turn on their lights against the building and, one after the other, they pull away and go out into the traffic.

'Duane,' Holly goes.

In this, too, she was right.

I could see the smallest things

I was in bed when I heard the gate. I listened carefully. I didn't hear anything else. But I heard that. I tried to wake Cliff. He was passed out. So I got up and went to the window. A big moon was laid over the mountains that went around the city. It was a white moon and covered with scars. Any damn fool could imagine a face there.

There was light enough so that I could see everything in the yard – lawn chairs, the willow tree, clothesline strung between the poles, the petunias, the fences, the gate standing wide open.

But nobody was moving around. There were no scary shadows. Everything lay in moonlight, and I could see the smallest things. The clothespins on the line, for instance.

I put my hands on the glass to block out the moon. I looked some more. I listened. Then I went back to bed.

But I couldn't get to sleep. I kept turning over. I thought about the gate standing open. It was like a dare.

Cliff's breathing was awful to listen to. His mouth gaped open and his arms hugged his pale chest. He was taking up his side of the bed and most of mine.

I pushed and pushed on him. But he just groaned.

I stayed still awhile longer until I decided it was no use. I got up and got my slippers. I went to the kitchen and made tea and sat with it at the kitchen table. I smoked one of Cliff's unfiltereds.

It was late. I didn't want to look at the time. I drank the tea and smoked another cigaret. After a while I decided I'd go out and fasten up the gate.

So I got my robe.

The moon lighted up everything – houses and trees, poles and power lines, the whole world. I peered around the backyard before I stepped off the porch. A little breeze came along that made me close the robe.

I started for the gate.

There was a noise at the fences that separated our place from Sam Lawton's place. I took a sharp look. Sam was leaning with his arms on his fence, there being two fences to lean on. He raised his fist to his mouth and gave a dry cough.

'Evening, Nancy,' Sam Lawton said.

I said, 'Sam, you scared me.' I said, 'What are you doing up?' 'Did you hear something?' I said. 'I heard my gate unlatch.'

He said, 'I didn't hear anything. Haven't seen anything, either. It might have been the wind.'

He was chewing something. He looked at the open gate and shrugged.

His hair was silvery in the moonlight and stood up on his head. I could see his long nose, the lines in his big sad face.

I said, 'What are you doing up, Sam?' and moved closer to the fence.

'Want to see something?' he said.

'I'll come around,' I said.

I let myself out and went along the walk. It felt funny walking around outside in my nightgown and my robe. I thought to myself that I should try to remember this, walking around outside like this.

Sam was standing over by the side of his house, his pajamas way up high over his tan-and-white shoes. He was holding a flashlight in one hand and a can of something in the other.

Sam and Cliff used to be friends. Then one night they got to drinking. They had words. The next thing, Sam had built a fence and then Cliff built one too.

That was after Sam had lost Millie, gotten married again, and become a father again all in the space of no time at all. Millie had been a good friend to me up until she died. She was only forty-five when she did it. Heart failure. It hit her just as she was coming into their drive. The car kept going and went on through the back of the carport.

'Look at this,' Sam said, hitching his pajama trousers and squatting down. He pointed his light at the ground.

I looked and saw some wormy things curled on a patch of dirt.

'Slugs,' he said. 'I just gave them a dose of this,' he said, raising a can of something that looked like Ajax. 'They're taking over,' he said, and worked whatever it was that he had in his mouth. He turned his head to one side and spit what could have been tobacco. 'I have to keep at this to just come close to staying up with them.' He turned his light on a jar that was filled with the things. 'I put bait out, and then every chance I get I come out here with this stuff. Bastards are all over. A crime what they can do. Look here,' he said.

He got up. He took my arm and moved me over to his rosebushes. He showed me the little holes in the leaves.

'Slugs,' he said. 'Everywhere you look around here at night. I lay out bait and then I come out and get them,' he said. 'An awful invention, the slug. I save them up in that jar there.' He moved his light to under the rosebush.

A plane passed overhead. I imagined the people on it sitting belted in their seats, some of them reading, some of them staring down at the ground.

'Sam,' I said, 'how's everybody?'

'They're fine,' he said, and shrugged.

He chewed on whatever it was he was chewing. 'How's Clifford?' he said.

I said, 'Same as ever.'

Sam said, 'Sometimes when I'm out here after the slugs, I'll look over in your direction.' He said, 'I wish me and Cliff was friends again. Look there now,' he said, and drew a sharp breath. 'There's one there. See him? Right there where my light is.' He had the beam directed onto the dirt under the rosebush. 'Watch this,' Sam said.

I closed my arms under my breasts and bent over to where he was shining his light. The thing stopped moving and turned its head from side to side. Then Sam was over it with his can of powder, sprinkling the powder down.

'Slimy things,' he said.

The slug was twisting this way and that. Then it curled and straightened out.

Sam picked up a toy shovel, and scooped the slug into it, and dumped it out in the jar.

'I quit, you know,' Sam said. 'Had to. For a while it was getting so I didn't know up from down. We still keep it around the house, but I don't have much to do with it anymore.'

I nodded. He looked at me and he kept looking.

'I'd better get back,' I said.

'Sure,' he said. 'I'll continue with what I'm doing and then when I'm finished, I'll head in too.'

I said, 'Good night, Sam.'

He said, 'Listen.' He stopped chewing. With his tongue, he pushed whatever it was behind his lower lip. 'Tell Cliff I said hello.'

I said, 'I'll tell him you said so, Sam.'

Sam ran his hand through his silvery hair as if he was going to make it sit down once and for all, and then he used his hand to wave.

In the bedroom, I took off the robe, folded it, put it within reach. Without looking at the time, I checked to make sure the stem was out on the clock. Then I got into the bed, pulled the covers up, and closed my eyes.

It was then that I remembered I'd forgotten to latch the gate.

I opened my eyes and lay there. I gave Cliff a little shake. He cleared his throat. He swallowed. Something caught and dribbled in his chest.

I don't know. It made me think of those things that Sam Lawton was dumping powder on.

I thought for a minute of the world outside my house, and then I didn't have any more thoughts except the thought that I had to hurry up and sleep.

Sacks

It's October, a damp day. From my hotel window I can see too much of this Midwestern city. I can see lights coming on in some of the buildings, smoke from the tall stacks rising in a thick climb. I wish I didn't have to look.

I want to pass along to you a story my father told me when I stopped over in Sacramento last year. It concerns some events that involved him two years before that time, that time being before he and my mother were divorced.

I'm a book salesman. I represent a well-known organization. We put out textbooks, and the home base is Chicago. My territory is Illinois, parts of Iowa and Wisconsin. I had been attending the Western Book Publishers Association convention in Los Angeles when it occurred to me to visit a few hours with my father. I had not seen him since the divorce, you understand. So I got his address out of my wallet and sent him a wire. The next morning I sent my things on to Chicago and boarded a plane for Sacramento.

It took me a minute to pick him out. He was standing where everyone else was — behind the gate, that is — white hair, glasses, brown Sta-Prest pants.

'Dad, how are you?' I said.

He said, 'Les.'

We shook hands and moved toward the terminal.

'How's Mary and the kids?' he said.

'Everyone's fine,' I said, which was not the truth.

He opened a white confectionary sack. He said, 'I picked up a little something you could maybe take back with you. Not much. Some Almond Roca for Mary, and some jelly-beans for the kids.'

'Thanks,' I said.

'Don't forget this when you leave,' he said.

We moved out of the way as some nuns came running for the boarding area.

'A drink or a cup of coffee?' I said.

'Anything you say,' he said. 'But I don't have a car,' he said.

We located the lounge, got drinks, lit cigarettes.

'Here we are,' I said.

'Well, yes,' he said.

I shrugged and said, 'Yes.'

I leaned back in the seat and drew a long breath, inhaling from what I took to be the air of woe that circled his head.

He said, 'I guess the Chicago airport would make four of this one.'

'More than that,' I said.

'Thought it was big,' he said.

'When did you start wearing glasses?' I said.

'A while ago,' he said.

He took a good swallow, and then he got right down to it.

'I liked to have died over it,' he said. He rested his heavy arms on either side of his glass. 'You're an educated man, Les. You'll be the one to figure it out.'

I turned the ashtray on its edge to read what was on the bottom: HARRAH'S CLUB/RENO AND LAKE TAHOE GOOD PLACES TO HAVE FUN.

'She was a Stanley Products woman. A little woman, small feet and hands and coal-black hair. She wasn't the most beautiful thing in the world. But she had these nice ways about her. She was thirty and had kids. But she was a decent woman, whatever happened.

'Your mother was always buying from her, a broom, a mop, some kind of pie filling. You know your mother. It was a Saturday, and I was home. Your mother was gone someplace. I don't know where she was. She wasn't working. I was in the front room reading the paper and having a cup of coffee when there was this knock on the door and it was this little woman. Sally Wain. She said she had some things for Mrs Palmer. "I'm Mr Palmer," I says. "Mrs Palmer is not here now," I says. I ask her just to step in, you know, and I'd pay her for the things. She didn't know whether she should or not. Just stands there holding this little paper sack and the receipt with it.

' "Here, I'll take that." I says. "Why don't you come in and sit down a minute till I see if I can find some money."

' "That's all right," she says. "You can owe it. I have lots of people do that. It's all right." She smiles to let me know it was all right, you see.

' "No, no," I says. "I've got it. I'd sooner pay it now. Save you a trip back and save me owing. Come in," I said, and I hold the screen door open. It wasn't polite to have her standing out there.'

He coughed and took one of my cigarettes. From down the bar a woman laughed. I looked at her and then I read from the ashtray again.

'She steps in, and I says. "Just a minute, please," and I go into the bedroom to look for my wallet. I look around on the dresser, but I can't find it. I find some change and matches and my comb, but I can't find my wallet. Your mother has gone through that morning cleaning up, you see. So I go back to the front room and says, "Well, I'll turn up some money yet."

' "Please, don't bother," she says.

' "No bother," I says. "Have to find my wallet, anyway. Make yourself at home."

' "Oh, I'm fine," she says.

' "Look here," I says. "You hear about that big holdup back East? I was just reading about it."

' "I saw it on the TV last night," she says.

' "They got away clean," I says.

' "Pretty slick," she says.

' "The perfect crime," I says.

' "Not many people get away with it," she says.

'I didn't know what else to say. We were just standing there looking at each other. So I went on out to the porch and looked for my pants in the hamper, where I figured your mother had put them. I found the wallet in my back pocket and went back to the other room and asked how much I owed.

'It was three or four dollars, and I paid her. Then, I don't know why, I asked her what she'd do with it if she had it, all the money those robbers got away with.

'She laughed and I saw her teeth.

'I don't know what came over me then, Les. Fifty-five years old. Grown kids. I knew better than that. This woman was half my age with little kids in school. She did this Stanley job just the hours they were in school, just to give her something to keep busy. She didn't have to work. They had enough to get by on. Her husband, Larry, he was a driver for Consolidated Freight. Made good money. Teamster, you know.'

He stopped and wiped his face.

'Anybody can make a mistake,' I said.

He shook his head.

'She had these two boys, Hank and Freddy. About a year apart. She showed me some pictures. Anyway, she laughs when I say that about the money, says she guessed she'd quit selling Stanley Products and move to Dago and buy a house. She said she had relations in Dago.'

I lit another cigarette. I looked at my watch. The bartender raised his eyebrows and I raised my glass.

'So she's sitting down on the sofa now and she asks me do I have a cigarette. Said she'd left hers in her other purse, and how she hadn't had a smoke since she left home. Says she hated to buy from a machine when she had a carton at home. I gave her a cigarette and I hold a match for her. But I can tell you, Les, my fingers were shaking.'

He stopped and studied the bottles for a minute. The woman who'd done the laughing had her arms locked through the arms of the men on either side of her.

'It's fuzzy after that. I remember I asked her if she wanted coffee. She said maybe she had time for one cup. I went out to the kitchen and waited for the coffee to heat. I tell you, Les, I'll swear before God, I never once stepped out on your mother the whole time we were man and wife. Not once. There were times when I felt like it and had the chance. I tell you, you don't know your mother like I do.'

I said. 'You don't have to say anything in that direction.'

'I took her her coffee, and she's taken off her coat by now. I sit down on the other end of the sofa from her and we get to talking more personal. She says she's got two kids in Roosevelt grade school, and Larry, he was a driver and was sometimes gone for a week or two. Up to Seattle, or down to L.A., or maybe to Phoenix. Always someplace. She says she met Larry when they were going to high school. Said she was proud of the fact she'd gone all the way through. Well, pretty soon she gives a little laugh at something I'd said. It was a thing that could maybe be taken two ways. Then she asks if I'd heard the one about the traveling shoe-salesman who called on the widow woman. We laughed over that one, and then I told her one a little worse. So then she laughs hard at that and smokes another cigarette. One thing's leading to another, is what's happening, don't you see.

'Well, I kissed her then. I put her head back on the sofa and I kissed her, and I can feel her tongue out there rushing to get in my mouth. You see what I'm saying? A man can go along obeying all the rules and then it don't matter a damn anymore. His luck just goes, you know?

'But it was all over in no time at all. And afterwards she says, "You must think I'm a whore or something," and then she just goes.

'I was so excited, you know? I fixed up the sofa and turned over the cushions. I folded all the newspapers and even washed the cups we'd used. I cleaned out the coffee pot. All the time what I was thinking about was how I was going to have to face your mother. I was scared.

'Well, that's how it started. Your mother and I went along the same as usual. But I took to seeing that woman regular.'

The woman down the bar got off her stool. She took some steps toward the center of the floor and commenced to dance. She tossed her head from side to side and snapped her fingers. The bartender stopped doing drinks. The woman raised her arms above her head and moved in a small circle in the middle of the floor. But then she stopped doing it and the bartender went back to work.

'Did you see that?' my father said.

But I didn't say anything at all.

'So that's the way it went,' he said. 'Larry has this schedule, and I'd be over there every time I had the chance. I'd tell your mother I was going here or going there.'

He took off his glasses and shut his eyes. 'I haven't told this to nobody.'

There was nothing to say to that. I looked out at the field and then at my watch.

'Listen,' he said. 'What time does your plane leave? Can you take a different plane? Let me buy us another drink, Les. Order us two more. I'll speed it up. I'll be through with this in a minute. *Listen*,' he said.

'She kept his picture in the bedroom by the bed. First it bothered me, seeing his picture there and all. But after a while I got used to it. You see how a man gets used to things?' He shook his head. 'Hard to believe. Well, it all come to a bad end. You know that. You know all about that.'

'I only know what you tell me,' I said.

'I'll tell you, Les. I'll tell you what's the most important thing involved here. You see, there are things. More important things than your mother leaving me. Now, you listen to this. We were in bed one time. It must have been around lunchtime. We were just laying there talking, I was dozing maybe. It's that funny kind of dreaming dozing, you know. But at the same time, I'm telling myself I better remember that pretty soon I got to get up and go. So it's like this when this car pulls into the driveway and somebody gets out and slams the door.

' "My God," she screams. "It's Larry!" '

'I must have gone crazy. I seem to remember thinking that if I run out the back door he's going to pin me up against this big fence in the yard and maybe kill me. Sally is making a funny kind of sound. Like she couldn't get her breath. She has her robe on, but it's not closed up, and she's standing in the kitchen shaking her head. All this is happening all at once, you understand. So there I am, almost naked with my clothes in my hand, and Larry is opening the front door. Well, I jump. I just jump right into their picture window, right in there through the glass.'

'You got away?' I said. 'He didn't come after you?'

My father looked at me as if I were crazy. He stared at his empty glass. I looked at my watch, stretched. I had a small headache behind my eyes.

I said, 'I guess I better be getting out there soon.' I ran my hand over my chin and straightened my collar. 'She still in Redding, that woman?'

'You don't know anything, do you?' my father said. 'You don't know anything at all. You don't know anything except how to sell books.'

It was almost time to go.

'Ah, God, I'm sorry,' he said. 'The man went all to pieces, is what. He got down on the floor and cried. She stayed out in the kitchen. She did her crying out there. She got down on her knees and she prayed to God, good and loud so the man would hear.'

My father started to say something more. But instead he shook his head. Maybe he wanted me to say something.

But then he said, 'No, you got to catch a plane.'

I helped him into his coat and we started out, my hand guiding him by the elbow.

'I'll put you in a cab,' I said.

He said, 'I'll see you off.'

'That's all right,' I said. 'Next time maybe.'

We shook hands. That was the last I've seen of him. On the way to Chicago, I remembered how I'd left his sack of gifts on the bar. Just as well. Mary didn't need candy, Almond Roca or anything else.

That was last year. She needs it now even less.

The bath

Saturday afternoon the mother drove to the bakery in the shopping center. After looking through a loose-leaf binder with photographs of cakes taped onto the pages, she ordered chocolate, the child's favorite. The cake she chose was decorated with a spaceship and a launching pad under a sprinkling of white stars. The name SCOTTY would be iced on in green as if it were the name of the spaceship.

The baker listened thoughtfully when the mother told him Scotty would be eight years old. He was an older man, this baker, and he wore a curious apron, a heavy thing with loops that went under his arms and around his back and then crossed in front again where they were tied in a very thick knot. He kept wiping his hands on the front of the apron as he listened to the woman, his wet eyes examining her lips as she studied the samples and talked.

He let her take her time. He was in no hurry.

The mother decided on the spaceship cake, and then she gave the baker her name and her telephone number. The cake would be ready Monday morning, in plenty of time for the party Monday afternoon. This was all the baker was willing to say. No pleasantries, just this small exchange, the barest information, nothing that was not necessary.

Monday morning, the boy was walking to school. He was in the company of another boy, the two boys passing a bag of potato chips back and forth between them. The birthday boy was trying to trick the other boy into telling what he was going to give in the way of a present.

At an intersection, without looking, the birthday boy stepped off the curb, and was promptly knocked down by a car. He fell on his side, his head in the gutter, his legs in the road moving as if he were climbing a wall.

The other boy stood holding the potato chips. He was wondering if he should finish the rest or continue on to school.

The birthday boy did not cry. But neither did he wish to talk anymore. He would not answer when the other boy asked what it felt like to be hit by a car. The birthday boy got up and turned back for home, at which time the other boy waved good-bye and headed off for school.

The birthday boy told his mother what had happened. They sat together on the sofa. She held his hands in her lap. This is what she was doing when the boy pulled his hands away and lay down on his back.

Of course, the birthday party never happened. The birthday boy was in the hospital instead. The mother sat by the bed. She was waiting for the boy to wake up. The father hurried over from his office. He sat next to the mother. So now the both of them waited for the boy to wake up. They waited for hours, and then the father went home to take a bath.

The man drove home from the hospital. He drove the streets faster than he should. It had been a good life till now. There had been work, fatherhood, family. The man had been lucky and happy. But fear made him want a bath.

He pulled into the driveway. He sat in the car trying to make his legs work. The child had been hit by a car and he was in the hospital, but he was going to be all right. The man got out of the car and went up to the door. The dog was barking and the telephone was ringing. It kept ringing while the man unlocked the door and felt the wall for the light switch.

He picked up the receiver. He said, 'I just got in the door!'

'There's a cake that wasn't picked up.'

This is what the voice on the other end said.

'What are you saying?' the father said.

'The cake,' the voice said. 'Sixteen dollars.'

The husband held the receiver against his ear, trying to understand. He said, 'I don't know anything about it.'

'Don't hand me that,' the voice said.

The husband hung up the telephone. He went into the kitchen and poured himself some whiskey. He called the hospital.

The child's condition remained the same.

While the water ran into the tub, the man lathered his face and shaved. He was in the tub when he heard the telephone again. He got himself out and hurried through the house, saying, 'Stupid, stupid,' because he wouldn't be doing this if he'd stayed where he was in the hospital. He picked up the receiver and shouted, 'Hello!'

The voice said, 'It's ready.'

The father got back to the hospital after midnight. The wife was sitting in the chair by the bed. She looked up at the husband and then she looked back at the child. From an apparatus over the bed hung a bottle with a tube running from the bottle to the child.

'What's this?' the father said.

'Glucose,' the mother said.

The husband put his hand to the back of the woman's head.

'He's going to wake up,' the man said.

'I know,' the woman said.

In a little while the man said, 'Go home and let me take over.'

She shook her head. 'No,' she said.

'Really,' he said. 'Go home for a while. You don't have to worry. He's sleeping, is all.'

A nurse pushed open the door. She nodded to them as she went to the bed. She took the left arm out from under the covers and put her fingers on the wrist. She put the arm back under the covers and wrote on the clipboard attached to the bed.

'How is he?' the mother said.

'Stable,' the nurse said. Then she said, 'Doctor will be in again shortly.'

'I was saying maybe she'd want to go home and get a little rest,' the man said. 'After the doctor comes.'

'She could do that,' the nurse said.

The woman said, 'We'll see what the doctor says,' She brought her hand up to her eyes and leaned her head forward.

The nurse said, 'Of course.'

The father gazed at his son, the small chest inflating and deflating under the covers. He felt more fear now. He began shaking his head. He talked to himself like this. The child is fine. Instead of sleeping at home, he's doing it here. Sleep is the same wherever you do it.

The doctor came in. He shook hands with the man. The woman got up from the chair.

'Ann,' the doctor said and nodded. The doctor said, 'Let's just see how he's doing.' He moved to the bed and touched the boy's wrist. He peeled back an eyelid and then the other. He turned back the covers and listened to the heart. He pressed his fingers here and there on the body. He went to the end of the bed and studied the chart. He noted the time, scribbled on the chart, and then he considered the mother and the father.

This doctor was a handsome man. His skin was moist and tan. He wore a three-piece suit, a vivid tie, and on his shirt were cufflinks.

The mother was talking to herself like this. He has just come from somewhere with an audience. They gave him a special medal.

The doctor said, 'Nothing to shout about, but nothing to worry about. He should wake up pretty soon.' The doctor looked at the boy again. 'We'll know more after the tests are in.'

'Oh no,' the mother said.

The doctor said, 'Sometimes you see this.'

The father said, 'You wouldn't call this a coma, then?'

The father waited and looked at the doctor.

'No, I don't want to call it that,' the doctor said. 'He's sleeping. It's restorative. The body is doing what it has to do.'

'It's a coma,' the mother said. 'A kind of coma.'

The doctor said. 'I wouldn't call it that.'

He took the woman's hands and patted them. He shook hands with the husband.

The woman put her fingers on the child's forehead and kept them there for a while. 'At least he doesn't have a fever,' she said. Then she said, 'I don't know. Feel his head.'

The man put his fingers on the boy's forehead. The man said. 'I think he's supposed to feel this way.'

The woman stood there awhile longer, working her lip with her teeth. Then she moved to her chair and sat down.

The husband sat in the chair beside her. He wanted to say something else. But there was no saying what it should be. He took her hand and put it in his lap. This made him feel better. It made him feel he was saying something. They sat like that for a while, watching the boy, not talking. From time to time he squeezed her hand until she took it away.

'I've been praying,' she said.

'Me too,' the father said. 'I've been praying too.'

A nurse came back in and checked the flow from the bottle.

A doctor came in and said what his name was. This doctor was wearing loafers.

'We're going to take him downstairs for more pictures,' he said. 'And we want to do a scan.'

'A scan?' the mother said. She stood between this new doctor and the bed.

'It's nothing,' he said.

'My God,' she said.

Two orderlies came in. They wheeled a thing like a bed. They unhooked the boy from the tube and slid him over onto the thing with wheels.

It was after sunup when they brought the birthday boy back out. The mother and father followed the orderlies into the elevator and up to the room. Once more the parents took up their places next to the bed.

They waited all day. The boy did not wake up. The doctor came again and examined the boy again and left after saying the same things again. Nurses came in. Doctors came in. A technician came in and took blood.

'I don't understand this,' the mother said to the technician.

'Doctor's orders,' the technician said.

The mother went to the window and looked out at the parking lot. Cars with their lights on were driving in and out. She stood at the window with her hands on the sill. She was talking to herself like this. We're into something now, something hard.

She was afraid.

She saw a car stop and a woman in a long coat get into it. She made believe she was that woman. She made believe she was driving away from here to someplace else.

The doctor came in. He looked tanned and healthier than ever. He went to the bed and examined the boy. He said, 'His signs are fine. Everything's good.'

The mother said, 'But he's sleeping.'

'Yes,' the doctor said.

The husband said, 'She's tired, She's starved.'

The doctor said, 'She should rest. She should eat. Ann,' the doctor said.

'Thank you,' the husband said.

He shook hands with the doctor and the doctor patted their shoulders and left.

*

'I suppose one of us should go home and check on things,' the man said. 'The dog needs to be fed.'

'Call the neighbors,' the wife said. 'Someone will feed him if you ask them to.'

She tried to think who. She closed her eyes and tried to think anything at all. After a time she said, 'Maybe I'll do it. Maybe if I'm not here watching, he'll wake up. Maybe it's because I'm watching that he won't.'

'That could be it,' the husband said.

'I'll go home and take a bath and put on something clean,' the woman said.

'I think you should do that,' the man said.

She picked up her purse. He helped her into her coat. She moved to the door, and looked back. She looked at the child, and then she looked at the father. The husband nodded and smiled.

She went past the nurses' station and down to the end of the corridor, where she turned and saw a little waiting room, a family in there, all sitting in wicker chairs, a man in a khaki shirt, a baseball cap pushed back on his head, a large woman wearing a housedress, slippers, a girl in jeans, hair in dozens of kinky braids, the table littered with flimsy wrappers and styrofoam and coffee sticks and packets of salt and pepper.

'Nelson,' the woman said. 'Is it about Nelson?'

The woman's eyes widened.

'Tell me now, lady,' the woman said. 'Is it about Nelson?'

The woman was trying to get up from her chair. But the man had his hand closed over her arm.

'Here, here,' the man said.

'I'm sorry,' the mother said. 'I'm looking for the elevator. My son is in the hospital. I can't find the elevator.'

'Elevator is down that way,' the man said, and he aimed a finger in the right direction.

'My son was hit by a car,' the mother said. 'But he's going to be all right. He's in shock now, but it might be some kind of coma too. That's what worries us, the coma part. I'm going out for a little while. Maybe I'll take a bath. But my husband is with him. He's watching. There's a chance everything will change when I'm gone. My name is Ann Weiss.'

The man shifted in his chair. He shook his head.

He said, 'Our Nelson.'

She pulled into the driveway. The dog ran out from behind the house. He ran in circles on the grass. She closed her eyes and leaned her head against the wheel. She listened to the ticking of the engine.

She got out of the car and went to the door. She turned on lights and put on water for tea. She opened a can and fed the dog. She sat down on the sofa with her tea.

The telephone rang.

'Yes!' she said. 'Hello!' she said.

'Mrs Weiss,' a man's voice said.

'Yes,' she said. 'This is Mrs Weiss. Is it about Scotty?' she said.

'Scotty,' the voice said. 'It is about Scotty,' the voice said. 'It has to do with Scotty, yes.'

Tell the women we're going

Bill Jamison had always been best friends with Jerry Roberts. The two grew up in the south area, near the old fairgrounds, went through grade school and junior high together, and then on to Eisenhower, where they took as many of the same teachers as they could manage, wore each other's shirts and sweaters and pegged pants, and dated and banged the same girls – whichever came up as a matter of course.

Summers they took jobs together – swamping peaches, picking cherries, stringing hops, anything they could do that paid a little and where there was no boss to get on your ass. And then they bought a car together. The summer before their senior year, they chipped in and bought a red '54 Plymouth for $325.

They shared it. It worked out fine.

But Jerry got married before the end of the first semester and dropped out of school to work steady at Robby's Mart.

As for Bill, he'd dated the girl too. Carol was her name, and she went just fine with Jerry, and Bill went over there every chance he got. It made him feel older, having married friends. He'd go over there for lunch or for supper, and they'd listen to Elvis or to Bill Haley and the Comets.

But sometimes Carol and Jerry would start making out right with Bill still there, and he'd have to get up and excuse himself and take a walk to Dezorn's Service Station to get some Coke because there was only one bed in the apartment, a hide-away that came down in the living room. Or sometimes Jerry and Carol would head off to the bathroom, and Bill would have to move to the kitchen and pretend to be interested in the cupboards and the refrigerator and not trying to listen.

So he stopped going over so much; and then June he graduated, took a job at the Darigold plant, and joined the National Guard. In a year he had a milk route of his own and was going steady with Linda. So Bill and Linda would go over to Jerry and Carol's, drink beer, and listen to records.

Carol and Linda got along fine, and Bill was flattered when Carol said that, confidentially, Linda was 'a real person.'

Jerry liked Linda too. 'She's great,' Jerry said.

When Bill and Linda got married, Jerry was best man. The reception, of course, was at the Donnelly Hotel, Jerry and Bill cutting up together and linking arms and tossing off glasses of spiked punch. But once, in the middle of all this happiness, Bill looked at Jerry and thought how much older Jerry looked, a lot older than twenty-two. By then Jerry was the happy father of two kids and had moved up to assistant manager at Robby's, and Carol had one in the oven again.

They saw each other every Saturday and Sunday, sometimes oftener if it was a holiday. If the weather was good, they'd be over at Jerry's to barbecue hot dogs and turn the kids loose in the wading pool Jerry had got for next to nothing, like a lot of other things he got from the Mart.

Jerry had a nice house. It was up on a hill overlooking the Naches. There were other houses around, but not too close. Jerry was doing all right. When Bill and Linda and Jerry and Carol got together, it was always at Jerry's place because Jerry had the barbecue and the records and too many kids to drag around.

It was Sunday at Jerry's place the time it happened.

The women were in the kitchen straightening up. Jerry's girls were out in the yard throwing a plastic ball into the wading pool, yelling, and splashing after it.

Jerry and Bill were sitting in the reclining chairs on the patio, drinking beer and just relaxing.

Bill was doing most of the talking – things about people they knew, about Darigold, about the four-door Pontiac Catalina he was thinking of buying.

Jerry was staring at the clothesline, or at the '68 Chevy hardtop that stood in the garage. Bill was thinking how Jerry was getting to be deep, the way he stared all the time and hardly did any talking at all.

Bill moved in his chair and lighted a cigarette.

He said, 'Anything wrong, man? I mean, you know.'

Jerry finished his beer and then mashed the can. He shrugged.

'You know,' he said.

Bill nodded.

Then Jerry said, 'How about a little run?'

'Sounds good to me,' Bill said. 'I'll tell the women we're going.'

They took the Naches River highway out to Gleed, Jerry driving. The day was sunny and warm, and air blew through the car.

'Where we headed?' Bill said.

'Let's shoot a few balls.'

'Fine with me,' Bill said. He felt a whole lot better just seeing Jerry brighten up.

'Guy's got to get out,' Jerry said. He looked at Bill. 'You know what I mean?'

Bill understood. He liked to get out with the guys from the plant for the Friday-night bowling league. He liked to stop off twice a week after work to have a few beers with Jack Broderick. He knew a guy's got to get out.

'Still standing,' Jerry said, as they pulled up onto the gravel in front of the Rec Center.

They went inside, Bill holding the door for Jerry, Jerry punching Bill lightly in the stomach as he went on by.

'Hey there!'

It was Riley.

'Hey, how you boys keeping?'

It was Riley coming around from behind the counter, grinning. He was a heavy man. He had on a short-sleeved Hawaiian shirt that hung outside his jeans. Riley said, 'So how you boys been keeping?'

'Ah, dry up and give us a couple of Olys,' Jerry said, winking at Bill. 'So how you been, Riley?' Jerry said.

Riley said, 'So how you boys doing? Where you been keeping yourselves? You boys getting any on the side? Jerry, the last time I seen you, your old lady was six months gone.'

Jerry stood a minute and blinked his eyes.

'So how about the Olys?' Bill said.

They took stools near the window. Jerry said, 'What kind of place is this, Riley, that it don't have any girls on a Sunday afternoon?'

Riley laughed. He said, 'I guess they're all in church praying for it.'

They each had five cans of beer and took two hours to play three racks of rotation and two racks of snooker, Riley sitting on a stool and talking and watching them play, Bill always looking at his watch and then looking at Jerry.

Bill said, 'So what do you think, Jerry? I mean, what do you think?' Bill said.

Jerry drained his can, mashed it, then stood for a time turning the can in his hand.

Back on the highway, Jerry opened it up – little jumps of eighty-five and ninety. They'd just passed an old pickup loaded with furniture when they saw the two girls.

'Look at that!' Jerry said, slowing. 'I could use some of that.'

Jerry drove another mile or so and then pulled off the road. 'Let's go back,' Jerry said, 'Let's try it.'

'Jesus,' Bill said. 'I don't know.'

'I could use some,' Jerry said.

Bill said, 'Yeah, but I don't know.'

'For Christ's sake,' Jerry said.

Bill glanced at his watch and then looked all around. He said, 'You do the talking. I'm rusty.'

Jerry hooted as he whipped the car around.

He slowed when he came nearly even with the girls. He pulled the Chevy onto the shoulder across from them. The girls kept on going on their bicycles, but they looked at each other and laughed. The one on the inside was dark-haired, tall, and willowy. The other was light-haired and smaller. They both wore shorts and halters.

'Bitches,' Jerry said. He waited for the cars to pass so he could pull a U.

'I'll take the brunette,' he said. He said, 'The little one's yours.'

Bill moved his back against the front seat and touched the bridge of his sunglasses. 'They're not going to do anything,' Bill said.

'They're going to be on your side,' Jerry said.

He pulled across the road and drove back. 'Get ready,' Jerry said.

'Hi,' Bill said as the girls bicycled up. 'My name's Bill,' Bill said.

'That's nice,' the brunette said.

'Where are you going?' Bill said.

The girls didn't answer. The little one laughed. They kept bicycling and Jerry kept driving.

'Oh, come on now. Where you going?' Bill said.

'No place,' the little one said.

'Where's no place?' Bill said.

'Wouldn't you like to know,' the little one said.

'I told you my name,' Bill said. 'What's yours? My friend's Jerry,' Bill said.

The girls looked at each other and laughed.

A car came up from behind. The driver hit his horn.

'Cram it!' Jerry shouted.

He pulled off a little and let the car go around. Then he pulled back up alongside the girls.

Bill said, 'We'll give you a lift. We'll take you where you want. That's a promise. You must be tired riding those bicycles. You look tired. Too much exercise isn't good for a person. Especially girls.'

The girls laughed.

'You see?' Bill said. 'Now tell us your names.'

'I'm Barbara, she's Sharon,' the little one said.

'All right!' Jerry said. 'Now find out where they're going.'

'Where you girls going?' Bill said. 'Barb?'

She laughed. 'No place,' she said. 'Just down the road.'

'Where down the road?'

'Do you want me to tell them?' she said to the other girl.

'I don't care,' the other girl said. 'It doesn't make any difference,' she said. 'I'm not going to go anyplace with anybody anyway,' the one named Sharon said.

'Where you going?' Bill said. 'Are you going to Picture Rock?'

The girls laughed.

'That's where they're going,' Jerry said.

He fed the Chevy gas and pulled up off onto the shoulder so that the girls had to come by on his side.

'Don't be that way,' Jerry said. He said, 'Come on.' He said, 'We're all introduced.'

The girls just rode on by.

'I won't bite you!' Jerry shouted.

The brunette glanced back. It seemed to Jerry she was looking at him in the right kind of way. But with a girl you could never be sure.

Jerry gunned it back onto the highway, dirt and pebbles flying from under the tires.

'We'll be seeing you!' Bill called as they went speeding by.

'It's in the bag,' Jerry said. 'You see the look that cunt gave me?'

'I don't know,' Bill said. 'Maybe we should cut for home.'

'We got it made!' Jerry said.

He pulled off the road under some trees. The highway forked here at Picture Rock, one road going on to Yakima, the other heading for Naches, Enumclaw, the Chinook Pass, Seattle.

A hundred yards off the road was a high, sloping, black mound of rock, part of a low range of hills, honeycombed with footpaths and small caves, Indian sign-painting here and there on the cave walls. The cliff side of the rock faced the highway and all over it there were things like this:

NACHES 67 – GLEED WILDCATS – JESUS SAVES – BEAT YAKIMA – REPENT NOW.

They sat in the car, smoking cigarettes. Mosquitoes came in and tried to get at their hands.

'Wish we had a beer now,' Jerry said. 'I sure could go for a beer,' he said.

Bill said, 'Me too,' and looked at his watch.

When the girls came into view, Jerry and Bill got out of the car. They leaned against the fender in front.

'Remember,' Jerry said, starting away from the car, 'the dark one's mine. You got the other one.'

The girls dropped their bicycles and started up one of the paths. They disappeared around a bend and then reappeared again, a little higher up. They were standing there and looking down.

'What're you guys following us for?' the brunette called down.

Jerry just started up the path.

The girls turned away and went off again at a trot.

Jerry and Bill kept climbing at a walking pace. Bill was smoking a cigaret, stopping every so often to get a good drag. When the path turned, he looked back and caught a glimpse of the car.

'Move it!' Jerry said.

'I'm coming,' Bill said.

They kept climbing. But then Bill had to catch his breath. He couldn't see the car now. He couldn't see the highway, either. To his left and all the way down, he could see a strip of the Naches like a strip of aluminum foil.

Jerry said, 'You go right and I'll go straight. We'll cut the cock-teasers off.'

Bill nodded. He was too winded to speak.

He went higher for a while, and then the path began to drop, turning toward the valley. He looked and saw the girls. He saw them crouched behind an outcrop. Maybe they were smiling.

Bill took out a cigarette. But he could not get it lit. Then Jerry showed up. It did not matter after that.

Bill had just wanted to fuck. Or even to see them naked. On the other hand, it was okay with him if it didn't work out.

He never knew what Jerry wanted. But it started and ended with a rock. Jerry used the same rock on both girls, first on the girl called Sharon and then on the one that was supposed to be Bill's.

After the denim

Edith Packer had the tape cassette plugged into her ear, and she was smoking one of his cigarettes. The TV played without any volume as she sat on the sofa with her legs tucked under her and turned the pages of a magazine. James Packer came out of the guest room, which was the room he had fixed up as an office, and Edith Packer took the cord from her ear. She put the cigarette in the ashtray and pointed her foot and wiggled her toes in greeting.

He said, 'Are we going or not?'

'I'm going,' she said.

Edith Packer liked classical music. James Packer did not. He was a retired accountant. But he still did returns for some old clients, and he didn't like to hear music when he did it.

'If we're going, let's go.'

He looked at the TV, and then went to turn it off.

'I'm going,' she said.

She closed the magazine and got up. She left the room and went to the back.

He followed her to make sure the back door was locked and also that the porch light was on. Then he stood waiting and waiting in the living room.

It was a ten-minute drive to the community center, which meant they were going to miss the first game.

In the place where James always parked, there was an old van with markings on it, so he had to keep going to the end of the block.

'Lots of cars tonight,' Edith said.

He said, 'There wouldn't be so many if we'd been on time.'

'There'd still be as many. It's just we wouldn't have seen them.' She pinched his sleeve, teasing.

He said, 'Edith, if we're going to play bingo, we ought to be here on time.'

'Hush,' Edith Packer said.

He found a parking space and turned into it. He switched off the engine and cut the lights. He said, 'I don't know if I feel lucky tonight. I think I felt lucky when I was doing Howard's taxes. But I don't think I feel lucky now. It's not lucky if you have to start out walking half a mile just to play.'

'You stick to me,' Edith Packer said. 'You'll feel lucky.'

'I don't feel lucky yet,' James said. 'Lock your door.'

There was a cold breeze. He zipped the windbreaker to his neck, and she pulled her coat closed. They could hear the surf breaking on the rocks at the bottom of the cliff behind the building.

She said, 'I'll take one of your cigarettes first.'

They stopped under the street lamp at the corner. It was a damaged street lamp, and wires had been added to support it. The wires moved in the wind, made shadows on the pavement.

'When are you going to stop?' he said, lighting his cigarette after he'd lighted hers.

'When you stop,' she said. 'I'll stop when you stop. Just like it was when you stopped drinking. Like that. Like you.'

'I can teach you to do needlework,' he said.

'One needleworker in the house is enough,' she said.

He took her arm and they kept on walking.

When they reached the entrance, she dropped her cigarette and stepped on it. They went up the steps and into the foyer. There was a sofa in the room, a wooden table, folding chairs stacked up. On the walls were hung photographs of fishing boats and naval vessels, one showing a boat that had turned over, a man standing on the keel and waving.

The Packers passed through the foyer, James taking Edith's arm as they entered the corridor.

Some clubwomen sat to the side of the far doorway signing people in as they entered the assembly hall, where a game was already in progress, the numbers being called by a woman who stood on the stage.

The Packers hurried to their regular table. But a young couple occupied the Packers' usual places. The girl wore denims, and so did the long-haired man with her. She had rings and bracelets and earrings that made her shiny in the milky light. Just as the Packers came up, the girl turned to the fellow with her and poked her finger at a number on his card. Then she pinched his arm. The fellow had his hair pulled back and tied behind his head, and something else the Packers saw – a tiny gold loop through his earlobe.

*

James guided Edith to another table, turning to look again before sitting down. First he took off his windbreaker and helped Edith with her coat, and then he stared at the couple who had taken their places. The girl was scanning her cards as the numbers were called, leaning over to check the man's cards too – as if, James thought, the fellow did not have sense enough to look after his own numbers.

James picked up the stack of bingo cards that had been set out on the table. He gave half to Edith. 'Pick some winners,' he said. 'Because I'm taking these three on top. It doesn't matter which ones I pick. Edith, I don't feel lucky tonight.'

'Don't you pay it any attention,' she said. 'They're not hurting anybody. They're just young, that's all.'

He said, 'This is regular Friday night bingo for the people of this community.'

She said, 'It's a free country.'

She handed back the stack of cards. He put them on the other side of the table. Then they served themselves from the bowl of beans.

James peeled a dollar bill from the roll of bills he kept for bingo nights. He put the dollar next to his cards. One of the clubwomen, a thin woman with bluish hair and a spot on her neck – the Packers knew her only as Alice – would presently come by with a coffee can. She would collect the coins and bills, making change from the can. It was this woman or another woman who paid off the wins.

The woman on the stage called 'I-25,' and someone in the hall yelled, 'Bingo!'

Alice made her way between the tables. She took up the winning card and held it in her hand as the woman on the stage read out the winning numbers.

'It's a bingo,' Alice confirmed.

'That bingo, ladies and gentlemen, is worth twelve dollars!' the woman on the stage announced. 'Congratulations to the winner!'

The Packers played another five games to no effect. James came close once on one of his cards. But then five numbers were called in succession, none of them his, the fifth a number that produced a bingo on somebody else's card.

'You almost had it that time,' Edith said. 'I was watching your card.'

'She was teasing me,' James said.

He tilted the card and let the beans slide into his hand. He closed his hand and made a fist. He shook the beans in his fist. Something came to him about a boy who'd thrown some beans out a window. The memory reached to him from a long way off, and it made him feel lonely.

'Change cards, maybe,' Edith said.

'It isn't my night,' James said.

He looked over at the young couple again. They were laughing at something the fellow had said. James could see they weren't paying attention to anyone else in the hall.

Alice came around collecting money for the next game, and just after the first number had been called, James saw the fellow in the denims put down a bean on a card he hadn't paid for. Another number was called, and James saw the fellow do it again. James was amazed. He could not concentrate on his own cards. He kept looking up to see what the fellow in denim was doing.

'James, look at your cards,' Edith said. 'You missed N-34. Pay attention.'

'That fellow over there who has our place is cheating. I can't believe my eyes,' James said.

'How is he cheating?' Edith said.

'He's playing a card that he hasn't paid for,' James said. 'Somebody ought to report him.'

'Not you, dear,' Edith said. She spoke slowly and tried to keep her eyes on her cards. She dropped a bean on a number.

'The fellow is cheating,' James said.

She extracted a bean from her palm and placed it on a number. 'Play your cards,' Edith said.

He looked back at his cards. But he knew he might as well write this game off. There was no telling how many numbers he had missed, how far behind he had fallen. He squeezed the beans in his fist.

The woman on the stage called, 'G-60.'

Someone yelled, 'Bingo!'

'Christ,' James Packer said.

A ten-minute break was announced. The game after the break would be a Blackout, one dollar a card, winner takes all, this week's jackpot ninety-eight dollars.

There was whistling and clapping.

James looked at the couple. The fellow was touching the ring in his ear and staring up at the ceiling. The girl had her hand on his leg.

'I have to go to the bathroom,' Edith said. 'Give me your cigarettes.'

James said, 'And I'll get us some raisin cookies and coffee.'

'I'll go to the bathroom,' Edith said.

But James Packer did not go to get cookies and coffee. Instead, he went to stand behind the chair of the fellow in denim.

'I see what you're doing,' James said.

The man turned around. 'Pardon me?' he said and stared. 'What am I doing?'

'You know,' James said.

The girl held her cookie in mid-bite.

'A word to the wise,' James said.

He walked back to his table. He was trembling.

When Edith came back, she handed him the cigarettes and sat down, not talking, not being her jovial self.

James looked at her closely. He said, 'Edith, has something happened?'

'I'm spotting again,' she said.

'Spotting?' he said. But he knew what she meant. 'Spotting,' he said again, very quietly.

'Oh, dear,' Edith Packer said, picking up some cards and sorting through them.

'I think we should go home,' he said.

She kept sorting through the cards. 'No, let's stay,' she said. 'It's just the spotting, is all.'

He touched her hand.

'We'll stay,' she said. 'It'll be all right.'

'This is the worst bingo night in history,' James Packer said.

They played the Blackout game, James watching the man in denim. The fellow was still at it, still playing a card he hadn't paid for. From time to time, James checked how Edith was doing. But there was no way of telling. She held her lips pursed together. It could mean anything – resolve, worry, pain. Or maybe she just liked having her lips that way for this particular game.

He had three numbers to go on one card and five numbers on another, and no chance at all on a third card when the girl with the man in denim began shrieking: 'Bingo! Bingo! Bingo! I have a bingo!'

The fellow clapped and shouted with her. 'She's got a bingo! She's got a bingo, folks! A bingo!'

The fellow in denim kept clapping.

It was the woman on the stage herself who went to the girl's table to check her card against the master list. She said, 'This young woman has a bingo, and that's a ninety-eight-dollar jackpot! Let's give her a round of applause, people! It's a bingo here! A Blackout!'

Edith clapped along with the rest. But James kept his hands on the table.

The fellow in denim hugged the girl when the woman from the stage handed over the cash.

'They'll use it to buy drugs,' James said.

They stayed for the rest of the games. They stayed until the last game was played. It was a game called the Progressive, the jackpot increasing from week to week if no one bingoed before so many numbers were called.

James put his money down and played his cards with no hope of winning. He waited for the fellow in denim to call 'Bingo!'

But no one won, and the jackpot would be carried over to the following week, the prize bigger than ever.

'That's bingo for tonight!' the woman on the stage proclaimed. 'Thank you all for coming. God bless you and good night.'

The Packers filed out of the assembly hall along with the rest, somehow managing to fall in behind the fellow in denim and his girl. They saw the girl pat her pocket. They saw the girl put her arm around the fellow's waist.

'Let those people get ahead of us,' James said into Edith's ear. 'I can't stand to look at them.'

Edith said nothing in reply. But she hung back a little to give the couple time to move ahead.

Outside, the wind was up. James thought sure he could hear the surf over the sound of engines starting.

He saw the couple stop at the van. Of course. He should have put two and two together.

'The dumbbell,' James Packer said.

Edith went into the bathroom and shut the door. James took off his windbreaker and put it down on the back of the sofa. He turned on the TV and took up his place and waited.

After a time, Edith came out of the bathroom. James concentrated his attention on the TV. Edith went to the kitchen and ran water. James heard her turn off the faucet. Edith came to the room and said, 'I guess I'll have to see Dr Crawford in the morning. I guess there really is something happening down there.'

'The lousy luck,' James said.

She stood there shaking her head. She covered her eyes and leaned into him when he came to put his arms around her.

'Edith, dearest Edith,' James Packer said.

He felt awkward and terrified. He stood with his arms more or less holding his wife.

She reached for his face and kissed his lips, and then she said good night.

He went to the refrigerator. He stood in front of the open door and drank tomato juice while he studied everything inside. Cold air blew out at him. He looked at the little packages and the containers of foodstuffs on the shelves, a chicken covered in plastic wrap, the neat, protected exhibits.

He shut the door and spit the last of the juice into the sink. Then he rinsed his mouth and made himself a cup of instant coffee. He carried it into the living room. He sat down in front of the TV and lit a cigarette. He understood that it took only one lunatic and a torch to bring everything to ruin.

He smoked and finished the coffee, and then he turned the TV off. He went to the bedroom door and listened for a time. He felt unworthy to be listening, to be standing.

Why not someone else? Why not those people tonight? Why not all those people who sail through life free as birds? Why not them instead of Edith?

He moved away from the bedroom door. He thought about going for a walk. But the wind was wild now, and he could hear the branches whining in the birch tree behind the house.

He sat in front of the TV again. But he did not turn it on. He smoked and thought of that sauntering, arrogant gait as the two of them moved just ahead. If only they knew. If only someone would tell them. Just once!

He closed his eyes. He would get up early and fix breakfast. He would go with her to see Crawford. If only they had to sit with him in the waiting room! He'd tell them what to expect! He'd set those floozies straight! He'd tell them what was waiting for you after the denim and the earrings, after touching each other and cheating at games.

He got up and went into the guest room and turned on the lamp over the bed. He glanced at his papers and at his account books and at the adding machine on his desk. He found a pair of pajamas in one of the drawers. He turned down the covers on the bed. Then he walked back through the house, snapping off lights and checking doors. For a while he stood looking out the kitchen window at the tree shaking under the force of the wind.

He left the porch light on and went back to the guest room. He pushed aside his knitting basket, took up his basket of embroidery, and then settled himself in the chair. He raised the lid of the basket and got out the metal hoop. There was fresh white linen stretched across it. Holding the tiny needle to the light, James Packer stabbed at the eye with a length of blue silk thread. Then he set to work — stitch after stitch — making believe he was waving like the man on the keel.

So much water
so close to home

My husband eats with a good appetite. But I don't think he's really hungry. He chews, arms on the table, and stares at something across the room. He looks at me and looks away. He wipes his mouth on the napkin. He shrugs, and goes on eating.

'What are you staring at me for?' he says. 'What is it?' he says and lays down his fork.

'Was I staring?' I say, and shake my head.

The telephone rings.

'Don't answer it,' he says.

'It might be your mother,' I say.

'Watch and see,' he says.

I pick up the receiver and listen. My husband stops eating.

'What did I tell you?' he says when I hang up. He starts to eat again. Then throws his napkin on his plate. He says, 'Goddamn it, why can't people mind their own business? Tell me what I did wrong and I'll listen! I wasn't the only man there. We talked it over and we all decided. We couldn't just turn around. We were five miles from the car. I won't have you passing judgment. Do you hear?'

'You know,' I say.

He says, 'What do I know, Claire? Tell me what I'm supposed to know. I don't know anything except one thing.' He gives me what he thinks is a meaningful look. 'She was dead,' he says. 'And I'm so sorry as anyone else. But she was dead.'

'That's the point,' I say.

He raises his hands. He pushes his chair away from the table. He takes out his cigarettes and goes out to the back with a can of beer. I see him sit in the lawn chair and pick up the newspaper again.

His name is in there on the first page. Along with the names of his friends.

I close my eyes and hold on to the sink. Then I rake my arm across the drainboard and send the dishes to the floor.

He doesn't move. I know he's heard. He lifts his head as if still listening. But he doesn't move otherwise. He doesn't turn around.

He and Gordon Johnson and Mel Dorn and Vern Williams, they play poker and bowl and fish. They fish every spring and early summer before visiting relatives can get in the way. They are decent men, family men, men who take care of their jobs. They have sons and daughters who go to school with our son, Dean.

Last Friday these family men left for the Naches River. They parked the car in the mountains and hiked to where they wanted to fish. They carried their bedrolls, their food, their playing cards, their whiskey.

They saw the girl before they set up camp. Mel Dorn found her. No clothes on her at all. She was wedged into some branches that stuck out over the water.

He called the others and they came to look. They talked about what to do. One of the men – my Stuart didn't say which – said they should start back at once. The others stirred the sand with their shoes, said they didn't feel inclined that way. They pleaded fatigue, the late hour, the fact that the girl wasn't going anywhere.

In the end they went ahead and set up the camp. They built a fire and drank their whiskey. When the moon came up, they talked about the girl. Someone said they should keep the body from drifting away. They took their flashlights and went back to the river. One of the men – it might have been Stuart – waded in and got her. He took her by the fingers and pulled her into shore. He got some nylon cord and tied it to her wrist and then looped the rest around a tree.

The next morning they cooked breakfast, drank coffee, and drank whiskey, and then split up to fish. That night they cooked fish, cooked potatoes, drank coffee, drank whiskey, then took their cooking things and eating things back down to the river and washed them where the girl was.

They played some cards later on. Maybe they played until they couldn't see them anymore. Vern Williams went to sleep. But the others told stories. Gordon Johnson said the trout they'd caught were hard because of the terrible coldness of the water.

The next morning they got up late, drank whiskey, fished a little, took down their tents, rolled their sleeping bags, gathered their stuff, and hiked out. They drove until they got to a telephone. It was Stuart who made the call while the others stood around in the sun and listened. He gave the sheriff their names. They had nothing to hide. They weren't ashamed. They said they'd wait until someone could come for better directions and take down their statements.

*

I was asleep when he got home. But I woke up when I heard him in the kitchen. I found him leaning against the refrigerator with a can of beer. He put his heavy arms around me and rubbed his big hands on my back. In bed he put his hands on me again and then waited as if thinking of something else. I turned and opened my legs. Afterwards, I think he stayed awake.

He was up that morning before I could get out of bed. To see if there was something in the paper, I suppose.

The telephone began ringing right after eight.

'Go to hell!' I heard him shout.

The telephone rang right again.

'I have nothing to add to what I already said to the sheriff!'

He slammed the receiver down.

'What is going on?' I said.

It was then that he told me what I just told you.

I sweep up the broken dishes and go outside. He is lying on his back on the grass now, the newspaper and can of beer within reach.

'Stuart, could we go for a drive?' I say.

He rolls over and looks at me. 'We'll pick up some beer,' he says. He gets to his feet and touches me on the hip as he goes past. 'Give me a minute,' he says.

We drive through town without speaking. He stops at a roadside market for beer. I notice a great stack of papers just inside the door. On the top step a fat woman in a print dress holds out a licorice stick to a little girl. Later on, we cross Everson Creek and turn into the picnic grounds. The creek runs under the bridge and into a large pond a few hundred yards away. I can see the men out there. I can see them out there fishing.

So much water so close to home.

I say, 'Why did you have to go miles away?'

'Don't rile me,' he says.

We sit on a bench in the sun. He opens us cans of beer. He says, 'Relax, Claire.'

'They said they were innocent. They said they were crazy.'

He says, 'Who?' He says, 'What are you talking about?'

'The Maddox brothers. They killed a girl named Arlene Hubly where I grew up. They cut off her head and threw her into the Cle Elum River. It happened when I was a girl.'

'You're going to get me riled,' he says.

I look at the creek. I'm right in it, eyes open, face down, staring at the moss on the bottom, dead.

'I don't know what's wrong with you,' he says on the way home. 'You're getting me more riled by the minute.'

There is nothing I can say to him.

He tries to concentrate on the road. But he keeps looking into the rear-view mirror.

He knows.

Stuart believes he is letting me sleep this morning. But I was awake long before the alarm went off. I was thinking, lying on the far side of the bed away from his hairy legs.

He gets Dean off for school, and then he shaves, dresses, and leaves for work. Twice he looks in and clears his throat. But I keep my eyes closed.

In the kitchen I find a note from him. It's signed 'Love.'

I sit in the breakfast nook and drink coffee and leave a ring on the note. I look at the newspaper and turn it this way and that on the table. Then I skid it close and read what it says. The body has been identified, claimed. But it took some examining it, some putting things into it, some cutting, some weighing, some measuring, some putting things back again and sewing them in.

I sit for a long time holding the newspaper and thinking. Then I call up to get a chair at the hairdresser's.

I sit under the dryer with a magazine on my lap and let Marnie do my nails.

'I am going to a funeral tomorrow,' I say.

'I'm sorry to hear that,' Marnie says.

'It was a murder,' I say.

'That's the worst kind,' Marnie says.

'We weren't all that close,' I say. 'But you know.'

'We'll get you fixed up for it,' Marnie says.

That night I make my bed on the sofa, and in the morning I get up first. I put on coffee and fix breakfast while he shaves.

He appears in the kitchen doorway, towel over his bare shoulder, appraising.

'Here's coffee,' I say. 'Eggs'll be ready in a minute.'

I wake Dean, and the three of us eat. Whenever Stuart looks at me, I ask Dean if he wants more milk, more toast, etc.

'I'll call you today.' Stuart says as he opens the door.

I say, 'I don't think I'll be home today.'

'All right,' he says. 'Sure.'

I dress carefully. I try on a hat and look at myself in the mirror. I write out a note for Dean.

Honey, Mommy has things to do this afternoon, but will be back later. You stay in or be in the backyard until one of us comes home.
Love, Mommy

I look at the word *Love* and then I underline it. Then I see the word *backyard*. Is it one word or two?

I drive through farm country, through fields of oats and sugar beets and past apple orchards, cattle grazing in pastures. Then everything changes, more like shacks than farmhouses and stands of timber instead of orchards. Then mountains, and on the right, far below, I sometimes see the Naches River.

A green pickup comes up behind me and stays behind me for miles. I keep slowing at the wrong times, hoping he will pass. Then I speed up. But this is at the wrong times, too. I grip the wheel until my fingers hurt.

On a long clear stretch he goes past. But he drives along beside for a bit, a crewcut man in a blue workshirt. We look each other over. Then he waves, toots his horn, and pulls on up ahead.

I slow down and find a place. I pull over and shut off the motor. I can hear the river down below the trees. Then I hear the pickup coming back.

I lock the doors and roll up the windows.

'You all right?' the man says. He raps on the glass. 'You okay?' He leans his arms on the door and brings his face to the window.

I stare at him. I can't think what else to do.

'Is everything all right in there? How come you're all locked up?'

I shake my head.

'Roll down your window,' He shakes his head and looks at the highway and then back at me. 'Roll it down now.'

'Please,' I say, 'I have to go.'

'Open the door,' he says as if he isn't listening. 'You're going to choke in there.'

He looks at my breasts, my legs. I can tell that's what he's doing.

'Hey, sugar,' he says. 'I'm just here to help is all.'

*

The casket is closed and covered with floral sprays. The organ starts up the minute I take a seat. People are coming in and finding chairs. There's a boy in flared pants and a yellow short-sleeved shirt. A door opens and the family comes in in a group and moves over to a curtained place off to one side. Chairs creak as everybody gets settled. Directly, a nice blond man in a nice dark suit stands and asks us to bow our heads. He says a prayer for us, the living, and when he finishes, he says a prayer for the soul of the departed.

Along with the others I go past the casket. Then I move out onto the front steps and into the afternoon light. There's a woman who limps as she goes down the stairs ahead of me. On the sidewalk she looks around. 'Well, they got him,' she says. 'If that's any consolation. They arrested him this morning. I heard it on the radio before I come. A boy right here in town.'

We move a few steps down the hot sidewalk. People are starting cars. I put out my hand and hold on to a parking meter. Polished hoods and polished fenders. My head swims.

I say, 'They have friends, these killers. You can't tell.'

'I have known that child since she was a little girl,' the woman says. 'She used to come over and I'd bake cookies for her and let her eat them in front of the TV.'

Back home, Stuart sits at the table with a drink of whiskey in front of him. For a crazy instant I think something's happened to Dean.

'Where is he?' I say. 'Where is Dean?'

'Outside,' my husband says.

He drains his glass and stands up. He says, 'I think I know what you need.'

He reaches an arm around my waist and with his other hand he begins to unbutton my jacket and then he goes on to the buttons of my blouse.

'First things first,' he says.

He says something else. But I don't need to listen. I can't hear a thing with so much water going.

'That's right,' I say, finishing the buttons myself. 'Before Dean comes. Hurry.'

The third thing
that killed my father off

I'll tell you what did my father in. The third thing was Dummy, that Dummy died. The first thing was Pearl Harbor. And the second thing was moving to my grandfather's farm near Wenatchee. That's where my father finished out his days, except they were probably finished before that.

My father blamed Dummy's death on Dummy's wife. Then he blamed it on the fish. And finally he blamed himself – because he was the one that showed Dummy the ad in the back of *Field and Stream* for live black bass shipped anywhere in the U.S.

It was after he got the fish that Dummy started acting peculiar. The fish changed Dummy's whole personality. That's what my father said.

I never knew Dummy's real name. If anyone did, I never heard it. Dummy it was then, and it's Dummy I remember him by now. He was a little wrinkled man, bald-headed, short but very powerful in the arms and legs. If he grinned, which was seldom, his lips folded back over brown, broken teeth. It gave him a crafty expression. His watery eyes stayed fastened on your mouth when you were talking – and if you weren't, they'd go to someplace queer on your body.

I don't think he was really deaf. At least not as deaf as he made out. But he sure couldn't talk, That was for certain.

Deaf or no, Dummy'd been on as a common laborer out at the sawmill since the 1920s. This was the Cascade Lumber Company in Yakima, Washington. The years I knew him, Dummy was working as a cleanup man. And all those years I never saw him with anything different on. Meaning a felt hat, a khaki workshirt, a denim jacket over a pair of coveralls. In his top pockets he carried rolls of toilet paper, as one of his jobs was to clean and supply the toilets. It kept him busy, seeing as how the men on nights used to walk off after their tours with a roll or two in their lunchboxes.

Dummy carried a flashlight, even though he worked days. He also carried wrenches, pliers, screwdrivers, friction tape, all the same things the millwrights carried. Well, it made them kid Dummy, the way he was, always carrying everything. Carl Lowe, Ted Slade,

Johnny Wait, they were the worst kidders of the ones that kidded Dummy. But Dummy took it all in stride. I think he'd gotten used to it.

My father never kidded Dummy. Not to my knowledge, anyway. Dad was a big, heavy-shouldered man with a crew-haircut, double chin, and a belly of real size. Dummy was always staring at that belly. He'd come to the filing room where my father worked, and he'd sit on a stool and watch my dad's belly while he used the big emery wheels on the saws.

Dummy had a house as good as anyone's.

It was a tarpaper-covered affair near the river, five or six miles from town. Half a mile behind the house, at the end of a pasture, there lay a big gravel pit that the state had dug when they were paving the roads around there. Three good-sized holes had been scooped out, and over the years they'd filled with water. By and by, the three ponds came together to make one.

It was deep. It had a darkish look to it.

Dummy had a wife as well as a house. She was a woman years younger and said to go around with Mexicans. Father said it was busybodies that said that, men like Lowe and Wait and Slade.

She was a small stout woman with glittery little eyes. The first time I saw her, I saw those eyes. It was when I was with Pete Jensen and we were on our bicycles and we stopped at Dummy's to get a glass of water.

When she opened the door, I told her I was Del Fraser's son. I said, 'He works with —' And then I realized. 'You know, your husband. We were on our bicycles and thought we could get a drink.'

'Wait here,' she said.

She came back with a little tin cup of water in each hand. I downed mine in a single gulp.

But she didn't offer us more. She watched us without saying anything. When we started to get on our bicycles, she came over to the edge of the porch.

'You little fellas had a car now, I might catch a ride with you.'

She grinned. Her teeth looked too big for her mouth.

'Let's go,' Pete said, and we went.

There weren't many places you could fish for bass in our part of the state. There was rainbow mostly, a few brook and Dolly Varden in some of the high mountain streams, and silvers in Blue Lake and Lake Rimrock. That was mostly it, except for the runs of steelhead and salmon in some of the freshwater rivers in late fall. But if you were a fisherman, it was enough to keep you busy. No one fished for bass. A lot of people I knew had never seen a bass except for pictures. But my father had seen plenty of them when he was growing up in Arkansas and Georgia, and he had high hopes to do with Dummy's bass, Dummy being a friend.

The day the fish arrived, I'd gone swimming at the city pool. I remember coming home and going out again to get them since Dad was going to give Dummy a hand – three tanks Parcel Post from Baton Rouge, Louisiana.

We went in Dummy's pickup, Dad and Dummy and me.

These tanks turned out to be barrels, really, the three of them crated in pine lath. They were standing in the shade out back of the train depot, and it took my dad and Dummy both to lift each crate into the truck.

Dummy drove very carefully through town and just as carefully all the way to his house. He went right through his yard without stopping. He went on down to within feet of the pond. By that time it was nearly dark, so he kept his headlights on and took out a hammer and a tire iron from under the seat, and then the two of them lugged the crates up close to the water and started tearing open the first one.

The barrel inside was wrapped in burlap, and there were these nickel-sized holes in the lid. They raised it off and Dummy aimed his flashlight in.

It looked like a million bass fingerlings were finning inside. It was the strangest sight, all those live things busy in there, like a little ocean that had come on the train.

Dummy scooted the barrel to the edge of the water and poured it out. He took his flashlight and shined it into the pond. But there was nothing to be seen anymore. You could hear the frogs going, but you could hear them going anytime it newly got dark.

'Let me get the other crates,' my father said, and he reached over as if to take the hammer from Dummy's coveralls. But Dummy pulled back and shook his head.

He undid the other two crates himself, leaving dark drops of blood on the lath where he ripped his hand doing it.

From that night on, Dummy was different.

Dummy wouldn't let anyone come around now anymore. He put up fencing all around the pasture, and then he fenced off the pond with electrical barbed wire. They said it cost him all his savings for that fence.

Of course, my father wouldn't have anything to do with Dummy after that. Not since Dummy ran him off. Not from fishing, mind you, because the bass were just babies still. But even from trying to get a look.

One evening two years after, when Dad was working late and I took him his food and a jar of iced tea, I found him standing talking with Syd Glover, the millwright. Just as I came in, I heard Dad saying, 'You'd reckon the fool was married to them fish, the way he acts.'

'From what I hear,' Syd said, 'he'd do better to put that fence round his house.'

My father saw me then, and I saw him signal Syd Glover with his eyes.

But a month later my dad finally made Dummy do it. What he did was, he told Dummy how you had to thin out the weak ones on account of keeping things fit for the rest of them. Dummy stood there pulling at his ear and staring at the floor. Dad said, Yeah, he'd be down to do it tomorrow because it had to be done. Dummy never said yes, actually. He just never said no, is all. All he did was pull on his ear some more.

When Dad got home that day, I was ready and waiting. I had his old bass plugs out and was testing the treble hooks with my finger.

'You set?' he called to me, jumping out of the car. 'I'll go to the toilet, you put the stuff in. You can drive us out there if you want.'

I'd stowed everything in the back seat and was trying out the wheel when he came back out wearing his fishing hat and eating a wedge of cake with both hands.

Mother was standing in the door watching. She was a fair-skinned woman, her blonde hair pulled back in a tight bun and fastened down with a rhinestone clip. I wonder if she ever went around back in those happy days, or what she ever really did.

I let out the handbrake. Mother watched until I'd shifted gears, and then, still unsmiling, she went back inside.

It was a fine afternoon. We had all the windows down to let the air in. We crossed the Moxee Bridge and swung west onto Slater Road. Alfalfa fields stood off to either side, and farther on it was cornfields.

Dad had his hand out the window. He was letting the wind carry it back. He was restless, I could see.

It wasn't long before we pulled up at Dummy's. He came out of the house wearing his hat. His wife was looking out the window.

'You got your frying pan ready?' Dad hollered out to Dummy, but Dummy just stood there eyeing the car. 'Hey, Dummy!' Dad yelled. 'Hey, Dummy, where's your pole, Dummy?'

Dummy jerked his head back and forth. He moved his weight from one leg to the other and looked at the ground and then at us. His tongue rested on his lower lip, and he began working his foot into the dirt.

I shouldered the creel. I handed Dad his pole and picked up my own.

'We set to go?' Dad said. 'Hey, Dummy, we set to go?'

Dummy took off his hat and, with the same hand, he wiped his wrist over his head. He turned abruptly, and we followed him across the spongy pasture. Every twenty feet or so a snipe sprang up from the clumps of grass at the edge of the old furrows.

At the end of the pasture, the ground sloped gently and became dry and rocky, nettle bushes and scub oaks scattered here and there. We cut to the right, following an old set of car tracks, going through a field of milkweed that came up to our waists, the dry pods at the tops of the stalks rattling angrily as we pushed through. Presently, I saw the sheen of water over Dummy's shoulder, and I heard Dad shout, 'Oh, Lord, look at that!'

But Dummy slowed down and kept bringing his hand up and moving his hat back and forth over his head, and then he just stopped flat.

Dad said, 'Well, what do you think, Dummy? One place good as another? Where do you say we should come onto it?'

Dummy wet his lower lip.

'What's the matter with you, Dummy?' Dad said. 'This your pond, ain't it?'

Dummy looked down and picked an ant off his coveralls.

'Well, hell,' Dad said, letting out his breath. He took out his watch. 'If it's still all right with you, we'll get to it before it gets too dark.'

Dummy stuck his hands in his pockets and turned back to the pond. He started walking again. We trailed along behind. We could see the whole pond now, the water dimpled with rising fish. Every so often a bass would leap clear and come down in a splash.

'Great God,' I heard my father say.

We came up to the pond at an open place, a gravel beach kind of.

Dad motioned to me and dropped into a crouch. I dropped too. He was peering into the water in front of us, and when I looked, I saw what had taken him so.

'Honest to God,' he whispered.

A school of bass was cruising, twenty, thirty, not one of them under two pounds. They veered off, and then they shifted and came back, so densely spaced they looked like they were bumping up against each other. I could see their big, heavy-lidded eyes watching us as they went by. They flashed away again, and again they came back.

They were asking for it. It didn't make any difference if we stayed squatted or stood up. The fish just didn't think a thing about us. I tell you, it was a sight to behold.

We sat there for quite a while, watching that school of bass go so innocently about their business, Dummy the whole time pulling at his fingers and looking around as if he expected someone to show up. All over the pond the bass were coming up to nuzzle the water, or jumping clear and falling back, or coming up to the surface to swim along with their dorsals sticking out.

Dad signaled, and we got up to cast. I tell you, I was shaky with excitement. I could hardly get the plug loose from the cork handle of my pole. It was while I was trying to get the hooks out that I felt Dummy seize my shoulder with his big fingers. I looked, and in answer Dummy worked his chin in Dad's direction. What he wanted was clear enough, no more than one pole.

Dad took off his hat and then put it back on and then he moved over to where I stood.

'You go on, Jack,' he said. 'That's all right, son – you do it now.'

I looked at Dummy just before I laid out my cast. His face had gone rigid, and there was a thin line of drool on his chin.

'Come back stout on the sucker when he strikes,' Dad said. 'Sons of bitches got mouths hard as doorknobs.'

I flipped off the drag lever and threw back my arm. I sent her out a good forty feet. The water was boiling even before I had time to take up the slack.

'Hit him!' Dad yelled. 'Hit the son of a bitch! Hit him good!'

I came back hard, twice. I had him, all right. The rod bowed over and jerked back and forth. Dad kept yelling what to do.

'Let him go, let him go! Let him run! Give him more line! Now wind in! Wind in! No, let him run! Woo-ee! Will you look at that!'

The bass danced around the pond. Every time it came up out of the water, it shook its head so hard you could hear the plug rattle. And then he'd take off again. But by and by I wore him out and had him in up close. He looked enormous, six or seven pounds maybe. He lay on his side, whipped, mouth open, gills working. My knees felt so weak I could hardly stand. But I held the rod up, the line tight.

Dad waded out over his shoes. But when he reached for the fish, Dummy started sputtering, shaking his head, waving his arms.

'Now what the hell's the matter with you, Dummy? The boy's got hold of the biggest bass I ever seen, and he ain't going to throw him back, by God!'

Dummy kept carrying on and gesturing toward the pond.

'I ain't about to let this boy's fish go. You hear me, Dummy? You got another think coming if you think I'm going to do that.'

Dummy reached for my line. Meanwhile, the bass had gained some strength back. He turned himself over and started swimming again. I yelled and then I lost my head and slammed down the brake on the reel and started winding. The bass made a last, furious run.

That was that. The line broke. I almost fell over on my back.

'Come on, Jack,' Dad said, and I saw him grabbing up his pole. 'Come on, goddamn the fool, before I knock the man down.'

That February the river flooded.

It had snowed pretty heavy the first weeks of December, and turned real cold before Christmas. The ground froze. The snow stayed where it was. But toward the end of January, the Chinook wind struck. I woke up one morning to hear the house getting buffeted and the steady drizzle of water running off the roof.

It blew for five days, and on the third day the river began to rise.

'She's up to fifteen feet,' my father said one evening, looking over his newspaper. 'Which is three feet over what you need to flood. Old Dummy going to lose his darlings.'

I wanted to go down to the Moxee Bridge to see how high the water was running. But my dad wouldn't let me. He said a flood was nothing to see.

Two days later the river crested, and after that the water began to subside.

Orin Marshall and Danny Owens and I bicycled out to Dummy's one morning a week after. We parked our bicycles and walked across the pasture that bordered Dummy's property.

It was a wet, blustery day, the clouds dark and broken, moving fast across the sky. The ground was soppy wet and we kept coming to puddles in the thick grass. Danny was just learning how to cuss, and he filled the air with the best he had every time he stepped in over his shoes. We could see the swollen river at the end of the pasture. The water was still high and out of its channel, surging around the trunks of trees and eating away at the edge of the land. Out toward the middle, the current moved heavy and swift, and now and then a bush floated by, or a tree with its branches sticking up.

We came to Dummy's fence and found a cow wedged in up against the wire. She was bloated and her skin was shiny-looking and gray. It was the first dead thing of any size I'd ever seen. I remember Orin took a stick and touched the open eyes.

We moved on down the fence, toward the river. We were afraid to go near the wire because we thought it might still have electricity in it. But at the edge of what looked like a deep canal, the fence came to an end. The ground had simply dropped into the water here, and the fence along with it.

We crossed over and followed the new channel that cut directly into Dummy's land and headed straight for his pond, going into it length-wise and forcing an outlet for itself at the other end, then twisting off until it joined up with the river farther on.

You didn't doubt that most of Dummy's fish had been carried off. But those that hadn't been were free to come and go.

Then I caught sight of Dummy. It scared me, seeing him. I motioned to the other fellows, and we all got down.

Dummy was standing at the far side of the pond near where the water was rushing out. He was just standing there, the saddest man I ever saw.

'I sure do feel sorry for old Dummy, though,' my father said at supper a few weeks after. 'Mind, the poor devil brought it on himself. But you can't help but be troubled for him.'

Dad went on to say George Laycock saw Dummy's wife sitting in the Sportsman's Club with a big Mexican fellow.

'And that ain't the half of it —'

Mother looked up at him sharply and then at me. But I just went on eating like I hadn't heard a thing.

Dad said, 'Damn it to hell, Bea, the boy's old enough!'

He'd changed a lot, Dummy had. He was never around any of the men anymore, not if he could help it. No one felt like joking with him either, not since he'd chased Carl Lowe with a two-by-four stud after Carl tipped Dummy's hat off. But the worst of it was that Dummy was missing from work a day or two a week on the average now, and there was some talk of his being laid off.

'The man's going off the deep end,' Dad said. 'Clear crazy if he don't watch out.'

Then on a Sunday afternoon just before my birthday, Dad and I were cleaning the garage. It was a warm, drifty day. You could see the dust hanging in the air. Mother came to the back door and said, 'Del, it's for you. I think it's Vern.'

I followed Dad in to wash up. When he was through talking, he put the phone down and turned to us.

'It's Dummy,' he said. 'Did in his wife with a hammer and drowned himself. Vern just heard it in town.'

When we got out there, cars were parked all around. The gate to the pasture stood open, and I could see tire marks that led on to the pond.

The screen door was propped ajar with a box, and there was this lean, pock-faced man in slacks and sports shirt and wearing a shoulder holster. He watched Dad and me get out of the car.

'I was his friend,' Dad said to the man.

The man shook his head. 'Don't care who you are. Clear off unless you got business here.'

'Did they find him?' Dad said.

'They're dragging,' the man said, and adjusted the fit of his gun.

'All right if we walk down? I knew him pretty well.'

The man said, 'Take your chances. They chase you off, don't say you wasn't warned.'

We went on across the pasture, taking pretty much the same route we had the day we tried fishing. There were motorboats going on the pond, dirty fluffs of exhaust hanging over it. You could see where the high water had cut away the ground and carried off trees and rocks. The two boats had uniformed men in them, and they were going back and forth, one man steering and the other man handling the rope and hooks.

An ambulance waited on the gravel beach where we'd set ourselves to cast for Dummy's bass. Two men in white lounged against the back, smoking cigarettes.

One of the motorboats cut off. We all looked up. The man in back stood up and started heaving on his rope. After a time, an arm came out of the water. It looked like the hooks had gotten Dummy in the side. The arm went back down and then it came out again, along with a bundle of something.

It's not him, I thought. It's something else that has been in there for years.

The man in the front of the boat moved to the back, and together the two men hauled the dripping thing over the side.

I looked at Dad. His face was funny the way it was set.

'Women,' he said. He said, 'That's what the wrong kind of woman can do to you, Jack.'

But I don't think Dad really believed it. I think he just didn't know who to blame or what to say.

It seemed to me everything took a bad turn for my father after that. Just like Dummy, he wasn't the same man anymore. That arm coming up and going back down in the water, it was like so long to good times and hello to bad. Because it was nothing but that all the years after Dummy drowned himself in that dark water.

Is that what happens when a friend dies? Bad luck for the pals he left behind?

But as I said, Pearl Harbor and having to move back to his dad's place didn't do my dad one bit of good, either.

A serious talk

Vera's car was there, no others, and Burt gave thanks for that. He pulled into the drive and stopped beside the pie he'd dropped the night before. It was still there, the aluminum pan upside down, a halo of pumpkin filling on the pavement. It was the day after Christmas.

He'd come on Christmas day to visit his wife and children. Vera had warned him beforehand. She'd told him the score. She'd said he had to be out by six o'clock because her friend and his children were coming for dinner.

They had sat in the living room and solemnly opened the presents Burt had brought over. They had opened his packages while other packages wrapped in festive paper lay piled under the tree waiting for after six o'clock.

He had watched the children open their gifts, waited while Vera undid the ribbon on hers. He saw her slip off the paper, lift the lid, take out the cashmere sweater.

'It's nice,' she said. 'Thank you, Burt.'

'Try it on,' his daughter said.

'Put it on,' his son said.

Burt looked at his son, grateful for his backing him up.

She did try it on. Vera went into the bedroom and came out with it on.

'It's nice,' she said.

'It's nice on *you*,' Burt said, and felt a welling in his chest.

He opened his gifts. From Vera, a gift certificate at Sondheim's men's store. From his daughter, a matching comb and brush. From his son, a ballpoint pen.

Vera served sodas, and they did a little talking. But mostly they looked at the tree. Then his daughter got up and began setting the dining-room table, and his son went off to his room.

But Burt liked it where he was. He liked it in front of the fireplace, a glass in his hand, his house, his home.

Then Vera went into the kitchen.

From time to time his daughter walked into the dining room with something for the table. Burt watched her. He watched her fold the linen napkins into the wine glasses. He watched her put a slender vase in the middle of the table. He watched her lower a flower into the vase, doing it ever so carefully.

A small wax and sawdust log burned on the grate. A carton of five more sat ready on the hearth. He got up from the sofa and put them all in the fireplace. He watched until they flamed. Then he finished his soda and made for the patio door. On the way, he saw the pies lined up on the sideboard. He stacked them in his arms, all six, one for every ten times she had ever betrayed him.

In the driveway in the dark, he'd let one fall as he fumbled with the door.

The front door was permanently locked since the night his key had broken off inside it. He went around to the back. There was a wreath on the patio door. He rapped on the glass. Vera was in her bathrobe. She looked out at him and frowned. She opened the door a little.

Burt said, 'I want to apologize to you for last night. I want to apologize to the kids, too.'

Vera said, 'They're not here.'

She stood in the doorway and he stood on the patio next to the philodendron plant. He pulled at some lint on his sleeve.

She said, 'I can't take any more. You tried to burn the house down.'

'I did not.'

'You did. Everybody here was a witness.'

He said, 'Can I come in and talk about it?'

She drew the robe together at her throat and moved back inside.

She said, 'I have to go somewhere in an hour.'

He looked around. The tree blinked on and off. There was a pile of colored tissue paper and shiny boxes at one end of the sofa. A turkey carcass sat on a platter in the center of the dining-room table, the leathery remains in a bed of parsley as if in a horrible nest. A cone of ash filled the fireplace. There were some empty Shasta cola cans in there too. A trail of smoke stains rose up the bricks to the mantel, where the wood that stopped them was scorched black.

He turned around and went back to the kitchen.

He said, 'What time did your friend leave last night?'

She said, 'If you're going to start that, you can go right now.'

He pulled a chair out and sat down at the kitchen table in front of the big ashtray. He closed his eyes and opened them. He moved the curtain aside and looked out at the backyard. He saw a bicycle without a front wheel standing upside down. He saw weeds growing along the redwood fence.

She ran water into a saucepan. 'Do you remember Thanksgiving?' she said. 'I said then that was the last holiday you were going to wreck for us. Eating bacon and eggs instead of turkey at ten o'clock at night.'

'I know it,' he said. 'I said I'm sorry.'

'Sorry isn't good enough.'

The pilot light was out again. She was at the stove trying to get the gas going under the pan of water.

'Don't burn yourself,' he said. 'Don't catch yourself on fire.'

He considered her robe catching fire, him jumping up from the table, throwing her down onto the floor and rolling her over and over into the living room, where he would cover her with his body. Or should he run to the bedroom for a blanket?'

'Vera?'

She looked at him.

'Do you have anything to drink? I could use a drink this morning.'

'There's some vodka in the freezer.'

'When did you start keeping vodka in the freezer?'

'Don't ask.'

'Okay,' he said, 'I won't ask.'

He got out the vodka and poured some into a cup he found on the counter.

She said, 'Are you just going to drink it like that, out of a cup?' She said. 'Jesus, Burt. What'd you want to talk about, anyway? I told you I have someplace to go. I have a flute lesson at one o'clock.'

'Are you still taking flute?'

'I just said so. What is it? Tell me what's on your mind, and then I have to get ready.'

'I wanted to say I was sorry.'

She said, 'You said that.'

He said, 'If you have any juice, I'll mix it with this vodka.'

She opened the refrigerator and moved things around.

'There's cranapple juice,' she said.

'That's fine,' he said.

'I'm going to the bathroom,' she said.

He drank the cup of cranapple juice and vodka. He lit a cigarette and tossed the match into the big ashtray that always sat on the kitchen table. He studied the butts in it. Some of them were Vera's brand, and some of them weren't. Some even were lavender-colored.

He got up and dumped it all under the sink.

The ashtray was not really an ashtray. It was a big dish of stone-ware they'd bought from a bearded potter on the mall in Santa Clara. He rinsed it out and dried it. He put it back on the table. And then he ground out his cigarette in it.

The water on the stove began to bubble just as the phone began to ring.

He heard her open the bathroom door and call to him through the living room. 'Answer that! I'm about to get into the shower.'

The kitchen phone was on the counter in a corner behind the roasting pan. He moved the roasting pan and picked up the receiver.

'Is Charlie there?' the voice said.

'No,' Burt said.

'Okay,' the voice said.

While he was seeing to the coffee, the phone rang again.

'Charlie?'

'Not here,' Burt said.

This time he left the receiver off the hook.

Vera came back into the kitchen wearing jeans and a sweater and brushing her hair.

He spooned the instant into the cups of hot water and then spilled some vodka into his. He carried the cups over to the table.

She picked up the receiver, listened. She said, 'What's this? Who was on the phone?'

'Nobody,' he said. 'Who smokes colored cigarettes?'

'I do.'

'I didn't know you did that.'

'Well, I do.'

She sat across from him and drank her coffee. They smoked and used the ashtray.

There were things he wanted to say, grieving things, consoling things, things like that.

'I'm smoking three packs a day,' Vera said. 'I mean, if you really want to know what goes on around here.'

'God almighty,' Burt said.

Vera nodded.

'I didn't come over here to hear that,' he said.

'What did you come over here to hear, then? You want to hear the house burned down?'

'Vera,' he said. 'It's Christmas. That's why I came.'

'It's the day after Christmas,' she said. 'Christmas has come and gone,' she said. 'I don't ever want to see another one.'

'What about me?' he said. 'You think I look forward to holidays?'

The phone rang again. Burt picked it up.

'It's someone wanting Charlie,' he said.

'What?'

'Charlie,' Burt said.

Vera took the phone. She kept her back to him as she talked. Then she turned to him and said, 'I'll take this call in the bedroom. So would you please hang up after I've picked it up in there? I can tell, so hang it up when I say.'

He took the receiver. She left the kitchen. He held the receiver to his ear and listened. He heard nothing. Then he heard a man clear his throat. Then he heard Vera pick up the other phone. She shouted. 'Okay, Burt! I have it now, Burt!'

He put down the receiver and stood looking at it. He opened the silverware drawer and pushed things around inside. He opened another drawer. He looked in the sink. He went into the dining room and got the carving knife. He held it under hot water until the grease broke and ran off. He wiped the blade on his sleeve. He moved to the phone, doubled the cord, and sawed through without any trouble at all. He examined the ends of the cord. Then he shoved the phone back into its corner behind the roasting pan.

She came in. She said, 'The phone went dead. Did you do anything to the telephone?' She looked at the phone and then picked it up from the counter.

'Son of a bitch!' she screamed. She screamed, 'Out, out, where you belong!' She was shaking the phone at him. 'That's it! I'm going to get a restraining order, that's what I'm going to get!'

The phone made a *ding* when she banged it down on the counter.

'I'm going next door to call the police if you don't get out of here now!'

He picked up the ashtray. He held it by its edge. He posed with it like a man preparing to hurl the discus.

'Please,' she said. 'That's our ashtray.'

He left through the patio door. He was not certain, but he thought

he had proved something. He hoped he had made something clear.
The thing was, they had to have a serious talk soon. There were things
that needed talking about, important things that had to be discussed.
They'd talk again. Maybe after the holidays were over and things got
back to normal. He'd tell her the goddamn ashtray was a goddamn
dish, for example.

He stepped around the pie in the driveway and got back into his
car. He started the car and put it into reverse. It was hard managing
until he put the ashtray down.

The calm

I was getting a haircut. I was in the chair and three men were sitting along the wall across from me. Two of the men waiting I'd never seen before. But one of them I recognized, though I couldn't exactly place him. I kept looking at him as the barber worked on my hair. The man was moving a toothpick around in his mouth, a heavyset man, short wavy hair. And then I saw him in a cap and uniform, little eyes watchful in the lobby of a bank.

Of the other two, one was considerably the older, with a full head of curly gray hair. He was smoking. The third, though not so old, was nearly bald on top, but the hair at the sides hung over his ears. He had on logging boots, pants shiny with machine oil.

The barber put a hand on top of my head to turn me for a better look. Then he said to the guard, 'Did you get your deer, Charles?'

I liked this barber. We weren't acquainted well enough to call each other by name. But when I came in for a haircut, he knew me. He knew I used to fish. So we'd talk fishing. I don't think he hunted. But he could talk on any subject. In this regard, he was a good barber.

'Bill, it's a funny story. The damnedest thing,' the guard said. He took out the toothpick and laid it in the ashtray. He shook his head. 'I did and I didn't. So yes and no to your question.'

I didn't like the man's voice. For a guard, the voice didn't fit. It wasn't the voice you'd expect.

The two other men looked up. The older man was turning the pages of a magazine, smoking, and the other fellow was holding a newspaper. They put down what they were looking at and turned to listen to the guard.

'Go on, Charles,' the barber said. 'Let's hear it.'

The barber turned my head again, and went back to work with his clippers.

'We were up on Fikle Ridge. My old man and me and the kid. We were hunting those draws. My old man was stationed at the head of one, and me and the kid were at the head of another. The kid had a hangover, goddamn his hide. The kid, he was green around the gills and drank water all day, mine and his both. It was in the afternoon and we'd been out since daybreak. But we had our hopes. We figured the hunters down below would move a deer in our direction. So we were sitting behind a log and watching the draw when we heard this shooting down in the valley.'

'There's orchards down there,' said the fellow with the newspaper. He was fidgeting a lot and kept crossing a leg, swinging his boot for a time, and then crossing his legs the other way. 'Those deer hang out around those orchards.'

'That's right,' said the guard. 'They'll go in there at night, the bastards, and eat those little green apples. Well, we heard this shooting and we're just sitting there on our hands when this big old buck comes up out of the underbrush not a hundred feet away. The kid sees him the same time I do, of course, and he throws down and starts banging. The knothead. That old buck wasn't in any danger. Not from the kid, as it turns out. But he can't tell where the shots are coming from. He doesn't know which way to jump. Then I get off a shot. But in all the commotion, I just stun him.'

'Stunned him?' the barber said.

'You know, stun him,' the guard said. 'It was a gut shot. It just like stuns him. So he drops his head and begins this trembling. He trembles all over. The kid's still shooting. Me, I felt like I was back in Korea. So I shot again but missed. Then old Mr Buck moves back into the brush. But now, by God, he doesn't have any oompf left in him. The kid has emptied his goddamn gun all to no purpose. But I hit solid. I'd rammed one right in his guts. That's what I meant by stunned him.'

'Then what?' said the fellow with the newspaper, who had rolled it and was tapping it against his knee. 'Then what? You must have trailed him. They find a hard place to die every time.'

'But you trailed him?' the older man asked, though it wasn't really a question.

'I did. Me and the kid, we trailed him. But the kid wasn't good for much. He gets sick on the trail, slows us down. That chucklehead.' The guard had to laugh now, thinking about that situation. 'Drinking beer and chasing all night, then saying he can hunt deer. He knows better now, by God. But, sure, we trailed him. A good trail, too. Blood on the ground and blood on the leaves. Blood everywhere. Never seen a buck with so much blood. I don't know how the sucker kept going.'

'Sometimes they'll go forever,' the fellow with the newspaper said. 'They find them a hard place to die every time.'

'I chewed the kid out for missing his shot, and when he smarted off at me, I cuffed him a good one. Right here.' The guard pointed to the side of his head and grinned. 'I boxed his goddamn ears for him, that goddamn kid. He's not too old. He needed it. So the point is, it got too dark to trail, what with the kid laying back to vomit and all.'

'Well, the coyotes will have that deer by now,' the fellow with the newspaper said. 'Them and the crows and the buzzards.'

He unrolled the newspaper, smoothed it all the way out, and put it off to one side. He crossed a leg again. He looked around at the rest of us and shook his head.

The older man had turned in his chair and was looking out the window. He lit a cigarette.

'I figure so,' the guard said. 'Pity too. He was a big old son of a bitch. So in answer to your question, Bill, I both got my deer and I didn't. But we had venison on the table anyway. Because it turns out the old man has got himself a little spike in the meantime. Already has him back to camp, hanging up and gutted slick as a whistle, liver, heart, and kidneys wrapped in waxed paper and already setting in the cooler. A spike. Just a little bastard. But the old man, he was tickled.'

The guard looked around the shop as if remembering. Then he picked up his toothpick and stuck it back in his mouth.

The older man put his cigarette out and turned to the guard. He drew a breath and said, 'You ought to be out there right now looking for that deer instead of in here getting a haircut.'

'You can't talk like that,' the guard said. 'You old fart. I've seen you someplace.'

'I've seen you too,' the old fellow said.

'Boys, that's enough. This is my barbershop,' the barber said.

'I ought to box *your* ears,' the old fellow said.

'You ought to try it,' the guard said.

'Charles,' the barber said.

The barber put his comb and scissors on the counter and his hands on my shoulders, as if he thought I was thinking to spring from the chair into the middle of it. 'Albert, I've been cutting Charles's head of hair, and his boy's too, for years now. I wish you wouldn't pursue this.'

The barber looked from one man to the other and kept his hands on my shoulders.

'Take it outside,' the fellow with the newspaper said, flushed and hoping for something.

'That'll be enough,' the barber said. 'Charles, I don't want to hear anything more on the subject. Albert, you're next in line. Now.' The barber turned to the fellow with the newspaper. 'I don't know you from Adam, mister, but I'd appreciate if you wouldn't put your oar in.'

The guard got up. He said, 'I think I'll come back for my cut later. Right now the company leaves something to be desired.'

The guard went out and pulled the door closed, hard.

The old fellow sat smoking his cigarette. He looked out the window. He examined something on the back of his hand. He got up and put on his hat.

'I'm sorry, Bill,' the old fellow said. 'I can go a few more days.'

'That's all right, Albert,' the barber said.

When the old fellow went out, the barber stepped over to the window to watch him go.

'Albert's about dead from emphysema,' the barber said from the window. 'We used to fish together. He taught me salmon inside out. The women. They used to crawl all over that old boy. He's picked up a temper, though. But in all honesty, there was provocation.'

The man with the newspaper couldn't sit still. He was on his feet and moving around, stopping to examine everything, the hat rack, the photos of Bill and his friends, the calendar from the hardware showing scenes for each month of the year. He flipped every page. He even went so far as to stand and scrutinize Bill's barbering license, which was up on the wall in a frame. Then he turned and said, 'I'm going too,' and out he went just like he said.

'Well, do you want me to finish barbering this hair or not?' the barber said to me as if I was the cause of everything.

The barber turned me in the chair to face the mirror. He put a hand to either side of my head. He positioned me a last time, and then he brought his head down next to mine.

We looked into the mirror together, his hands still framing my head.

I was looking at myself, and he was looking at me too. But if the barber saw something, he didn't offer comment.

He ran his fingers through my hair. He did it slowly, as if thinking about something else. He ran his fingers through my hair. He did it tenderly, as a lover would.

That was in Crescent City, California, up near the Oregon border. I left soon after. But today I was thinking of that place, of Crescent City, and of how I was trying out a new life there with my wife, and how, in the barber's chair that morning, I had made up my mind to go. I was thinking today about the calm I felt when I closed my eyes and let the barber's fingers move through my hair, the sweetness of those fingers, the hair already starting to grow.

Popular mechanics

Early that day the weather turned and the snow was melting into dirty water. Streaks of it ran down from the little shoulder-high window that faced the backyard. Cars slushed by on the street outside, where it was getting dark. But it was getting dark on the inside too.

He was in the bedroom pushing clothes into a suitcase when she came to the door.

I'm glad you're leaving! I'm glad you're leaving! she said. Do you hear?

He kept on putting his things into the suitcase.

Son of a bitch! I'm so glad you're leaving! She began to cry. You can't even look me in the face, can you?'

Then she noticed the baby's picture on the bed and picked it up.

He looked at her and she wiped her eyes and stared at him before turning and going back to the living room.

Bring that back, he said.

Just get your things and get out, she said.

He did not answer. He fastened the suitcase, put on his coat, looked around the bedroom before turning off the light. Then he went out to the living room.

She stood in the doorway of the little kitchen, holding the baby.

I want the baby, he said.

Are you crazy?

No, but I want the baby. I'll get someone to come by for his things.

You're not touching this baby, she said.

The baby had begun to cry and she uncovered the blanket from around his head.

Oh, oh, she said, looking at the baby.

He moved toward her.

For God's sake! she said. She took a step back into the kitchen.

I want the baby.

Get out of here!

She turned and tried to hold the baby over in a corner behind the stove.

But he came up. He reached across the stove and tightened his hands on the baby.

Let go of him, he said.

Get away, get away! she cried.

The baby was red-faced and screaming. In the scuffle they knocked down a flowerpot that hung behind the stove.

He crowded her into the wall then, trying to break her grip. He held on to the baby and pushed with all his weight.

Let go of him, he said.

Don't, she said. You're hurting the baby, she said.

I'm not hurting the baby, he said.

The kitchen window gave no light. In the near-dark he worked on her fisted fingers with one hand and with the other hand he gripped the screaming baby up under an arm near the shoulder.

She felt her fingers being forced open. She felt the baby going from her.

No! she screamed just as her hands came loose.

She would have it, this baby. She grabbed for the baby's other arm. She caught the baby around the wrist and leaned back.

But he would not let go. He felt the baby slipping out of his hands and he pulled back very hard.

In this manner, the issue was decided.

Everything
stuck to him

She's in Milan for Christmas and wants to know what it was like when she was a kid.

Tell me, she says. Tell me what it was like when I was a kid. She sips Strega, waits, eyes him closely.

She is a cool, slim, attractive girl, a survivor from top to bottom.

That was a long time ago. That was twenty years ago, he says.

You can remember, she says. Go on.

What do you want to hear? he says. What else can I tell you? I could tell you about something that happened when you were a baby. It involves you, he says. But only in a minor way.

Tell me, she says. But first fix us another so you won't have to stop in the middle.

He comes back from the kitchen with drinks, settles into his chair, begins.

They were kids themselves, but they were crazy in love, this eighteen-year-old boy and this seventeen-year-old girl when they married. Not all that long afterwards they had a daughter.

The baby came along in late November during a cold spell that just happened to coincide with the peak of the waterfowl season. The boy loved to hunt, you see. That's part of it.

The boy and girl, husband and wife, father and mother, they lived in a little apartment under a dentist's office. Each night they cleaned the dentist's place upstairs in exchange for rent and utilities. In summer they were expected to maintain the lawn and the flowers. In winter the boy shoveled snow and spread rock salt on the walks. Are you still with me? Are you getting the picture?

I am, she says.

That's good, he says. So one day the dentist finds out they were using his letterhead for their personal correspondence. But that's another story.

He gets up from his chair and looks out the window. He sees the tile rooftops and the snow that is falling steadily on them.

Tell the story, she says.

The two kids were very much in love. On top of this they had great ambitions. They were always talking about the things they were going to do and the places they were going to go.

Now the boy and girl slept in the bedroom, and the baby slept in the living room. Let's say the baby was about three months old and had only just begun to sleep through the night.

On this one Saturday night after finishing his work upstairs, the boy stayed in the dentist's office and called an old hunting friend of his father's.

Carl, he said when the man picked up the receiver, believe it or not, I'm a father.

Congratulations, Carl said. How is the wife?

She's fine, Carl. Everybody's fine.

That's good, Carl said, I'm glad to hear it. But if you called about going hunting, I'll tell you something. The geese are flying to beat the band. I don't think I've ever seen so many. Got five today. Going back in the morning, so come along if you want to.

I want to, the boy said.

The boy hung up the telephone and went downstairs to tell the girl. She watched while he laid out his things. Hunting coat, shell bag, boots, socks, hunting cap, long underwear, pump gun.

What time will you be back? the girl said.

Probably around noon, the boy said. But maybe as late as six o'clock. Would that be too late?

It's fine, she said. The baby and I will get along fine. You go and have some fun. When you get back, we'll dress the baby up and go visit Sally.

The boy said, Sounds like a good idea.

Sally was the girl's sister. She was striking. I don't know if you've seen pictures of her. The boy was a little in love with Sally, just as he was a little in love with Betsy, who was another sister the girl had. The boy used to say to the girl, If we weren't married, I could go for Sally.

What about Betsy? the girl used to say. I hate to admit it, but I truly feel she's better looking than Sally and me. What about Betsy?

Betsy too, the boy used to say.

After dinner he turned up the furnace and helped her bathe the baby. He marveled again at the infant who had half his features and half the girl's. He powdered the tiny body. He powdered between fingers and toes.

He emptied the bath into the sink and went upstairs to check the air. It was overcast and cold. The grass, what there was of it, looked like canvas, stiff and gray under the street light.

Snow lay in piles beside the walk. A car went by. He heard sand under the tires. He let himself imagine what it might be like tomorrow, geese beating the air over his head, shotgun plunging against his shoulder.

Then he locked the door and went downstairs.

In bed they tried to read. But both of them fell asleep, she first, letting the magazine sink to the quilt.

It was the baby's cries that woke him up.

The light was on out there, and the girl was standing next to the crib rocking the baby in her arms. She put the baby down, turned out the light, and came back to the bed.

He heard the baby cry. This time the girl stayed where she was. The baby cried fitfully and stopped. The boy listened, then dozed. But the baby's cries woke him again. The living room light was burning. He sat up and turned on the lamp.

I don't know what's wrong, the girl said, walking back and forth with the baby. I've changed her and fed her, but she keeps on crying. I'm so tired I'm afraid I might drop her.

You come back to bed, the boy said. I'll hold her for a while.

He got up and took the baby, and the girl went to lie down again.

Just rock her for a few minutes, the girl said from the bedroom. Maybe she'll go back to sleep.

The boy sat on the sofa and held the baby. He juggled it in his lap until he got its eyes to close, his own eyes closing right along. He rose carefully and put the baby back in the crib.

It was a quarter to four, which gave him forty-five minutes. He crawled into bed and dropped off. But a few minutes later the baby was crying again, and this time they both got up.

The boy did a terrible thing. He swore.

For God's sake, what's the matter with you? the girl said to the boy. Maybe she's sick or something. Maybe we shouldn't have given her the bath.

The boy picked up the baby. The baby kicked its feet and smiled.

Look, the boy said, I really don't think there's anything wrong with her.

How do you know that? the girl said. Here, let me have her. I know

I ought to give her something, but I don't know what it's supposed to be.

The girl put the baby down again. The boy and the girl looked at the baby, and the baby began to cry.

The girl took the baby. Baby, baby, the girl said with tears in her eyes.

Probably it's something on her stomach, the boy said.

The girl didn't answer. She went on rocking the baby, paying no attention to the boy.

The boy waited. He went to the kitchen and put on water for coffee. He drew his woolen underwear on over his shorts and T-shirt, buttoned up, then got into his clothes.

What are you doing? the girl said.

Going hunting, the boy said.

I don't think you should, she said. I don't want to be left alone with her like this.

Carl's planning on me going, the boy said. We've planned it.

I don't care about what you and Carl planned, she said. And I don't care about Carl, either. I don't even know Carl.

You've met Carl before. You know him, the boy said. What do you mean you don't know him?

That's not the point and you know it, the girl said.

What is the point? the boy said. The point is we planned it.

The girl said, I'm your wife. This is your baby. She's sick or something. Look at her. Why else is she crying?

I know you're my wife, the boy said.

The girl began to cry. She put the baby back in the crib. But the baby started up again. The girl dried her eyes on the sleeve of her nightgown and picked the baby up.

The boy laced up his boots. He put on his shirt, his sweater, his coat. The kettle whistled on the stove in the kitchen.

You're going to have to choose, the girl said. Carl or us. I mean it.

What do you mean? the boy said.

You heard what I said, the girl said. If you want a family, you're going to have to choose.

They stared at each other. Then the boy took up his hunting gear and went outside. He started the car. He went around to the car windows and, making a job of it, scraped away the ice.

He turned off the motor and sat awhile. And then he got out and went back inside.

The living-room light was on. The girl was asleep on the bed. The baby was asleep beside her.

The boy took off his boots. Then he took off everything else. In his socks and his long underwear, he sat on the sofa and read the Sunday paper.

The girl and the baby slept on. After a while, the boy went to the kitchen and started frying bacon.

The girl came out in her robe and put her arms around the boy.

Hey, the boy said.

I'm sorry, the girl said.

It's all right, the boy said.

I didn't mean to snap like that.

It was my fault, he said.

You sit down, the girl said. How does a waffle sound with bacon?

Sounds great, the boy said.

She took the bacon out of the pan and made waffle batter. He sat at the table and watched her move around the kitchen.

She put a plate in front of him with bacon, a waffle. He spread butter and poured syrup. But when he started to cut, he turned the plate into his lap.

I don't believe it, he said, jumping up from the table.

If you could see yourself, the girl said.

The boy looked down at himself, at everything stuck to his underwear.

I was starved, he said, shaking his head.

You were starved, she said, laughing.

He peeled off the woolen underwear and threw it at the bathroom door. Then he opened his arms and the girl moved into them.

We won't fight anymore, she said.

The boy said, We won't.

He gets up from his chair and refills their glasses.

That's it, he says. End of story. I admit it's not much of a story.

I was interested, she says.

He shrugs and carries his drink over to the window. It's dark now but still snowing.

Things change, he says. I don't know how they do. But they do without your realizing it or wanting them to.

Yes, that's true, only – But she does not finish what she started.

She drops the subject. In the window's reflection he sees her study her nails. Then she raises her head. Speaking brightly, she asks if he is going to show her the city, after all.

He says, Put your boots on and let's go.

But he stays by the window, remembering. They had laughed. They had leaned on each other and laughed until the tears had come, while everything else – the cold, and where he'd go in it – was outside, for a while anyway.

What we talk about
when we talk about love

My friend Mel McGinnis was talking. Mel McGinnis is a cardio-
logist, and sometimes that give him the right.

The four of us were sitting around his kitchen table drinking gin.
Sunlight filled the kitchen from the big window behind the sink.
There were Mel and me and his second wife, Teresa – Terri, we called
her – and my wife, Laura. We lived in Albuquerque then. But we were
all from somewhere else.

There was an ice bucket on the table. The gin and the tonic water
kept going around, and we somehow got on the subject of love. Mel
thought real love was nothing less than spiritual love. He said he'd
spent five years in a seminary before quitting to go to medical school.
He said he still looked back on those years in the seminary as the most
important years in his life.

Terri said the man she lived with before she lived with Mel loved
her so much he tried to kill her. Then Terri said, 'He beat me up one
night. He dragged me around the living room by my ankles. He kept
saying, 'I love you, I love you, you bitch.' He went on dragging me
around the living room. My head kept knocking on things.' Terri
looked around the table. 'What do you do with love like that?'

She was a bone-thin woman with a pretty face, dark eyes, and
brown hair that hung down her back. She liked necklaces made of
turquoise, and long pendant earrings.

'My God, don't be silly. That's not love, and you know it,' Mel said.
'I don't know what you'd call it, but I sure know you wouldn't call it
love.'

'Say what you want to, but I know it was,' Terri said. 'It may sound
crazy to you, but it's true just the same. People are different, Mel.
Sure, sometimes he may have acted crazy. Okay. But he loved me. In
his own way maybe, but he loved me. There was love there, Mel.
Don't say there wasn't.'

Mel let out his breath. He held his glass and turned to Laura and
me. 'The man threatened to kill me,' Mel said. He finished his drink
and reached for the gin bottle. 'Terri's a romantic. Terri's of the
kick-me-so-I'll-know-you-love-me school. Terri, hon, don't look that

way.' Mel reached across the table and touched Terri's cheek with his fingers. He grinned at her.

'Now he wants to make up,' Terri said.

'Make up what?' Mel said. 'What is there to make up? I know what I know. That's all.'

'How'd we get started on this subject, anyway?' Terri said. She raised her glass and drank from it. 'Mel always has love on his mind,' she said. 'Don't you honey?' She smiled. And I thought that was the last of it.

'I just wouldn't call Ed's behavior love. That's all I'm saying, honey,' Mel said. 'What about you guys?' Mel said to Laura and me. 'Does that sound like love to you?'

'I'm the wrong person to ask,' I said. 'I didn't even know the man. I've only heard his name mentioned in passing. I wouldn't know. You'd have to know the particulars. But I think what you're saying is that love is an absolute.'

Mel said, 'The kind of love I'm talking about is. The kind of love I'm talking about, you don't try to kill people.'

Laura said, 'I don't know anything about Ed, or anything about the situation. But who can judge anyone else's situation?'

I touched the back of Laura's hand. She gave me a quick smile. I picked up Laura's hand. It was warm, the nails polished, perfectly manicured. I encircled the broad wrist with my fingers, and I held her.

'When I left, he drank rat poison,' Terri said. She clasped her arms with her hands. 'They took him to the hospital in Santa Fe. That's where we lived then, about ten miles out. They saved his life. But his gums went crazy from it. I mean they pulled away from his teeth. After that, his teeth stood out like fangs. My God,' Terri said. She waited a minute, then let go of her arms and picked up her glass.

'What people won't do!' Laura said.

'He's out of the action now,' Mel said. 'He's dead.'

Mel handed me the saucer of limes. I took a section, squeezed it over my drink, and stirred the ice cubes with my finger.

'It gets worse,' Terri said. 'He shot himself in the mouth. But he bungled that too, Poor Ed,' she said. Terri shook her head.

'Poor Ed nothing,' Mel said. 'He was dangerous.'

Mel was forty-five years old. He was tall and rangy with curly soft hair. His face and arms were brown from the tennis he played. When he was sober, his gestures, all his movements, were precise, very careful.

'He did love me though, Mel. Grant me that,' Terri said. 'That's all I'm asking. He didn't love me the way you love me. I'm not saying that, But he loved me. You can grant me that, can't you?'

'What do you mean, he bungled it?' I said.

Laura leaned forward with her glass. She put her elbows on the table and held her glass in both hands. She glanced from Mel to Terri and waited with a look of bewilderment on her open face, as if amazed that such things happened to people you were friendly with.

'How'd he bungle it when he killed himself?' I said.

'I'll tell you what happened,' Mel said. 'He took this twenty-two pistol he'd bought to threaten Terri and me with. Oh, I'm serious, the man was always threatening. You should have seen the way we lived in those days. Like fugitives. I even bought a gun myself. Can you believe it? A guy like me? But I did. I bought one for self-defense and carried it in the glove compartment. Sometimes I'd have to leave the apartment in the middle of the night. To go to the hospital, you know? Terri and I weren't married then, and my first wife had the house and kids, the dog, everything, and Terri and I were living in this apartment here. Sometimes, as I say, I'd get a call in the middle of the night and have to go in to the hospital at two or three in the morning. It'd be dark out there in the parking lot, and I'd break into a sweat before I could even get to my car. I never knew if he was going to come up out of the shrubbery or from behind a car and start shooting. I mean, the man was crazy. He was capable of wiring a bomb, anything. He used to call my service at all hours and say he needed to talk to the doctor, and when I'd return the call, he'd say, 'Son of a bitch, your days are numbered.' Little things like that. It was scary, I'm telling you.'

'I still feel sorry for him,' Terri said.

'It sounds like a nightmare,' Laura said. 'But what exactly happened after he shot himself?'

Laura is a legal secretary. We'd met in a professional capacity. Before we knew it, it was a courtship. She's thirty-five, three years younger than I am. In addition to being in love, we like each other and enjoy one another's company. She's easy to be with.

'What happened?' Laura said.

Mel said, 'He shot himself in the mouth in his room. Someone heard the shot and told the manager. They came in with a passkey, saw what had happened, and called an ambulance. I happened to be there when they brought him in, alive but past recall. The man lived for three days. His head swelled up to twice the size of a normal head. I'd never seen anything like it, and I hope I never do again. Terri wanted to go in and sit with him when she found out about it. We had a fight over it. I didn't think she should see him like that. I didn't think she should see him, and I still don't.'

'Who won the fight?' Laura said.

'I was in the room with him when he died,' Terri said. 'He never came up out of it. But I sat with him. He didn't have anyone else.'

'He was dangerous,' Mel said. 'If you call that love, you can have it.'

'It was love,' Terri said. 'Sure, it's abnormal in most people's eyes. But he was willing to die for it. He did die for it.'

'I sure as hell wouldn't call it love,' Mel said. 'I mean, no one knows what he did it for. I've seen a lot of suicides, and I couldn't say anyone ever knew what they did it for.'

Mel put his hands behind his neck and tilted his chair back. 'I'm not interested in that kind of love,' he said. 'If that's love, you can have it.'

Terri said, 'We were afraid. Mel even made a will out and wrote to his brother in California who used to be a Green Beret. Mel told him who to look for if something happened to him.'

Terri drank from her glass. She said, 'But Mel's right – we lived like fugitives. We were afraid. Mel was, weren't you, honey? I even called the police at one point, but they were no help. They said they couldn't do anything until Ed actually did something. Isn't that a laugh?' Terri said.

She poured the last of the gin into her glass and waggled the bottle. Mel got up from the table and went to the cupboard. He took down another bottle.

'Well, Nick and I know what love is,' Laura said. 'For us, I mean,' Laura said. She bumped my knee with her knee. 'You're supposed to say something now,' Laura said, and turned her smile on me.

For an answer, I took Laura's hand and raised it to my lips. I made a big production out of kissing her hand. Everyone was amused.

'We're lucky,' I said.

'You guys,' Terri said. 'Stop that now. You're making me sick.

You're still on the honeymoon, for God's sake. You're still gaga, for crying out loud. Just wait. How long have you been together now? How long has it been? A year? Longer than a year?'

'Going on a year and a half,' Laura said, flushed and smiling.

'Oh, now,' Terri said. 'Wait awhile.'

She held her drink and gazed at Laura.

'I'm only kidding,' Terri said.

Mel opened the gin and went around the table with the bottle.

'Here, you guys,' he said. 'Let's have a toast. I want to propose a toast. A toast to love. To true love,' Mel said.

We touched glasses.

'To love,' we said.

Outside in the backyard, one of the dogs began to bark. The leaves of the aspen that leaned past the window ticked against the glass. The afternoon sun was like a presence in this room, the spacious light of ease and generosity. We could have been anywhere, somewhere enchanted. We raised our glasses again and grinned at each other like children who had agreed on something forbidden.

'I'll tell you what real love is,' Mel said. 'I mean, I'll give you a good example. And then you can draw your own conclusions.' He poured more gin into his glass. He added an ice cube and a sliver of lime. We waited and sipped our drinks. Laura and I touched knees again. I put a hand on her warm thigh and left it there.

'What do any of us really know about love?' Mel said. 'It seems to me we're just beginners at love. We say we love each other and we do, I don't doubt it. I love Terri and Terri loves me, and you guys love each other too. You know the kind of love I'm talking about now. Physical love, that impulse that drives you to someone special, as well as love of the other person's being, his or her essence, as it were. Carnal love and, well, call it sentimental love, the day-to-day caring about the other person. But sometimes I have a hard time accounting for the fact that I must have loved my first wife too. But I did, I know I did. So I suppose I am like Terri in that regard. Terri and Ed.' He thought about it and then he went on. 'There was a time when I thought I loved my first wife more than life itself. But now I hate her guts. I do. How do you explain that? What happened to that love? What happened to it, is what I'd like to know. I wish someone could tell me. Then there's Ed. Okay, we're back to Ed. He loves Terri so much he tries to kill her and he winds up killing himself.' Mel stopped talking and swallowed from his glass. 'You guys have been together eighteen months and you love each other. It shows all over you. You glow with it. But you both loved other people before you met each other. You've both been married before, just like us. And you probably loved other people before that too, even. Terri and I have been together five years, been married for four. And the terrible thing, the terrible thing is, but the good thing too, the saving grace, you might say, is that if something happened to one of us – excuse me for saying this – but if something happened to one of us tomorrow, I think the other one, the other person, would grieve for a while, you know, but then the surviving party would go out and love again, have someone else soon enough. All this, all of this love we're talking about, it would just be a memory. Maybe not even a memory. Am I wrong? Am I way off base? Because I want you to set me straight if you think I'm wrong. I want to know. I mean, I don't know anything, and I'm the first one to admit it.'

'Mel, for God's sake,' Terri said. She reached out and took hold of his wrist. 'Are you getting drunk? Honey? Are you drunk?'

'Honey, I'm just talking,' Mel said. 'All right? I don't have to be drunk to say what I think. I mean, we're all just talking, right?' Mel said. He fixed his eyes on her.

'Sweetie, I'm not criticizing,' Terri said.

She picked up her glass.

'I'm not on call today,' Mel said. 'Let me remind you of that. I am not on call,' he said.

'Mel, we love you,' Laura said.

Mel looked at Laura. He looked at her as if he could not place her, as if she was not the woman she was.

'Love you too, Laura,' Mel said. 'And you, Nick, love you too. You know something?' Mel said. 'You guys are our pals,' Mel said.

He picked up his glass.

Mel said, 'I was going to tell you about something. I mean, I was going to prove a point. You see, this happened a few months ago, but it's still going on right now, and it ought to make us feel ashamed when we talk like we know what we talking about when we talk about love.'

'Come on now,' Terri said. 'Don't talk like you're drunk if you're not drunk.'

'Just shut up for once in your life,' Mel said very quietly. 'Will you do me a favor and do that for a minute? So as I was saying, there's this old couple who had this car wreck out on the interstate. A kid hit them and they were all torn to shit and nobody was giving them much chance to pull through.'

Terri looked at us and then back at Mel. She seemed anxious, or maybe that's too strong a word.

Mel was handing the bottle around the table.

'I was on call that night,' Mel said. 'It was May or maybe it was June. Terri and I had just sat down to dinner when the hospital called. There'd been this thing out on the interstate. Drunk kid, teenager, plowed his dad's pickup into this camper with this old couple in it. They were up in their mid-seventies, that couple. The kid – eighteen, nineteen, something – he was DOA. Taken the steering wheel through his sternum. The old couple, they were alive, you understand. I mean, just barely. But they had everything. Multiple fractures, internal injuries, hemorrhaging, contusions, lacerations, the works, and they each of them had themselves concussions. They were in a bad way, believe me. And, of course, their age was two strikes against them. I'd say she was worse off than he was. Ruptured spleen along with everything else. Both kneecaps broken. But they'd been wearing their seatbelts and, God knows, that's what saved them for the time being.'

'Folks, this is an advertisement for the National Safety Council,' Terri said. 'This is your spokesman, Dr Melvin R. McGinnis, talking.' Terri laughed. 'Mel,' she said, 'sometimes you're just too much. But I love you, hon,' she said.

'Honey, I love you,' Mel said.

He leaned across the table. Terri met him halfway. They kissed.

'Terri's right,' Mel said as he settled himself again. 'Get those seatbelts on. But seriously, they were in some shape, those oldsters. By the time I got down there, the kid was dead, as I said. He was off in a corner, laid out on a gurney. I took one look at the old couple and told the ER nurse to get me a neurologist and an orthopedic man and a couple of surgeons down there right away.'

He drank from his glass. 'I'll try to keep this short,' he said. 'So we took the two of them up to the OR and worked like fuck on them most of the night. They had these incredible reserves, those two. You see that once in a while. So we did everything that could be done, and toward morning we're giving them a fifty-fifty chance, maybe less than that for her. So here they are, still alive the next morning. So, okay, we move them into the ICU, which is where they both kept plugging away at it for two weeks, hitting it better and better on all the scopes. So we transfer them out to their own room.'

Mel stopped talking. 'Here,' he said, 'let's drink this cheapo gin the hell up. Then we're going to dinner, right? Terri and I know a new place. That's where we'll go, to this new place we know about. But we're not going until we finish up this cut-rate, lousy gin.'

Terri said, 'We haven't actually eaten there yet. But it looks good. From the outside, you know.'

'I like food,' Mel said. 'If I had it to do all over again, I'd be a chef, you know? Right, Terri?' Mel said.

He laughed. He fingered the ice in his glass.

'Terri knows,' he said. 'Terri can tell you. But let me say this. If I could come back again in a different life, a different time and all, you know what? I'd like to come back as a knight. You were pretty safe wearing all that armor. It was all right being a knight until gun-powder and muskets and pistols came along.'

'Mel would like to ride a horse and carry a lance,' Terri said.

'Carry a woman's scarf with you everywhere,' Laura said.

'Or just a woman,' Mel said.

'Shame on you,' Laura said.

Terri said, 'Suppose you came back as a serf. The serfs didn't have it so good in those days,' Terri said.

'The serfs never had it good,' Mel said. 'But I guess even the knights were vessels to someone. Isn't that the way it worked? But then everyone is always a vessel to someone. Isn't that right? Terri? But what I liked about knights, besides their ladies, was that they had that suit of armor, you know, and they couldn't get hurt very easy. No cars in those days, you know? No drunk teenagers to tear into your ass.'

'Vassals,' Terri said.

'What?' Mel said.

'Vassals,' Terri said. 'They were called vassals, not vessels.'

'Vassals, vessels,' Mel said, 'what the fuck's the difference? You knew what I meant anyway. All right,' Mel said. 'So I'm not educated. I learned my stuff. I'm a heart surgeon, sure, but I'm just a mechanic. I go in and I fuck around and I fix things. Shit,' Mel said.

'Modesty doesn't become you,' Terri said.

'He's just a humble sawbones,' I said. 'But sometimes they suffocated in all that armor, Mel. They'd even have heart attacks if it got too hot and they were too tired and worn out. I read somewhere that they'd fall off their horses and not be able to get up because they were too tired to stand with all that armor on them. They got trampled by their own horses sometimes.'

'That's terrible,' Mel said. 'That's a terrible thing, Nicky. I guess they'd just lay there and wait until somebody came along and made a shish kebab out of them.'

'Some other vessel,' Terri said.

'That's right,' Mel said. 'Some vassal would come along and spear the bastard in the name of love. Or whatever the fuck it was they fought over in those days.'

'Same things we fight over these days,' Terri said.

Laura said, 'Nothing's changed.'

The color was still high in Laura's cheeks. Her eyes were bright. She brought her glass to her lips.

Mel poured himself another drink. He looked at the label closely as if studying a long row of numbers. Then he slowly put the bottle down on the table and slowly reached for the tonic water.

'What about the old couple?' Laura said. 'You didn't finish that story you started.'

Laura was having a hard time lighting her cigarette. Her matches kept going out.

The sunshine inside the room was different now, changing, getting thinner. But the leaves outside the window were still shimmering, and I stared at the pattern they made on the panes and on the Formica counter. They weren't the same patterns, of course.

'What about the old couple?' I said.

'Older but wiser,' Terri said.

Mel stared at her.

Terri said, 'Go on with your story, hon. I was only kidding. Then what happened?'

'Terri, sometimes,' Mel said.

'Please, Mel,' Terri said. 'Don't always be so serious, sweetie. Can't you take a joke?'

'Where's the joke?' Mel said.

He held his glass and gazed steadily at his wife.

'What happened?' Laura said.

Mel fastened his eyes on Laura. He said, 'Laura, if I didn't have

Terri and if I didn't love her so much, and if Nick wasn't my best friend, I'd fall in love with you. I'd carry you off, honey,' he said.

'Tell your story,' Terri said. 'Then we'll go to that new place, okay?'

'Okay,' Mel said. 'Where was I?' he said. He stared at the table and then he began again.

'I dropped in to see each of them every day, sometimes twice a day if I was up doing other calls anyway. Casts and bandages, head to foot, the both of them. You know, you've seen it in the movies. That's just the way they looked, just like in the movies. Little eye-holes and nose-holes and mouth-holes. And she had to have her legs slung up on top of it. Well, the husband was very depressed for the longest while. Even after he found out that his wife was going to pull through, he was still very depressed. Not about the accident, though. I mean, the accident was one thing, but it wasn't everything. I'd get up to his mouth-hole, you know, and he'd say no, it wasn't the accident exactly but it was because he couldn't see her through his eye-holes. He said that was what was making him feel so bad. Can you imagine? I'm telling you, the man's heart was breaking because he couldn't turn his goddamn head and *see* his goddamn wife.'

Mel looked around the table and shook his head at what he was going to say.

'I mean, it was killing the old fart just because he couldn't *look* at the fucking woman.'

We all looked at Mel.

'Do you see what I'm saying?' he said.

Maybe we were a little drunk by then. I know it was hard keeping things in focus. The light was draining out of the room, going back through the window where it had come from. Yet nobody made a move to get up from the table to turn on the overhead light.

'Listen,' Mel said. 'Let's finish this fucking gin. There's about enough left here for one shooter all around. Then let's go eat. Let's go to the new place.'

'He's depressed,' Terri said. 'Mel, why don't you take a pill?'

Mel shook his head. 'I've taken everything there is.'

'We all need a pill now and then,' I said.

'Some people are born needing them,' Terri said.

She was using her finger to rub at something on the table. Then she stopped rubbing.

'I think I want to call my kids,' Mel said. 'Is that all right with everybody? I'll call my kids,' he said.

Terri said, 'What if Marjorie answers the phone? You guys, you've heard us on the subject of Marjorie? Honey, you know you don't want to talk to Marjorie. It'll make you feel even worse.'

'I don't want to talk to Marjorie,' Mel said. 'But I want to talk to my kids.'

'There isn't a day goes by that Mel doesn't say he wishes she'd get married again. Or else die,' Terri said. 'For one thing,' Terri said, 'she's bankrupting us. Mel says it's just to spite him that she won't get married again. She has a boyfriend who lives with her and the kids, so Mel is supporting the boyfriend too.'

'She's allergic to bees,' Mel said. 'If I'm not praying she'll get married again, I'm praying she'll get herself stung to death by a swarm of fucking bees.'

'Shame on you,' Laura said.

'Bzzzzzz,' Mel said, turning his fingers into bees and buzzing them at Terri's throat. Then he let his hands drop all the way to his sides.

'She's vicious,' Mel said. 'Sometimes I think I'll go up there dressed like a beekeeper. You know, that hat that's like a helmet with the plate that comes down over your face, the big gloves, and the padded coat? I'll knock on the door and let loose a hive of bees in the house. But first I'd make sure the kids were out, of course.'

He cross one leg over the other. It seemed to take him a lot of time to do it. Then he put both feet on the floor and leaned forward, elbows on the table, his chin cupped in his hands.

'Maybe I won't call the kids, after all. Maybe it isn't such a hot idea. Maybe we'll just go eat. How does that sound?'

'Sounds fine to me,' I said. 'Eat or not eat. Or keep drinking. I could head right on out into the sunset.'

'What does that mean, honey?' Laura said.

'It just means what I said,' I said. 'It means I could just keep going. That's all it means.'

'I could eat something myself,' Laura said. 'I don't think I've ever been so hungry in my life. Is there something to nibble on?'

'I'll put out some cheese and crackers,' Terri said.

But Terri just sat there. She did not get up to get anything.

Mel turned his glass over. He spilled it out on the table.

'Gin's gone,' Mel said.

Terri said, 'Now what?'

I could hear my heart beating. I could hear everyone's heart. I could hear the human noise we sat there making, not one of us moving, not even when the room went dark.

One more thing

L.D.'s wife, Maxine, told him to get out the night she came home from work and found L.D. drunk again and being abusive to Rae, their fifteen-year-old. L.D. and Rae were at the kitchen table, arguing. Maxine didn't have time to put her purse away or take off her coat.

Rae said, 'Tell him, Mom. Tell him what we talked about.'

L.D. turned the glass in his hand, but he didn't drink from it. Maxine had him in a fierce and disquieting gaze.

'Keep your nose out of things you don't know anything about,' L.D. said. L.D. said, 'I can't take anybody seriously who sits around all day reading astrology magazines.'

'This has nothing to do with astrology,' Rae said. 'You don't have to insult me.'

As for Rae, she hadn't been to school for weeks. She said no one could make her go. Maxine said it was another tragedy in a long line of low-rent tragedies.

'Why don't you both shut up!' Maxine said. 'My God, I already have a headache.'

'Tell him, Mom,' Rae said. 'Tell him it's all in his head. Anybody who knows anything about it will tell you that's where it is!'

'How about sugar diabetes?' L.D. said. 'What about epilepsy? Can the brain control that?'

He raised the glass right under Maxine's eyes and finished his drink.

'Diabetes, too,' Rae said. 'Epilepsy. Anything! The brain is the most powerful organ in the body, for your information.'

She picked up his cigarettes and lit one for herself.

'Cancer. What about cancer?' L.D. said.

He thought he might have her there. He looked at Maxine.

'I don't know how we got started on this,' L.D. said to Maxine.

'Cancer,' Rae said, and shook her head at his simplicity. 'Cancer, too. Cancer *starts* in the brain.'

'That's crazy!' L.D. said. He hit the table with the flat of his hand. The ashtray jumped. His glass fell on its side and rolled off. 'You're crazy, Rae! Do you know that?'

'Shut up!' Maxine said.

She unbuttoned her coat and put her purse down on the counter. She looked at L.D. and said, 'L.D., I've had it. So has Rae. So has everyone who knows you. I've been thinking it over. I want you out of here. Tonight. This minute. Now. Get the hell out of here right now.'

L.D. had no intention of going anywhere. He looked from Maxine to the jar of pickles that had been on the table since lunch. He picked up the jar and pitched it through the kitchen window.

Rae jumped away from her chair. 'God! He's crazy!'

She went to stand next to her mother. She took in little breaths through her mouth.

'Call the police,' Maxine said. 'He's violent. Get out of the kitchen before he hurts you. Call the police,' Maxine said.

They started backing out of the kitchen.

'I'm going,' L.D. said. 'All right, I'm going right now.' he said. 'It suits me to a tee. You're nuts here, anyway. This is a nuthouse. There's another life out there. Believe me, this is no picnic, this nuthouse.'

He could feel air from the hole in the window on his face.

'That's where I'm going,' he said. 'Out there,' he said and pointed.

'Good,' Maxine said.

'All right, I'm going,' L.D. said.

He slammed down his hand on the table. He kicked back his chair. He stood up.

'You won't ever see me again,' L.D. said.

'You've given me plenty to remember you by,' Maxine said.

'Okay,' L.D. said.

'Go on, get out,' Maxine said. 'I'm paying the rent here, and I'm saying go. Now.'

'I'm going,' he said. 'Don't push me,' he said. 'I'm going.'

'Just go,' Maxine said.

'I'm leaving this nuthouse,' L.D. said.

He made his way into the bedroom and took one of her suitcases from the closet. It was an old white Naugahyde suitcase with a broken clasp. She'd used to pack it full of sweater sets and carry it with her to college. He had gone to college too. He threw the suitcase onto the bed and began putting in his underwear, his trousers, his shirts, his sweaters, his old leather belt with the brass buckle, his socks, and everything else he had. From the nightstand he took magazines for reading material. He took the ashtray. He put everything he could into the suitcase, everything it could hold. He fastened the one good side, secured the strap, and then he remembered his bathroom things. He found the vinyl shaving bag up on the closet shelf behind her hats. Into it went his razor and his shaving cream, his talcum powder and his stick deodorant and his toothbrush. He took the toothpaste, too. And then he got the dental floss.

He could hear them in the living room talking in their low voices.

He washed his face. He put the soap and towel into the shaving bag. Then he put in the soap dish and the glass from over the sink and the fingernail clippers and her eyelash curlers.

He couldn't get the shaving bag closed, but that was okay. He put on his coat and picked up the suitcase. He went into the living room.

When she saw him, Maxine put her arm around Rae's shoulders.

'This is it,' L.D. said. 'This is good-bye,' he said. 'I don't know what else to say except I guess I'll never see you again. You too,' L.D. said to Rae. 'You and your crackpot ideas.'

'Go,' Maxine said. She took Rae's hand. 'Haven't you done enough damage in this house already? Go on, L.D. Get out of here and leave us in peace.'

'Just remember,' Rae said. 'It's in your head.'

'I'm going, that's all I can say,' L.D. said. 'Anyplace. Away from this nuthouse,' he said. 'That's the main thing.'

He took a last look around the living room and then he moved the suitcase from one hand to the other and put the shaving bag under his arm. 'I'll be in touch, Rae. Maxine, you're better off out of this nuthouse yourself.'

'You made it into a nuthouse,' Maxine said. 'If it's a nuthouse, then that's what you made it.'

He put the suitcase down and the shaving bag on top of the suitcase. He drew himself up and faced them.

They moved back.

'Watch it, Mom,' Rae said.

'I'm not afraid of him,' Maxine said.

L.D. put the shaving bag under his arm and picked up the suitcase. He said, 'I just want to say one more thing.'

But then he could not think what it could possibly be.

Cathedral

For Tess Gallagher
and in memory of John Gardner

Feathers

This friend of mine from work, Bud, he asked Fran and me to supper. I didn't know his wife and he didn't know Fran. That made us even. But Bud and I were friends. And I knew there was a little baby at Bud's house. That baby must have been eight months old when Bud asked us to supper. Where'd those eight months go? Hell, where's the time gone since? I remember the day Bud came to work with a box of cigars. He handed them out in the lunchroom. They were drugstore cigars. Dutch Masters. But each cigar had a red sticker on it and a wrapper that said IT'S A BOY! I didn't smoke cigars, but I took one anyway. 'Take a couple,' Bud said. He shook the box. 'I don't like cigars either. This is her idea.' He was talking about his wife. Olla.

I'd never met Bud's wife, but once I'd heard her voice over the telephone. It was a Saturday afternoon, and I didn't have anything I wanted to do. So I called Bud to see if he wanted to do anything. This woman picked up the phone and said, 'Hello.' I blanked and couldn't remember her name. Bud's wife. Bud had said her name to me any number of times. But it went in one ear and out the other. 'Hello!' the woman said again. I could hear a TV going. Then the woman said, 'Who is this?' I heard a baby start up. 'Bud!' the woman called. 'What?' I heard Bud say. I still couldn't remember her name. So I hung up. The next time I saw Bud at work I sure as hell didn't tell him I'd called. But I made a point of getting him to mention his wife's name. 'Olla,' he said. Olla, I said to myself. *Olla.*

'No big deal,' Bud said. We were in the lunchroom drinking coffee. 'Just the four of us. You and your missus, and me and Olla. Nothing fancy. Come around seven. She feeds the baby at six. She'll put him down after that, and then we'll eat. Our place isn't hard to find. But here's a map.' He gave me a sheet of paper with all kinds of lines indicating major and minor roads, lanes and such, with arrows pointing to the four poles of the compass. A large X marked the location of his house. I said, 'We're looking forward to it.' But Fran wasn't too thrilled.

That evening, watching TV, I asked her if we should take anything to Bud's.

'Like what?' Fran said. 'Did he say to bring something? How

should I know? I don't have any idea.' She shrugged and gave me this look. She'd heard me before on the subject of Bud. But she didn't know him and she wasn't interested in knowing him. 'We could take a bottle of wine,' she said. 'But I don't care. Why don't you take some wine?' She shook her head. Her long hair swung back and forth over her shoulders. Why do we need other people? she seemed to be saying. We have each other. 'Come here,' I said. She moved a little closer so I could hug her. Fran's a big tall drink of water. She has this blond hair that hangs down her back. I picked up some of her hair and sniffed it. I wound my hand in her hair. She let me hug her. I put my face right up in her hair and hugged her some more.

Sometimes when her hair gets in her way she has to pick it up and push it over her shoulder. She gets mad at it. 'This hair,' she says. 'Nothing but trouble.' Fran works in a creamery and has to wear her hair up when she goes to work. She has to wash it every night and take a brush to it when we're sitting in front of the TV. Now and then she threatens to cut it off. But I don't think she'd do that. She knows I like it too much. She knows I'm crazy about it. I tell her I fell in love with her because of her hair. I tell her I might stop loving her if she cut it. Sometimes I call her 'Swede.' She could pass for a Swede. Those times together in the evening she'd brush her hair and we'd wish out loud for things we didn't have. We wished for a new car, that's one of the things we wished for. And we wished we could spend a couple of weeks in Canada. But one thing we didn't wish for was kids. The reason we didn't have kids was that we didn't want kids. Maybe sometime, we said to each other. But right then, we were waiting. We thought we might keep on waiting. Some nights we went to a movie. Other nights we just stayed in and watched TV. Sometimes Fran baked things for me and we'd eat whatever it was all in a sitting.

'Maybe they don't drink wine,' I said.

'Take some wine anyway,' Fran said. 'If they don't drink it, we'll drink it.'

'White or red?' I said.

'We'll take something sweet,' she said, not paying me any attention. 'But I don't care if we take anything. This is your show. Let's not make a production out of it, or else I don't want to go. I can make a raspberry coffee ring. Or else some cupcakes.'

'They'll have dessert,' I said. 'You don't invite people to supper without fixing a dessert.'

'They might have rice pudding. Or Jell-O! Something we don't like,' she said. 'I don't know anything about the woman. How do we know what she'll have? What if she gives us Jell-O?' Fran shook her head. I shrugged. But she was right. 'Those old cigars he gave you,' she said. 'Take them. Then you and him can go off to the parlor after supper and smoke cigars and drink port wine, or whatever those people in movies drink.'

'Okay, we'll just take ourselves,' I said.

Fran said, 'We'll take a loaf of my bread.'

Bud and Olla lived twenty miles or so from town. We'd lived in that town for three years, but, damn it, Fran and I hadn't so much as taken a spin in the country. It felt good driving those winding little roads. It was early evening, nice and warm, and we saw pastures, rail fences, milk cows moving slowly toward old barns. We saw red-winged blackbirds on the fences, and pigeons circling around haylofts. There were gardens and such, wildflowers in bloom, and little houses set back from the road. I said, 'I wish we had us a place out here.' It was just an idle thought, another wish that wouldn't amount to anything. Fran didn't answer. She was busy looking at Bud's map. We came to the four-way stop he'd marked. We turned right like the map said and drove exactly three and three-tenths miles. On the left side of the road, I saw a field of corn, a mailbox, and a long, graveled driveway. At the end of the driveway, back in some trees, stood a house with a front porch. There was a chimney on the house. But it was summer, so, of course, no smoke rose from the chimney. But I thought it was a pretty picture, and I said so to Fran.

'It's the sticks out here,' she said.

I turned into the drive. Corn rose up on both sides of the drive. Corn stood higher than the car. I could hear gravel crunching under the tires. As we got up close to the house, we could see a garden with green things the size of baseballs hanging from the vines.

'What's that?' I said.

'How should I know?' she said. 'Squash, maybe, I don't have a clue.'

'Hey, Fran,' I said. 'Take it easy.'

She didn't say anything. She drew in her lower lip and let it go. She turned off the radio as we got close to the house.

A baby's swing-set stood in the front yard and some toys lay on the porch. I pulled up in front and stopped the car. It was then that we heard this awful squall. There was a baby in the house, right, but this

294 Stories by Raymond Carver

cry was too loud for a baby.

'What's that sound?' Fran said.

Then something as big as a vulture flapped heavily down from one of the trees and landed just in front of the car. It shook itself. It turned its long neck toward the car, raised its head, and regarded us.

'Goddamn it,' I said. I sat there with my hands on the wheel and stared at the thing.

'Can you believe it?' Fran said. 'I never saw a real one before.'

We both knew it was a peacock, sure, but we didn't say the word out loud. We just watched it. The bird turned its head up in the air and made this harsh cry again. It had fluffed itself out and looked about twice the size it'd been when it landed.

'Goddamn,' I said again. We stayed where we were in the front seat.

The bird moved forward a little. Then it turned its head to the side and braced itself. It kept its bright, wild eye right on us. Its tail was raised, and it was like a big fan folding in and out. There was every color in the rainbow shining from that tail.

'My God,' Fran said quietly. She moved her hand over to my knee.

'Goddamn,' I said. There was nothing else to say.

The bird made this strange wailing sound once more. *'May-awe, may-awe!'* it went. If it'd been something I was hearing late at night and for the first time, I'd have thought it was somebody dying, or else something wild and dangerous.

The front door opened and Bud came out on the porch. He was buttoning his shirt. His hair was wet. It looked like he'd just come from the shower.

'Shut yourself up, Joey!' he said to the peacock. He clapped his hands at the bird, and the thing moved back a little. 'That's enough now. That's right, shut up! You shut up, you old devil!' Bud came down the steps. He tucked in his shirt as he came over to the car. He was wearing what he always wore to work – blue jeans and a denim shirt. I had on my slacks and a short-sleeved sport shirt. My good loafers. When I saw what Bud was wearing, I didn't like it that I was dressed up.

'Glad you could make it,' Bud said as he came over beside the car. 'Come on inside.'

'Hey, Bud,' I said.

Fran and I got out of the car. The peacock stood off a little to one side, dodging its mean-looking head this way and that. We were careful to keep some distance between it and us.

'Any trouble finding the place?' Bud said to me. He hadn't looked at Fran. He was waiting to be introduced.

'Good directions,' I said. 'Hey, Bud, this is Fran. Fran, Bud. She's got the word on you, Bud.'

He laughed and they shook hands. Fran was taller than Bud. Bud had to look up.

'He talks about you,' Fran said. She took her hand back. 'Bud this, Bud that. You're about the only person down there he talks about. I feel like I know you.' She was keeping an eye on the peacock. It had moved over near the porch.

'This here's my friend,' Bud said. 'He *ought* to talk about me.' Bud said this and then he grinned and gave me a little punch on the arm.

Fran went on holding her loaf of bread. She didn't know what to do with it. She gave it to Bud. 'We brought you something.'

Bud took the load. He turned it over and looked at it as if it was the first loaf of bread he'd ever seen. 'This is real nice of you.' He brought the loaf up to his face and sniffed it.

'Fran baked that bread,' I told Bud.

Bud nodded. Then he said, 'Let's go inside and meet the wife and mother.'

He was talking about Olla, sure. Olla was the only mother around. Bud had told me his own mother was dead and that his dad had pulled out when Bud was a kid.

The peacock scuttled ahead of us, then hopped onto the porch when Bud opened the door. It was trying to get inside the house.

'Oh,' said Fran as the peacock pressed itself against her leg.

'Joey, goddamn it,' Bud said. He thumped the bird on the top of its head. The peacock backed up on the porch and shook itself. The quills in its train rattled as it shook. Bud made as if to kick it, and the peacock backed up some more. Then Bud held the door for us. 'She lets the goddamn thing in the house. Before long, it'll be wanting to eat at the goddamn table and sleep in the goddamn bed.'

Fran stopped just inside the door. She looked back at the cornfield. 'You have a nice place,' she said. Bud was still holding the door. 'Don't they, Jack?'

'You bet,' I said. I was surprised to hear her say it.

'A place like this is not all it's cracked up to be,' Bud said, still holding the door. He made a threatening move toward the peacock.

'Keeps you going. Never a dull moment.' Then he said, 'Step on inside, folks.'

I said, 'Hey, Bud, what's that growing there?'

'Them's tomatoes,' Bud said.

'Some farmer I got,' Fran said, and shook her head.

Bud laughed. We went inside. This plump little woman with her hair done up in a bun was waiting for us in the living room. She had her hands rolled up in her apron. The cheeks of her face were bright red. I thought at first she might be out of breath, or else mad at something. She gave me the once-over, and then her eyes went to Fran. Not unfriendly, just looking. She stared at Fran and continued to blush.

Bud said, 'Olla, this is Fran. And this is my friend Jack. You know all about Jack. Folks, this is Olla.' He handed Olla the bread.

'What's this?' she said. 'Oh, it's homemade bread. Well, thanks. Sit down anywhere. Make yourselves at home. Bud, why don't you ask them what they'd like to drink. I've got something on the stove.' Olla said that and went back into the kitchen with the bread.

'Have a seat,' Bud said. Fran and I plunked ourselves down on the sofa. I reached for my cigarettes. Bud said, 'Here's an ashtray.' He picked up something heavy from the top of the TV. 'Use this,' he said, and he put the thing down on the coffee table in front of me. It was one of those glass ashtrays made to look like a swan. I lit up and dropped the match into the opening in the swan's back. I watched a little wisp of smoke drift out of the swan.

The color TV was going, so we looked at that for a minute. On the screen, stock cars were tearing around a track. The announcer talked in a grave voice. But it was like he was holding back some excitement, too. 'We're still waiting to have official confirmation,' the announcer said.

'You want to watch this?' Bud said. He was still standing.

I said I didn't care. And I didn't. Fran shrugged. What difference could it make to her? she seemed to say. The day was shot anyway.

'There's only about twenty laps left,' Bud said. 'It's close now. There was a big pile-up earlier. Knocked out half-a-dozen cars. Some drivers got hurt. They haven't said yet how bad.'

'Leave it on,' I said. 'Let's watch it.'

'Maybe one of those damn cars will explode right in front of us,' Fran said. 'Or else maybe one'll run up into the grandstand and smash the guy selling the crummy hot dogs.' She took a strand of hair between her fingers and kept her eyes fixed on the TV.

Bud looked at Fran to see if she was kidding. 'That other business, that pile-up, was something. One thing led to another. Cars, parts of cars, people all over the place. Well, what can I get you? We have ale, and there's a bottle of Old Crow.'

'What are you drinking?' I said to Bud.

'Ale,' Bud said, 'It's good and cold.'

'I'll have ale,' I said.

'I'll have some of that Old Crow and a little water,' Fran said. 'In a tall glass, please. With some ice. Thank you, Bud.'

'Can do,' Bud said. He threw another look at the TV and moved off to the kitchen.

Fran nudged me and nodded in the direction of the TV. 'Look up on top,' she whispered. 'Do you see what I see?' I looked at where she was looking. There was a slender red vase into which somebody had stuck a few garden daisies. Next to the vase, on the doily, sat an old plaster-of-Paris cast of the most crooked, jaggedy teeth in the world. There were no lips to the awful-looking thing, and no jaw either, just these old plaster teeth packed into something that resembled thick yellow gums.

Just then Olla came back with a can of mixed nuts and a bottle of root beer. She had her apron off now. She put the can of nuts onto the coffee table next to the swan. She said, 'Help yourselves. Bud's getting your drinks.' Olla's face came on red again as she said this. She sat down in an old cane rocking chair and set it in motion. She drank from her root beer and looked at the TV. Bud came back carrying a little wooden tray with Fran's glass of whiskey and water and my bottle of ale. He had a bottle of ale on the tray for himself.

'You want a glass?' he asked me.

I shook my head. He tapped me on the knee and turned to Fran.

She took her glass from Bud and said, 'Thanks.' Her eyes went to the teeth again. Bud saw where she was looking. The cars screamed around the track. I took the ale and gave my attention to the screen. The teeth were none of my business. 'Them's what Olla's teeth looked like before she had her braces put on,' Bud said to Fran. 'I've got used to them. But I guess they look funny up there. For the life of me, I don't know why she keeps them around.' He looked over at Olla.

Then he looked at me and winked. He sat down in his La-Z-Boy and crossed one leg over the other. He drank from his ale and gazed at Olla.

Olla turned red once more. She was holding her bottle of root beer. She took a drink of it. Then she said, 'They're to remind me how much I owe Bud.'

· 'What was that?' Fran said. She was picking through the can of nuts, helping herself to the cashews. Fran stopped what she was doing and looked at Olla. 'Sorry, but I missed that.' Fran stared at the woman and waited for whatever thing it was she'd say next.

Olla's face turned red again. 'I've got lots of things to be thankful for,' she said. 'That's one of the things I'm thankful for. I keep them around to remind me how much I owe Bud.' She drank from her root beer. Then she lowered the bottle and said, 'You've got pretty teeth, Fran. I noticed right away. But these teeth of mine, they came in crooked when I was a kid.' With her fingernail, she tapped a couple of her front teeth. She said, 'My folks couldn't afford to fix teeth. These teeth of mine came in just any which way. My first husband didn't care what I looked like. No, he didn't! He didn't care about anything except where his next drink was coming from. He had one friend only in this world, and that was his bottle.' She shook her head. 'Then Bud come along and got me out of that mess. After we were together, the first thing Bud said was, 'We're going to have them teeth fixed.' That mold was made right after Bud and I met, on the occasion of my second visit to the orthodontist. Right before the braces went on.'

Olla's face stayed red. She looked at the picture on the screen. She drank from her root beer and didn't seem to have any more to say.

'That orthodontist must have been a whiz,' Fran said. She looked back at the horror-show teeth on top of the TV.

'He was great,' Olla said. She turned in her chair and said, 'See?' She opened her mouth and showed us her teeth once more, not a bit shy now.

Bud had gone to the TV and picked up the teeth. He walked over to Olla and held them up against Olla's cheek. 'Before and after,' Bud said.

Olla reached up and took the mold from Bud. 'You know something? That orthodontist wanted to keep this.' She was holding it in her lap while she talked. 'I said nothing doing. I pointed out to him they were *my* teeth. So he took pictures of the mold instead. He told me he was going to put the pictures in a magazine.'

Bud said, 'Imagine what kind of magazine that'd be. Not much call for that kind of publication, I don't think,' he said, and we all laughed.

'After I got the braces off, I kept putting my hand up to my mouth when I laughed. Like this,' she said. 'Sometimes I still do it. Habit. One day Bud said, 'You can stop doing that anytime, Olla. You don't have to hide teeth as pretty as that. You have nice teeth now.' Olla looked over at Bud. Bud winked at her. She grinned and lowered her eyes.

Fran drank from her glass. I took some of my ale. I didn't know what to say to this. Neither did Fran. But I knew Fran would have plenty to say about it later.

I said, 'Olla, I called here once. You answered the phone. But I hung up. I don't know why I hung up.' I said that and then sipped my ale. I didn't know why I'd brought it up now.

'I don't remember,' Olla said. 'When was that?'

'A while back.'

'I don't remember,' she said and shook her head. She fingered the plaster teeth in her lap. She looked at the race and went back to rocking.

Fran turned her eyes to me. She drew her lip under. But she didn't say anything.

Bud said, 'Well, what else is new?'

'Have some more nuts,' Olla said. 'Supper'll be ready in a little while.'

There was a cry from a room in the back of the house.

'Not him,' Olla said to Bud, and made a face.

'Old Junior boy,' Bud said. He leaned back in his chair, and we watched the rest of the race, three or four laps, no sound.

Once or twice we heard the baby again, little fretful cries coming from the room in the back of the house.

'I don't know,' Olla said. She got up from her chair. 'Everything's about ready for us to sit down. I just have to take up the gravy. But I'd better look in on him first. Why don't you folks go out and sit down at the table? I'll just be a minute.'

'I'd like to see the baby,' Fran said.

Olla was still holding the teeth. She went over and put them back on top of the TV. 'It might upset him just now,' she said. 'He's not used to strangers. Wait and see if I can get him back to sleep. Then you can peek in. While he's asleep.' She said this and then she went down the hall to a room, where she opened a door. She eased in and shut the door behind her. The baby stopped crying.

Bud killed the picture and we went in to sit at the table. Bud and I talked about things at work. Fran listened. Now and then she even asked a question. But I could tell she was bored, and maybe feeling put out with Olla for not letting her see the baby. She looked around Olla's kitchen. She wrapped a strand of hair around her fingers and checked out Olla's things.

Olla came back into the kitchen and said, 'I changed him and gave him his rubber duck. Maybe he'll let us eat now. But don't bet on it.' She raised a lid and took a pan off the stove. She poured red gravy into a bowl and put the bowl on the table. She took lids off some other pots and looked to see that everything was ready. On the table were baked ham, sweet potatoes, mashed potatoes, lima beans, corn on the cob, salad greens. Fran's loaf of bread was in a prominent place next to the ham.

'I forgot the napkins,' Olla said. 'You all get started. Who wants what to drink? Bud drinks milk with all of his meals.'

'Milk's fine,' I said.

'Water for me,' Fran said. 'But I can get it. I don't want you waiting on me. You have enough to do.' She made as if to get up from her chair.

Olla said, 'Please. You're company. Sit still. Let me get it.' She was blushing again.

We sat with our hands in our laps and waited. I thought about those plaster teeth. Olla came back with napkins, big glasses of milk for Bud and me, and a glass of ice water for Fran. Fran said, 'Thanks.'

'You're welcome,' Olla said. Then she seated herself. Bud cleared his throat. He bowed his head and said a few words of grace. He talked in a voice so low I could hardly make out the words. But I got the drift of things – he was thanking the Higher Power for the food we were about to put away.

'Amen,' Olla said when he'd finished.

Bud passed me the platter of ham and helped himself to some mashed potatoes. We got down to it then. We didn't say much except now and then Bud or I would say, 'This is real good ham.' Or, 'This sweet corn is the best sweet corn I ever ate.'

'This bread is what's special,' Olla said.

'I'll have some more salad, please, Olla,' Fran said, softening up maybe a little.

'Have more of this,' Bud would say as he passed me the platter of ham, or else the bowl of red gravy.

From time to time, we heard the baby make its noise. Olla would turn her head to listen, then, satisfied it was just fussing, she would give her attention back to her food.

'The baby's out of sorts tonight,' Olla said to Bud.

'I'd still like to see him,' Fran said. 'My sister has a little baby. But she and the baby live in Denver. When will I ever get to Denver? I have a niece I haven't even seen.' Fran thought about this for a minute, and then she went back to eating.

Olla forked some ham into her mouth. 'Let's hope he'll drop off to sleep,' she said.

Bud said, 'There's a lot more of everything. Have some more ham and sweet potatoes, everybody.'

'I can't eat another bite,' Fran said. She laid her fork on her plate. 'It's great, but I can't eat any more.'

'Save room,' Bud said. 'Olla's made rhubarb pie.'

Fran said, 'I guess I could eat a little piece of that. When everybody else is ready.'

'Me, too,' I said. But I said it to be polite. I'd hated rhubarb pie since I was thirteen years old and had got sick on it, eating it with strawberry ice cream.

We finished what was on our plates. Then we heard that damn peacock again. The thing was on the roof this time. We could hear it over our heads. It made a ticking sound as it walked back and forth on the shingles.

Bud shook his head. 'Joey will knock it off in a minute. He'll get tired and turn in pretty soon,' Bud said. 'He sleeps in one of them trees.'

The bird let go with its cry once more. *'May-awe!'* it went. Nobody said anything. What was there to say?

Then Olla said, 'He wants in, Bud.'

'Well, he can't come in,' Bud said. 'We got company, in case you hadn't noticed. These people don't want a goddamn old bird in the house. That dirty bird and your old pair of teeth! What're people going to think?' He shook his head. He laughed. We all laughed. Fran laughed along with the rest of us.

'He's not *dirty*, Bud,' Olla said. 'What's gotten into you? You like Joey. Since when did you start calling him dirty?'

'Since he shit on the rug that time,' Bud said. 'Pardon the French,' he said to Fran. 'But, I'll tell you, sometimes I could wring that old bird's neck for him. He's not even worth killing, is he, Olla? Sometimes, in the middle of the night he'll bring me up out of bed with that cry of his. He's not worth a nickel — right, Olla?'

Olla shook her head at Bud's nonsense. She moved a few lima beans around on her plate.

'How'd you get a peacock in the first place?' Fran wanted to know.

Olla looked up from her plate. She said, 'I always dreamed of having me a peacock. Since I was a girl and found a picture of one in a magazine. I thought it was the most beautiful thing I ever saw. I cut the picture out and put it over my bed. I kept that picture for the longest time. Then when Bud and I got this place, I saw my chance. I said, 'Bud, I want a peacock.' Bud laughed at the idea.'

'I finally asked around,' Bud said. 'I heard tell of an old boy who raised them over in the next county. Birds of paradise, he called them. We paid a hundred bucks for that bird of paradise,' he said. He smacked his forehead. 'God Almighty, I got me a woman with expensive tastes.' He grinned at Olla.

'Bud,' Olla said, 'you know that isn't true. Besides everything else, Joey's a good watchdog,' she said to Fran. 'We don't need a watchdog with Joey. He can hear just about anything.'

'If times get tough, as they might, I'll put Joey in a pot,' Bud said. 'Feathers and all.'

'Bud! That's not funny,' Olla said. But she laughed and we got a good look at her teeth again.

The baby started up once more. It was serious crying this time. Olla put down her napkin and got up from the table.

Bud said, 'If it's not one thing, it's another. Bring him on out here, Olla.'

'I'm going to,' Olla said, and went to get the baby.

The peacock wailed again, and I could feel the hair on the back of my neck. I looked at Fran. She picked up her napkin and then put it down. I looked toward the kitchen window. It was dark outside. The window was raised, and there was a screen in the frame. I thought I heard the bird on the front porch.

Fran turned her eyes to look down the hall. She was watching for Olla and the baby.

After a time, Olla came back with it. I looked at the baby and drew a breath. Olla sat down at the table with the baby. She held it up

under its arms so it could stand on her lap and face us. She looked at
Fran and then at me. She wasn't blushing now. She waited for one of
us to comment.

'Ah!' said Fran.

'What is it?' Olla said quickly.

'Nothing,' Fran said. 'I thought I saw something at the window. I
thought I saw a bat.'

'We don't have any bats around here,' Olla said.

'Maybe it was a moth,' Fran said. 'It was something. Well,' she
said, 'isn't that some baby.'

Bud was looking at the baby. Then he looked over at Fran. He
tipped his chair onto its back legs and nodded. He nodded again, and
said. 'That's all right, don't worry any. We know he wouldn't win no
beauty contests right now. He's no Clark Gable. But give him time.
With any luck, you know, he'll grow up to look like his old man.'

The baby stood on Olla's lap, looking around the table at us. Olla
had moved her hands down to its middle so that the baby could rock
back and forth on its fat legs. Bar none, it was the ugliest baby I'd ever
seen. It was so ugly I couldn't say anything. No words would come
out of my mouth. I don't mean it was diseased or disfigured. Nothing
like that. It was just ugly. It had a big red face, pop eyes, a broad
forehead, and these big fat lips. It had no neck to speak of, and it had
three or four fat chins. Its chins rolled right up under its ears, and its
ears stuck out from its bald head. Fat hung over its wrists. Its arms
and fingers were fat. Even calling it ugly does it credit.

The ugly baby made its noise and jumped up and down on its
mother's lap. Then it stopped jumping. It leaned forward and tried to
reach its fat hand into Olla's plate.

I've seen babies. When I was growing up, my two sisters had a total
of six babies. I was around babies a lot when I was a kid. I've seen
babies in stores and so on. But this baby beat anything. Fran stared at
it, too. I guess she didn't know what to say either.

'He's a big fellow, isn't he?' I said.

Bud said, 'He'll by God be turning out for football before long. He
sure as hell won't go without meals around this house.'

As if to make sure of this, Olla plunged her fork into some sweet
potatoes and brought the fork up to the baby's mouth. 'He's my baby,
isn't he?' she said to the fat thing, ignoring us.

The baby leaned forward and opened up for the sweet potatoes. It reached for Olla's fork as she guided the sweet potatoes into its mouth, then clamped down. The baby chewed the stuff and rocked some more on Olla's lap. It was so pop-eyed, it was like it was plugged into something.

Fran said, 'He's some baby, Olla.'

The baby's face screwed up. It began to fuss all over again.

'Let Joey in,' Olla said to Bud.

Bud let the legs of his chair come down on the floor. 'I think we should at least ask these people if they mind,' Bud said.

Olla looked at Fran and then she looked at me. Her face had gone red again. The baby kept prancing in her lap, squirming to get down.

'We're friends here,' I said. 'Do whatever you want.'

Bud said, 'Maybe they don't want a big old bird like Joey in the house. Did you ever think of that, Olla?'

'Do you folks mind?' Olla said to us. 'If Joey comes inside? Things got headed in the wrong direction with that bird tonight. The baby, too, I think. He's used to having Joey come in and fool around with him a little before his bedtime. Neither of them can settle down tonight.'

'Don't ask us,' Fran said. 'I don't mind if he comes in. I've never been up close to one before. But I don't mind.' She looked at me. I suppose I could tell she wanted me to say something.

'Hell, no,' I said. 'Let him in.' I picked up my glass and finished the milk.

Bud got up from his chair. He went to the front door and opened it. He flicked on the yard lights.

'What's your baby's name?' Fran wanted to know.

'Harold,' Olla said. She gave Harold some more sweet potatoes from her plate. 'He's real smart. Sharp as a tack. Always knows what you're saying to him. Don't you, Harold? You wait until you get your own baby, Fran. You'll see.'

Fran just looked at her. I heard the front door open and then close.

'He's smart, all right,' Bud said as he came back into the kitchen. 'He takes after Olla's dad. Now there was one smart old boy for you.'

I looked around behind Bud and could see that peacock hanging back in the living room, turning its head this way and that, like you'd turn a hand mirror. It shook itself, and the sound was like a deck of cards being shuffled in the other room.

It moved forward a step. Then another step.

'Can I hold the baby?' Fran said. She said it like it would be a favor if Olla would let her.

Olla handed the baby across the table to her.

Fran tried to get the baby settled in her lap. But the baby began to squirm and make its noises.

'Harold,' Fran said.

Olla watched Fran with the baby. She said, 'When Harold's grandpa was sixteen years old, he set out to read the encyclopedia from A to Z. He did it, too. He finished when he was twenty. Just before he met my mama.'

'Where's he now?' I asked. 'What's he do?' I wanted to know what had become of a man who'd set himself a goal like that.

'He's dead,' Olla said. She was watching Fran, who by now had the baby down on its back and across her knees. Fran chucked the baby under one of its chins. She started to talk baby talk to it.

'He worked in the woods,' Bud said. 'Loggers dropped a tree on him.'

'Mama got some insurance money,' Olla said. 'But she spent that. Bud sends her something every month.'

'Not much,' Bud said. 'Don't have much ourselves. But she's Olla's mother.'

By this time, the peacock had gathered its courage and was beginning to move slowly, with little swaying and jerking motions, into the kitchen. Its head was erect but at an angle, its red eyes fixed on us. Its crest, a little sprig of feathers, stood a few inches over its head. Plumes rose from its tail. The bird stopped a few feet away from the table and looked us over.

'They don't call them birds of paradise for nothing,' Bud said.

Fran didn't look up. She was giving all her attention to the baby. She'd begun to patty-cake with it, which pleased the baby somewhat. I mean, at least the thing had stopped fussing. She brought it up to her neck and whispered something into its ear.

'Now,' she said. 'don't tell anyone what I said.'

The baby stared at her with its pop eyes. Then it reached and got itself a baby handful of Fran's blond hair. The peacock stepped closer to the table. None of us said anything. We just sat still. Baby Harold saw the bird. It let go of Fran's hair and stood up on her lap. It pointed its fat fingers at the bird. It jumped up and down and made noises.

The peacock walked quickly around the table and went for the baby. It ran its long neck across the baby's legs. It pushed its beak in under the baby's pajama top and shook its stiff head back and forth. The baby laughed and kicked its feet. Scooting onto its back, the baby worked its way over Fran's knees and down onto the floor. The peacock kept pushing against the baby, as if it was a game they were playing. Fran held the baby against her legs while the baby strained forward.

'I just don't believe this,' she said.

'That peacock is crazy, that's what,' Bud said. 'Damn bird doesn't know it's a bird, that's its major trouble.'

Olla grinned and showed her teeth again. She looked over at Bud. Bud pushed his chair away from the table and nodded.

It *was* an ugly baby. But, for all I know, I guess it didn't matter that much to Bud and Olla. Or if it did, maybe they simply thought, So okay if it's ugly. It's our baby. And this is just a stage. Pretty soon there'll be another stage. There is this stage and then there is the next stage. Things will be okay in the long run, once all the stages have been gone through. They might have thought something like that.

Bud picked up the baby and swung him over his head until Harold shrieked. The peacock ruffled its feathers and watched.

Fran shook her head again. She smoothed out her dress where the baby had been. Olla picked up her fork and was working at some lima beans on her plate.

Bud shifted the baby onto his hip and said, 'There's pie and coffee yet.'

That evening at Bud and Olla's was special. I knew it was special. That evening I felt good about almost everything in my life. I couldn't wait to be alone with Fran to talk to her about what I was feeling. I made a wish that evening. Sitting there at the table, I closed my eyes for a minute and thought hard. What I wished for was that I'd never forget or otherwise let go of that evening. That's one wish of mine that came true. And it was bad luck for me that it did. But, of course, I couldn't know that then.

'What are you thinking about, Jack?' Bud said to me.

'I'm just thinking,' I said. I grinned at him.

'A penny,' Olla said.

I just grinned some more and shook my head.

After we got home from Bud and Olla's that night, and we were under the covers, Fran said, 'Honey, fill me up with your seed!' When she said that, I heard her all the way down to my toes, and I hollered and let go.

Later, after things had changed for us, and the kid had come along, all of that, Fran would look back on that evening at Bud's place as the beginning of the change. But she's wrong, The change came later — and when it came, it was like something that happened to other people, not something that could have happened to us.

'Goddamn those people and their ugly baby,' Fran will say, for no apparent reason, while we're watching TV late at night. 'And that smelly bird,' she'll say. 'Christ, who needs it!' Fran will say. She says this kind of stuff a lot, even though she hasn't seen Bud and Olla since that one time.

Fran doesn't work at the creamery anymore, and she cut her hair a long time ago. She's gotten fat on me, too. We don't talk about it. What's to say?

I still see Bud at the plant. We work together and we open our lunch pails together. If I ask, he tells me about Olla and Harold. Joey's out of the picture. He flew into his tree one night and that was it for him. He didn't come down. Old age, maybe, Bud says. Then the owls took over. Bud shrugs. He eats his sandwich and says Harold's going to be a linebacker someday. 'You ought to see that kid,' Bud says. I nod. We're still friends. That hasn't changed any. But I've gotten careful with what I say to him. And I know he feels that and wishes it could be different. I wish it could be, too.

Once in a blue moon, he asks about my family. When he does, I tell him everybody's fine. 'Everybody's fine,' I say. I close the lunch pail and take out my cigarettes. Bud nods and sips his coffee. The truth is, my kid has a conniving streak in him. But I don't talk about it. Not even with his mother. Especially her. She and I talk less and less as it is. Mostly it's just the TV. But I remember that night. I recall the way the peacock picked up its gray feet and inched around the table. And then my friend and his wife saying goodnight to us on the porch. Olla giving Fran some peacock feathers to take home. I remember all of us shaking hands, hugging each other, saying things. In the car, Fran sat close to me as we drove away. She kept her hand on my leg. We drove home like that from my friend's house.

Chef's house

That summer Wes rented a furnished house north of Eureka from a recovered alcoholic named Chef. Then he called to ask me to forget what I had going and to move up there and live with him. He said he was on the wagon. I knew about that wagon. But he wouldn't take no for an answer. He called again and said, Edna, you can see the ocean from the front window. You can smell salt in the air. I listened to him talk. He didn't slur his words. I said, I'll think about it. And I did. A week later he called again and said, Are you coming? I said I was still thinking. He said, We'll start over. I said, If I come up there, I want you to do something for me. Name it, Wes said. I said, I want you to try and be the Wes I used to know. The old Wes. The Wes I married. Wes began to cry, but I took it as a sign of his good intentions. So I said, All right, I'll come up.

Wes had quit his girlfriend, or she'd quit him — I didn't know, didn't care. When I made up my mind to go with Wes, I had to say goodbye to my friend. My friend said, You're making a mistake. He said, Don't do this to me. What about us? he said. I said, I have to do it for Wes's sake. He's trying to stay sober. You remember what that's like. I remember my friend said, but I don't want you to go. I said, I'll go for the summer. Then I'll see. I'll come back, I said. He said, What about me? What about *my* sake? Don't come back, he said.

We drank coffee, pop, and all kinds of fruit juice that summer. The whole summer, that's what we had to drink. I found myself wishing the summer wouldn't end. I knew better, but after a month of being with Wes in Chef's house, I put my wedding ring back on. I hadn't worn the ring in two years. Not since the night Wes was drunk and threw his ring into a peach orchard.

Wes had a little money, so I didn't have to work. And it turned out Chef was letting us have the house for almost nothing. We didn't have a telephone. We paid the gas and light and shopped for specials at the Safeway. One Sunday afternoon Wes went out to get a sprinkler and came back with something for me. He came back with a nice bunch of daisies and a straw hat. Tuesday evenings we'd go to a movie. Other nights Wes would go to what he called his Don't Drink meetings. Chef would pick him up in his car at the door and drive him home again afterward. Some days Wes and I would go fishing for trout in one of the freshwater lagoons nearby. We'd fish off the bank and take all day to catch a few little ones. They'll do fine, I'd say, and that night I'd fry them for supper. Sometimes I'd take off my hat and fall asleep on a blanket next to my fishing pole. The last thing I'd remember would be clouds passing overhead toward the central valley. At night, Wes would take me in his arms and ask me if I was still his girl.

Our kids kept their distance. Cheryl lived with some people on a farm in Oregon. She looked after a herd of goats and sold the milk. She kept bees and put up jars of honey. She had her own life, and I didn't blame her. She didn't care one way or the other about what her dad and I did so long as we didn't get her into it. Bobby was in Washington working in the hay. After the haying season, he planned to work in the apples. He had a girl and was saving his money. I wrote letters and signed them. 'Love always.'

One afternoon Wes was in the yard pulling weeds when Chef drove up in front of the house. I was working at the sink. I looked and saw Chef's big car pull in. I could see his car, the access road and the freeway, and, behind the freeway, the dunes and the ocean. Clouds hung over the water. Chef got out of his car and hitched his pants. I knew there was something. Wes stopped what he was doing and stood up. He was wearing his gloves and a canvas hat. He took off the hat and wiped his face with the back of his hand. Chef walked over and put his arm around Wes's shoulders. Wes took off one of his gloves. I went to the door. I heard Chef say to Wes God knows he was sorry but he was going to have to ask us to leave at the end of the month. Wes pulled off his other glove. Why's that, Chef? Chef said his daughter, Linda, the woman Wes used to call Fat Linda from the time of his drinking days, needed a place to live and this place was it. Chef told Wes that Linda's husband had taken his fishing boat out a few weeks back and nobody had heard from him since. She's my own blood, Chef said to Wes. She's lost her husband. She's lost her baby's father. I can help. I'm glad I'm in a position to help, Chef said. I'm sorry, Wes, but you'll have to look for another house. Then Chef hugged Wes again, hitched his pants, and got in his big car and drove away.

Wes came inside the house. He dropped his hat and gloves on the carpet and sat down in the big chair. Chef's chair, it occurred to me. Chef's carpet, even. Wes looked pale. I poured two cups of coffee and gave one to him.

It's all right, I said. Wes, don't worry about it, I said. I sat down on Chef's sofa with my coffee.

Fat Linda's going to live here now instead of us, Wes said. He held his cup, but he didn't drink from it.

Wes, don't get stirred up, I said.

Her man will turn up in Ketchikan, Wes said. Fat Linda's husband has simply pulled out on them. And who could blame him? Wes said. Wes said if it came to that, he'd go down with his ship, too, rather than live the rest of his days with Fat Linda and her kid. Then Wes put his cup down next to his gloves. This has been a happy house up to now, he said.

We'll get another house, I said.

Not like this one, Wes said. It wouldn't be the same, anyway. This house has been a good house for us. This house has good memories to it. Now Fat Linda and her kid will be in here, Wes said. He picked up his cup and tasted from it.

It's Chef's house, I said. He has to do what he has to do.

I know that, Wes said. But I don't have to like it.

Wes had this look about him. I knew that look. He kept touching his lips with his tongue. He kept thumbing his shirt under his waist-band. He got up from the chair and went to the window. He stood looking out at the ocean and at the clouds, which were building up. He patted his chin with his fingers like he was thinking about something. And he *was* thinking.

Go easy, Wes, I said.

She wants me to go easy, Wes said. He kept standing there.

But in a minute he came over and sat next to me on the sofa. He crossed one leg over the other and began fooling with the buttons on his shirt. I took his hand. I started to talk. I talked about the summer. But I caught myself talking like it was something that had happened in the past. Maybe years back. At any rate, like something that was over. Then I started talking about the kids. Wes said he wished he could do it over again and do it right this time.

They love you, I said.

No, they don't, he said.

I said, Someday, they'll understand things.

Maybe, Wes said. But it won't matter then.

You don't know, I said.

I know a few things, Wes said, and looked at me. I know I'm glad you came up here. I won't forget you did it, Wes said.

I'm glad, too, I said. I'm glad you found this house, I said.

Wes snorted. Then he laughed. We both laughed. That Chef, Wes said, and shook his head. He threw us a knuckle-ball, that son of a bitch. But I'm glad you wore your ring. I'm glad we had us this time together, Wes said.

Then I said something. I said, Suppose, just suppose, nothing had ever happened. Suppose this was for the first time. Just suppose. It doesn't hurt to suppose. Say none of the other had ever happened. You know what I mean? Then what? I said.

Wes fixed his eyes on me. He said, Then I suppose we'd have to be somebody else if that was the case. Somebody we're not. I don't have that kind of supposing left in me. We were born who we are. Don't you see what I'm saying?

I said I hadn't thrown away a good thing and come six hundred miles to hear him talk like this.

He said, I'm sorry, but I can't talk like somebody I'm not. I'm not somebody else. If I was somebody else, I sure as hell wouldn't be here. If I was somebody else, I wouldn't be me. But I'm who I am. Don't you see?

Wes, it's all right, I said. I brought his hand to my cheek. Then, I don't know, I remembered how he was when he was nineteen, the way he looked running across this field to where his dad sat on a tractor, hand over his eyes, watching Wes run toward him. We'd just driven up from California. I got out with Cheryl and Bobby and said, There's Grandpa. But they were just babies.

Wes sat next to me patting his chin, like he was trying to figure out the next thing. Wes's dad was gone and our kids were grown up. I looked at Wes and then I looked around Chef's living room at Chef's things, and I thought, We have to do something now and do it quick.

Hon, I said. Wes, listen to me.

What do you want? he said. But that's all he said. He seemed to have made up his mind. But, having made up his mind, he was in no hurry. He leaned back on the sofa, folded his hands in his lap, and closed his eyes. He didn't say anything else. He didn't have to.

I said his name to myself. It was an easy name to say, and I'd been used to saying it for a long time. Then I said it once more. This time I said it out loud. Wes, I said.

He opened his eyes. But he didn't look at me. He just sat where he was and looked toward the window. Fat Linda, he said. But I knew it wasn't her. She was nothing. Just a name. Wes got up and pulled the drapes and the ocean was gone just like that. I went in to start supper. We still had some fish in the icebox. There wasn't much else. We'll clean it up tonight, I thought, and that will be the end of it.

Preservation

Sandy's husband had been on the sofa ever since he'd been termi-
nated three months ago. That day, three months ago, he'd come home
looking pale and scared and with all his work things in a box. 'Happy
Valentine's Day,' he said to Sandy and put a heart-shaped box of
candy and a bottle of Jim Beam on the kitchen table. He took off his
cap and laid that on the table, too. 'I got canned today. Hey, what do
you think's going to happen to us now?'

Sandy and her husband sat at the table and drank whiskey and ate
the chocolates. They talked about what he might be able to do instead
of putting roofs on new houses. But they couldn't think of anything.
'Something will turn up,' Sandy said. She wanted to be encouraging.
But she was scared, too. Finally, he said he'd sleep on it. And he did.
He made his bed on the sofa that night, and that's where he'd slept
every night since it had happened.

The day after his termination there were unemployment benefits to
see about. He went downtown to the state office to fill out papers and
look for another job. But there were no jobs in his line of work, or in
any other line of work. His face began to sweat as he tried to describe
to Sandy the milling crowd of men and women down there. That
evening he got back on the sofa. He began spending all of his time
there, as if, she thought, it was the thing he was supposed to do now
that he no longer had any work. Once in a while he had to go talk to
somebody about a job possibility, and every two weeks he had to go
sign something to collect his unemployment compensation. But the
rest of the time he stayed on the sofa. It's like he *lives* there, Sandy
thought. He *lives* in the living room. Now and then he looked through
magazines she brought home from the grocery store; and every so
often she came in to find him looking at this big book she'd got as a
bonus for joining a book club – something called *Mysteries of the Past*.
He held the book in front of him with both hands, his head inclined
over the pages, as if he were being drawn in by what he was reading.
But after a while she noticed that he didn't seem to be making any
progress in it; he still seemed to be at about the same place – somewhere around chapter two, she guessed. Sandy picked it up once and
opened it to his place. There she read about a man who had been

discovered after spending two thousand years in a peat bog in the Netherlands. A photograph appeared on one page. The man's brow was furrowed, but there was a serene expression to his face. He wore a leather cap and lay on his side. The man's hands and feet had shriveled, but otherwise he didn't look so awful. She read in the book a little further, then put it back where she'd gotten it. Her husband kept it within easy reach on the coffee table that stood in front of the sofa. That goddamn sofa! As far as she was concerned, she didn't even want to sit on it again. She couldn't imagine them ever having lain down there in the past to make love.

The newspaper came to the house every day. He read it from the first page to the last. She saw him read everything, right down to the obituary section, and the part showing the temperatures of the major cities, as well as the Business News section which told about mergers and interest rates. Mornings, he got up before she did and used the bathroom. Then he turned the TV on and made coffee. She thought he seemed upbeat and cheerful at that hour of the day. But by the time she left for work, he'd made his place on the sofa and the TV was going. Most often it would still be going when she came in again that afternoon. He'd be sitting up on the sofa, or else lying down on it, dressed in what he used to wear to work – jeans and a flannel shirt. But sometimes the TV would be off and he'd be sitting there holding his book.

'How's it going?' he'd say when she looked in on him.

'Okay,' she'd say. 'How's it with you?'

'Okay.'

He always had a pot of coffee warming on the stove for her. In the living room, she'd sit in the big chair and he'd sit on the sofa while they talked about her day. They'd hold their cups and drink their coffee as if they were normal people, Sandy thought.

Sandy still loved him, even though she knew things were getting weird. She was thankful to have her job, but she didn't know what was going to happen to them or to anybody else in the world. She had a girlfriend at work she confided in one time about her husband – about his being on the sofa all the time. For some reason, her friend didn't seem to think it was anything very strange, which both surprised and depressed Sandy. Her friend told her about her uncle in Tennessee – when her uncle had turned forty, he got into his bed and wouldn't get up anymore. And he cried a lot – he cried at least once every day. She told Sandy she guessed her uncle was afraid of getting old. She guessed maybe he was afraid of a heart attack or something. But the man was sixty-three now and still breathing, she said. When Sandy heard this, she was stunned. If this woman was telling the truth, she thought, the man has been in bed for twenty-three years. Sandy's husband was only thirty-one. Thirty-one and twenty-three is fifty-four. That'd put her in her fifties then, too. My God, a person couldn't live the whole rest of his life in bed, or else on the sofa. If her husband had been wounded or was ill, or had been hurt in a car accident, that'd be different. She could understand that. If something like that was the case, she knew she could bear it. Then if he had to live on the sofa, and she had to bring him his food out there, maybe carry the spoon up to his mouth — there was even something like romance in that kind of thing. But for her husband, a young and otherwise healthy man, to take to the sofa in this way and not want to get up except to go to the bathroom or to turn the TV on in the morning or off at night, this was different. It made her ashamed; and except for that one time, she didn't talk about it to anybody. She didn't say any more about it to her friend, whose uncle had gotten into bed twenty-three years ago and was still there, as far as Sandy knew.

Late one afternoon she came home from work, parked the car, and went inside the house. She could hear the TV going in the living room as she let herself in the door to the kitchen. The coffee pot was on the stove, and the burner was on low. From where she stood in the kitchen, holding her purse, she could look into the living room and see the back of the sofa and the TV screen. Figures moved across the screen. Her husband's bare feet stuck out from one end of the sofa. At the other end, on a pillow which lay across the arm of the sofa, she could see the crown of his head. He didn't stir. He may or may not have been asleep, and he may or may not have heard her come in. But she decided it didn't make any difference one way or the other. She put her purse on the table and went over to the fridge to get herself some yogurt. But when she opened the door, warm, boxed-in air came out at her. She couldn't believe the mess inside. The ice cream from the freezer had melted and run down into the leftover fish sticks and cole slaw. Ice cream had gotten into the bowl of Spanish rice and pooled on the bottom of the fridge. Ice cream was everywhere. She opened the door to the freezer compartment. An awful smell puffed out at her that made her want to gag. Ice cream covered the bottom of the compartment and puddled around a three-pound package of hamburger. She pressed her finger into the cellophane wrapper covering the meat, and her finger sank into the package. The pork chops had thawed, too. Everything had thawed, including some more fish sticks, a package of Steak-ums, and two Chef Sammy Chinese food dinners. The hot dogs and homemade spaghetti sauce had thawed. She closed the door to the freezer and reached into the fridge for her carton of yogurt. She raised the lid on the yogurt and sniffed. That's when she yelled at her husband.

'What is it?' he said, sitting up and looking over the back of the sofa. 'Hey, what's wrong?' He pushed his hand through his hair a couple of times. She couldn't tell if he'd been asleep all this time or what.

'This goddamn fridge has gone out,' Sandy said. 'That's what.'

Her husband got up off the sofa and lowered the volume on the TV. Then he turned it off and came out to the kitchen. 'Let me see this,' he said. 'Hey, I don't believe this.'

'See for yourself,' she said. 'Everything's going to spoil.'

Her husband looked inside the fridge, and his face assumed a very grave expression. Then he poked around in the freezer and saw what things were like in there.

'Tell me what next,' he said.

A bunch of things suddenly flew into her head, but she didn't say anything.

'Goddamn it,' he said, 'when it rains, it pours. Hey, this fridge can't be more than ten years old. It was nearly new when we bought it. Listen, my folks had a fridge that lasted them twenty-five years. They gave it to my brother when he got married. It was working fine. Hey, what's going on?' He moved over so that he could see into the narrow space between the fridge and the wall. 'I don't get it,' he said and shook his head. 'It's plugged in.' Then he took hold of the fridge and rocked it back and forth. He put his shoulder against it and pushed and jerked the appliance a few inches out into the kitchen. Something inside the fridge fell off a shelf and broke. 'Hells bells,' he said.

Sandy realized she was still holding the yogurt. She went over to the garbage can, raised the lid, and dropped the carton inside. 'I have to cook everything tonight,' she said. She saw herself at the stove frying meat, fixing things in pans on the stove and in the oven. 'We need a new fridge,' she said.

He didn't say anything. He looked into the freezer compartment once more and turned his head back and forth.

She moved in front of him and started taking things off the shelves and putting stuff on the table. He helped. He took the meat out of the freezer and put the packages on the table. Then he took the other things out of the freezer and put them in a different place on the table. He took everything out and then found the paper towels and the dishcloth and started wiping up inside.

'We lost our Freon,' he said and stopped wiping. 'That's what happened. I can smell it. The Freon leaked out. Something happened and the Freon went. Hey, I saw this happen to somebody else's box once.' He was calm now. He started wiping again. 'It's the Freon,' he said.

She stopped what she was doing and looked at him. 'We need another fridge,' she said.

'You said that. Hey, where are we going to get one? They don't grow on trees.'

'We have to have one,' she said. 'Don't we need a fridge? Maybe we don't. Maybe we can keep our perishables on the window sill like those people in tenements do. Or else we could get one of those little Styrofoam coolers and buy some ice every day.' She put a head of lettuce and some tomatoes on the table next to the packages of meat. Then she sat down on one of the dinette chairs and brought her hands up to her face.

'We'll get us another fridge,' her husband said. 'Hell, yes. We need one, don't we? We can't get along without one. The question is, where do we get one and how much can we pay for it? There must be zillions of used ones in the classifieds. Just hold on and we'll see what's in the paper. Hey, I'm an expert on the classifieds,' he said.

She brought her hands down from her face and looked at him.

'Sandy, we'll find us a good used box out of the paper,' he went on. 'Most of your fridges are built to last a lifetime. This one of ours, Jesus, I don't know what happened to it. It's only the second one in my life I ever heard about going on the fritz like this.' He switched his gaze to the fridge again. 'Goddamn lousy luck,' he said.

'Bring the paper out here,' she said. 'Let's see what there is.'

'Don't worry,' he said. He went out to the coffee table, sorted through the stack of newspapers, and came back to the kitchen with the classified section. She pushed the food to one side so that he could spread the pages out. He took one of the chairs.

She glanced down at the paper, then at the food that had thawed. 'I've got to fry pork chops tonight,' she said. 'And I have to cook up that hamburger. And those sandwich steaks and the fish sticks. Don't forget the TV dinners, either.'

'That goddamn Freon,' he said. 'You can smell it.'

They began to go through the classifieds. He ran his finger down one column and then another. He passed quickly over the JOBS AVAILABLE section. She saw checks beside a couple of things, but she didn't look to see what he'd marked. It didn't matter. There was a column headlined OUTDOOR CAMPING SUPPLIES. Then they found it - APPLIANCES NEW AND OLD.

'Here,' she said, and put her finger down on the paper.

He moved her finger. 'Let me see,' he said.

She put her finger back where it'd been. ' "Refrigerators, Ranges, Washers, Dryers, etc.," ' she said, reading from the ad boxed in the column. ' "Auction Barn." What's that? Auction Barn.' She went on reading. ' "New and used appliances and more every Thursday night. Auction at seven o'clock." That's today. Today's Thursday,' she said. 'This auction's tonight. And this place is not very far away. It's down on Pine Street. I must have driven by there a hundred times. You, too. You know where it is. It's down there close to that Baskin-Robbins.'

Her husband didn't say anything. He stared at the ad. He brought his hand up and pulled at his lower lip with two of his fingers. 'Auction Barn,' he said.

She fixed her eyes on him. 'Let's go to it. What do you say? It'll do you good to get out, and we'll see if we can't find us a fridge. Two birds with one stone,' she said.

'I've never been to an auction in my life,' he said. 'I don't believe I want to go to one now.'

'Come *on*,' Sandy said. 'What's the matter with you? They're fun. I haven't been to one in years, not since I was a kid. I used to go to them with my dad.' She suddenly wanted to go to this auction very much.

'Your dad,' he said.

'Yeah, my dad.' She looked at her husband, waiting for him to say something else. The least thing. But he didn't.

'Auctions are fun,' she said.

'They probably are, but I don't want to go.'

'I need a bed lamp, too,' she went on. 'They'll have bed lamps.'

'Hey, we need lots of things. But I don't have a job, remember?'

'I'm going to this auction,' she said. 'Whether you go or not. You might as well come along. But I don't care. If you want the truth, it's immaterial to me. But I'm going.'

'I'll go with you. Who said I wouldn't go?' He looked at her and then looked away. He picked up the paper and read the ad again. 'I don't know the first thing about auctions. But, sure, I'll try anything once. Whoever said anything about us buying an icebox at an auction?'

'Nobody,' she said. 'But we'll do it anyway.'

'Okay,' he said.

'Good,' she said. 'But only if you really want to.'

He nodded.

She said, 'I guess I'd better start cooking. I'll cook the goddamn pork chops now, and we'll eat. The rest of this stuff can wait. I'll cook everything else later. After we go to this auction. But we have to get moving. The paper said seven o'clock.'

'Seven o'clock,' he said. He got up from the table and made his way into the living room, where he looked out the bay window for a minute. A car passed on the street outside. He brought his fingers up to his lip. She watched him sit down on the sofa and take up his book. He opened it to his place. But in a minute he put it down and lay back on the sofa. She saw his head come down on the pillow that lay across the arm of the sofa. He adjusted the pillow under his head and put his hands behind his neck. Then he lay still. Pretty soon she saw his arms move down to his sides.

She folded the paper. She got up from the chair and went quietly out to the living room, where she looked over the back of the sofa. His eyes were shut. His chest seemed to barely rise and then fall. She went back to the kitchen and put a frying pan on the burner. She turned the burner on and poured oil into the pan. She started frying pork chops. She'd gone to auctions with her dad. Most of those auctions had to do with farm animals. She seemed to remember her dad was always trying to sell a calf, or else buy one. Sometimes there'd be farm equipment and household items at the auctions. But mostly it was farm animals. Then, after her dad and mom had divorced, and she'd gone away to live with her mom, her dad wrote to say he missed going to auctions with her. The last letter he wrote to her, after she'd grown up and was living with her husband, he said he'd bought a peach of a car at this auction for two hundred dollars. If she'd been there, he said, he'd have bought one for her, too. Three weeks later, in the middle of the night, a telephone call told her that he was dead. The car he'd bought leaked carbon monoxide up through the floorboards and caused him to pass out behind the wheel. He lived in the country. The motor went on running until there was no more gas in the tank. He stayed in the car until somebody found him a few days later.

The pan was starting to smoke. She poured in more oil and turned on the fan. She hadn't been to an auction in twenty years, and now she was getting ready to go to one tonight. But first she had to dry these pork chops. It was bad luck their fridge had gone flooey, but she found herself looking forward to this auction. She began missing her dad. She even missed her mom now, though the two of them used to argue all the time before she met her husband and began living with him. She stood at the stove, turning the meat, and missing both her dad and her mom.

Still missing them, she took a pot holder and moved the pan off the stove. Smoke was being drawn up through the vent over the stove. She stepped to the doorway with the pan and looked into the living room. The pan was still smoking and drops of oil and grease jumped over the sides as she held it. In the darkened room, she could just make out her husband's head, and his bare feet. 'Come on out here,' she said. 'It's ready.'

'Okay,' he said.

She saw his head come up from the end of the sofa. She put the pan back on the stove and turned to the cupboard. She took down a couple of plates and put them on the counter. She used her spatula to raise one of the pork chops. Then she lifted it onto a plate. The meat didn't look like meat. It looked like part of an old shoulder blade, or a digging instrument. But she knew it was a pork chop, and she took the other one out of the pan and put that on a plate, too.

In a minute, her husband came into the kitchen. He looked at the fridge once more, which was standing there with its door open. And then his eyes took in the pork chops. His mouth dropped open, but he didn't say anything. She waited for him to say something, anything, but he didn't. She put salt and pepper on the table and told him to sit down.

'Sit down,' she said and gave him a plate on which lay the remains of a pork chop. 'I want you to eat this,' she said. He took the plate. But he just stood there and looked at it. Then she turned to get her own plate.

Sandy cleared the newspaper away and shoved the food to the far side of the table. 'Sit down,' she said to her husband once more. He moved his plate from one hand to the other. But he kept standing there. It was then she saw puddles of water on the table. She heard water, too. It was dripping off the table and onto the linoleum.

She looked down at her husband's bare feet. She stared at his feet next to the pool of water. She knew she'd never again in her life see anything so unusual. But she didn't know what to make of it yet. She thought she'd better put on some lipstick, get her coat, and go ahead to the auction. But she couldn't take her eyes from her husband's feet. She put her plate on the table and watched until the feet left the kitchen and went back into the living room.

The compartment

Myers was traveling through France in a first-class rail car on his way to visit his son in Strasbourg, who was a student at the university there. He hadn't seen the boy in eight years. There had been no phone calls between them during this time, not even a postcard since Myers and the boy's mother had gone their separate ways – the boy staying with her. The final break-up was hastened along, Myers always believed, by the boy's malign interference in their personal affairs.

The last time Myers had seen his son, the boy had lunged for him during a violent quarrel. Myers's wife had been standing by the sideboard, dropping one dish of china after the other onto the dining-room floor. Then she'd gone on to the cups. 'That's enough,' Myers had said, and at that instant the boy charged him. Myers sidestepped and got him in a headlock while the boy wept and pummeled Myers on the back and kidneys. Myers had him, and while he had him, he made the most of it. He slammed him into the wall and threatened to kill him. He meant it. 'I gave you life,' Myers remembered himself shouting, 'and I can take it back!'

Thinking about that horrible scene now, Myers shook his head as if it had happened to someone else. And it had. He was simply not that same person. These days he lived alone and had little to do with anybody outside of his work. At night, he listened to classical music and read books on water-fowl decoys.

He lit a cigarette and continued to gaze out the train window, ignoring the man who sat in the seat next to the door and who slept with a hat pulled over his eyes. It was early in the morning and mist hung over the green fields that passed by outside. Now and then Myers saw a farmhouse and its outbuildings, everything surrounded by a wall. He thought this might be a good way to live – in an old house surrounded by a wall.

It was just past six o'clock. Myers hadn't slept since he'd boarded the train in Milan at eleven the night before. When the train had left Milan, he'd considered himself lucky to have the compartment to himself. He kept the light on and looked at guidebooks. He read things he wished he'd read before he'd been to the place they were about. He discovered much that he should have seen and done. In a way, he was sorry to be finding out certain things about the country now, just as he was leaving Italy behind after his first and, no doubt, last visit.

He put the guidebooks away in his suitcase, put the suitcase in the overhead rack, and took off his coat so he could use it for a blanket. He switched off the light and sat there in the darkened compartment with his eyes closed, hoping sleep would come.

After what seemed a long time, and just when he thought he was going to drop off, the train began to slow. It came to a stop at a little station outside of Basel. There, a middle-aged man in a dark suit, and wearing a hat, entered the compartment. The man said something to Myers in a language Myers didn't understand, and then the man put his leather bag up into the rack. He sat down on the other side of the compartment and straightened his shoulders. Then he pulled his hat over his eyes. By the time the train was moving again, the man was asleep and snoring quietly. Myers envied him. In a few minutes, a Swiss official opened the door of the compartment and turned on the light. In English, and in some other language – German, Myers assumed – the official asked to see their passports. The man in the compartment with Myers pushed the hat back on his head, blinked his eyes, and reached into his coat pocket. The official studied the passport, looked at the man closely, and gave him back the document. Myers handed over his own passport. The official read the data, examined the photograph, and then looked at Myers before nodding and giving it back. He turned off the light as he went out. The man across from Myers pulled the hat over his eyes and put out his legs. Myers supposed he'd go right back to sleep, and once again he felt envy.

He stayed awake after that and began to think of the meeting with his son, which was now only a few hours away. How would he act when he saw the boy at the station? Should he embrace him? He felt uncomfortable with that prospect. Or should he merely offer his hand, smile as if these eight years had never occurred, and then pat the boy on the shoulder? Maybe the boy would say a few words – I'm glad to see you – how was your trip? And Myers would say – something. He really didn't know what he was going to say.

The French *contrôleur* walked by the compartment. He looked in on Myers and at the man sleeping across from Myers. This same *contrôleur* had already punched their tickets, so Myers turned his head and went back to looking out the window. More houses began to appear. But now there were no walls, and the houses were smaller and set closer together. Soon, Myers was sure, he'd see a French village. The haze was lifting. The train blew its whistle and sped past a crossing over which a barrier had been lowered. He saw a young woman with her hair pinned up and wearing a sweater, standing with her bicycle as she watched the cars whip past.

How's your mother? he might say to the boy after they had walked a little way from the station. *What do you hear from your mother?* For a wild instant, it occurred to Myers she could be dead. But then he understood that it couldn't be so, he'd have heard something – one way or the other, he'd have heard. He knew if he let himself go on thinking about these things, his heart could break. He closed the top button of his shirt and fixed his tie. He laid his coat across the seat next to him. He laced his shoes, got up, and stepped over the legs of the sleeping man. He let himself out of the compartment.

Myers had to put his hand against the windows along the corridor to steady himself as he moved toward the end of the car. He closed the door to the little toilet and locked it. Then he ran water and splashed his face. The train moved into a curve, still at the same high speed, and Myers had to hold on to the sink for balance.

The boy's letter had come to him a couple of months ago. The letter had been brief. He wrote that he'd been living in France and studying for the past year at the university in Strasbourg. There was no other information about what had possessed him to go to France, or what he'd been doing with himself during those years before France. Appropriately enough, Myers thought, no mention was made in the letter of the boy's mother – not a clue to her condition or whereabouts. But, inexplicably, the boy had closed the letter with the word *Love*, and Myers had pondered this for a long while. Finally, he'd answered the letter. After some deliberation, Myers wrote to say he had been thinking for some time of making a little trip to Europe. Would the boy like to meet him at the station in Strasbourg? He signed his letter, 'Love, Dad.' He'd heard back from the boy and then he made his arrangements. It struck him that there was really no one, besides his secretary and a few business associates, that he felt it was necessary to tell he was going away. He had accumulated six weeks of vacation at the engineering firm where he worked, and he decided he would take all of the time coming to him for this trip. He was glad he'd done this, even though he now had no intention of spending all that time in Europe.

He'd gone first to Rome. But after the first few hours, walking around by himself on the streets, he was sorry he hadn't arranged to be with a group. He was lonely. He went to Venice, a city he and his wife had always talked of visiting. But Venice was a disappointment. He saw a man with one arm eating fried squid, and there were grimy, water-stained buildings everywhere he looked. He took a train to Milan, where he checked into a four-star hotel and spent the night watching a soccer match on a Sony color TV until the station went off the air. He got up the next morning and wandered around the city until it was time to go to the station. He'd planned the stopover in Strasbourg as the culmination of his trip. After a day or two, or three days — he'd see how it went — he would travel to Paris and fly home. He was tired of trying to make himself understood to strangers and would be glad to get back.

Someone tried the door to the WC. Myers finished tucking his shirt. He fastened his belt. Then he unlocked the door and, swaying with the movement of the train, walked back to his compartment. As he opened the door, he saw at once that his coat had been moved. It lay across a different seat from the one where he'd left it. He felt he had entered into a ludicrous but potentially serious situation. His heart began to race as he picked up the coat. He put his hand into the inside pocket and took out his passport. He carried his wallet in his hip pocket. So he still had his wallet and the passport. He went through the other coat pockets. What was missing was the gift he'd bought for the boy — an expensive Japanese wristwatch purchased at a shop in Rome. He had carried the watch in his inside coat pocket for safe-keeping. Now the watch was gone.

'Pardon,' he said to the man who slumped in the seat, legs out, the hat over his eyes. 'Pardon.' The man pushed the hat back and opened his eyes. He pulled himself up and looked at Myers. His eyes were large. He might have been dreaming. But he might not.

Myers said, 'Did you see somebody come in here?'

But it was clear the man didn't know what Myers was saying. He continued to stare at him with what Myers took to be a look of total incomprehension. But maybe it was something else, Myers thought. Maybe the look masked slyness and deceit. Myers shook his coat to focus the man's attention. Then he put his hand into the pocket and rummaged. He pulled his sleeve back and showed the man his own wristwatch. The man looked at Myers and then at Myers's watch. He seemed mystified. Myers tapped the face of his watch. He put his other hand back into his coat pocket and made a gesture as if he were fishing for something. Myers pointed at the watch once more and waggled his fingers, hoping to signify the wristwatch taking flight out the door.

The man shrugged and shook his head.

'Goddamn it,' Myers said in frustration. He put his coat on and went out into the corridor. He couldn't stay in the compartment another minute. He was afraid he might strike the man. He looked up and down the corridor, as if hoping he could see and recognize the thief. But there was no one around. Maybe the man who shared his compartment hadn't taken the watch. Maybe someone else, the person who tried the door to the WC, had walked past the compartment, spotted the coat and the sleeping man, and simply opened the door, gone through the pockets, closed the door, and gone away again.

Myers walked slowly to the end of the car, peering into the other compartments. It was not crowded in this first-class car, but there were one or two people in each compartment. Most of them were asleep, or seemed to be. Their eyes were closed, and their heads were thrown back against the seats. In one compartment, a man about his own age sat by the window looking out at the countryside. When Myers stopped at the glass and looked in at him, the man turned and regarded him fiercely.

Myers crossed into the second-class car. The compartments in this car were crowded – sometimes five or six passengers in each, and the people, he could tell at a glance, were more desperate. Many of them were awake – it was too uncomfortable to sleep – and they turned their eyes on him as he passed. Foreigners, he thought. It was clear to him that if the man in his compartment hadn't taken the watch, then the thief was from one of these compartments. But what could he do? It was hopeless. The watch was gone. It was in someone else's pocket now. He couldn't hope to make the *contrôleur* understand what had happened. And even if he could, then what? He made his way back to his own compartment. He looked in and saw that the man had stretched out again with his hat over his eyes.

Myers stepped over the man's legs and sat down in his seat by the window. He felt dazed with anger. They were on the outskirts of the city now. Farms and grazing land had given over to industrial plants with unpronounceable names on the fronts of the buildings. The train began slowing. Myers could see automobiles on city streets, and others waiting in line at the crossings for the train to pass. He got up and took his suitcase down. He held it on his lap while he looked out the window at this hateful place.

It came to him that he didn't want to see the boy after all. He was shocked by this realization and for a moment felt diminished by the meanness of it. He shook his head. In a lifetime of foolish actions, this trip was possibly the most foolish thing he'd ever done. But the fact was, he really had no desire to see this boy whose behavior had long ago isolated him from Myers's affections. He suddenly, and with great clarity, recalled the boy's face when he had lunged that time, and a wave of bitterness passed over Myers. This boy had devoured Myers's youth, had turned the young girl he had courted and wed into a nervous, alcoholic woman whom the boy alternately pitied and bullied. Why on earth, Myers asked himself, would he come all this way to see someone he disliked? He didn't want to shake the boy's hand, the hand of his enemy, nor have to clap him on the shoulder and make small-talk. He didn't want to have to ask him about his mother.

He sat forward in the seat as the train pulled into the station. An announcement was called out in French over the train's intercom. The man across from Myers began to stir. He adjusted his hat and sat up in the seat as something else in French came over the speaker. Myers didn't understand anything that was said. He grew more agitated as the train slowed and then came to a stop. He decided he wasn't going to leave the compartment. He was going to sit where he was until the train pulled away. When it did, he'd be on it, going on with the train to Paris, and that would be that. He looked out the window cautiously, afraid he'd see the boy's face at the glass. He didn't know what he'd do if that happened. He was afraid he might shake his fist. He saw a few people on the platform wearing coats and scarves who stood next to their suitcases, waiting to board the train. A few other people waited, without luggage, hands in their pockets, obviously expecting to meet someone. His son was not one of those waiting, but, of course, that didn't mean he wasn't out there somewhere. Myers moved the suitcase off his lap onto the floor and inched down in his seat.

The man across from him was yawning and looking out the window. Now he turned his gaze on Myers. He took off his hat and ran his hand through his hair. Then he put the hat back on, got to his feet, and pulled his bag down from the rack. He opened the compartment door. But before he went out, he turned around and gestured in the direction of the station.

'Strasbourg,' the man said.

Myers turned away.

The man waited an instant longer, and then went out into the corridor with his bag and, Myers felt certain, with the wristwatch. But that was the least of his concerns now. He looked out the train window once again. He saw a man in an apron standing in the door of the station, smoking a cigarette. The man was watching two trainmen explaining something to a woman in a long skirt who held a baby in her arms. The woman listened and then nodded and listened some more. She moved the baby from one arm to the other. The men kept talking. She listened. One of the men chucked the baby under its chin. The woman looked down and smiled. She moved the baby again and listened some more. Myers saw a young couple embracing on the platform a little distance from his car. Then the young man let go of the young woman. He said something, picked up his valise, and moved to board the train. The woman watched him go. She brought a hand up to her face, touched one eye and then the other with the heel of her hand. In a minute, Myers saw her moving down the platform, her eyes fixed on his car, as if following someone. He glanced away from the woman and looked at the big clock over the station's waiting room. He looked up and down the platform. The boy was nowhere in sight. It was possible he had overslept or it might be that he, too, had changed his mind. In any case, Myers felt relieved. He looked at the clock again, then at the young woman who was hurrying up to the window where he sat. Myers drew back as if she were going to strike the glass.

The door to the compartment opened. The young man he'd seen outside closed the door behind him and said, *'Bonjour.'* Without waiting for a reply, he threw his valise into the overhead rack and stepped over to the window. *'Pardonnez-moi.'* He pulled the window down. 'Marie,' he said. The young woman began to smile and cry at the same time. The young man brought her hands up and began kissing her fingers.

Myers looked away and clamped his teeth. He heard the final shouts of the trainmen. Someone blew a whistle. Presently, the train began to move away from the platform. The young man had let go of the woman's hands, but he continued to wave at her as the train rolled forward.

But the train went only a short distance, into the open air of the railyard, and then Myers felt it come to an abrupt stop. The young man closed the window and moved over to the seat by the door. He took a newspaper from his coat and began to read. Myers got up and opened the door. He went to the end of the corridor, where the cars were coupled together. He didn't know why they had stopped. Maybe something was wrong. He moved to the window. But all he could see was an intricate system of tracks where trains were being made up, cars taken off or switched from one train to another. He stepped back from the window. The sign on the door to the next car said, POUSSEZ. Myers struck the sign with his fist, and the door slid open. He was in the second-class car again. He passed along a row of compartments filled with people settling down, as if making ready for a long trip. He needed to find out from someone where this train was going. He had understood, at the time he purchased the ticket, that the train to Strasbourg went on to Paris. But he felt it would be humiliating to put his head into one of the compartments and say, 'Paree?' or however they said it – as if asking if they'd arrived at a destination. He heard a loud clanking, and the train backed up a little. He could see the station again, and once more he thought of his son. Maybe he was standing back there, breathless from having rushed to get to the station, wondering what had happened to his father. Myers shook his head.

The car he was in creaked and groaned under him, then something caught and fell heavily into place. Myers looked out at the maze of tracks and realized that the train had begun to move again. He turned and hurried back to the end of the car and crossed back into the car he'd been traveling in. He walked down the corridor to his compartment. But the young man with the newspaper was gone. And Myers's suitcase was gone. It was not his compartment after all. He realized with a start they must have uncoupled his car while the train was in the yard and attached another second-class car to the train. The compartment he stood in front of was nearly filled with small, dark-skinned men who spoke rapidly in a language Myers had never heard before. One of the men signaled him to come inside. Myers moved into the compartment, and the men made room for him. There seemed to be a jovial air in the compartment. The man who'd signaled him laughed and patted the space next to him. Myers sat down with his back to the front of the train. The countryside out the window began to pass faster and faster. For a moment, Myers had the impression of the landscape shooting away from him. He was going somewhere, he knew that. And if it was the wrong direction, sooner or later he'd find out.

He leaned against the seat and closed his eyes. The men went on talking and laughing. Their voices came to him as if from a distance. Soon the voices became part of the train's movements – and gradually Myers felt himself being carried, then pulled back, into sleep.

A small
good thing

Saturday afternoon she drove to the bakery in the shopping center. After looking through a loose-leaf binder with photographs of cakes taped onto the pages, she ordered chocolate, the child's favorite. The cake she chose was decorated with a space ship and launching pad under a sprinkling of white stars, and a planet made of red frosting at the other end. His name, SCOTTY, would be in green letters beneath the planet. The baker, who was an older man with a thick neck, listened without saying anything when she told him the child would be eight years old next Monday. The baker wore a white apron that looked like a smock. Straps cut under his arms, went around in back and then to the front again, where they were secured under his heavy waist. He wiped his hands on his apron as he listened to her. He kept his eyes down on the photographs and let her talk. He let her take her time. He'd just come to work and he'd be there all night, baking, and he was in no real hurry.

She gave the baker her name, Ann Weiss, and her telephone number. The cake would be ready on Monday morning, just out of the oven, in plenty of time for the child's party that afternoon. The baker was not jolly. There were no pleasantries between them, just the minimum exchange of words, the necessary information. He made her feel uncomfortable, and she didn't like that. While he was bent over the counter with the pencil in his hand, she studied his coarse features and wondered if he'd ever done anything else with his life besides be a baker. She was a mother and thirty-three years old, and it seemed to her that everyone, especially someone the baker's age – a man old enough to be her father – must have children who'd gone through this special time of cakes and birthday parties. There must be that between them, she thought. But he was abrupt with her – not rude, just abrupt. She gave up trying to make friends with him. She looked into the back of the bakery and could see a long, heavy wooden table with aluminum pie pans stacked at one end; and beside the table a metal container filled with empty racks. There was an enormous oven. A radio was playing country-Western music.

The baker finished printing the information on the special order card and closed up the binder. He looked at her and said, 'Monday morning.' She thanked him and drove home.

On Monday morning, the birthday boy was walking to school with another boy. They were passing a bag of potato chips back and forth and the birthday boy was trying to find out what his friend intended to give him for his birthday that afternoon. Without looking, the birthday boy stepped off the curb at an intersection and was immediately knocked down by a car. He fell on his side with his head in the gutter and his legs out in the road. His eyes were closed, but his legs moved back and forth as if he were trying to climb over something. His friend dropped the potato chips and started to cry. The car had gone a hundred feet or so and stopped in the middle of the road. The man in the driver's seat looked back over his shoulder. He waited until the boy got unsteadily to his feet. The boy wobbled a little. He looked dazed, but okay. The driver put the car into gear and drove away.

The birthday boy didn't cry, but he didn't have anything to say about anything either. He wouldn't answer when his friend asked him what it felt like to be hit by a car. He walked home, and his friend went on to school. But after the birthday boy was inside his house and was telling his mother about it – she sitting beside him on the sofa, holding his hands in her lap, saying, 'Scotty, honey, are you sure you feel all right, baby?' thinking she would call the doctor anyway – he suddenly lay back on the sofa, closed his eyes, and went limp. When she couldn't wake him up, she hurried to the telephone and called her husband at work. Howard told her to remain calm, remain calm, and then he called an ambulance for the child and left for the hospital himself.

Of course, the birthday party was canceled. The child was in the hospital with a mild concussion and suffering from shock. There'd been vomiting, and his lungs had taken in fluid which needed pumping out that afternoon. Now he simply seemed to be in a very deep sleep – but no coma, Dr. Francis had emphasized, no coma, when he saw the alarm in the parents' eyes. At eleven o'clock that night, when the boy seemed to be resting comfortably enough after the many X-rays and the lab work, and it was just a matter of his waking up and coming around, Howard left the hospital. He and Ann had been at the hospital with the child since that afternoon, and he was going home for a short while to bathe and change clothes. 'I'll be back in an hour,' he said. She nodded. 'It's fine,' she said. 'I'll be right here.' He kissed her on the forehead, and they touched hands. She sat in the chair beside the bed and looked at the child. She was waiting for him to wake up and be all right. Then she could begin to relax.

Howard drove home from the hospital. He took the wet, dark streets very fast, then caught himself and slowed down. Until now, his life had gone smoothly and to his satisfaction – college, marriage, another year of college for the advanced degree in business, a junior partnership in an investment firm. Fatherhood. He was happy and, so far, lucky – he knew that. His parents were still living, his brothers and his sister were established, his friends from college had gone out to take their places in the world. So far, he had kept away from any real harm, from those forces he knew existed and that could cripple or bring down a man if the luck went bad, if things suddenly turned. He pulled into the driveway and parked. His left leg began to tremble. He sat in the car for a minute and tried to deal with the present situation in a rational manner. Scotty had been hit by a car and was in the hospital, but he was going to be all right. Howard closed his eyes and ran his hand over his face. He got out of the car and went up to the front door. The dog was barking inside the house. The telephone rang and rang while he unlocked the door and fumbled for the light switch. He shouldn't have left the hospital, he shouldn't have. 'Goddamn it!' he said. He picked up the receiver and said, 'I just walked in the door!'

'There's a cake here that wasn't picked up,' the voice on the other end of the line said.

'What are you saying?' Howard asked.

'A cake,' the voice said. 'A sixteen-dollar cake.'

Howard held the receiver against his ear, trying to understand. 'I don't know anything about a cake,' he said. 'Jesus, what are you talking about?'

'Don't hand me that,' the voice said.

Howard hung up the telephone. He went into the kitchen and poured himself some whiskey. He called the hospital. But the child's condition remained the same; he was still sleeping and nothing had changed there. While water poured into the tub, Howard lathered his face and shaved. He'd just stretched out in the tub and closed his eyes when the telephone rang again. He hauled himself out, grabbed a towel, and hurried through the house, saying, 'Stupid, stupid,' for having left the hospital. But when he picked up the receiver and shouted, 'Hello!' there was no sound at the other end of the line. Then the caller hung up.

*

He arrived back at the hospital a little after midnight. Ann still sat in the chair beside the bed. She looked up at Howard, and then she looked back at the child. The child's eyes stayed closed, the head was still wrapped in bandages. His breathing was quiet and regular. From an apparatus over the bed hung a bottle of glucose with a tube running from the bottle to the boy's arm.

'How is he?' Howard said. 'What's all this?' waving at the glucose and the tube.

'Dr Francis's orders,' she said. 'He needs nourishment. He needs to keep up his strength. Why doesn't he wake up, Howard? I don't understand, if he's all right.'

Howard put his hand against the back of her head. He ran his fingers through her hair. 'He's going to be all right. He'll wake up in a little while. Dr Francis knows what's what.'

After a time, he said. 'Maybe you should go home and get some rest. I'll stay here. Just don't put up with this creep who keeps calling. Hang up right away.'

'Who's calling?' she asked.

'I don't know who, just somebody with nothing better to do than call up people. You go on now.'

She shook her head. 'No,' she said, 'I'm fine.'

'Really,' he said. 'Go home for a while, and then come back and spell me in the morning. It'll be all right. What did Dr Francis say? He said Scotty's going to be all right. We don't have to worry. He's just sleeping now, that's all.'

A nurse pushed the door open. She nodded at them as she went to the bedside. She took the left arm out from under the covers and put her fingers on the wrist, found the pulse, then consulted her watch. In a little while, she put the arm back under the covers and moved to the foot of the bed, where she wrote something on a clipboard attached to the bed.

'How is he?' Ann said. Howard's hand was a weight on her shoulder. She was aware of the pressure from his fingers.

'He's stable,' the nurse said. Then she said, 'Doctor will be in again shortly. Doctor's back in the hospital. He's making rounds right now.'

'I was saying maybe she'd want to go home and get a little rest,' Howard said. 'After the doctor comes,' he said.

'She could do that,' the nurse said. 'I think you should both feel free to do that, if you wish.' The nurse was a big Scandinavian woman with blond hair. There was the trace of an accent in her speech.

'We'll see what the doctor says,' Ann said. 'I want to talk to the doctor. I don't think he should keep sleeping like this. I don't think that's a good sign.' She brought her hand up to her eyes and let her head come forward a little. Howard's grip tightened on her shoulder, and then his hand moved up to her neck, where his fingers began to knead the muscles there.

'Dr Francis will be here in a few minutes,' the nurse said. Then she left the room.

Howard gazed at his son for a time, the small chest quietly rising and falling under the covers. For the first time since the terrible minutes after Ann's telephone call to him at his office, he felt a genuine fear starting in his limbs. He began shaking his head. Scotty was fine, but instead of sleeping at home in his own bed, he was in a hospital bed with bandages around his head and a tube in his arm. But this help was what he needed right now.

Dr Francis came in and shook hands with Howard, though they'd just seen each other a few hours before. Ann got up from the chair. 'Doctor?'

'Ann,' he said and nodded. 'Let's just first see how he's doing,' the doctor said. He moved to the side of the bed and took the boy's pulse. He peeled back one eyelid and then the other. Howard and Ann stood beside the doctor and watched. Then the doctor turned back the covers and listened to the boy's heart and lungs with his stethoscope. He pressed his fingers here and there on the abdomen. When he was finished, he went to the end of the bed and studied the chart. He noted the time, scribbled something on the chart, and then looked at Howard and Ann.

'Doctor, how is he?' Howard said. 'What's the matter with him exactly?'

'Why doesn't he wake up?' Ann said.

The doctor was handsome, big-shouldered man with a tanned face. He wore a three-piece blue suit, a striped tie, and ivory cufflinks. His gray hair was combed along the sides of his head, and he looked as if he had just come from a concert. 'He's all right,' the doctor said. 'Nothing to shout about, he could be better, I think. But he's all right. Still, I wish he'd wake up. He should wake up pretty soon.' The doctor looked at the boy again. 'We'll know some more in a couple of hours, after the results of a few more tests are in. But he's all right, believe me, except for the hairline fracture of the skull. He does have that.'

'Oh, no,' Ann said.

'And a bit of a concussion, as I said before. Of course, you know he's in shock,' the doctor said. 'Sometimes you see this in shock cases. This sleeping.'

'But he's out of any real danger?' Howard said. 'You said before he's not in a coma. You wouldn't call this a coma, then – would you, doctor?' Howard waited. He looked at the doctor.

'No, I don't want to call it a coma,' the doctor said and glanced over at the boy once more. 'He's just in a very deep sleep. It's a restorative measure the body is taking on its own. He's out of any real danger, I'd say that for certain, yes. But we'll know more when he wakes up and the other tests are in,' the doctor said.

'It's a coma,' Ann said. 'Of sorts.'

'It's not a coma yet, not exactly,' the doctor said. 'I wouldn't want to call it coma. Not yet, anyway. He's suffered shock. In shock cases, this kind of reaction is common enough; it's a temporary reaction to bodily trauma. Coma. Well, coma is a deep, prolonged unconsciousness, something that could go on for days, or weeks even. Scotty's not in that area, not as far as we can tell. I'm certain his condition will show improvement by morning. I'm betting that it will. We'll know more when he wakes up, which shouldn't be long now. Of course, you may do as you like, stay here or go home for a time. But by all means feel free to leave the hospital for a while if you want. This is not easy, I know.' The doctor gazed at the boy again, watching him, and then he turned to Ann and said, 'You try not to worry, little mother. Believe me, we're doing all that can be done. It's just a question of a little more time now.' He nodded at her, shook hands with Howard again, and then he left the room.

Ann put her hand over the child's forehead. 'At least he doesn't have a fever,' she said. Then she said, 'My God, he feels so cold, though. Howard? Is he supposed to feel like this? Feel his head.'

Howard touched the child's temples. His own breathing had slowed. 'I think he's supposed to feel this way right now,' he said. 'He's in shock, remember? That's what the doctor said. The doctor was just in here. He would have said something if Scotty wasn't okay.'

Ann stood there a while longer, working her lip with her teeth. Then she moved over to her chair and sat down.

Howard sat in the chair next to her chair. They looked at each other. He wanted to say something else and reassure her, but he was afraid, too. He took her hand and put it in his lap, and this made him feel better, her hand being there. He picked up her hand and squeezed it. Then he just held her hand. They sat like that for a while, watching the boy and not talking. From time to time, he squeezed her hand. Finally, she took her hand away.

'I've been praying,' she said.

He nodded.

She said, 'I almost thought I'd forgotten how, but it came back to me. All I had to do was close my eyes and say, 'Please God, help us – help Scotty,' and then the rest was easy. The words were right there. Maybe if you prayed, too,' she said to him.

'I've already prayed,' he said. 'I prayed this afternoon – yesterday afternoon, I mean – after you called, while I was driving to the hospital. I've been praying,' he said.

'That's good,' she said. For the first time, she felt they were together in it, this trouble. She realized with a start that, until now, it had only been happening to her and to Scotty. She hadn't let Howard into it, though he was there and needed all along. She felt glad to be his wife.

The same nurse came in and took the boy's pulse again and checked the flow from the bottle hanging above the bed.

In an hour, another doctor came in. He said his name was Parsons, from Radiology. He had a bushy mustache. He was wearing loafers, a Western shirt, and a pair of jeans.

'We're going to take him downstairs for more pictures,' he told them. 'We need to do some more pictures, and we want to do a scan.'

'What's that?' Ann said. 'A scan?' She stood between this new doctor and the bed. 'I thought you'd already taken all your X-rays.'

'I'm afraid we need some more,' he said. 'Nothing to be alarmed about. We just need some more pictures, and we want to do a brain scan on him.'

'My God,' Ann said.

'It's perfectly normal procedure in cases like this,' this new doctor said. 'We just need to find out for sure why he isn't back awake yet. It's normal medical procedure, and nothing to be alarmed about. We'll be taking him down in a few minutes,' this doctor said.

In a little while, two orderlies came into the room with a gurney. They were black-haired, dark-complexioned men in white uniforms, and they said a few words to each other in a foreign tongue as they unhooked the boy from the tube and moved him from his bed to the gurney. Then they wheeled him from the room. Howard and Ann got on the same elevator. Ann gazed at the child. She closed her eyes as the elevator began its descent. The orderlies stood at either end of the gurney without saying anything, though once one of the men made a comment to the other in their own language, and the other man nodded slowly in response.

Later that morning, just as the sun was beginning to lighten the windows in the waiting room outside the X-ray department, they brought the boy out and moved him back up to his room. Howard and Ann rode up on the elevator with him once more, and once more they took up their places beside the bed.

They waited all day, but still the boy did not wake up. Occasionally, one of them would leave the room to go downstairs to the cafeteria to drink coffee and then, as if suddenly remembering and feeling guilty, get up from the table and hurry back to the room. Dr Francis came again that afternoon and examined the boy once more and then left after telling them he was coming along and could wake up at any minute now. Nurses, different nurses from the night before, came in from time to time. Then a young woman from the lab knocked and entered the room. She wore white slacks and a white blouse and carried a little tray of things which she put on the stand beside the bed. Without a word to them, she took blood from the boy's arm. Howard closed his eyes as the woman found the right place on the boy's arm and pushed the needle in.

'I don't understand this,' Ann said to the woman.

'Doctor's orders,' the young woman said. 'I do what I'm told. They say draw that one, I draw. What's wrong with him, anyway?' she said. 'He's a sweetie.'

'He was hit by a car,' Howard said. 'A hit-and-run.'

The young woman shook her head and looked again at the boy. Then she took her tray and left the room.

'Why won't he wake up?' Ann said. 'Howard? I want some answers from these people.'

Howard didn't say anything. He sat down again in the chair and crossed one leg over the other. He rubbed his face. He looked at his son and then he settled back in the chair, closed his eyes, and went to sleep.

Ann walked to the window and looked out at the parking lot. It was night, and cars were driving into and out of the parking lot with their lights on. She stood at the window with her hands gripping the sill, and knew in her heart that they were into something now, something hard. She was afraid, and her teeth began to chatter until she tightened her jaws. She saw a big car stop in front of the hospital and someone, a woman in a long coat, get into the car. She wished she were that woman and somebody, anybody, was driving her away from here to somewhere else, a place where she would find Scotty waiting for her when she stepped out of the car, ready to say *Mom* and let her gather him in her arms.

In a little while, Howard woke up. He looked at the boy again. Then he got up from the chair, stretched, and went over to stand beside her at the window. They both stared out at the parking lot. They didn't say anything. But they seemed to feel each other's insides now, as though the worry had made them transparent in a perfectly natural way.

The door opened and Dr Francis came in. He was wearing a different suit and tie this time. His gray hair was combed along the sides of his head, and he looked as if he had just shaved. He went straight to the bed and examined the boy. 'He ought to have come around by now. There's just no good reason for this,' he said. 'But I can tell you we're all convinced he's out of any danger. We'll just feel better when he wakes up. There's no reason, absolutely none, why he shouldn't come around. Very soon. Oh, he'll have himself a dilly of a headache when he does, you can count on that. But all of his signs are fine. They're as normal as can be.'

'It is a coma, then?' Ann said.

The doctor rubbed his smooth cheek. 'We'll call it that for the time being, until he wakes up. But you must be worn out. This is hard. I know this is hard. Feel free to go out for a bite,' he said. 'It would do you good. I'll put a nurse in here while you're gone if you'll feel better about going. Go and have yourselves something to eat.'

'I couldn't eat anything,' Ann said.

'Do what you need to do, of course,' the doctor said. 'Anyway, I wanted to tell you that all the signs are good, the tests are negative, nothing showed up at all, and just as soon as he wakes up he'll be over the hill.'

'Thank you, doctor,' Howard said. He shook hands with the doctor again. The doctor patted Howard's shoulder and went out.

'I suppose one of us should go home and check on things,' Howard said. 'Slug needs to be fed, for one thing.'

'Call one of the neighbors,' Ann said. 'Call the Morgans. Anyone will feed a dog if you ask them to.'

'All right,' Howard said. After a while, he said, 'Honey, why don't *you* do it? Why don't you go home and check on things, and then come back? It'll do you good. I'll be right here with him. Seriously,' he said. 'We need to keep up our strength on this. We'll want to be here for a while even after he wakes up.'

'Why don't *you* go?' she said. 'Feed Slug. Feed yourself.'

'I already went,' he said. 'I was gone for exactly an hour and fifteen minutes. You go home for an hour and freshen up. Then come back.'

She tried to think about it, but she was too tired. She closed her eyes and tried to think about it again. After a time, she said, 'Maybe I *will* go home for a few minutes. Maybe if I'm not just sitting right here watching him every second, he'll wake up and be all right. You know? Maybe he'll wake up if I'm not here. I'll go home and take a bath and put on clean clothes. I'll feed Slug. Then I'll come back.'

'I'll be right here,' he said. 'You go on home, honey. I'll keep an eye on things here.' His eyes were bloodshot and small, as if he'd been drinking for a long time. His clothes were rumpled. His beard had come out again. She touched his face, and then she took her hand back. She understood he wanted to be by himself for a while, not have to talk or share his worry for a time. She picked her purse up from the nightstand, and he helped her into her coat.

'I won't be gone long,' she said.

'Just sit and rest for a little while when you get home,' he said. 'Eat something. Take a bath. After you get out of the bath, just sit for a while and rest. It'll do you a world of good, you'll see. Then come back.' he said. 'Let's try not to worry. You heard what Dr Francis said.'

She stood in her coat for a minute trying to recall the doctor's exact words, looking for any nuances, any hint of something behind his words other than what he had said. She tried to remember if his expression had changed any when he bent over to examine the child. She remembered the way his features had composed themselves as he rolled back the child's eyelids and then listened to his breathing.

She went to the door, where she turned and looked back. She looked at the child, and then she looked at the father. Howard nodded. She stepped out of the room and pulled the door closed behind her.

She went past the nurses' station and down to the end of the corridor, looking for the elevator. At the end of the corridor, she turned to her right and entered a little waiting room where a Negro family sat in wicker chairs. There was a middle-aged man in a khaki shirt and pants, a baseball cap pushed back on his head. A large woman wearing a housedress and slippers was slumped in one of the chairs. A teenaged girl in jeans, hair done in dozens of little braids, lay stretched out in one of the chairs smoking a cigarette, her legs crossed at the ankles. The family swung their eyes to Ann as she entered the room. The little table was littered with hamburger wrappers and Styrofoam cups.

'Franklin,' the large woman said as she roused herself. 'Is it about Franklin?' Her eyes widened. 'Tell me now, lady,' the woman said. 'Is it about Franklin?' She was trying to rise from her chair, but the man had closed his hand over her arm.

'Here, here,' he said. 'Evelyn.'

'I'm sorry,' Ann said. 'I'm looking for the elevator. My son is in the hospital, and now I can't find the elevator.'

'Elevator is down that way, turn left,' the man said as he aimed a finger.

The girl drew on her cigarette and stared at Ann. Her eyes were narrowed to slits, and her broad lips parted slowly as she let the smoke escape. The Negro woman let her head fall on her shoulder and looked away from Ann, no longer interested.

'My son was hit by a car,' Ann said to the man. She seemed to need to explain herself. 'He has a concussion and a little skull fracture, but he's going to be all right. He's in shock now, but it might be some kind of coma, too. That's what really worries us, the coma part. I'm going out for a little while, but my husband is with him. Maybe he'll wake up while I'm gone.'

'That's too bad,' the man said and shifted in the chair. He shook his head. He looked down at the table, and then he looked back at Ann. She was still standing there. He said, 'Our Franklin, he's on the operating table. Somebody cut him. Tried to kill him. There was a fight where he was at. At this party. They say he was just standing and watching. Not bothering nobody. But that don't mean nothing these days. Now he's on the operating table. We're just hoping and praying, that's all we can do now.' He gazed at her steadily.

Ann looked at the girl again, who was still watching her, and at the older woman, who kept her head down, but whose eyes were now closed. Ann saw the lips moving silently, making words. She had an urge to ask what those words were. She wanted to talk more with these people who were in the same kind of waiting she was in. She was afraid, and they were afraid. They had that in common. She would have liked to have said something else about the accident, told them more about Scotty, that it had happened on the day of his birthday, Monday, and that he was still unconscious. Yet she didn't know how to begin. She stood looking at them without saying anything more.

She went down the corridor the man had indicated and found the elevator. She waited a minute in front of the closed doors, still wondering if she was doing the right thing. Then she put out her finger and touched the button.

She pulled into the driveway and cut the engine. She closed her eyes and leaned her head against the wheel for a minute. She listened to the ticking sounds the engine made as it began to cool. Then she got out of the car. She could hear the dog barking inside the house. She went to the front door, which was unlocked. She went inside and turned on lights and put on a kettle of water for tea. She opened some dogfood and fed Slug on the back porch. The dog ate in hungry little smacks. It kept running into the kitchen to see that she was going to stay. As she sat down on the sofa with her tea, the telephone rang.

'Yes!' she said as she answered. 'Hello!'

'Mrs Weiss,' a man's voice said. It was five o'clock in the morning, and she thought she could hear machinery or equipment of some kind in the background.

'Yes, yes! What is it?' she said. 'This is Mrs Weiss. This is she. What is it, please?' She listened to whatever it was in the background. 'Is it Scotty, for Christ's sake?'

'Scotty,' the man's voice said. 'It's about Scotty, yes. It has to do with Scotty, that problem. Have you forgotten about Scotty?' the man said. Then he hung up.

She dialed the hospital's number and asked for the third floor. She demanded information about her son from the nurse who answered the telephone. Then she asked to speak to her husband. It was, she said, an emergency.

She waited, turning the telephone cord in her fingers. She closed her eyes and felt sick at her stomach. She would have to make herself eat. Slug came in from the back porch and lay down near her feet. He wagged his tail. She pulled at his ear while he licked her fingers. Howard was on the line.

'Somebody just called here,' she said. She twisted the telephone cord. 'He said it was about Scotty,' she cried.

'Scotty's fine,' Howard told her. 'I mean, he's still sleeping. There's been no change. The nurse has been in twice since you've been gone. A nurse or else a doctor, He's all right.'

'This man called. He said it was about Scotty,' she told him.

'Honey, you rest for a little while, you need the rest. It must be that same caller I had. Just forget it. Come back down here after you've rested. Then we'll have breakfast or something.'

'Breakfast,' she said. 'I don't want any breakfast.'

'You know what I mean,' he said. 'Juice, something. I don't know. I don't know anything, Ann. Jesus, I'm not hungry, either. Ann, it's hard to talk now. I'm standing here at the desk. Dr Francis is coming again at eight o'clock this morning. He's going to have something to tell us then, something more definite. That's what one of the nurses said. She didn't know any more than that. Ann? Honey, maybe we'll know something more then. At eight o'clock. Come back here before eight. Meanwhile, I'm right here and Scotty's all right. He's still the same,' he added.

'I was drinking a cup of tea,' she said. 'when the telephone rang. They said it was about Scotty. There was a noise in the background. Was there a noise in the background on that call you had, Howard?'

'I don't remember,' he said. 'Maybe the driver of the car, maybe he's a psychopath and found out about Scotty somehow. But I'm here with him. Just rest like you were going to do. Take a bath and come back by seven or so, and we'll talk to the doctor together when he gets here. It's going to be all right, honey. I'm here, and there are doctors and nurses around. They say his condition is stable.'

'I'm scared to death,' she said.

She ran water, undressed, and got into the tub. She washed and dried quickly, not taking the time to wash her hair. She put on clean underwear, wool slacks, and a sweater. She went into the living room, where the dog looked up at her and let its tail thump once against the floor. It was just starting to get light outside when she went out to the car.

She drove into the parking lot of the hospital and found a space close to the front door. She felt she was in some obscure way responsible for what had happened to the child. She let her thoughts move to the Negro family. She remembered the name Franklin and the table that was covered with hamburger papers, and the teenaged girl staring at her as she drew on her cigarette. 'Don't have children,' she told the girl's image as she entered the front door of the hospital. 'For God's sake, don't.'

*

She took the elevator up to the third floor with two nurses who were just going on duty. It was Wednesday morning, a few minutes before seven. There was a page for a Dr Madison as the elevator doors slid open on the third floor. She got off behind the nurses, who turned in the other direction and continued the conversation she had interrupted when she'd gotten into the elevator. She walked down the corridor to the little alcove where the Negro family had been waiting. They were gone now, but the chairs were scattered in such a way that it looked as if people had just jumped up from them the minute before. The tabletop was cluttered with the same cups and papers, the ashtray was filled with cigarette butts.

She stopped at the nurses' station. A nurse was standing behind the counter, brushing her hair and yawning.

'There was a Negro boy in surgery last night,' Ann said. 'Franklin was his name. His family was in the waiting room, I'd like to inquire about his condition.'

A nurse who was sitting at a desk behind the counter looked up from a chart in front of her. The telephone buzzed and she picked up the receiver, but she kept her eyes on Ann.

'He passed away,' said the nurse at the counter. The nurse held the hairbrush and kept looking at her. 'Are you a friend of the family or what?'

'I met the family last night,' Ann said. 'My own son is in the hospital. I guess he's in shock. We don't know for sure what's wrong. I just wondered about Franklin, that's all. Thank you.' She moved down the corridor. Elevator doors the same color as the walls slid open and a gaunt, bald man in white pants and white canvas shoes pulled a heavy cart off the elevator. She hadn't noticed these doors last night. The man wheeled the cart out into the corridor and stopped in front of the room nearest the elevator and consulted a clipboard. Then he reached down and slid a tray out of the cart. He rapped lightly on the door and entered the room. She could smell the unpleasant odors of warm food as she passed the cart. She hurried on without looking at any of the nurses and pushed open the door to the child's room.

Howard was standing at the window with his hands behind his back. He turned around as she came in.

'How is he?' she said. She went over to the bed. She dropped her purse on the floor beside the nightstand. It seemed to her she had been gone a long time. She touched the child's face. 'Howard?'

'Dr Francis was here a little while ago,' Howard said. She looked at him closely and thought his shoulders were bunched a little.

'I thought he wasn't coming until eight o'clock this morning,' she said quickly.

'There was another doctor with him. A neurologist.'

'A neurologist,' she said.

Howard nodded. His shoulders were bunching, she could see that. 'What'd they say, Howard? For Christ's sake, what'd they say? What is it?'

'They said they're going to take him down and run more tests on him, Ann. They think they're going to operate, honey. Honey, they *are* going to operate. They can't figure out why he won't wake up. It's more than just shock or concussion, they know that much now. It's in his skull, the fracture, it has something, something to do with that, they think. So they're going to operate. I tried to call you, but I guess you'd already left the house.'

'Oh, God,' she said. 'Oh, please, Howard, please,' she said, taking his arms.

'Look!' Howard said. 'Scotty! Look, Ann!' He turned her toward the bed.

The boy had opened his eyes, then closed them. He opened them again now. The eyes stared straight ahead for a minute, then moved slowly in his head until they rested on Howard and Ann, then traveled away again.

'Scotty,' his mother said, moving to the bed.

'Hey, Scott,' his father said. 'Hey, son.'

They leaned over the bed. Howard took the child's hand in his hands and began to pat and squeeze the hand. Ann bent over the boy and kissed his forehead again and again. She put her hands on either side of his face. 'Scotty, honey, it's Mummy and Daddy,' she said. 'Scotty?'

The boy looked at them, but without any sign of recognition. Then his mouth opened, his eyes scrunched closed, and he howled until he had no more air in his lungs. His face seemed to relax and soften then. His lips parted as his last breath was puffed through his throat and exhaled gently through the clenched teeth.

The doctors called it a hidden occlusion and said it was a one-in-a-million circumstance. Maybe if it could have been detected somehow and surgery undertaken immediately, they could have saved him. But more than likely not. In any case, what would they have been looking for? Nothing had shown up in the tests or in the X-rays.

Dr Francis was shaken. 'I can't tell you how badly I feel. I'm so very sorry, I can't tell you,' he said as he led them into the doctors' lounge. There was a doctor sitting in a chair with his legs hooked over the back of another chair, watching an early-morning TV show. He was wearing a green delivery-room outfit, loose green pants and green blouse, and a green cap that covered his hair. He looked at Howard and Ann and then looked at Dr Francis. He got to his feet and turned off the set and went out of the room. Dr Francis guided Ann to the sofa, sat down beside her, and began to talk in a low, consoling voice. At one point, he leaned over and embraced her. She could feel his chest rising and falling evenly against her shoulder. She kept her eyes open and let him hold her. Howard went into the bathroom, but he left the door open. After a violent fit of weeping, he ran water and washed his face. Then he came out and sat down at the little table that held a telephone. He looked at the telephone as though deciding what to do first. He made some calls. After a time, Dr Francis used the telephone.

'Is there anything else I can do for the moment?' he asked them.

Howard shook his head. Ann stared at Dr Francis as if unable to comprehend his words.

The doctor walked them to the hospital's front door. People were entering and leaving the hospital. It was eleven o'clock in the morning. Ann was aware of how slowly, almost reluctantly, she moved her feet. It seemed to her that Dr Francis was making them leave when she felt they should stay, when it would be more the right thing to do to stay. She gazed out into the parking lot and then turned around and looked back at the front of the hospital. She began shaking her head. 'No, no,' she said. 'I can't leave him here, no.' She heard herself say that and thought how unfair it was that the only words that came out were the sort of words used on TV shows where people were stunned by violent or sudden deaths. She wanted her words to be her own. 'No,' she said, and for some reason the memory of the Negro woman's head lolling on the woman's shoulder came to her. 'No,' she said again.

'I'll be talking to you later in the day,' the doctor was saying to Howard. 'There are still some things that have to be done, things that have to be cleared up to our satisfaction. Some things that need explaining.'

'An autopsy,' Howard said.

Dr Francis nodded.

'I understand,' Howard said. Then he said, 'Oh, Jesus. No, I don't understand, doctor. I can't, I can't. I just can't.'

Dr Francis put his arm around Howard's shoulders. 'I'm sorry. God, how I'm sorry.' He let go of Howard's shoulders and held out his hand. Howard looked at the hand, and then he took it. Dr Francis put his arms around Ann once more. He seemed full of some goodness she didn't understand. She let her head rest on his shoulder, but her eyes stayed open. She kept looking at the hospital. As they drove out of the parking lot, she looked back at the hospital.

At home, she sat on the sofa with her hands in her coat pockets. Howard closed the door to the child's room. He got the coffee-maker going and then he found an empty box. He had thought to pick up some of the child's things that were scattered around the living room. But instead he sat down beside her on the sofa, pushed the box to one side, and leaned forward, arms between his knees. He began to weep. She pulled his head over into her lap and patted his shoulder. 'He's gone,' she said. She kept patting his shoulder. Over his sobs, she could hear the coffee-maker hissing in the kitchen. 'There, there,' she said tenderly. 'Howard, he's gone. He's gone and now we'll have to get used to that. To being alone.'

In a little while, Howard got up and began moving aimlessly around the room with the box, not putting anything into it, but collecting some things together on the floor at one end of the sofa. She continued to sit with her hands in her coat pockets. Howard put the box down and brought coffee into the living room. Later, Ann made calls to relatives. After each call had been placed and the party had answered, Ann would blurt out a few words and cry for a minute. Then she would quietly explain, in a measured voice, what had happened and tell them about arrangements. Howard took the box out to the garage, where he saw the child's bicycle. He dropped the box and sat down on the pavement beside the bicycle. He took hold of the bicycle awkwardly so that it leaned against his chest. He held it, the rubber pedal sticking into his chest. He gave the wheel a turn.

Ann hung up the telephone after talking to her sister. She was looking up another number when the telephone rang. She picked it up on the first ring.

'Hello,' she said, and she heard something in the background, a humming noise. 'Hello!' she said. 'For God's sake,' she said. 'Who is this? What is it you want?'

'You're Scotty, I got him ready for you,' the man's voice said. 'Did you forget him?'

'You evil bastard!' she shouted into the receiver. 'How can you do this, you evil son of a bitch?'

'Scotty,' the man said. 'Have you forgotten about Scotty?' Then the man hung up on her.

Howard heard the shouting and came in to find her with her head on her arms over the table, weeping. He picked up the receiver and listened to the dial tone.

Much later, just before midnight, after they had dealt with many things, the telephone rang again.

'You answer it,' she said. 'Howard, it's him, I know.' They were sitting at the kitchen table with coffee in front of them. Howard had a small glass of whiskey beside his cup. He answered on the third ring.

'Hello,' he said. 'Who is this? Hello! Hello!' The line went dead. 'He hung up,' Howard said. 'Whoever it was.'

'It was him,' she said. 'That bastard. I'd like to kill him,' she said. 'I'd like to shoot him and watch him kick,' she said.

'Ann, my God,' he said.

'Could you hear anything?' she said. 'In the background? A noise, machinery, something humming?'

'Nothing, really. Nothing like that,' he said. 'There wasn't much time. I think there was some radio music. Yes, there was a radio going, that's all I could tell. I don't know what in God's name is going on,' he said.

She shook her head. 'If I could, could get my hands on him.' It came to her then. She knew who it was. Scotty, the cake, the telephone number. She pushed the chair away from the table and got up. 'Drive me down to the shopping center,' she said. 'Howard.'

'What are you saying?'

'The shopping center. I know who it is who's calling. I know who it is. It's the baker, the son-of-a-bitching baker, Howard. I had him bake a cake for Scotty's birthday. That's who's calling. That's who has the number and keeps calling us. To harass us about that cake. The baker, that bastard.'

They drove down to the shopping center. The sky was clear and stars were out. It was cold, and they ran the heater in the car. They parked in front of the bakery. All of the shops and stores were closed, but there were cars at the far end of the lot in front of the movie theater. The bakery windows were dark, but when they looked through the glass they could see a light in the back room and, now and then, a big man in an apron moving in and out of the white, even light. Through the glass, she could see the display cases and some little tables with chairs. She tried the door. She rapped on the glass. But if the baker heard them, he gave no sign. He didn't look in their direction.

They drove around behind the bakery and parked. They got out of the car. There was a lighted window too high up for them to see inside. A sign near the back door said THE PANTRY BAKERY, SPECIAL ORDERS. She could hear faintly a radio playing inside and something creak — an oven door as it was pulled down? She knocked on the door and waited. Then she knocked again, louder. The radio was turned down and there was a scraping sound now, the distinct sound of something, a drawer, being pulled open and then closed.

Someone unlocked the door and opened it. The baker stood in the light and peered out at them. 'I'm closed for business,' he said. 'What do you want at this hour? It's midnight. Are you drunk or something?'

She stepped into the light that fell through the open door. He blinked his heavy eyelids as he recognized her. 'It's you,' he said.

'It's me,' she said. 'Scotty's mother. This is Scotty's father. We'd like to come in.'

The baker said, 'I'm busy now. I have work to do.'

She had stepped inside the doorway anyway. Howard came in behind her. The baker moved back. 'It smells like a bakery in here. Doesn't it smell like a bakery in here, Howard?'

'What do you want?' the baker said. 'Maybe you want your cake? That's it, you decided you want your cake. You ordered a cake, didn't you?'

'You're pretty smart for a baker,' she said. 'Howard, this is the man who's been calling us.' She clenched her fists. She stared at him fiercely. There was a deep burning inside her, an anger that made her feel larger than herself, larger than either of these men.

'Just a minute here,' the baker said. 'You want to pick up your three-day-old cake? That it? I don't want to argue with you, lady. There it sits over there, getting stale. I'll give it to you for half of what I quoted you. No. You want it? You can have it. It's no good to me, no good to anyone now. It cost me time and money to make that cake. If you want it, okay, if you don't, that's okay, too. I have to get back to work.' He looked at them and rolled his tongue behind his teeth.

'More cakes,' she said. She knew she was in control of it, of what was increasing in her. She was calm.

'Lady, I work sixteen hours a day in this place to earn a living,' the baker said. He wiped his hands on his apron. 'I work night and day in here, trying to make ends meet.' A look crossed Ann's face that made the baker move back and say, 'No trouble, now.' He reached to the counter and picked up a rolling pin with his right hand and began to tap it against the palm of his other hand. 'You want the cake or not? I have to get back to work. Bakers work at night,' he said again. His eyes were small, mean-looking, she thought, nearly lost in the bristly flesh around his cheeks. His neck was thick with fat.

'I know bakers work at night,' Ann said. 'They make phone calls at night, too. You bastard,' she said.

The baker continued to tap the rolling pin against his hand. He glanced at Howard. 'Careful, careful,' he said to Howard.

'My son's dead,' she said with a cold, even finality. 'He was hit by a car Monday morning. We've been waiting with him until he died. But, of course, you couldn't be expected to know that, could you? Bakers can't know everything – can they, Mr Baker? But he's dead. He's dead, you bastard!' Just as suddenly as it had welled in her, the anger dwindled, gave way to something else, a dizzy feeling of nausea. She leaned against the wooden table that was sprinkled with flour, put her hands over her face, and began to cry, her shoulders rocking back and forth. 'It isn't fair,' she said. 'It isn't, isn't fair.'

Howard put his hand at the small of her back and looked at the baker. 'Shame on you,' Howard said to him. 'Shame.'

The baker put the rolling pin back on the counter. He undid his apron and threw it on the counter. He looked at them, and then he shook his head slowly. He pulled a chair out from under the card table that held papers and receipts, an adding machine, and a telephone directory. 'Please sit down,' he said. 'Let me get you a chair,' he said to Howard. 'Sit down now, please.' The baker went into the front of the shop and returned with two little wrought-iron chairs. 'Please sit down, you people.'

Ann wiped her eyes and looked at the baker. 'I wanted to kill you,' she said. 'I wanted you dead.'

The baker had cleared a space for them at the table. He shoved the adding machine to one side, along with the stacks of notepaper and receipts. He pushed the telephone directory onto the floor, where it landed with a thud. Howard and Ann sat down and pulled their chairs up to the table. The baker sat down, too.

'Let me say how sorry I am,' the baker said, putting his elbows on the table. 'God alone knows how sorry. Listen to me. I'm just a baker. I don't claim to be anything else. Maybe once, maybe years ago, I was a different kind of human being. I've forgotten, I don't know for sure. But I'm not any longer, if I ever was. Now I'm just a baker. That don't excuse my doing what I did, I know. But I'm deeply sorry. I'm sorry for your son, and sorry for my part in this,' the baker said. He spread his hands out on the table and turned them over to reveal his palms. 'I don't have any children myself, so I can only imagine what you must be feeling. All I can say to you now is that I'm sorry. Forgive me, if you can,' the baker said. 'I'm not an evil man, I don't think. Not evil, like you said on the phone. You got to understand what it comes down to is I don't know how to act anymore, it would seem. Please,' the man said, 'let me ask you if you can find it in your hearts to forgive me?'

It was warm inside the bakery. Howard stood up from the table and took off his coat. He helped Ann from her coat. The baker looked at them for a minute and then nodded and got up from the table. He went to the oven and turned off some switches. He found cups and poured coffee from an electric coffee-maker. He put a carton of cream on the table, and a bowl of sugar.

'You probably need to eat something,' the baker said. 'I hope you'll eat some of my hot rolls. You have to eat and keep going. Eating is a small, good thing in a time like this,' he said.

He served them warm cinnamon rolls just out of the oven, the icing still runny. He put butter on the table and knives to spread the butter. Then the baker sat down at the table with them. He waited. He waited until they each took a roll from the platter and began to eat. 'It's good to eat something,' he said, watching them. 'There's more. Eat up. Eat all you want. There's all the rolls in the world in here.'

They ate rolls and drank coffee. Ann was suddenly hungry, and the rolls were warm and sweet. She ate three of them, which pleased the baker. Then he began to talk. They listened carefully. Although they were tired and in anguish, they listened to what the baker had to say. They nodded when the baker began to speak of loneliness, and of the sense of doubt and limitation that had come to him in his middle years. He told them what it was like to be childless all these years. To repeat the days with the ovens endlessly full and endlessly empty. The party food, the celebrations he'd worked over. Icing knuckle-deep. The tiny wedding couples stuck into cakes. Hundreds of them, no, thousands by now. Birthdays. Just imagine all those candles burning. He had a necessary trade. He was a baker. He was glad he wasn't a florist. It was better to be feeding people. This was a better smell anytime than flowers.

'Smell this,' the baker said, breaking open a dark loaf. 'It's a heavy bread, but rich.' They smelled it, then he had them taste it. It had the taste of molasses and coarse grains. They listened to him. They ate what they could. They swallowed the dark bread. It was like daylight under the fluorescent trays of light. They talked on into the early morning, the high, pale cast of light in the windows, and they did not think of leaving.

Vitamins

I had a job and Patti didn't. I worked a few hours a night for the hospital. It was a nothing job. I did some work, signed the card for eight hours, went drinking with the nurses. After a while, Patti wanted a job. She said she needed a job for her self-respect. So she started selling multiple vitamins door to door.

For a while, she was just another girl who went up and down blocks in strange neighborhoods, knocking on doors. But she learned the ropes. She was quick and had excelled at things in school. She had personality. Pretty soon the company gave her a promotion. Some of the girls who weren't doing so hot were put to work under her. Before long, she had herself a crew and a little office out in the mall. But the girls who worked for her were always changing. Some would quit after a couple of days – after a couple of hours, sometimes. But sometimes there were girls who were good at it. They could sell vitamins. These were the girls that stuck with Patti. They formed the core of the crew. But there were girls who couldn't give away vitamins.

The girls who couldn't cut it would just quit. Just not show up for work. If they had a phone, they'd take it off the hook. They wouldn't answer the door. Patti took these losses to heart, like the girls were new converts who had lost their way. She blamed herself. But she got over it. There were too many not to get over it.

Once in a while a girl would freeze and not be able to push the doorbell. Or maybe she'd get to the door and something would happen to her voice. Or she'd get the greeting mixed up with something she shouldn't be saying until she got inside. A girl like this, she'd decide to pack it in, take the sample case, head for the car, hang around until Patti and the others finished. There'd be a conference. Then they'd all ride back to the office. They'd say things to buck themselves up. 'When the going gets tough, the tough get going.' And, 'Do the right things and the right things will happen.' Things like that.

Sometimes a girl just disappeared in the field, sample case and all. She'd hitch a ride into town, then beat it. But there were always girls to take her place. Girls were coming and going in those days. Patti had a list. Every few weeks she'd run a little ad in *The Pennysaver*. There'd be more girls and more training. There was no end of girls.

The core group was made up of Patti, Donna, and Sheila. Patti was a looker. Donna and Sheila were only medium-pretty. One night this Sheila said to Patti that she loved her more than anything on earth. Patti told me these were the words. Patti had driven Sheila home and they were sitting in front of Sheila's place. Patti said to Sheila she loved her, too. Patti said to Sheila she loved all her girls. But not in the way Sheila had in mind. Then Sheila touched Patti's breast. Patti said she took Sheila's hand and held it. She said she told her she didn't swing that way. She said Sheila didn't bat an eye, that she only nodded, held on to Patti's hand, kissed it, and got out of the car.

That was around Christmas. The vitamin business was pretty bad off back then, so we thought we'd have a party to cheer everybody up. It seemed like a good idea at the time. Sheila was the first to get drunk and pass out. She passed out on her feet, fell over, and didn't wake up for hours. One minute she was standing in the middle of the living room, then her eyes closed, the legs buckled, and she went down with a glass in her hand. The hand holding the drink smacked the coffee table when she fell. She didn't make a sound otherwise. The drink poured out onto the rug. Patti and I and somebody else lugged her out to the back porch and put her down on a cot and did what we could to forget about her.

Everybody got drunk and went home. Patti went to bed. I wanted to keep on, so I sat at the table with a drink until it began to get light out. Then Sheila came in from the porch and started up. She said she had this headache that was so bad it was like somebody was sticking wires in her brain. She said it was such a bad headache she was afraid it was going to leave her with a permanent squint. And she was sure her little finger was broken. She showed it to me. It looked purple. She bitched about us letting her sleep all night with her contacts in. She wanted to know didn't anybody give a shit. She brought the finger up close and looked at it. She shook her head. She held the finger as far away as she could and looked some more. It was like she couldn't believe the things that must have happened to her that night. Her face was puffy, and her hair was all over. She ran cold water on her finger. 'God. Oh, God,' she said and cried some over the sink. But she'd made a serious pass at Patti, a declaration of love, and I didn't have any sympathy.

I was drinking Scotch and milk with a sliver of ice. Sheila was leaning on the drainboard. She watched me from her little slits of eyes. I took some of my drink. I didn't say anything. She went back to telling me how bad she felt. She said she needed to see a doctor. She said she was going to wake Patti. She said she was quitting, leaving the state, going to Portland. That she had to say goodbye to Patti first. She kept on. She wanted Patti to drive her to the hospital for her finger and her eyes.

'I'll drive you,' I said. I didn't want to do it, but I would.

'I wanted Patti to drive me,' Sheila said.

She was holding the wrist of her bad hand with her good hand, the little finger as big as a pocket flashlight. 'Besides, we need to talk. I need to tell her I'm going to Portland. I need to say goodbye.'

I said, 'I guess I'll have to tell her for you. She's asleep.'

Sheila turned mean. 'We're *friends*,' she said. 'I have to talk to her. I have to tell her myself.'

I shook my head. 'She's asleep. I just said so.'

'We're friends and we love each other,' Sheila said. 'I have to say goodbye to her.'

Sheila made to leave the kitchen.

I started to get up. I said, 'I said I'll drive you.'

'You're drunk! You haven't even been to bed yet.' She looked at her finger again and said, 'Goddamn, why'd this have to happen?'

'Not too drunk to drive you to the hospital,' I said.

'I won't ride with you!' Sheila yelled.

'Suit yourself. But you're not going to wake Patti. Lesbo bitch,' I said.

'Bastard,' she said.

That's what she said, and then she went out of the kitchen and out the front door without using the bathroom or even washing her face. I got up and looked through the window. She was walking down the road toward Euclid. Nobody else was up. It was too early.

I finished my drink and thought about fixing another one.

I fixed it.

Nobody saw any more of Sheila after that. None of us vitamin-related people, anyway. She walked to Euclid Avenue and out of our lives.

Later on Patti said, 'What happened to Sheila?' and I said, 'She went to Portland.'

I had the hots for Donna, the other member of the core group. We'd

danced to some Duke Ellington records that night of the party. I'd
held her pretty tight, smelled her hair, kept a hand low on her back as
I moved her over the rug. It was great dancing with her. I was the only
fellow at the party, and there were seven girls, six of them dancing
with each other. It was great just looking around the living room.

I was in the kitchen when Donna came in with her empty glass. We
were alone for a bit. I got her into a little embrace. She hugged me
back. We stood there and hugged.

Then she said, 'Don't. Not now.'

When I heard that 'Not now,' I let go. I figured it was money in the
bank.

I'd been at the table thinking about that hug when Sheila came in
with her finger.

I thought some more about Donna. I finished the drink. I took the
phone off the hook and headed for the bedroom. I took off my clothes
and got in next to Patti. I lay for a while, winding down. Then I
started in. But she didn't wake up. Afterwards, I closed my eyes.

It was the afternoon when I opened them again. I was in bed alone.
Rain was blowing against the window. A sugar doughnut was lying
on Patti's pillow, and a glass of old water was on the nightstand. I was
still drunk and couldn't figure anything out. I knew it was Sunday
and close to Christmas. I ate the doughnut and drank the water. I
went back to sleep until I heard Patti running the vacuum. She came
into the bedroom and asked about Sheila. That's when I told her, said
she'd gone to Portland.

A week or so into the new year, Patti and I were having a drink. She'd
just come home from work. It wasn't so late, but it was dark and
rainy. I was going to work in a couple of hours. But first we were
having us some Scotch and talking. Patti was tired. She was down in
the dumps and into her third drink. Nobody was buying vitamins. All
she had was Donna and Pam, a semi-new girl who was a klepto. We
were talking about things like negative weather and the number of
parking tickets you could get away with. Then we got to talking about
how we'd be better off if we moved to Arizona, someplace like that.

I fixed us another one. I looked out the window. Arizona wasn't a
bad idea.

Patti said, 'Vitamins.' She picked up her glass and spun the ice.
'For shit's sake!' she said. 'I mean, when I was a girl, this is the last
thing I ever saw myself doing. Jesus, I never thought I'd grow up to

sell vitamins. Door-to-door vitamins. This beats all. This really blows my mind.'

'I never thought so either, honey,' I said.

'That's right,' she said. 'You said it in a nutshell.'

'Honey.'

'Don't honey me,' she said. 'This is hard, brother. This life is not easy, any way you cut it.'

She seemed to think things over for a bit. She shook her head. Then she finished her drink. She said, 'I even dream of vitamins when I'm asleep. I don't have any relief. There's no relief! At least you can walk away from your job and leave it behind. I'll bet you haven't had one dream about it. I'll bet you don't dream about waxing floors or whatever you do down there. After you've left the goddamn place, you don't come home and dream about it, do you?' she screamed.

I said, 'I can't remember what I dream. Maybe I don't dream. I don't remember anything when I wake up.' I shrugged. I didn't keep track of what went on in my head when I was asleep. I didn't care.

'You dream!' Patti said. 'Even if you don't remember. Everybody dreams. If you didn't dream, you'd go crazy. I read about it. It's an outlet. People dream when they're asleep. Or else they'd go nuts. But when I dream, I dream of vitamins. Do you see what I'm saying?' She had her eyes fixed on me.

'Yes and no,' I said.

It wasn't a simple question.

'I dream I'm pitching vitamins,' she said. 'I'm selling vitamins day and night. Jesus, what a life,' she said.

She finished her drink.

'How's Pam doing?' I said. 'She still stealing things?' I wanted to get us off this subject. But there wasn't anything else I could think of.

Patti said, 'Shit,' and shook her head like I didn't know anything. We listened to it rain.

'Nobody's selling vitamins,' Patti said. She picked up her glass. But it was empty. 'Nobody's buying vitamins. That's what I'm telling you. Didn't you hear me?'

I got up to fix us another. 'Donna doing anything?' I said. I read the label on the bottle and waited.

Patti said, 'She made a little sale two days ago. That's all. That's all that any of us has done this week. It wouldn't surprise me if she quit. I wouldn't blame her,' Patti said. 'If I was in her place, I'd quit. But if she quits, then what? Then I'm back at the start, that's what. Ground zero. Middle of winter, people sick all over the state, people dying, and nobody thinks they need vitamins. I'm sick as hell myself.'

'What's wrong, honey?' I put the drinks on the table and sat down. She went on like I hadn't said anything. Maybe I hadn't.

'I'm my only customer,' she said. 'I think taking all these vitamins is doing something to my skin. Does my skin look okay to you? Can a person get overdosed on vitamins? I'm getting to where I can't even take a crap like a normal person.'

'Honey,' I said.

Patti said. 'You don't care if I take vitamins. That's the point. You don't care about anything. The windshield wiper quit this afternoon in the rain. I almost had a wreck. I came this close.'

We went on drinking and talking until it was time for me to go to work. Patti said she was going to soak in a tub if she didn't fall asleep first. 'I'm asleep on my feet,' she said. She said, 'Vitamins. That's all there is anymore.' She looked around the kitchen. She looked at her empty glass. She was drunk. But she let me kiss her. Then I left for work.

There was a place I went to after work. I'd started going for the music and because I could get a drink there after closing hours. It was a place called the Off-Broadway. It was a spade place in a spade neighborhood. It was run by a spade named Khaki. People would show up after the other places had stopped serving. They'd ask for house specials – RC Colas with a shooter of whiskey – or else they'd bring in their own stuff under their coats, order RC, and build their own. Musicians showed up to jam, and the drinkers who wanted to keep drinking came to drink and listen to the music. Sometimes people danced. But mainly they sat around and drank and listened.

Now and then a spade hit a spade in the head with a bottle. A story went around once that somebody had followed somebody into the Gents and cut the man's throat while he had his hands down pissing. But I never saw any trouble. Nothing that Khaki couldn't handle. Khaki was a big spade with a bald head that lit up weird under the fluorescents. He wore Hawaiian shirts that hung over his pants. I think he carried something inside his waistband. At least a sap, maybe. If somebody started to get out of line, Khaki would go over to where it was beginning. He'd rest his big hand on the party's shoulder and say a few words and that was that. I'd been going there off and on for months. I was pleased that he'd say things to me, things like,

'How're you doing tonight, friend?' Or, 'Friend, I haven't seen you for a spell.'

The Off-Broadway is where I took Donna on our date. It was the one date we ever had.

I'd walked out of the hospital just after midnight. It'd cleared up and stars were out. I still had this buzz on from the Scotch I'd had with Patti. But I was thinking to hit New Jimmy's for a quick one on the way home. Donna's car was parked in the space next to my car, and Donna was inside the car. I remembered that hug we'd had in the kitchen. 'Not now,' she'd said.

She rolled the window down and knocked ashes from her cigarette.

'I couldn't sleep,' she said. 'I have some things on my mind, and I couldn't sleep.'

I said, 'Donna. Hey, I'm glad to see you, Donna.'

'I don't know what's wrong with me,' she said.

'You want to go someplace for a drink?' I said.

'Patti's my friend,' she said.

'She's my friend, too,' I said. Then I said, 'Let's go.'

'Just so you know,' she said.

'There's this place. It's a spade place.' I said. 'They have music. We can get a drink, listen to some music.'

'You want to drive me?' Donna said.

I said, 'Scoot over.'

She started right in about vitamins. Vitamins were on the skids, vitamins had taken a nosedive. The bottom had fallen out of the vitamin market.

Donna said, 'I hate to do this to Patti. She's my best friend, and she's trying to build things up for us. But I may have to quit. This is between us. Swear it! But I have to eat. I have to pay rent. I need new shoes and a new coat. Vitamins can't cut it,' Donna said. 'I don't think vitamins is where it's at anymore. I haven't said anything to Patti. Like I said, I'm still just thinking about it.'

Donna laid her hand next to my leg. I reached down and squeezed her fingers. She squeezed back. Then she took her hand away and pushed in the lighter. After she had her cigarette going, she put the hand back. 'Worse than anything, I hate to let Patti down. You know what I'm saying? We were a team.' She reached me her cigarette. 'I know it's a different brand,' she said 'but try it, go ahead.'

I pulled into the lot for the Off-Broadway. Three spades were up against an old Chrysler that had a cracked windshield. They were just lounging, passing a bottle in a sack. They looked us over. I got out and went around to open up for Donna. I checked the doors, took her arm, and we headed for the street. The spades just watched us.

I said, 'You're not thinking about moving to Portland, are you?'

We were on the sidewalk. I put my arm around her waist.

'I don't know anything about Portland. Portland hasn't crossed my mind once.'

The front half of the Off-Broadway was like a regular café and bar. A few spades sat at the counter and a few more worked over plates of food at tables with red oilcloth. We went through the café and into the big room in back. There was a long counter with booths against the wall and farther back a platform where musicians could set up. In front of the platform was what passed for a dance floor. The bars and nightclubs were still serving, so people hadn't turned up in any real numbers yet. I helped Donna take off her coat. We picked a booth and put our cigarettes on the table. The spade waitress named Hannah came over. Hannah and me nodded. She looked at Donna. I ordered us two RC specials and decided to feel good about things.

After the drinks came and I'd paid and we'd each had a sip, we started hugging. We carried on like this for a while, squeezing and patting, kissing each other's face. Every so often Donna would stop and draw back, push me away a little, then hold me by the wrists. She'd gaze into my eyes. Then her lids would close slowly and we'd fall to kissing again. Pretty soon the place began to fill up. We stopped kissing. But I kept my arm around her. She put her fingers on my leg. A couple of spade horn-players and a white drummer began fooling around with something. I figured Donna and me would have another drink and listen to the set. Then we'd leave and go to her place to finish things.

I'd just ordered two more from Hannah when this spade named Benny came over with this other spade – this big, dressed-up spade. This big spade had little red eyes and was wearing a three-piece pinstripe. He had on a rose-colored shirt, a tie, a topcoat, a fedora – all of it.

'How's my man?' said Benny.

Benny stuck out his hand for a brother handshake. Benny and I had talked. He knew I liked the music, and he used to come over to talk whenever we were both in the place. He liked to talk about Johnny Hodges, how he'd played sax back-up for Johnny. He'd say things like, 'When Johnny and me had this gig in Mason City.'

'Hi, Benny,' I said.

'I want you to meet Nelson,' Benny said. 'He just back from Nam today. This morning. He here to listen to some of these good sounds. He got on his dancing shoes in case.' Benny looked at Nelson and nodded. 'This here is Nelson.'

I was looking at Nelson's shiny shoes, and then I looked at Nelson. He seemed to want to place me from somewhere. He studied me. Then he let loose a rolling grin that showed his teeth.

'This is Donna,' I said. 'Donna, this is Benny, and this is Nelson. Nelson, this is Donna.'

'Hello, girl,' Nelson said, and Donna said right back, 'Hello there, Nelson. Hello, Benny.'

'Maybe we'll just slide in and join you folks?' Benny said. 'Okay?'

I said, 'Sure.'

But I was sorry they hadn't found someplace else.

'We're not going to be here long,' I said. 'Just long enough to finish this drink, is all.'

'I know, man, I know,' Benny said. He sat across from me after Nelson had let himself down into the booth. 'Things to do, places to go. Yes sir, Benny knows,' Benny said, and winked.

Nelson looked across the booth to Donna. Then he took off the hat. He seemed to be looking for something on the brim as he turned the hat around in his big hands. He made room for the hat on the table. He looked up at Donna. He grinned and squared his shoulders. He had to square his shoulders every few minutes. It was like he was very tired of carrying them around.

'You real good friends with him, I bet,' Nelson said to Donna.

'We're good friends,' Donna said.

Hannah came over. Benny asked for RCs. Hannah went away, and Nelson worked a pint of whiskey from his topcoat.

'Good friends,' Nelson said. 'Real good friends.' He unscrewed the cap on his whiskey.

'Watch it, Nelson,' Benny said. 'Keep that out of sight. Nelson just got off the plane from Nam,' Benny said.

Nelson raised the bottle and drank some of his whiskey. He screwed the cap back on, laid the bottle on the table, and put his hat down on top of it. 'Real good friends,' he said.

Benny looked at me and rolled his eyes. But he was drunk, too. 'I got to get into shape,' he said to me. He drank RC from both of their glasses and then held the glasses under the table and poured whiskey. He put the bottle in his coat pocket. 'Man, I ain't put my lips to a reed for a month now. I got to get with it.'

We were bunched in the booth, glasses in front of us, Nelson's hat on the table. 'You,' Nelson said to me. 'You with somebody else, ain't you? This beautiful woman, she ain't your wife. I know that. But you real good friends with this woman. Ain't I right?'

I had some of my drink. I couldn't taste the whiskey. I couldn't taste anything, I said, 'Is all that shit about Vietnam true we see on the TV?'

Nelson had his red eyes fixed on me. He said, 'What I want to say is, do you know where your wife is? I bet she out with some dude and she be seizing his nipples for him and pulling his pud for him while you setting here big as life with your good friend. I bet she have herself a good friend, too.'

'Nelson,' Benny said.

'Nelson nothing,' Nelson said.

Benny said, 'Nelson, let's leave these people be. There's somebody in that other booth. Somebody I told you about. Nelson just this morning got off a plane,' Benny said.

'I bet I know what you thinking,' Nelson said. 'I bet you thinking, "Now here a big drunk nigger and what am I going to do with him? Maybe I have to whip his ass for him!" That what you thinking?'

I looked around the room. I saw Khaki standing near the platform, the musicians working away behind him. Some dancers were on the floor. I thought Khaki looked right at me – but if he did, he looked away again.

'Ain't it your turn to talk?' Nelson said. 'I just teasing you. I ain't done any teasing since I left Nam. I teased the gooks some.' He grinned again, his big lips rolling back. Then he stopped grinning and just stared.

'Show them that ear,' Benny said. He put his glass on the table. 'Nelson got himself an ear off one of them little dudes,' Benny said. 'He carry it with him. Show them, Nelson.'

Nelson sat there. Then he started feeling the pockets of his topcoat. He took things out of one pocket. He took out some keys and a box of cough drops.

Donna said, 'I don't want to see an ear. Ugh. Double ugh. Jesus.' She looked at me.

'We have to go,' I said.

Nelson was still feeling in his pockets. He took a wallet from a pocket inside the suit coat and put it on the table. He patted the wallet. 'Five big ones there. Listen here,' he said to Donna. 'I going to give you two bills. You with me? I give you two big ones, and then you French me. Just like his woman doing some other big fellow. You hear? You know she got her mouth on somebody's hammer right this minute while he here with his hand up your skirt. Fair's fair. Here.' He pulled the corners of the bills from his wallet. 'Hell, here another hundred for your good friend, so he won't feel left out. He don't have to do nothing. You don't have to do nothing,' Nelson said to me. 'You just sit there and drink your drink and listen to the music. Good music. Me and this woman walk out together like good friends. And she walk back in by herself. Won't be long, she be back.'

'Nelson,' Benny said, 'this is no way to talk, Nelson.'

Nelson grinned. 'I finished talking,' he said.

He found what he'd been feeling for. It was a silver cigarette case. He opened it up. I looked at the ear inside. It sat on a bed of cotton. It looked like a dried mushroom. But it was a real ear, and it was hooked up to a key chain.

'Jesus,' said Donna. 'Yuck.'

'Ain't that something?' Nelson said. He was watching Donna.

'No way. Fuck off,' Donna said.

'Girl,' Nelson said.

'Nelson,' I said. And then Nelson fixed his red eyes on me. He pushed the hat and wallet and cigarette case out of his way.

'What do you want?' Nelson said. 'I give you what you want.'

Khaki had a hand on my shoulder and the other one on Benny's shoulder. He leaned over the table, his head shining under the lights. 'How you folks? You all having fun?'

'Everything all right, Khaki,' Benny said. 'Everything A-okay. These people here was just fixing to leave. Me and Nelson going to sit and listen to the music.'

'That's good,' Khaki said. 'Folks be happy is my motto.'

He looked around the booth. He looked at Nelson's wallet on the table and at the open cigarette case next to the wallet. He saw the ear.

'That a real ear?' Khaki said.

Benny said, 'It is. Show him that ear, Nelson. Nelson just stepped off the plan from Nam with this ear. This ear has traveled halfway around the world to be on this table tonight. Nelson, show him,' Benny said.

Nelson picked up the case and handed it to Khaki.

Khaki examined the ear. He took up the chain and dangled the ear in front of his face. He looked at it. He let it swing back and forth on the chain. 'I heard about these dried-up ears and dicks and such.'

'I took it off one of them gooks,' Nelson said. 'He couldn't hear nothing with it no more. I wanted me a keepsake.'

Khaki turned the ear on its chain.

Donna and I began getting out of the booth.

'Girl, don't go,' Nelson said.

'Nelson,' Benny said.

Khaki was watching Nelson now. I stood beside the booth with Donna's coat. My legs were crazy.

Nelson raised his voice. He said, 'You go with this mother here, you let him put his face in your sweets, you both going to have a deal with me.'

We started to move away from the booth. People were looking.

'Nelson just got off the plane from Nam this morning,' I heard Benny say. 'We been drinking all day. This been the longest day on record. But me and him, we going to be fine, Khaki.'

Nelson yelled something over the music. He yelled, 'It ain't going to do no good! Whatever you do, it ain't going to help none!' I heard him say that, and then I couldn't hear anymore. The music stopped, and then it started again. We didn't look back. We kept going. We got out to the sidewalk.

I opened the door for her. I started us back to the hospital. Donna stayed over on her side. She'd used the lighter on a cigarette, but she wouldn't talk.

I tried to say something. I said, 'Look, Donna, don't get on a downer because of this. I'm sorry it happened,' I said.

'I could of used the money,' Donna said. 'That's what I was thinking.'

I kept driving and didn't look at her.

'It's true,' she said. 'I could of used the money.' She shook her head. 'I don't know,' she said. She put her chin down and cried.

'Don't cry,' I said.

'I'm not going in to work tomorrow, today, whenever it is the alarm goes off,' she said. 'I'm not going in. I'm leaving town. I take what happened back there as a sign.' She pushed in the lighter and waited for it to pop out.

I pulled in beside my car and killed the engine. I looked in the rearview, half thinking I'd see that old Chrysler drive into the lot behind me with Nelson in the seat. I kept my hands on the wheel for a minute, and then dropped them to my lap. I didn't want to touch Donna. The hug we'd given each other in my kitchen that night, the kissing we'd done at the Off-Broadway, that was all over.

I said, 'What are you going to do?' But I didn't care. Right then she could have died of a heart attack and it wouldn't have meant anything.

'Maybe I could go up to Portland,' she said. 'There must be something in Portland. Portland's on everybody's mind these days. Portland's a drawing card. Portland this, Portland that. Portland's as good a place as any. It's all the same.'

'Donna,' I said, 'I'd better go.'

I started to let myself out. I cracked the door, and the overhead light came on.

'For Christ's sake, turn off that light!'

I got out in a hurry. ''Night, Donna,' I said.

I left her staring at the dashboard. I started up my car and turned on the lights. I slipped it in gear and fed it the gas.

I poured Scotch, drank some of it, and took the glass into the bathroom. I brushed my teeth. Then I pulled open a drawer. Patti yelled something from the bedroom. She opened the bathroom door. She was still dressed. She'd been sleeping with her clothes on, I guess.

'What time is it?' she screamed. 'I've overslept! Jesus, oh my God! You've let me oversleep, goddamn you!'

She was wild. She stood in the doorway with her clothes on. She could have been fixing to go to work. But there was no sample case, no vitamins. She was having a bad dream, is all. She began shaking her head from side to side.

I couldn't take any more tonight. 'Go back to sleep, honey. I'm looking for something,' I said. I knocked some stuff out of the medicine chest. Things rolled into the sink. 'Where's the aspirin?' I said. I knocked down some more things. I didn't care. Things kept falling.

Careful

After a lot of talking – what his wife, Inez, called *assessment* – Lloyd moved out of the house and into his own place. He had two rooms and a bath on the top floor of a three-story house. Inside the rooms, the roof slanted down sharply. If he walked around, he had to duck his head. He had to stoop to look from his windows and be careful getting in and out of bed. There were two keys. One key let him into the house itself. Then he climbed some stairs that passed through the house to a landing. He went up another flight of stairs to the door of his room and used the other key on that lock.

Once, when he was coming back to his place in the afternoon, carrying a sack with three bottles of André champagne and some lunch meat, he stopped on the landing and looked into his landlady's living room. He saw the old woman lying on her back on the carpet. She seemed to be asleep. Then it occurred to him she might be dead. But the TV was going, so he chose to think she was asleep. He didn't know what to make of it. He moved the sack from one arm to the other. It was then that the woman gave a little cough, brought her hand to her side, and went back to being quiet and still again. Lloyd continued on up the stairs and unlocked his door. Later that day, toward evening, as he looked from his kitchen window, he saw the old woman down in the yard, wearing a straw hat and holding her hand against her side. She was using a little watering can on some pansies.

In his kitchen, he had a combination refrigerator and stove. The refrigerator and stove was a tiny affair wedged into a space between the sink and the wall. He had to bend over, almost get down on his knees, to get anything out of the refrigerator. But it was all right because he didn't keep much in there, anyway – except fruit juice, lunch meat, and champagne. The stove had two burners. Now and then he heated water in a saucepan and made instant coffee. But some days he didn't drink any coffee. He forgot, or else he just didn't feel like coffee. One morning he woke up and promptly fell to eating crumb doughnuts and drinking champagne. There'd been a time, some years back, when he would have laughed at having a breakfast like this. Now, there didn't seem to be anything very unusual about it. In fact, he hadn't thought anything about it until he was in bed and trying to recall the things he'd done that day, starting with when he'd gotten up that morning. At first, he couldn't remember anything noteworthy. Then he remembered eating those doughnuts and drinking champagne. Time was when he would have considered this a mildly crazy thing to do, something to tell friends about. Then, the more he thought about it, the more he could see it didn't matter much one way or the other. He'd had doughnuts and champagne for breakfast. So what?

In his furnished rooms, he also had a dinette set, a little sofa, an old easy chair, and a TV set that stood on a coffee table. He wasn't paying the electricity here, it wasn't even his TV, so sometimes he left the set on all day and all night. But he kept the volume down unless he saw there was something he wanted to watch. He did not have a telephone, which was fine with him. He didn't want a telephone. There was a bedroom with a double bed, a nightstand, a chest of drawers, a bathroom.

The one time Inez came to visit, it was eleven o'clock in the morning. He'd been in his new place for two weeks, and he'd been wondering if she were going to drop by. But he was trying to do something about his drinking, too, so he was glad to be alone. He'd made that much clear – being alone was the thing he needed most. The day she came, he was on the sofa, in his pajamas, hitting his fist against the right side of his head. Just before he could hit himself again, he heard voices downstairs on the landing. He could make out his wife's voice. The sound was like the murmur of voices from a faraway crowd, but he knew it was Inez and somehow knew the visit was an important one. He gave his head another jolt with his fist, then got to his feet.

He'd awakened that morning and found that his ear had stopped up with wax. He couldn't hear anything clearly, and he seemed to have lost his sense of balance, his equilibrium, in the process. For the last hour, he'd been on the sofa, working frustratedly on his ear, now and again slamming his head with his fist. Once in a while he'd massage the gristly underpart of his ear, or else tug at his lobe. Then he'd dig furiously in his ear with his little finger and open his mouth, simulating yawns. But he'd tried everything he could think of, and he was nearing the end of his rope. He could hear the voices below break off their murmuring. He pounded his head a good one and finished the glass of champagne. He turned off the TV and carried the glass to the sink. He picked up the open bottle of champagne from the drainboard and took it into the bathroom, where he put it behind the stool. Then he went to answer the door.

'Hi, Lloyd,' Inez said. She didn't smile. She stood in the doorway in a bright spring outfit. He hadn't seen these clothes before. She was holding a canvas handbag that had sunflowers stitched onto its sides. He hadn't seen the handbag before, either.

'I didn't think you heard me,' she said. 'I thought you might be gone or something. But the woman downstairs — what's her name? Mrs Matthews — she thought you were up here.'

'I heard you,' Lloyd said. 'But just barely.' He hitched his pajamas and ran a hand through his hair. 'Actually, I'm in one hell of a shape. Come on in.'

'It's eleven o'clock,' she said. She came inside and shut the door behind her. She acted as if she hadn't heard him. Maybe she hadn't.

'I know what time it is,' he said. 'I've been up for a long time. I've been up since eight. I watched part of the *Today* show. But just now I'm about to go crazy with something. My ear's plugged up. You remember that other time it happened? We were living in that place near the Chinese take-out joint. Where the kids found that bulldog dragging its chain? I had to go to the doctor then and have my ears flushed out. I know you remember. You drove me and we had to wait a long time. Well, it's like that now. I mean it's that bad. Only I can't go to a doctor this morning. I don't have a doctor for one thing. I'm about to go nuts, Inez. I feel like I want to cut my head off or something.'

He sat down at one end of the sofa, and she sat down at the other end. But it was a small sofa, and they were still sitting close to each other. They were so close he could have put out his hand and touched her knee. But he didn't. She glanced around the room and then fixed her eyes on him again. He knew he hadn't shaved and that his hair stood up. But she was his wife, and she knew everything there was to know about him.

'What have you tried?' she said. She looked in her purse and brought up a cigarette. 'I mean, what have you done for it so far?'

'What'd you say?' He turned the left side of his head to her. 'Inez, I swear, I'm not exaggerating. This thing is driving me crazy. When I talk, I feel like I'm talking inside a barrel. My head rumbles. And I can't hear good, either. When *you* talk, it sounds like you're talking through a lead pipe.'

'Do you have any Q-tips, or else Wesson oil?' Inez said.

'Honey, this is serious,' he said. 'I don't have any Q-tips or Wesson oil. Are you kidding?'

'If we had some Wesson oil, I could heat it and put some of that in your ear. My mother used to do that,' she said. 'It might soften things up in there.'

He shook his head. His head felt full and like it was awash with fluid. It felt like it had when he used to swim near the bottom of the municipal pool and come up with his ears filled with water. But back then it'd been easy to clear the water out. All he had to do was fill his lungs with air, close his mouth, and clamp down on his nose. Then he'd blow out his cheeks and force air into his head. His ears would pop, and for a few seconds he'd have the pleasant sensation of water running out of his head and dripping onto his shoulders. Then he'd heave himself out of the pool.

Inez finished her cigarette and put it out. 'Lloyd, we have things to talk about. But I guess we'll have to take things one at a time. Go sit in the chair. Not *that* chair, the chair in the kitchen! So we can have some light on the situation.'

He whacked his head once more. Then he went over to sit on a dinette chair. She moved over and stood behind him. She touched his hair with her fingers. Then she moved the hair away from his ears. He reached for her hand, but she drew it away.

'Which ear did you say it was?' she said.

'The right ear,' he said. 'The right one.'

'First,' she said, 'you have to sit here and not move. I'll find a hairpin and some tissue paper. I'll try to get in there with that. Maybe it'll do the trick.'

He was alarmed at the prospect of her putting a hairpin inside his ear. He said something to that effect.

'What?' she said. 'Christ, I can't hear you, either. Maybe this is catching.'

'When I was a kid, in school,' Lloyd said, 'we had this health teacher. She was like a nurse, too. She said we should never put anything smaller than an elbow into our ear.' He vaguely remembered a wall chart showing a massive diagram of the ear, along with an intricate system of canals, passageways, and walls.

'Well, your nurse was never faced with this exact problem,' Inez said. 'Anyway, we need to try *something*. We'll try this first. If it doesn't work, we'll try something else. That's life, isn't it?'

'Does that have a hidden meaning or something?' Lloyd said.

'It means just what I said. But you're free to think as you please. I mean, it's a free country,' she said. 'Now, let me get fixed up with what I need. You just sit there.'

She went through her purse, but she didn't find what she was looking for. Finally, she emptied the purse out onto the sofa. 'No hairpins,' she said. 'Damn.' But it was as if she were saying the words from another room. In a way, it was almost as if he'd imagined her saying them. There'd been a time, long ago, when they used to feel they had ESP when it came to what the other one was thinking. They could finish sentences that the other had started.

She picked up some nail clippers, worked for a minute, and then he saw the device separate in her fingers and part of it swing away from the other part. A nail file protruded from the clippers. It looked to him as if she were holding a small dagger.

'You're going to put that in my ear?' he said.

'Maybe you have a better idea,' she said. 'It's this, or else I don't know what. Maybe you have a pencil? You want me to use that? Or maybe you have a screwdriver around,' she said and laughed. 'Don't worry. Listen, Lloyd, I won't hurt you. I said I'd be careful. I'll wrap some tissue around the end of this. It'll be all right. I'll be careful, like I said. You just stay where you are, and I'll get some tissue for this. I'll make a swab.'

She went into the bathroom. She was gone for a time. He stayed where he was on the dinette chair. He began thinking of things he ought to say to her. He wanted to tell her he was limiting himself to champagne and champagne only. He wanted to tell her he was tapering off the champagne, too. It was only a matter of time now. But when she came back into the room, he couldn't say anything. He didn't know where to start. But she didn't look at him, anyway. She fished a cigarette from the heap of things she'd emptied onto the sofa cushion. She lit the cigarette with her lighter and went to stand by the window that faced onto the street. She said something, but he couldn't make out the words. When she stopped talking, he didn't ask her what it was she'd said. Whatever it was, he knew he didn't want her to say it again. She put out the cigarette. But she went on standing at the window, leaning forward, the slope of the roof just inches from her head.

'Inez,' he said.

She turned and came over to him. He could see tissue on the point of the nail file.

'Turn your head to the side and keep it that way,' she said. 'That's right. Sit still now and don't move. Don't move,' she said again.

'Be careful,' he said. 'For Christ's sake.'

She didn't answer him.

'Please, please,' he said. Then he didn't say any more. He was afraid. He closed his eyes and held his breath as he felt the nail file turn past the inner part of his ear and begin its probe. He was sure his heart would stop beating. Then she went a little farther and began turning the blade back and forth, working at whatever it was in there. Inside his ear, he heard a squeaking sound.

'Ouch!' he said.

'Did I hurt you?' She took the nail file out of his ear and moved back a step. 'Does anything feel different, Lloyd?'

He brought his hands up to his ears and lowered his head.

'It's just the same,' he said.

She looked at him and bit her lips.

'Let me go to the bathroom,' he said. 'Before we go any farther, I have to go to the bathroom.'

'Go ahead,' Inez said. 'I think I'll go downstairs and see if your landlady has any Wesson oil, or anything like that. She might even have some Q-tips. I don't know why I didn't think of that before. Of asking her.'

'That's a good idea,' he said. 'I'll go to the bathroom.'

She stopped at the door and looked at him, and then she opened the door and went out. He crossed the living room, went into his bedroom, and opened the bathroom door. He reached down behind the stool and brought up the bottle of champagne. He took a long drink. It was warm but it went right down. He took some more. In the beginning, he'd really thought he could continue drinking if he limited himself to champagne. But in no time he found he was drinking three or four bottles a day. He knew he'd have to deal with this pretty soon. But first, he'd have to get his hearing back. One thing at a time, just like she'd said. He finished off the rest of the champagne and put the empty bottle in its place behind the stool. Then he ran water and brushed his teeth. After he'd used the towel, he went back into the other room.

Inez had returned and was at the stove heating something in a little pan. She glanced in his direction, but didn't say anything at first. He looked past her shoulder and out the window. A bird flew from one tree to another and preened its feathers. But if it made any kind of bird noise, he didn't hear it.

She said something that he didn't catch.

'Say again,' he said.

She shook her head and turned back to the stove. But then she turned again and said, loud enough and slow enough so he could hear it: 'I found your stash in the bathroom.'

'I'm trying to cut back,' he said.

She said something else. 'What?' he said. 'What'd you say?' He really hadn't heard her.

'We'll talk later,' she said. 'We have things to discuss, Lloyd. Money is one thing. But there are other things, too. First we have to see about this ear.' She put her finger into the pan and then took the pan off the stove. 'I'll let it cool for a minute,' she said. 'It's too hot right now. Sit down. Put this towel around your shoulders.'

He did as he was told. He sat on a chair and put the towel around his neck and shoulders. Then he hit the side of his head with his fist.

'Goddamn it,' he said.

She didn't look up. She put her finger into the pan once more, testing. Then she poured the liquid from the pan into his plastic glass. She picked up the glass and came over to him.

'Don't be scared,' she said. 'It's just some of your landlady's baby oil, that's all it is. I told her what was wrong, and she thought this might help. No guarantees,' Inez said. 'But maybe this'll loosen things up in there. She said it used to happen to her husband. She said this one time she saw a piece of wax fall out of his ear, and it was like a big plug of something. It was ear wax, was what it was. She said try this. And she didn't have any Q-tips. That part really surprises me.'

'Okay,' he said. 'All right. I'm willing to try anything. Inez, if I had to go on like this, I think I'd rather be dead. You know? I mean it, Inez.'

'Tilt your head all the way to the side now,' she said. 'Don't move. I'll pour this in until your ear fills up, then I'll stopper it with this dishrag. And you just sit there for ten minutes, say. Then we'll see. If this doesn't do it, well, I don't have any other suggestions. I just don't know what to do then.'

'This'll work,' he said. 'If this doesn't work, I'll find a gun and shoot myself. I'm serious. That's what I feel like doing, anyway.'

He turned his head to the side and let it hang down. He looked at the things in the room from this new perspective. But it wasn't any different from the old way of looking, except that everything was on its side.

'Farther,' she said. He held on to the chair for balance and lowered his head even more. All of the objects in his vision, all of the objects in his life, it seemed, were at the far end of this room. He could feel the warm liquid pour into his ear. Then she brought the dishrag up and held it there. In a little while, she began to massage the area around his ear. She pressed into the soft part of the flesh between his jaw and skull. She moved her fingers to the area over his ear and began to work the tips of her fingers back and forth. After a while, he didn't know how long he'd been sitting there. It could have been ten minutes. It could have been longer. He was still holding on to the chair. Now and then, as her fingers pressed the side of his head, he could feel the warm oil she'd poured in there wash back and forth in the canals inside his ear. When she pressed a certain way, he imagined he could hear, inside his head, a soft, swishing sound.

'Sit up straight,' Inez said. He sat up and pressed the heel of his hand against his head while the liquid poured out of his ear. She caught it in the towel. Then she wiped the outside of his ear.

Inez was breathing through her nose. Lloyd heard the sound her breath made as it came and went. He heard a car pass on the street outside the house and, at the back of the house, down below his kitchen window, the clear *snick-snick* of pruning shears.

'Well?' Inez said. She waited with her hands on her hips, frowning.

'I can hear you,' he said. 'I'm all right! I mean, I can *hear*. It doesn't sound like you're talking underwater anymore. It's fine now. It's okay. God, I thought for a while I was going to go crazy. But I feel fine now. I can hear everything. Listen, honey, I'll make coffee. There's some juice, too.'

'I have to go,' she said. 'I'm late for something. But I'll come back. We'll go out for lunch sometime. We need to talk.'

'I just can't sleep on this side of my head, is all,' he went on. He followed her into the living room. She lit a cigarette. 'That's what happened. I slept all night on this side of my head, and my ear plugged up. I think I'll be all right as long as I don't forget and sleep on this side of my head. If I'm careful. You know what I'm saying? If I can just sleep on my back, or else on my left side.'

She didn't look at him.

'Not forever, of course not, I know that. I couldn't do that. I couldn't do it the rest of my life. But for a while, anyway. Just my left side, or else flat on my back.'

But even as he said this, he began to feel afraid of the night that was coming. He began to fear the moment he would begin to make his preparations for bed and what might happen afterward. That time was hours away, but already he was afraid. What if, in the middle of the night, he accidentally turned onto his right side, and the weight of his head pressing into the pillow were to seal the wax again into the dark canals of his ear? What if he woke up then, unable to hear, the ceiling inches from his head?

'Good God,' he said. 'Jesus, this is awful. Inez, I just had something like a terrible nightmare. Inez, where do you have to go?'

'I told you,' she said, as she put everything back into her purse and made ready to leave. She looked at her watch. 'I'm late for something.' She went to the door. But at the door she turned and said something else to him. He didn't listen. He didn't want to. He watched her lips move until she'd said what she had to say. When she'd finished, she said, 'Goodbye.' Then she opened the door and closed it behind her.

He went into the bedroom to dress. But in a minute he hurried out, wearing only his trousers, and went to the door. He opened it and stood there, listening. On the landing below, he heard Inez thank Mrs Matthews for the oil. He heard the old woman say, 'You're welcome.' And then he heard her draw a connection between her late husband and himself. He heard her say, 'Leave me your number. I'll call if something happens. You never know.'

'I hope you don't have to,' Inez said. 'But I'll give it to you, anyway. Do you have something to write it down with?'

Lloyd heard Mrs Matthews open a drawer and rummage through it. Then her old woman's voice said, 'Okay.'

Inez gave her their telephone number at home. 'Thanks,' she said.

'It was nice meeting you,' Mrs Matthews said.

He listened as Inez went on down the stairs and opened the front door. Then he heard it close. He waited until he heard her start their car and drive away. Then he shut the door and went back into the bedroom to finish dressing.

After he'd put on his shoes and tied the laces, he lay down on the bed and pulled the covers up to his chin. He let his arms rest under the covers at his sides. He closed his eyes and pretended it was night and pretended he was going to fall asleep. Then he brought his arms up and crossed them over his chest to see how this position would suit him. He kept his eyes closed, trying it out. All right, he thought. Okay. If he didn't want that ear to plug up again, he'd have to sleep on his back, that was all. He knew he could do it. He just couldn't forget, even in his sleep, and turn onto the wrong side. Four or five hours' sleep a night was all he needed, anyway. He'd manage. Worse things could happen to a man. In a way, it was a challenge. But he was up to it. He knew he was. In a minute, he threw back the covers and got up.

He still had the better part of the day ahead of him. He went into the kitchen, bent down in front of the little refrigerator, and took out a fresh bottle of champagne. He worked the plastic cork out of the bottle as carefully as he could, but there was still the festive *pop* of champagne being opened. He rinsed the baby oil out of his glass, then poured it full of champagne. He took the glass over to the sofa and sat down. He put the glass on the coffee table. Up went his feet onto the coffee table, next to the champagne. He leaned back. But after a time he began to worry some more about the night that was coming on. What if, despite all his efforts, the wax decided to plug his other ear? He closed his eyes and shook his head. Pretty soon he got up and went into the bedroom. He undressed and put his pajamas back on. Then he moved back into the living room. He sat down on the sofa once more, and once more put his feet up. He reached over and turned the TV on. He adjusted the volume. He knew he couldn't keep from worrying about what might happen when he went to bed. It was just something he'd have to learn to live with. In a way, this whole business reminded him of the thing with the doughnuts and champagne. It was not that remarkable at all, if you thought about it. He took some champagne. But it didn't taste right. He ran his tongue over his lips, then wiped his mouth on his sleeve. He looked and saw a film of oil on the champagne.

He got up and carried the glass to the sink, where he poured it into the drain. He took the bottle of champagne into the living room and made himself comfortable on the sofa. He held the bottle by its neck as he drank. He wasn't in the habit of drinking from the bottle, but it didn't seem that much out of the ordinary. He decided that even if he were to fall asleep sitting up on the sofa in the middle of the afternoon, it wouldn't be any more strange than somebody having to lie on his back for hours at a time. He lowered his head to peer out the window. Judging from the angle of sunlight, and the shadows that had entered the room, he guessed it was about three o'clock.

Where I'm
calling from

J.P. and I are on the front porch at Frank Martin's drying-out facility. Like the rest of us at Frank Martin's, J.P. is first and foremost a drunk. But he's also a chimney sweep. It's his first time here, and he's scared. I've been here once before. What's to say? I'm back. J.P.'s real name is Joe Penny, but he says I should call him J.P. He's about thirty years old. Younger than I am. Not much younger, but a little. He's telling me how he decided to go into his line of work, and he wants to use his hands when he talks. But his hands tremble. I mean, they won't keep still. 'This has never happened to me before,' he says. He means the trembling. I tell him I sympathize. I tell him the shakes will idle down. And they will. But it takes time.

We've only been in here a couple of days. We're not out of the woods yet. J.P. has these shakes, and every so often a nerve – maybe it isn't a nerve, but it's something – begins to jerk in my shoulder. Sometimes it's at the side of my neck. When this happens, my mouth dries up. It's an effort just to swallow then. I know something's about to happen and I want to head it off. I want to hide from it, that's what I want to do. Just close my eyes and let it pass by, let it take the next man. J.P. can wait a minute.

I saw a seizure yesterday morning. A guy they call Tiny. A big fat guy, an electrician from Santa Rosa. They said he'd been in here for nearly two weeks and that he was over the hump. He was going home in a day or two and would spend New Year's Eve with his wife in front of the TV. On New Year's Eve, Tiny planned to drink hot chocolate and eat cookies. Yesterday morning he seemed just fine when he came down for breakfast. He was letting out with quacking noises, showing some guy how he called ducks right down onto his head. 'Blam. Blam,' said Tiny, picking off a couple. Tiny's hair was damp and was slicked back along the sides of his head. He'd just come out of the shower. He'd also nicked himself on the chin with his razor. But so what? Just about everybody at Frank Martin's has nicks on his face. It's something that happens. Tiny edged in at the head of the table and began telling about something that had happened on one of his drinking bouts. People at the table laughed and shook their heads as they shoveled up their eggs. Tiny would say something, grin, then look around the table for a sign of recognition. We'd all done things just as bad and crazy, so, sure, that's why we laughed. Tiny had scrambled eggs on his plate, and some biscuits and honey. I was at the table, but I wasn't hungry. I had some coffee in front of me. Suddenly, Tiny wasn't there anymore. He'd gone over in his chair with a big clatter. He was on his back on the floor with his eyes closed, his heels drumming the linoleum. People hollered for Frank Martin. But he was right there. A couple of guys got down on the floor beside Tiny. One of the guys put his fingers inside Tiny's mouth and tried to hold his tongue. Frank Martin yelled, 'Everybody stand back!' Then I noticed that the bunch of us were leaning over Tiny, just looking at him, not able to take our eyes off him. 'Give him air!' Frank Martin said. Then he ran into the office and called the ambulance.

Tiny is on board again today. Talk about bouncing back. This morning Frank Martin drove the station wagon to the hospital to get him. Tiny got back too late for his eggs, but he took some coffee into the dining room and sat down at the table anyway. Somebody in the kitchen made toast for him, but Tiny didn't eat it. He just sat with his coffee and looked into his cup. Every now and then he moved his cup back and forth in front of him.

I'd like to ask him if he had any signal just before it happened. I'd like to know if he felt his ticker skip a beat, or else begin to race. Did his eyelid twitch? But I'm not about to say anything. He doesn't look like he's hot to talk about it, anyway. But what happened to Tiny is something I won't ever forget. Old Tiny flat on the floor, kicking his heels. So every time this little flitter starts up anywhere, I draw some breath and wait to find myself on my back, looking up, somebody's fingers in my mouth.

In his chair on the front porch, J.P. keeps his hands in his lap. I smoke cigarettes and use an old coal bucket for an ashtray. I listen to J.P. ramble on. It's eleven o'clock in the morning – an hour and a half until lunch. Neither one of us is hungry. But just the same we look forward to going inside and sitting down at the table. Maybe we'll get hungry.

What's J.P. talking about, anyway? He's saying how when he was twelve years old he fell into a well in the vicinity of the farm he grew up on. It was a dry well, lucky for him. 'Or unlucky,' he says, looking around him and shaking his head. He says how late that afternoon, after he'd been located, his dad hauled him out with a rope. J.P. had wet his pants down there. He'd suffered all kinds of terror in that well, hollering for help, waiting, and then hollering some more. He hollered himself hoarse before it was over. But he told me that being at the bottom of that well had made a lasting impression. He'd sat there and looked up at the well mouth. Way up at the top, he could see a circle of blue sky. Every once in a while a white cloud passed over. A flock of birds flew across, and it seemed to J.P. their wingbeats set up this odd commotion. He heard other things. He heard tiny rustlings above him in the well, which made him wonder if things might fall down into his hair. He was thinking of insects. He heard wind blow over the well mouth, and that sound made an impression on him, too. In short, everything about his life was different for him at the bottom of that well. But nothing fell on him and nothing closed off that little circle of blue. Then his dad came along with the rope, and it wasn't long before J.P. was back in the world he'd always lived in.

'Keep talking, J.P. Then what?' I say.

When he was eighteen or nineteen years old and out of high school and had nothing whatsoever he wanted to do with his life, he went across town one afternoon to visit a friend. This friend lived in a house with a fireplace. J.P. and his friend sat around drinking beer and batting the breeze. They played some records. Then the doorbell rings. The friend goes to the door. This young woman chimney sweep is there with her cleaning things. She's wearing a top hat, the sight of which knocked J.P. for a loop. She tells J.P.'s friend that she has an appointment to clean the fireplace. The friend lets her in and bows. The young woman doesn't pay him any mind. She spreads a blanket on the hearth and lays out her gear. She's wearing these black pants, black shirt, black shoes and socks. Of course, by now she's taken her hat off. J.P. says it nearly drove him nuts to look at her. She does the work, she cleans the chimney, while J.P. and his friend play records and drink beer. But they watch her and they watch what she does. Now and then J.P. and his friend look at each other and grin, or else they wink. They raise their eyebrows when the upper half of the young woman disappears into the chimney. She was all-right-looking, too, J.P. said.

When she'd finished her work, she rolled her things up in the blanket. From J.P.'s friend, she took a check that had been made out to her by his parents. And then she asks the friend if he wants to kiss her. 'It's supposed to bring good luck,' she says. That does it for J.P. The friend rolls his eyes. He clowns some more. Then, probably blushing, he kisses her on the cheek. At this minute, J.P. made his

mind up about something. He put his beer down. He got up from the
sofa. He went over to the young woman as she was starting to go out
the door.

'Me, too?' J.P. said to her.

She swept her eyes over him. J.P. says he could feel his heart
knocking. The young woman's name, it turns out, was Roxy.

'Sure,' Roxy says. 'Why not? I've got some extra kisses.' And she
kissed him a good one right on the lips and then turned to go.

Like that, quick as a wink, J.P. followed her onto the porch. He held
the porch screen door for her. He went down the steps with her and
out to the drive, where she'd parked her panel truck. It was something
that was out of his hands. Nothing else in the world counted for
anything. He knew he'd met somebody who could set his legs
atremble. He could feel her kiss still burning on his lips, etc. J.P.
couldn't begin to sort anything out. He was filled with sensations that
were carrying him every which way.

He opened the rear door of the panel truck for her. He helped her
store her things inside. 'Thanks,' she told him. Then he blurted it out
– that he'd like to see her again. Would she go to a movie with him
sometime? He'd realized, too, what he wanted to do with his life. He
wanted to do what she did. He wanted to be a chimney sweep. But he
didn't tell her that then.

J.P. says she put her hands on her hips and looked him over. Then
she found a business card in the front seat of her truck. She gave it to
him. She said, 'Call this number after ten tonight. We can talk. I have
to go now.' She put the top hat on and then took it off. She looked at
J.P. once more. She must have liked what she saw, because this time
she grinned. He told her there was a smudge near her mouth. Then
she got into her truck, tooted the horn, and drove away.

'Then what?' I say. 'Don't stop now, J.P.'

I was interested. But I would have listened if he'd been going on
about how one day he'd decided to start pitching horseshoes.

It rained last night. The clouds are banked up against the hills across
the valley. J.P. clears his throat and looks at the hills and the clouds.
He pulls his chin. Then he goes on with what he was saying.

Roxy starts going out with him on dates. And little by little he talks
her into letting him go along on jobs with her. But Roxy's in business
with her father and brother and they've got just the right amount of
work. They don't need anybody else. Besides, who was this guy J.P.?

J.P. what? Watch out, they warned her.

So she and J.P. saw some movies together. They went to a few dances. But mainly the courtship revolved around their cleaning chimneys together. Before you know it, J.P. says, they're talking about tying the knot. And after a while they do it, they get married. J.P.'s new father-in-law takes him in as a full partner. In a year or so, Roxy has a kid. She's quit being a chimney sweep. At any rate, she's quit doing the work. Pretty soon she has another kid. J.P.'s in his mid-twenties by now. He's buying a house. He says he was happy with his life. 'I was happy with the way things were going,' he says. 'I had everything I wanted. I had a wife and kids I loved, and I was doing what I wanted to do with my life.' But for some reason – who knows why we do what we do? – his drinking picks up. For a long time he drinks beer and beer only. Any kind of beer – it didn't matter. He says he could drink beer twenty-four hours a day. He'd drink beer at night while he watched TV. Sure, once in a while he drank hard stuff. But that was only if they went out on the town, which was not often, or else when they had company over. Then a time comes, he doesn't know why, when he makes the switch from beer to gin-and-tonic. And he'd have more gin-and-tonic after dinner, sitting in front of the TV. There was always a glass of gin-and-tonic in his hand. He says he actually liked the taste of it. He began stopping off after work for drinks before he went home to have more drinks. Then he began missing some dinners. He just wouldn't show up. Or else he'd show up, but he wouldn't want anything to eat. He'd filled up on snacks at the bar. Sometimes he'd walk in the door and for no good reason throw his lunch pail across the living room. When Roxy yelled at him, he'd turn around and go out again. He moved his drinking time up to early afternoon, while he was still supposed to be working. He tells me that he was starting off the morning with a couple of drinks. He'd have a belt of the stuff before he brushed his teeth. Then he'd have his coffee. He'd go to work with a thermos bottle of vodka in his lunch pail.

J.P. quits talking. He just clams up. What's going on? I'm listening. It's helping me relax, for one thing. It's taking me away from my own situation. After a minute, I say, 'What the hell? Go on, J.P.' He's pulling his chin. But pretty soon he starts talking again.

J.P. and Roxy are having some real fights now. I mean *fights*. J.P. says that one time she hit him in the face with her fist and broke his nose. 'Look at this,' he says. 'Right here.' He shows me a line across the bridge of his nose. 'That's a broken nose.' He returned the favor. He dislocated her shoulder for her. Another time he split her lip. They beat on each other in front of the kids. Things got out of hand. But he kept on drinking. He couldn't stop. And nothing could make him stop. Not even with Roxy's dad and her brother threatening to beat the hell out of him. They told Roxy she should take the kids and clear out. But Roxy said it was her problem. She got herself into it, and she'd solve it.

Now J.P. gets real quiet again. He hunches his shoulders and pulls down in his chair. He watches a car driving down the road between this place and the hills.

I say, 'I want to hear the rest of this, J.P. You better keep talking.'

'I just don't know,' he says. He shrugs.

'It's all right,' I say. And I mean it's okay for him to tell it. 'Go on J.P.'

One way she tried to fix things, J.P. says, was by finding a boy-friend. J.P. would like to know how she found the time with the house and kids.

I look at him and I'm surprised. He's a grown man. 'If you want to do that,' I say, 'you find the time. You make the time.'

J.P. shakes his head. 'I guess so,' he says.

Anyway, he found out about it – about Roxy's boyfriend – and he went wild. He manages to get Roxy's wedding ring off her finger. And when he does, he cuts it into several pieces with a pair of wire-cutters. Good, solid fun. They'd already gone a couple of rounds on this occasion. On his way to work the next morning, he gets arrested on a drunk charge. He loses his driver's license. He can't drive the truck to work anymore. Just as well, he says. He'd already fallen off a roof the week before and broken his thumb. It was just a matter of time until he broke his neck, he says.

He was here at Frank Martin's to dry out and to figure how to get his life back on track. But he wasn't here against his will, any more than I was. We weren't locked up. We could leave any time we wanted. But a minimum stay of a week was recommended, and two weeks or a month was, as they put it, 'strongly advised.'

As I said, this is my second time at Frank Martin's. When I was trying to sign a check to pay in advance for a week's stay, Frank Martin said, 'The holidays are always bad. Maybe you should think of sticking around a little longer this time? Think in terms of a couple of weeks. Can you do a couple of weeks? Think about it, anyway. You don't have to decide anything right now,' he said. He held his thumb on the check and I signed my name. Then I walked my girlfriend to the front door and said goodbye. 'Goodbye,' she said, and she lurched into the doorjamb and then onto the porch. It's late afternoon. It's raining. I go from the door to the window. I move the curtain and watch her drive away. She's in my car. She's drunk. But I'm drunk, too, and there's nothing I can do. I make it to a big chair that's close to the radiator, and I sit down. Some guys look up from their TV. Then they shift back to what they were watching. I just sit there. Now and then I look up at something that's happening on the screen.

Later that afternoon the front door banged open and J.P. was brought in between these two big guys – his father-in-law and brother-in-law, I find out afterward. They steered J.P. across the room. The old guy signed him in and gave Frank Martin a check. Then these two guys helped J.P. upstairs. I guess they put him to bed. Pretty soon the old guy and the other guy came downstairs and headed for the front door. They couldn't seem to get out of this place fast enough. It was like they couldn't wait to wash their hands of all this. I didn't blame them. Hell, no. I don't know how I'd act if I was in their shoes.

A day and a half later J.P. and I meet up on the front porch. We shake hands and comment on the weather. J.P. has a case of the shakes. We sit down and prop our feet up on the railing. We lean back in our chairs like we're just out there taking our ease, like we might be getting ready to talk about our bird dogs. That's when J.P. gets going with his story.

It's cold out, but not too cold. It's a little overcast. Frank Martin comes outside to finish his cigar. He has on a sweater buttoned all the way up. Frank Martin is short and heavy-set. He has curly gray hair and a small head. His head is too small for the rest of his body. Frank Martin puts the cigar in his mouth and stands with his arms crossed over his chest. He works that cigar in his mouth and looks across the valley. He stands there like a prizefighter, like somebody who knows the score.

J.P. gets quiet again. I mean, he's hardly breathing. I toss my cigarette into the coal bucket and look hard at J.P., who scoots farther down in his chair. J.P. pulls up his collar. What the hell's going on? I wonder. Frank Martin uncrosses his arms and takes a puff on the cigar. He lets the smoke carry out of his mouth. Then he raises his chin toward the hills and says, 'Jack London used to have a big place on the other side of this valley. Right over there behind that green hill you're looking at. But alcohol killed him. Let that be a lesson to you. He was a better man than any of us. But he couldn't handle the stuff, either.' Frank Martin looks at what's left of his cigar. It's gone out. He tosses it into the bucket. 'You guys want to read something while you're here, read that book of his, *The Call of the Wild*. You know the one I'm talking about? We have it inside if you want to read something. It's about this animal that's half dog and half wolf. End of sermon,' he says, and then hitches his pants up and tugs his sweater down. 'I'm going inside,' he says. 'See you at lunch.'

'I feel like a bug when he's around,' J.P. says. 'He makes me feel like a bug.' J.P. shakes his head. Then he says, 'Jack London. What a name! I wish I had me a name like that. Instead of the name I got.'

My wife brought me up here the first time. That's when we were still together, trying to make things work out. She brought me here and she stayed around for an hour or two, talking to Frank Martin in private. Then she left. The next morning Frank Martin got me aside and said, 'We can help you. If you want help and want to listen to what we say.' But I didn't know if they could help me or not. Part of me wanted help. But there was another part.

This time around, it was my girlfriend who drove me here. She was driving my car. She drove us through a rainstorm. We drank champagne all the way. We were both drunk when she pulled up in the drive. She intended to drop me off, turn around, and drive home again. She had things to do. One thing she had to do was to go to work the next day. She was a secretary. She had an okay job with this electronic-parts firm. She also had this mouthy teenaged son. I wanted her to get a room in town, spend the night, and then drive home. I don't know if she got the room or not. I haven't heard from her since she led me up the front steps the other day and walked me into Frank Martin's office and said, 'Guess who's here.'

But I wasn't mad at her. In the first place, she didn't have any idea what she was letting herself in for when she said I could stay with her after my wife asked me to leave. I felt sorry for her. The reason I felt sorry for her was that on the day before Christmas her Pap smear came back, and the news was not cheery. She'd have to go back to the doctor, and real soon. That kind of news was reason enough for both of us to start drinking. So what we did was get ourselves good and drunk. And on Christmas Day we were still drunk. We had to go out to a restaurant to eat, because she didn't feel like cooking. The two of us and her mouthy teenaged son opened some presents, and then we went to this steakhouse near her apartment. I wasn't hungry. I had some soup and a hot roll. I drank a bottle of wine with the soup. She drank some wine, too. Then we started in on Bloody Marys. For the next couple of days, I didn't eat anything except salted nuts. But I drank a lot of bourbon. Then I said to her, 'Sugar, I think I'd better pack up. I better go back to Frank Martin's.'

She tried to explain to her son that she was going to be gone for a while and he'd have to get his own food. But right as we were going out the door, this mouthy kid screamed at us. He screamed, 'The hell with you! I hope you never come back. I hope you kill yourselves!' Imagine this kid!

Before we left town, I had her stop at the package store, where I bought us the champagne. We stopped someplace else for plastic glasses. Then we picked up a bucket of fried chicken. We set out for Frank Martin's in this rainstorm, drinking and listening to music. She drove. I looked after the radio and poured. We tried to make a little party of it. But we were sad, too. There was that fried chicken, but we didn't eat any.

I guess she got home okay. I think I would have heard something if she didn't. But she hasn't called me, and I haven't called her. Maybe she's had some news about herself by now. Then again, maybe she hasn't heard anything. Maybe it was all a mistake. Maybe it was somebody else's smear. But she has my car, and I have things at her house. I know we'll be seeing each other again.

They clang an old farm bell here to call you for mealtime. J.P. and I get out of our chairs and we go inside. It's starting to get too cold on the porch, anyway. We can see our breath drifting out from us as we talk.

New Year's Eve morning I try to call my wife. There's no answer. It's okay. But even if it wasn't okay, what am I supposed to do? The last time we talked on the phone, a couple of weeks ago, we screamed at each other. I hung a few names on her. 'Wet brain!' she said, and put the phone back where it belonged.

But I wanted to talk to her now. Something had to be done about my stuff. I still had things at her house, too.

One of the guys here is a guy who travels. He goes to Europe and places. That's what he says, anyway. Business, he says. He also says he has his drinking under control and he doesn't have any idea why he's here at Frank Martin's. But he doesn't remember getting here. He laughs about it, about his not remembering. 'Anyone can have a blackout,' he says. 'That doesn't prove a thing.' He's not a drunk – he tells us this and we listen. 'That's a serious charge to make,' he says. 'That kind of talk can ruin a good man's prospects.' He says that if he'd only stick to whiskey and water, no ice, he'd never have these blackouts. It's the ice they put into your drink that does it. 'Who do you know in Egypt?' he asks me. 'I can use a few names over there.'

For New Year's Eve dinner Frank Martin serves steak and baked potato. My appetite's coming back. I clean up everything on my plate and I could eat more. I look over at Tiny's plate. Hell, he's hardly touched a thing. His steak is just sitting there. Tiny is not the same old Tiny. The poor bastard had planned to be at home tonight. He'd planned to be in his robe and slippers in front of the TV, holding hands with his wife. Now he's afraid to leave. I can understand. One seizure means you're ready for another. Tiny hasn't told any more nutty stories on himself since it happened. He's stayed quiet and kept to himself. I ask him if I can have his steak, and he pushes his plate over to me.

Some of us are still up, sitting around the TV, watching Times Square, when Frank Martin comes in to show us his cake. He brings it around and shows it to each of us. I know he didn't make it. It's just a bakery cake. But it's still a cake. It's a big white cake. Across the top there's writing in pink letters. The writing says, HAPPY NEW YEAR – ONE DAY AT A TIME.

'I don't want any stupid cake,' says the guy who goes to Europe and places. 'Where's the champagne?' he says, and laughs.

We all go into the dining room. Frank Martin cuts the cake. I sit next to J.P. J.P. eats two pieces and drinks a Coke. I eat a piece and wrap another piece in a napkin, thinking of later.

J.P. lights a cigarette – his hands are steady now – and he tells me his wife is coming in the morning, the first day of the new year.

'That's great,' I say. I nod. I lick the frosting off my finger. 'That's good news, J.P.'

'I'll introduce you,' he says.

'I look forward to it,' I say.

We say goodnight. We say Happy New Year. I use a napkin on my fingers. We shake hands.

I go to the phone, put in a dime, and call my wife collect. But nobody answers this time, either. I think about calling my girlfriend, and I'm dialing her number when I realize I really don't want to talk to her. She's probably at home watching the same thing on TV that I've been watching. Anyway, I don't want to talk to her. I hope she's okay. But if she has something wrong with her, I don't want to know about it.

After breakfast, J.P. and I take coffee out to the porch. The sky is clear, but it's cold enough for sweaters and jackets.

'She asked me if she should bring the kids,' J.P. says. 'I told her she should keep the kids at home. Can you imagine? My God, I don't want my kids up here.'

We use the coal bucket for an ashtray. We look across the valley to where Jack London used to live. We're drinking more coffee when this car turns off the road and comes down the drive.

'That's her!' J.P. says. He puts his cup next to his chair. He gets up and goes down the steps.

I see this woman stop the car and set the brake. I see J.P. open the door. I watch her get out, and I see them hug each other. I look away. Then I look back. J.P. takes her by the arm and they come up the stairs. This woman broke a man's nose once. She has had two kids, and much trouble, but she loves this man who has her by the arm. I get up from the chair.

'This is my friend,' J.P. says to his wife. 'Hey, this is Roxy.'

Roxy takes my hand. She's a tall, good-looking woman in a knit cap. She has on a coat, a heavy sweater, and slacks. I recall what J.P. told me about the boyfriend and the wire-cutters. I don't see any wedding ring. That's in pieces somewhere, I guess. Her hands are broad and the fingers have these big knuckles. This is a woman who can make fists if she has to.

'I've heard about you,' I say. 'J.P. told me how you got acquainted. Something about a chimney, J.P. said.'

'Yes, a chimney,' she says. 'There's probably a lot else he didn't tell you,' she says. 'I bet he didn't tell you everything,' she says, and laughs. Then – she can't wait any longer – she slips her arm around J.P. and kisses him on the cheek. They start to move to the door. 'Nice meeting you,' she says. 'Hey, did he tell you he's the best sweep in the business?'

'Come on now, Roxy,' J.P. says. He has his hand on the doorknob.

'He told me he learned everything he knew from you,' I say.

'Well, that much is sure true,' she says. She laughs again. But it's like she's thinking about something else. J.P. turns the doorknob. Roxy lays her hand over his. 'Joe, can't we go into town for lunch? Can't I take you someplace?'

J.P. clears his throat. He says, 'It hasn't been a week yet.' He takes his hand off the doorknob and brings his fingers to his chin. 'I think they'd like it if I didn't leave the place for a little while yet. We can have some coffee here,' he says.

'That's fine,' she says. Her eyes work over to me again. 'I'm glad Joe's made a friend. Nice to meet you,' she says.

They start to go inside. I know it's a dumb thing to do, but I do it anyway. 'Roxy,' I say. And they stop in the doorway and look at me. 'I need some luck,' I say. 'No kidding. I could do with a kiss myself.'

J.P. looks down. He's still holding the knob, even though the door is open. He turns the knob back and forth. But I keep looking at her. Roxy grins. 'I'm not a sweep anymore,' she says. 'Not for years. Didn't Joe tell you that? But, sure, I'll kiss you, sure.'

She moves over. She takes me by the shoulders — I'm a big man — and she plants this kiss on my lips. 'How's that?' she says.

'That's fine,' I say.

'Nothing to it,' she says. She's still holding me by the shoulders. She's looking me right in the eyes. 'Good luck,' she says, and then she lets go of me.

'See you later, pal,' J.P. says. He opens the door all the way, and they go in.

I sit down on the front steps and light a cigarette. I watch what my hand does, then I blow out the match. I've got the shakes. I started out with them this morning. This morning I wanted something to drink. It's depressing, but I didn't say anything about it to J.P. I try to put my mind on something else.

I'm thinking about chimney sweeps — all that stuff I heard from J.P. — when for some reason I start to think about a house my wife and I once lived in. That house didn't have a chimney, so I don't know what makes me remember it now. But I remember the house and how we'd only been in there a few weeks when I heard a noise outside one morning. It was Sunday morning and it was still dark in the bedroom.

But there was this pale light coming in from the bedroom window. I listened. I could hear something scrape against the side of the house. I jumped out of bed and went to look.

'My God!' my wife says, sitting up in bed and shaking the hair away from her face. Then she starts to laugh. 'It's Mr Venturini,' she says. 'I forgot to tell you. He said he was coming to paint the house today. Early. Before it gets too hot. I forgot all about it,' she says, and laughs. 'Come on back to bed, honey. It's just him.'

'In a minute,' I say.

I push the curtain away from the window. Outside, this old guy in white coveralls is standing next to his ladder. The sun is just starting to break above the mountains. The old guy and I look each other over. It's the landlord, all right – this old guy in coveralls. But his coveralls are too big for him. He needs a shave, too. And he's wearing this baseball cap to cover his bald head. Goddamn it, I think, if he isn't a weird old fellow. And a wave of happiness comes over me that I'm not him – that I'm me and that I'm inside this bedroom with my wife.

He jerks his thumb toward the sun. He pretends to wipe his forehead. He's letting me know he doesn't have all that much time. The old fart breaks into a grin. It's then I realize I'm naked. I look down at myself. I look at him again and shrug. What did he expect?

My wife laughs. 'Come *on*,' she says. 'Get back in this bed. Right now. This minute. Come on back to bed.'

I let go of the curtain. But I keep standing there at the window. I can see the old fellow nod to himself like he's saying, 'Go on, sonny, go back to bed. I understand.' He tugs on the bill of his cap. Then he sets about his business. He picks up his bucket. He starts climbing the ladder.

I lean back into the step behind me now and cross one leg over the other. Maybe later this afternoon I'll try calling my wife again. And then I'll call to see what's happening with my girlfriend. But I don't want to get her mouthy kid on the line. If I do call, I hope he'll be out somewhere doing whatever he does when he's not around the house. I try to remember if I ever read any Jack London books. I can't remember. But there was a story of his I read in high school. 'To Build a Fire,' it was called. This guy in the Yukon is freezing. Imagine it – he's actually going to freeze to death if he can't get a fire going. With a fire, he can dry his socks and things and warm himself.

He gets his fire going, but then something happens to it. A branchful of snow drops on it. It goes out. Meanwhile, it's getting colder. Night is coming on.

I bring some change out of my pocket. I'll try my wife first. If she answers, I'll wish her a Happy New Year. But that's it. I won't bring up business. I won't raise my voice. Not even if she starts something. She'll ask me where I'm calling from, and I'll have to tell her. I won't say anything about New Year's resolutions. There's no way to make a joke out of this. After I talk to her, I'll call my girlfriend. Maybe I'll call her first. I'll just have to hope I don't get her kid on the line. 'Hello, sugar,' I'll say when she answers. 'It's me.'

The train

For John Cheever

The woman was called Miss Dent, and earlier that evening she'd held a gun on a man. She'd made him get down in the dirt and plead for his life. While the man's eyes welled with tears and his fingers picked at leaves, she pointed the revolver at him and told him things about himself. She tried to make him see that he couldn't keep trampling on people's feelings. 'Be still!' she'd said, although the man was only digging his fingers into the dirt and moving his legs a little out of fear. When she had finished talking, when she had said all she could think of to say to him, she put her foot on the back of his head and pushed his face into the dirt. Then she put the revolver into her handbag and walked back to the railway station.

She sat on a bench in the deserted waiting room with the handbag on her lap. The ticket office was closed; no one was around. Even the parking lot outside the station was empty. She let her eyes rest on the big wall clock. She wanted to stop thinking about the man and how he'd acted toward her after taking what he wanted. But she knew she would remember for a long time the sound he made through his nose as he got down on his knees. She took a breath, closed her eyes, and listened for the sound of a train.

The waiting-room door opened. Miss Dent looked in that direction as two people came inside. One person was an old man with white hair and a white silk cravat; the other was a middle-aged woman wearing eye-shadow, lipstick, and a rose-colored knit dress. The evening had turned cool, but neither of the people wore a coat, and the old man was without shoes. They stopped in the doorway, seemingly astounded at finding someone in the waiting room. They tried to act as if her presence there was not a disappointment. The woman said something to the old man, but Miss Dent didn't catch what it was the woman had said. The couple moved on into the room. It seemed to Miss Dent that they gave off an air of agitation, of having just left somewhere in a great hurry and not yet being able to find a way to talk about it. It might be, Miss Dent thought, that they'd had too much to drink as well. The woman and the white-haired old man looked at the clock, as if it might tell them something about their situation and what they were supposed to do next.

Miss Dent also turned her eyes to the clock. There was nothing in the waiting room that announced when trains arrived and departed. But she was prepared to wait for any length of time. She knew if she waited long enough, a train would come along, and she could board it, and it would take her away from this place.

'Good evening,' the old man said to Miss Dent. He said this, she thought, as if it had been a normal summer's night and he were an important old man wearing shoes and an evening jacket.

'Good evening,' Miss Dent said.

The woman in the knit dress looked at her in a way that was calculated to let Miss Dent know the woman was not happy at finding her in the waiting room.

The old man and the woman seated themselves on a bench directly across the lobby from Miss Dent. She watched as the old man gave the knees of his trousers a little tug and then crossed one leg over the other and began to wag his stockinged foot. He took a pack of cigarettes and a cigarette holder from his shirt pocket. He inserted the cigarette into the holder and brought his hand up to his shirt pocket. Then he reached into his trouser pockets.

'I don't have a light,' he said to the woman.

'I don't smoke,' the woman said. 'I should think if you knew anything about me, you'd know that much. If you really must smoke, *she* may have a match.' The woman raised her chin and looked sharply at Miss Dent.

But Miss Dent shook her head. She pulled the handbag closer. She held her knees together, her fingers gripping the bag.

'So on top of everything else, no matches,' the white-haired old man said. He checked his pockets once more. Then he sighed and removed the cigarette from the holder. He pushed the cigarette back into the pack. He put the cigarettes and the cigarette holder into his shirt pocket.

The woman began to speak in a language that Miss Dent did not understand. She thought it might be Italian because the rapid-fire words sounded like words she'd heard Sophia Loren use in a film.

The old man shook his head. 'I can't follow you, you know. You're going too fast for me. 'You'll have to slow down. You'll have to speak English. I can't follow you,' he said.

Miss Dent released her grasp on the handbag and moved it from her lap to a place next to her on the bench. She stared at the catch on the handbag. She wasn't sure what she should do. It was a small waiting room, and she hated to get up suddenly and move somewhere else to sit. Her eyes traveled to the clock.

'I can't get over that bunch of nuts back there,' the woman said. 'It's colossal! It's simply too much for words. My God!' The woman said this and shook her head. She slumped against the bench as if exhausted. She raised her eyes and stared briefly at the ceiling.

The old man took the silk cravat between his fingers and began idly to rub the material back and forth. He opened a button on his shirt and tucked the cravat inside. He seemed to be thinking about something else as the woman went on.

'It's that girl I feel sorry for,' the woman said. 'That poor soul alone in a house filled with simps and vipers. She's the one I feel sorry for. And she'll be the one to pay! None of the rest of them. Certainly not that imbecile they call Captain Nick! He isn't responsible for anything. Not him,' the woman said.

The old man raised his eyes and looked around the waiting room. He gazed for a time at Miss Dent.

Miss Dent looked past his shoulder and through the window. There she could see the tall lamp post, its light shining on the empty parking lot. She held her hands together in her lap and tried to keep her attention on her own affairs. But she couldn't help hearing what these people said.

'I can tell you this much,' the woman said. 'The girl is the extent of my concern. Who cares about the rest of that tribe? Their entire existence is taken up with *café au lait* and cigarettes, their precious Swiss chocolate and those goddamned macaws. Nothing else means anything to them,' the woman said. 'What do they care? If I never see that outfit again, it'll be too soon. Do you understand me?'

'Sure, I understand,' the old man said. 'Of course.' He put his feet on the floor and then brought his other leg up over his knee. 'But don't fret about it now,' he said.

'Don't fret about it,' he says. Why don't you take a look at yourself in the mirror?' the woman said.

'Don't worry about me,' the old man said. 'Worse things have happened to me, and I'm still here.' He laughed quietly and shook his head. 'Don't worry about me.'

'How can I help not worrying about you?' the woman said. 'Who else is going to worry about you? Is this woman with the handbag going to worry about you?' she said, stopping long enough to glare at Miss Dent. 'I'm serious, *amico mio*. Just look at yourself! My God, if I didn't already have so many things on my mind, I could have a nervous breakdown right here. Tell me who else there is to worry about you if I don't worry? I'm asking a serious question. You know so much,' the woman said, 'so answer me that.'

The white-haired old man got to his feet and then sat down again. 'Just don't worry about me,' he said. 'Worry about someone else. Worry about the girl and Captain Nick, if you want to worry. You were in another room when he said, 'I'm not serious, but I'm in love with her.' Those were his exact words.'

'I knew something like that was coming!' the woman cried. She closed her fingers and brought her hands up to her temples. 'I knew you'd tell me something like that! But I'm not surprised, either. No, I'm not. A leopard doesn't change its spots. Truer words were never spoken. Live and learn. But when are you going to wake up, you old fool? Answer me that,' she said to him. 'Are you like the mule that first has to be hit between the eyes with a two-by-four? *O Dio mio!* Why don't you go look at yourself in the mirror?' the woman said. 'Take a good long look while you're at it.'

The old man got up from the bench and moved over to the drinking fountain. He put one hand behind his back, turned the knob, and bent over to drink. Then he straightened up and dabbed his chin with the back of his hand. He put both hands behind his back and began to stroll around the waiting room as if he were on a promenade.

But Miss Dent could see his eyes scanning the floor, the empty benches, the ashtrays. She understood he was looking for matches, and she was sorry she didn't have any.

The woman had turned to follow the old man's progress. She raised her voice and said: 'Kentucky Fried Chicken at the North Pole! Colonel Sanders in a parka and boots. That tore it! That was the limit!'

The old man didn't answer. He continued his circumnavigation of the room and came to a stop at the front window. He stood at the window, hands behind his back, and looked out onto the empty parking lot.

The woman turned around to Miss Dent. She pulled at the material under the arm of her dress. 'The next time I want to see home movies about Point Barrow, Alaska, and its native American Eskimos, I'll ask for them. My God, it was priceless! Some people will go to any lengths. Some people will try to kill their enemies with boredom. But you'd have needed to be there.' The woman stared hotly at Miss Dent as if daring her to contradict.

Miss Dent picked up the handbag and placed it on her lap. She looked at the clock, which seemed to be moving very slowly, if at all.

'You don't say much,' the woman said to Miss Dent. 'But I'll wager you could say a lot if someone got you started. Couldn't you? But you're a sly boots. You'd rather just sit with your prim little mouth while other people talk their heads off. Am I right? Still waters. Is that your name?' the woman asked. 'What *do* they call you?'

'Miss Dent. But I don't know you,' Miss Dent said.

'I sure as hell don't know you, either!' the woman said. 'Don't know you and don't care to know you. Sit there and think what you want. It won't change anything. But I know what I think, and I think it stinks!'

The old man left his place at the window and went outside. When he came back in a minute later, he had a cigarette burning in his holder and he seemed in better spirits. He carried his shoulders back and his chin out. He sat down beside the woman.

'I found some matches,' he said. 'There they were, a book of matches right next to the curb. Someone must have dropped them.'

'Basically, you're lucky,' the woman said. 'And that's a plus in your situation. I always knew that about you, even if no one else did. Luck is important.' The woman looked over at Miss Dent and said: 'Young lady, I'll wager you've had your share of trial and error in this life. I know you have. The expression on your face tells me so. But you aren't going to talk about it. Go ahead then, don't talk. Let us do the talking. But you'll get older. Then you'll have something to talk about. Wait until you're my age. Or his age,' the woman said and jerked her thumb at the old man. 'God forbid. But it'll all come to you. In its own sweet time, it'll come. You won't have to hunt for it, either. It'll find you.'

Miss Dent got up from the bench with her handbag and went over to the water fountain. She drank from the fountain and turned to look at them. The old man had finished smoking. He took what was left of his cigarette from the holder and dropped it under the bench. He tapped the holder against his palm, blew into the mouthpiece, and returned the holder to his shirt pocket. Now he, too, gave his attention to Miss Dent. He fixed his eyes on her and waited along with the woman. Miss Dent gathered herself to speak. She wasn't sure where to begin, but she thought she might start by saying she had a gun in her handbag. She might even tell them she'd already killed a man earlier that night.

But at that moment they heard the train. First they heard the whistle, then a clanging sound, an alarm bell, as the guard rails went down at the crossing. The woman and the white-haired old man got up from the bench and moved toward the door. The old man opened the door for his companion, and then he smiled and made a little movement with his fingers for Miss Dent to precede him. She held the handbag against the front of her blouse and followed the older woman outside.

The train tooted its whistle once more as it slowed and then ground to a stop in front of the station. The light on the cab of the engine went back and forth over the track. The two cars that made up this little train were well lighted, so it was easy for the three people on the platform to see that the train was nearly empty. But this didn't surprise them. At this hour, they were surprised to see anyone at all on the train.

The few passengers in the cars looked out through the glass and thought it strange to find these people on the platform, making ready to board a train at this time of night. What business could have taken them out? This was the hour when people should be thinking of going to bed. The kitchens in the houses up on the hills behind the station were clean and orderly; the dishwashers had long ago finished their cycle, all things were in their places. Night-lights burned in children's bedrooms. A few teenaged girls might still be reading novels, their fingers twisting a strand of hair as they did so. But television sets were going off now. Husbands and wives were making their own preparations for the night. The half-dozen or so passengers, sitting by themselves in the two cars, looked through the glass and wondered about the three people on the platform.

They saw a heavily made-up, middle-aged woman wearing a rose-colored knit dress mount the steps and enter the train. Behind her came a younger woman dressed in a summer blouse and skirt who clutched a handbag. They were followed onto the train by an old man who moved slowly and who carried himself in a dignified manner. The old man had white hair and a white silk cravat, but he was without shoes. The passengers naturally assumed that the three people boarding were together; and they felt sure that whatever these people's business had been that night, it had not come to a happy conclusion. But the passengers had seen things more various than this in their lifetime. The world is filled with business of every sort, as they well knew. This still was not as bad, perhaps, as it could be. For this reason, they scarcely gave another thought to these three who moved down the aisle and took up their places – the woman and the white-haired old man next to each other, the young woman with the handbag a few seats behind. Instead, the passengers gazed out at the station and went back to thinking about their own business, those things that had engaged them before the station stop.

The conductor looked up the track. Then he glanced back in the direction the train had come from. He raised his arm and, with his lantern, signaled the engineer. This was what the engineer was waiting for. He turned a dial and pushed down on a lever. The train began to move forward. It went slowly at first, but it began to pick up speed. It moved faster until once more it sped through the dark countryside, its brilliant cars throwing light onto the roadbed.

Fever

Carlyle was in a spot. He'd been in a spot all summer, since early June when his wife had left him. But up until a little while ago, just a few days before he had to start meeting his classes at the high school, Carlyle hadn't needed a sitter. He'd been the sitter. Every day and every night he'd attended to the children. Their mother, he told them, was away on a long trip.

Debbie, the first sitter he contacted, was a fat girl, nineteen years old, who told Carlyle she came from a big family. Kids loved her, she said. She offered a couple of names for reference. She penciled them on a piece of notebook paper. Carlyle took the names, folded the piece of paper, and put it in his shirt pocket. He told her he had meetings the next day. He said she could start to work for him the next morning. She said, 'Okay.'

He understood that his life was entering a new period. Eileen had left while Carlyle was still filling out his grade reports. She'd said she was going to Southern California to begin a new life for herself there. She'd gone with Richard Hoopes, one of Carlyle's colleagues at the high school. Hoopes was a drama teacher and glass-blowing instructor who'd apparently turned his grades in on time, taken his things, and left town in a hurry with Eileen. Now, the long and painful summer nearly behind him, and his classes about to resume, Carlyle had finally turned his attention to this matter of finding a baby-sitter. His first efforts had not been successful. In his desperation to find someone – anyone – he'd taken Debbie on.

In the beginning, he was grateful to have this girl turn up in response to his call. He'd yielded up the house and children to her as if she were a relative. So he had no one to blame but himself, his own carelessness, he was convinced, when he came home early from school one day that first week and pulled into the drive next to a car that had a big pair of flannel dice hanging from the rearview mirror. To his astonishment, he saw his children in the front yard, their clothes filthy, playing with a dog big enough to bite off their hands. His son, Keith, had the hiccups and had been crying. Sarah, his daughter, began to cry when she saw him get out of the car. They were sitting on the grass, and the dog was licking their hands and faces. The dog growled at him and then moved off a little as Carlyle made for his children. He picked up Keith and then he picked up Sarah. One child under each arm, he made for his front door. Inside the house, the phonograph was turned up so high the front windows vibrated.

In the living room, three teenaged boys jumped to their feet from where they'd been sitting around the coffee table. Beer bottles stood on the table and cigarettes burned in the ashtray. Rod Stewart screamed from the stereo. On the sofa, Debbie, the fat girl, sat with another teenaged boy. She stared at Carlyle with dumb disbelief as he entered the living room. The fat girl's blouse was unbuttoned. She had her legs drawn under her, and she was smoking a cigarette. The living room was filled with smoke and music. The fat girl and her friend got off the sofa in a hurry.

'Mr Carlyle, wait a minute,' Debbie said. 'I can explain.'

'Don't explain,' Carlyle said. 'Get the hell out of here. All of you. Before I throw you out.' He tightened his grip on the children.

'You owe me for four days,' the fat girl said, as she tried to button her blouse. She still had the cigarette between her fingers. Ashes fell from the cigarette as she tried to button up. 'Forget today. You don't owe me for today. Mr Carlyle, it's not what it looks like. They dropped by to listen to this record.'

'I understand, Debbie,' he said. He let the children down onto the carpet. But they stayed close to his legs and watched the people in the living room. Debbie looked at them and shook her head slowly, as if she'd never laid eyes on them before. 'Goddamn it, get out!' Carlyle said. 'Now. Get going. All of you.'

He went over and opened the front door. The boys acted as if they were in no real hurry. They picked up their beer and started slowly for the door. The Rod Stewart record was still playing. One of them said, 'That's my record.'

'Get it,' Carlyle said. He took a step toward the boy and then stopped.

'Don't touch me, okay? Just don't touch me,' the boy said. He went over to the phonograph, picked up the arm, swung it back, and took his record off while the turntable was still spinning.

Carlyle's hands were shaking. 'If that car's not out of the drive in one minute – one minute – I'm calling the police.' He felt sick and dizzy with his anger. He saw, really saw, spots dance in front of his eyes.

'Hey, listen, we're on our way, all right? We're going,' the boy said.

They filed out of the house. Outside, the fat girl stumbled a little. She weaved as she moved toward the car. Carlyle saw her stop and bring her hands up to her face. She stood like that in the drive for a minute. Then one of the boys pushed her from behind and said her name. She dropped her hands and got into the back seat of the car.

'Daddy will get you into some clean clothes,' Carlyle told his children, trying to keep his voice steady. 'I'll give you a bath, and put you into some clean clothes. Then we'll go out for some pizza. How does pizza sound to you?'

'Where's Debbie?' Sarah asked him.

'She's gone,' Carlyle said.

That evening, after he'd put the children to bed, he called Carol, the woman from school he'd been seeing for the past month. He told her what had happened with his sitter.

'My kids were out in the yard with this big dog,' he said. 'The dog was as big as a wolf. The baby-sitter was in the house with a bunch of hoodlum boyfriends. They had Rod Stewart going full blast, and they were tying one on while my kids were outside playing with this strange dog.' He brought his fingers to his temples and held them there while he talked.

'My God,' Carol said. 'Poor sweetie, I'm so sorry.' Her voice sounded indistinct. He pictured her letting the receiver slide down to her chin, as she was in the habit of doing while talking on the phone. He'd seen her do it before. It was a habit of hers he found vaguely irritating. Did he want her to come over to his place? she asked. She would. She thought maybe she'd better do that. She'd call her sitter. Then she'd drive to his place. She wanted to. He shouldn't be afraid to say when he needed affection, she said. Carol was one of the secretaries in the principal's office at the high school where Carlyle taught art classes. She was divorced and had one child, a neurotic ten-year-old the father had named Dodge, after his automobile.

'No, that's all right,' Carlyle said. 'But thanks. _Thanks_ Carol. The kids are in bed, but I think I'd feel a little funny, you know, having company tonight.'

She didn't offer again. 'Sweetie, I'm sorry about what happened. But I understand your wanting to be alone tonight. I respect that. I'll see you at school tomorrow.'

He could hear her waiting for him to say something else. 'That's two baby-sitters in less than a week,' he said. 'I'm going out of my tree with this.'

'Honey, don't let it get you down,' she said. 'Something will turn up. I'll help you find somebody this weekend. It'll be all right, you'll see.'

'Thanks again for being there when I need you,' he said. 'You're one in a million, you know.'

''Night, Carlyle,' she said.

After he'd hung up, he wished he could have thought of something else to say to her instead of what he'd just said. He'd never talked that way before in his life. They weren't having a love affair, he wouldn't call it that, but he liked her. She knew it was a hard time for him, and she didn't make demands.

After Eileen had left for California, Carlyle had spent every waking minute for the first month with his children. He supposed the shock of her going had caused this, but he didn't want to let the children out of his sight. He'd certainly not been interested in seeing other women, and for a time he didn't think he ever would be. He felt as if he were in mourning. His days and nights were passed in the company of his children. He cooked for them – he had no appetite himself – washed and ironed their clothes, drove them into the country, where they picked flowers and ate sandwiches wrapped up in waxed paper. He took them to the supermarket and let them pick out what they liked. And every few days they went to the park, or else to the library, or the zoo. They took old bread to the zoo so they could feed the ducks. At night, before tucking them in, Carlyle read to them – Aesop, Hans Christian Andersen, the Brothers Grimm.

'When is Mama coming back?' one of them might ask him in the middle of a fairy tale.

'Soon,' he'd say. 'One of these days. Now listen to this.' Then he'd read the tale to its conclusion, kiss them, and turn off the light.

And while they'd slept, he had wandered the rooms of his house with a glass in his hand, telling himself that, yes, sooner or later, Eileen would come back. In the next breath, he would say, 'I never want to see your face again. I'll never forgive you for this, you crazy bitch.' Then, a minute later, 'Come back, sweetheart, please. I love you and need you. The kids need you, too.' Some nights that summer he fell asleep in front of the TV and woke up with the set still going and the screen filled with snow. This was the period when he didn't think he would be seeing any women for a long time, if ever. At night, sitting in front of the TV with an unopened book or magazine next to him on the sofa, he often thought of Eileen. When he did, he might remember her sweet laugh, or else her hand rubbing his neck if he complained of a soreness there. It was at these times that he thought he could weep. He thought, You hear about stuff like this happening to other people.

Just before the incident with Debbie, when some of the shock and grief had worn off, he'd phoned an employment service to tell them something of his predicament and his requirements. Someone took down the information and said they would get back to him. Not many people wanted to do housework *and* baby-sit, they said, but they'd find somebody. A few days before he had to be at the high school for meetings and registration, he called again and was told there'd be somebody at his house first thing the next morning.

That person was a thirty-five-year-old woman with hairy arms and run-over shoes. She shook hands with him and listened to him talk without asking a single question about the children – not even their names. When he took her into the back of the house where the children were playing, she simply stared at them for a minute without saying anything. When she finally smiled, Carlyle noticed for the first time that she had a tooth missing. Sarah left her crayons and got up to come over and stand next to him. She took Carlyle's hand and stared at the woman. Keith stared at her, too. Then he went back to his coloring. Carlyle thanked the woman for her time and said he would be in touch.

That afternoon he took down a number from an index card tacked to the bulletin board at the supermarket. Someone was offering baby-sitting services. References furnished on request. Carlyle called the number and got Debbie, the fat girl.

Over the summer, Eileen had sent a few cards, letters, and photographs of herself to the children, and some pen-and-ink drawings of her own that she'd done since she'd gone away. She also sent Carlyle long, rambling letters in which she asked for his understanding in this matter – this matter – but told him that she was happy. Happy. As if, Carlyle thought, happiness was all there was to life. She told him that if he really loved her, as he said he did, and as she really believed – she loved him, too, don't forget – then he would understand and accept things as they were. She wrote, 'That which is truly bonded can never become unbonded.' Carlyle didn't know if she was talking about their own relationship or her way of life out in California. He hated the word *bonded*. What did it have to do with the two of them? Did she think they were a corporation? He thought Eileen must be losing her mind to talk like that. He read that part again and then crumpled the letter.

But a few hours later he retrieved the letter from the trash can where he'd thrown it, and put it with her other cards and letters in a box on the shelf in his closet. In one of the envelopes, there was a photograph of her in a big, floppy hat, wearing a bathing suit. And there was a pencil drawing on heavy paper of a woman on a riverbank in a filmy gown, her hands covering her eyes, her shoulders slumped. It was, Carlyle assumed, Eileen showing her heartbreak over the situation. In college, she had majored in art, and even though she'd agreed to marry him, she said she intended to do something with her talent. Carlyle said he wouldn't have it any other way. She owed it to herself, he said. She owed it to both of them. They had loved each other in those days. He knew they had. He couldn't imagine ever loving anyone again the way he'd loved her. And he'd felt loved, too. Then, after eight years of being married to him, Eileen had pulled out. She was, she said in her letter, 'going for it.'

After talking to Carol, he looked in on the children, who were asleep. Then he went into the kitchen and made himself a drink. He thought of calling Eileen to talk to her about the baby-sitting crisis, but decided against it. He had her phone number and her address out there, of course. But he'd only called once and, so far, had not written a letter. This was partly out of anger and humiliation. Once, earlier in the summer, after a few drinks, he'd chanced humiliation and called. Richard Hoopes answered the phone. Richard had said, 'Hey, Carlyle,' as if he were still Carlyle's friend. And then, as if remembering something, he said, 'Just a minute, all right?'

Eileen had come on the line and said, 'Carlyle, how are you? How are the kids? Tell me about yourself.' He told her the kids were fine. But before he could say anything else, she interrupted him to say, 'I know *they're* fine. What about *you*?' Then she went on to tell him that her head was in the right place for the first time in a long time. Next she wanted to talk about his head and his karma. She'd looked into his karma. It was going to improve any time now, she said. Carlyle listened, hardly able to believe his ears. Then he said, 'I have to go now, Eileen.' And he hung up. The phone rang a minute or so later, but he let it ring. When it stopped ringing, he took the phone off the hook and left it off until he was ready for bed.

He wanted to call her now, but he was afraid to call. He still missed her and wanted to confide in her. He longed to hear her voice – sweet, steady, not manic as it had been for months now – but if he dialed her number, Richard Hoopes might answer the telephone. Carlyle knew he didn't want to hear that man's voice again. Richard had been a colleague for three years and, Carlyle supposed, a kind of friend. At least he was someone Carlyle ate lunch with in the faculty dining room, someone who talked about Tennessee Williams and the photographs of Ansel Adams. But even if Eileen answered the telephone, she might launch into something about his karma.

While he was sitting there with the glass in his hand, trying to remember what it had felt like to be married and intimate with someone, the phone rang. He picked up the receiver, heard a trace of static on the line, and knew, even before she'd said his name, that it was Eileen.

'I was just thinking about you,' Carlyle said, and at once regretted saying it.

'See! I knew I was on your mind, Carlyle. Well, I was thinking about you, too. That's why I called.' He drew a breath. She *was* losing her mind. That much was clear to him. She kept talking. 'Now listen,' she said. 'The big reason I called is that I know things are in kind of a mess out there right now. Don't ask me how, but I know. I'm sorry, Carlyle. But here's the thing. You're still in need of a good house-keeper and sitter combined, right? Well, she's practically right there in the neighborhood! Oh, you may have found someone already, and that's good, if that's the case. If so, it's supposed to be that way. But see, just in case you're having trouble in that area, there's this woman who used to work for Richard's mother. I told Richard about the potential problem, and he put himself to work on it. You want to know what he did? Are you listening? He called his mother, who used to have this woman who kept house for her. The woman's name is Mrs Webster. She looked after things for Richard's mother before his aunt and her daughter moved in there. Richard was able to get a number through his mother. He talked to Mrs Webster today. Richard did. Mrs Webster is going to call you tonight. Or else maybe she'll call you in the morning. One or the other. Anyway, she's going to volunteer her services, if you need her. You might, you never can tell. Even if your situation is okay right now, which I hope it is. But some time or another you might need her. You know what I'm saying? If not this minute, some other time. Okay? How are the kids? What are they up to?'

'The children are fine, Eileen. They're asleep now,' he said. Maybe he should tell her they cried themselves to sleep every night. He wondered if he should tell her the truth – that they hadn't asked about her even once in the last couple of weeks. He decided not to say anything.

'I called earlier, but the line was busy. I told Richard you were probably talking to your girlfriend,' Eileen said and laughed. 'Think positive thoughts. You sound depressed,' she said.

'I have to go, Eileen.' He started to hang up, and he took the receiver from his ear. But she was still talking.

'Tell Keith and Sarah I love them. Tell them I'm sending some more pictures. Tell them that. I don't want them to forget their mother is an artist. Maybe not a great artist yet, that's not important. But, you know, an artist. It's important they shouldn't forget that.'

Carlyle said, 'I'll tell them.'

'Richard says hello.'

Carlyle didn't say anything. He said the word to himself – *hello*. What could the man possibly mean by this? Then he said, 'Thanks for calling. Thanks for talking to that woman.'

'Mrs Webster!'

'Yes. I'd better get off the phone now. I don't want to run up your nickel.'

Eileen laughed. 'It's only money. Money's not important except as a necessary medium of exchange. There are more important things than money. But then you already know that.'

He held the receiver out in front of him. He looked at the instrument from which her voice was issuing.

'Carlyle, things are going to get better for you. I *know* they are. You may think I'm crazy or something,' she said. 'But just remember.'

Remember what? Carlyle wondered in alarm, thinking he must have missed something she'd said. He brought the receiver in close. 'Eileen, thanks for calling,' he said.

'We have to stay in touch,' Eileen said. 'We have to keep all lines of communication open. I think the worst is over. For both of us. I've suffered, too. But we're going to get what we're supposed to get out of this life, both of us, and we're going to be made *stronger* for it in the long run.'

'Goodnight,' he said. He put the receiver back. Then he looked at the phone. He waited. It didn't ring again. But an hour later it did ring. He answered it.

'Mr Carlyle.' It was an old woman's voice. 'You don't know me, but my name is Mrs Jim Webster. I was supposed to get in touch.'

'Mrs Webster. Yes,' he said. Eileen's mention of the woman came back to him. 'Mrs Webster, can you come to my house in the morning? Early. Say seven o'clock?'

'I can do that easily,' the old woman said. 'Seven o'clock. Give me your address.'

'I'd like to be able to count on you,' Carlyle said.

'You can count on me,' she said.

'I can't tell you how important it is,' Carlyle said.

'Don't you worry,' the old woman said.

The next morning, when the alarm went off, he wanted to keep his eyes closed and keep on with the dream he was having. Something about a farmhouse. And there was a waterfall in there, too. Someone, he didn't know who, was walking along the road carrying something. Maybe it was a picnic hamper. He was not made uneasy by the dream. In the dream, there seemed to exist a sense of well-being.

Finally, he rolled over and pushed something to stop the buzzing. He lay in bed awhile longer. Then he got up, put his feet into his slippers, and went out to the kitchen to start the coffee.

He shaved and dressed for the day. Then he sat down at the kitchen table with coffee and a cigarette. The children were still in bed. But in five minutes or so he planned to put boxes of cereal on the table and lay out bowls and spoons, then go in to wake them for breakfast. He really couldn't believe that the old woman who'd phoned him last night would show up this morning, as she'd said she would. He decided he'd wait until five minutes after seven o'clock, and then he'd call in, take the day off, and make every effort in the book to locate someone reliable. He brought the cup of coffee to his lips.

It was then that he heard a rumbling sound out in the street. He left his cup and got up from the table to look out the window. A pickup truck had pulled over to the curb in front of his house. The pickup cab shook as the engine idled. Carlyle went to the front door, opened it, and waved. An old woman waved back and then let herself out of the vehicle. Carlyle saw the driver lean over and disappear under the dash. The truck gasped, shook itself once more, and fell still.

'Mr Carlyle?' the old woman said, as she came slowly up his walk carrying a large purse.

'Mrs Webster,' he said. 'Come on inside. Is that your husband? Ask him in. I just made coffee.'

'It's okay,' she said. 'He has his thermos.'

Carlyle shrugged. He held the door for her. She stepped inside and they shook hands. Mrs Webster smiled. Carlyle nodded. They moved out to the kitchen. 'Did you want me today, then?' she asked.

'Let me get the children up,' he said. 'I'd like them to meet you before I leave for school.'

'That'd be good,' she said. She looked around his kitchen. She put her purse on the drainboard.

'Why don't I get the children?' he said. 'I'll just be a minute or two.'

In a little while, he brought the children out and introduced them. They were still in their pajamas. Sarah was rubbing her eyes. Keith was wide awake. 'This is Keith,' Carlyle said. 'And this one here, this is my Sarah.' He held on to Sarah's hand and turned to Mrs Webster. 'They need someone, you see. We need someone we can count on. I guess that's our problem.'

Mrs Webster moved over to the children. She fastened the top button of Keith's pajamas. She moved the hair away from Sarah's face. They let her do it. 'Don't you kids worry, now,' she said to them. 'Mr Carlyle, it'll be all right. We're going to be fine. Give us a day or two to get to know each other, that's all. But if I'm going to stay, why don't you give Mr Webster the all-clear sign? Just wave at him through the window,' she said, and then she gave her attention back to the children.

Carlyle stepped to the bay window and drew the curtain. An old man was watching the house from the cab of the truck. He was just bringing a thermos cup to his lips. Carlyle waved to him, and with his free hand the man waved back. Carlyle watched him roll down the truck window and throw out what was left in his cup. Then he bent down under the dash again – Carlyle imagined him touching some wires together – and in a minute the truck started and began to shake. The old man put the truck in gear and pulled away from the curb.

Carlyle turned from the window. 'Mrs Webster,' he said, 'I'm glad you're here.'

'Likewise, Mr Carlyle,' she said. 'Now you go on about your business before you're late. Don't worry about anything. We're going to be fine. Aren't we, kids?'

The children nodded their heads. Keith held on to her dress with one hand. He put the thumb of his other hand into his mouth.

'Thank you,' Carlyle said. 'I feel, I really feel a hundred percent better.' He shook his head and grinned. He felt a welling in his chest as he kissed each of his children goodbye. He told Mrs Webster what time she could expect him home, put on his coat, said goodbye once more, and went out of the house. For the first time in months, it seemed, he felt his burden had lifted a little. Driving to school, he listened to some music on the radio.

During first-period art-history class, he lingered over slides of Byzantine paintings. He patiently explained the nuances of detail and motif. He pointed out the emotional power and fitness of the work. But he took so long trying to place the anonymous artists in their social milieu that some of his students began to scrape their shoes on the floor, or else clear their throats. They covered only a third of the lesson plan that day. He was still talking when the bell rang.

In his next class, watercolor painting, he felt unusually calm and insightful. 'Like this, like this,' he said, guiding their hands. 'Delicately. Like a breath of air on the paper. Just a touch. Like so. See?' he'd say and felt on the edge of discovery himself. '*Suggestion* is what it's all about,' he said, holding lightly to Sue Colvin's fingers as he guided her brush. 'You've got to work with your mistakes until they look intended. Understand?'

As he moved down the lunch line in the faculty dining room, he saw Carol a few places ahead of him. She paid for her food. He waited impatiently while his own bill was being rung up. Carol was halfway across the room by the time he caught up with her. He slipped his hand under her elbow and guided her to an empty table near the window.

'God, Carlyle,' she said after they'd seated themselves. She picked up her glass of iced tea. Her face was flushed. 'Did you see the look Mrs Storr gave us? What's wrong with you? Everybody will know.' She sipped from her iced tea and put the glass down.

'The hell with Mrs Storr,' Carlyle said. 'Hey, let me tell you something. Honey, I feel light-years better than I did this time yesterday. Jesus,' he said.

'What's happened?' Carol said. 'Carlyle, tell me.' She moved her fruit cup to one side of her tray and shook cheese over her spaghetti. But she didn't eat anything. She waited for him to go on. 'Tell me what it is.'

He told her about Mrs Webster. He even told her about Mr Webster. Carlyle ate his tapioca while he talked. Then he ate the garlic bread. He drank Carol's iced tea down before he realized he was doing it.

'You're nuts, Carlyle,' she said, nodding at the spaghetti in his plate that he hadn't touched.

He shook his head. 'My *God*, Carol. God, I feel good, you know? I feel better than I have all summer.' He lowered his voice. 'Come over tonight, will you?'

He reached under the table and put his hand on her knee. She turned red again. She raised her eyes and looked around the dining room. But no one was paying any attention to them. She nodded quickly. Then she reached under the table and touched his hand.

That afternoon he arrived home to find his house neat and orderly and his children in clean clothes. In the kitchen, Keith and Sarah stood on chairs, helping Mrs Webster with gingerbread cookies. Sarah's hair was out of her face and held back with a barrette.

'Daddy!' his children cried, happy, when they saw him.

'Keith, Sarah,' he said. 'Mrs Webster, I –' But she didn't let him finish.

'We've had a fine day, Mr Carlyle,' Mrs Webster said quickly. She wiped her fingers on the apron she was wearing. It was an old apron with blue windmills on it and it had belonged to Eileen. 'Such beautiful children. They're a treasure. Just a treasure.'

'I don't know what to say.' Carlyle stood by the drainboard and watched Sarah press out some dough. He could smell the spice. He took off his coat and sat down at the kitchen table. He loosened his tie.

'Today was a get-acquainted day,' Mrs Webster said. 'Tomorrow we have some other plans. I thought we'd walk to the park. We ought to take advantage of this good weather.'

'That's a fine idea,' Carlyle said. 'That's just fine. Good. Good for you, Mrs Webster.'

'I'll finish putting these cookies in the oven. and by that time Mr Webster should be here. You said four o'clock? I told him to come at four.'

Carlyle nodded, his heart full.

'You had a call today,' she said as she went over to the sink with the mixing bowl. 'Mrs Carlyle called.'

'Mrs Carlyle,' he said. He waited for whatever it was Mrs Webster might say next.

'Yes. I identified myself, but she didn't seem surprised to find me here. She said a few words to each of the children.'

Carlyle glanced at Keith and Sarah, but they weren't paying any attention. They were lining up cookies on another baking sheet.

Mrs Webster continued. 'She left a message. Let me see, I wrote it down, but I think I can remember it. She said, 'Tell him' – that is, tell you – 'what goes around, comes around.' I think that's right. She said you'd understand.'

Carlyle stared at her. He heard Mr Webster's truck outside.

'That's Mr Webster,' she said and took off the apron.

Carlyle nodded.

'Seven o'clock in the morning?' she asked.

'That will be fine,' he said. 'And thank you again.'

That evening he bathed each of the children, got them into their pajamas, and then read to them. He listened to their prayers, tucked in their covers, and turned out the light. It was nearly nine o'clock. He made himself a drink and watched something on TV until he heard Carol's car pull into the drive.

Around ten, while they were in bed together, the phone rang. He swore, but he didn't get up to answer it. It kept ringing.

'It might be important,' Carol said, sitting up. 'It might be my sitter. She has this number.'

'It's my wife,' Carlyle said. 'I know it's her. She's losing her mind. She's going crazy. I'm not going to answer it.'

'I have to go pretty soon anyway,' Carol said. 'It was real sweet tonight, honey.' She touched his face.

It was the middle of the fall term. Mrs Webster had been with him for nearly six weeks. During this time, Carlyle's life had undergone a number of changes. For one thing, he was becoming reconciled to the fact that Eileen was gone and, as far as he could understand it, had no intention of coming back. He had stopped imagining that this might change. It was only late at night, on the nights he was not with Carol, that he wished for an end to the love he still had for Eileen and felt tormented as to why all of this had happened. But for the most part he and the children were happy; they thrived under Mrs Webster's attentions. Lately, she'd gotten into the routine of making their dinner and keeping it in the oven, warming, until his arrival home from school. He'd walk in the door to the smell of something good coming from the kitchen and find Keith and Sarah helping to set the dining-room table. Now and again he asked Mrs Webster if she would care for overtime work on Saturdays. She agreed, as long as it wouldn't entail her being at his house before noon. Saturday mornings, she said, she had things to do for Mr Webster and herself. On these days, Carol would leave Dodge with Carlyle's children, all of them under Mrs Webster's care, and Carol and he would drive to a restaurant out in the country for dinner. He believed his life was beginning again. Though he hadn't heard from Eileen since that call six weeks ago, he found himself able to think about her now without either being angry or else feeling close to tears.

At school, they were just leaving the medieval period and about to enter the Gothic. The Renaissance was still some time off, at least not until after the Christmas recess. It was during this time that Carlyle got sick. Overnight, it seemed, his chest tightened and his head began to hurt. The joints of his body became stiff. He felt dizzy when he moved around. The headache got worse. He woke up with it on a Sunday and thought of calling Mrs Webster to ask her to come and take the children somewhere. They'd been sweet to him, bringing him glasses of juice and some soda pop. But he couldn't take care of them. On the second morning of his illness, he was just able to get to the phone to call in sick. He gave his name, his school, department, and the nature of his illness to the person who answered the number. Then he recommended Mel Fisher as his substitute. Fisher was a man who painted abstract oils three or four days a week, sixteen hours a day, but who didn't sell or even show his work. He was a friend of Carlyle's. 'Get Mel Fisher,' Carlyle told the woman on the other end of the line. 'Fisher,' he whispered.

He made it back to his bed, got under the covers, and went to sleep. In his sleep, he heard the pickup engine running outside, and then the backfire it made as the engine was turned off. Sometime later he heard Mrs Webster's voice outside the bedroom door.

'Mr Carlyle?'

'Yes, Mrs Webster.' His voice sounded strange to him. He kept his eyes shut. 'I'm sick today. I called the school. I'm going to stay in bed today.'

'I see. Don't worry, then,' she said. 'I'll look after things at this end.'

He shut his eyes. Directly, still in a state between sleeping and waking, he thought he heard his front door open and close. He listened. Out in the kitchen, he heard a man say something in a low voice, and a chair being pulled away from the table. Pretty soon he heard the voices of the children. Sometime later – he wasn't sure how much time had passed – he heard Mrs Webster outside his door.

'Mr Carlyle, should I call the doctor?'

'No, that's all right,' he said. 'I think it's just a bad cold. But I feel hot all over. I think I have too many covers. And it's too warm in the house. Maybe you'll turn down the furnace.' Then he felt himself drift back into sleep.

In a little while, he heard the children talking to Mrs Webster in the living room. Were they coming inside or going out? Carlyle wondered. Could it be the next day already?

He went back to sleep. But then he was aware of his door opening. Mrs Webster appeared beside his bed. She put her hand on his forehead.

'You're burning up,' she said. 'You have a fever.'

'I'll be all right,' Carlyle said. 'I just need to sleep a little longer. And maybe you could turn the furnace down. Please, I'd appreciate it if you could get me some aspirin. I have an awful headache.'

Mrs Webster left the room. But his door stood open. Carlyle could hear the TV going out there. 'Keep it down, Jim,' he heard her say, and the volume was lowered at once. Carlyle fell asleep again.

But he couldn't have slept more than a minute, because Mrs Webster was suddenly back in his room with a tray. She sat down on the side of his bed. He roused himself and tried to sit up. She put a pillow behind his back.

'Take these,' she said and gave him some tablets. 'Drink this.' She held a glass of juice for him. 'I also brought you some Cream of Wheat. I want you to eat it. It'll be good for you.'

He took the aspirin and drank the juice. He nodded. But he shut his eyes once more. He was going back to sleep.

'Mr Carlyle,' she said.

He opened his eyes. 'I'm awake,' he said. 'I'm sorry.' He sat up a little. 'I'm too warm, that's all. What time is it? Is it eight-thirty yet?'

'It's a little after nine-thirty,' she said.

'Nine-thirty,' he said.

'Now I'm going to feed this cereal to you. And you're going to open up and eat it. Six bites, that's all. Here, here's the first bite. Open,' she said. 'You're going to feel better after you eat this. Then I'll let you go back to sleep. You eat this, and then you can sleep all you want.'

He ate the cereal she spooned to him and asked for more juice. He drank the juice, and then he pulled down in the bed again. Just as he was going off to sleep, he felt her covering him with another blanket.

The next time he awoke, it was afternoon. He could tell it was afternoon by the pale light that came through his window. He reached up and pulled the curtain back. He could see that it was overcast outside; the wintry sun was behind the clouds. He got out of bed slowly, found his slippers, and put on his robe. He went into the bathroom and looked at himself in the mirror. Then he washed his face and took some more aspirin. He used the towel and then went out to the living room.

On the dining-room table, Mrs Webster had spread some newspaper, and she and the children were pinching clay figures together. They had already made some things that had long necks and bulging eyes, things that resembled giraffes, or else dinosaurs. Mrs Webster looked up as he walked by the table.

'How are you feeling?' Mrs Webster asked him as he settled onto the sofa. He could see into the dining-room area, where Mrs Webster and the children sat at the table.

'Better, thanks. A little better,' he said. 'I still have a headache, and I feel a little warm.' He brought the back of his hand up to his forehead. 'But I'm better. Yes, I'm better. Thanks for your help this morning.'

'Can I get you anything now?' Mrs Webster said. 'Some more juice or some tea? I don't think coffee would hurt, but I think tea would be better. Some juice would be best of all.'

'No, no thanks,' he said. 'I'll just sit here for a while. It's good to be out of bed. I feel a little weak is all. Mrs Webster?'

She looked at him and waited.

'Did I hear Mr Webster in the house this morning? It's fine, of course. I'm just sorry I didn't get a chance to meet him and say hello.'

'It was him,' she said. 'He wanted to meet you, too. I asked him to come in. He just picked the wrong morning, what with you being sick and all. I'd wanted to tell you something about our plans, Mr Webster's and mine, but this morning wasn't a good time for it.'

'Tell me what?' he said, alert, fear plucking at his heart.

She shook her head. 'It's all right,' she said. 'It can wait.'

'Tell him what?' Sarah said. 'Tell him what?'

'What, what?' Keith picked it up. The children stopped what they were doing.

'Just a minute, you two,' Mrs Webster said as she got to her feet.

'Mrs Webster, Mrs Webster!' Keith cried.

'Now see here, little man,' Mrs Webster said. 'I need to talk to your father. Your father is sick today. You just take it easy. You go on and play with your clay. If you don't watch it, your sister is going to get ahead of you with these creatures.'

Just as she began to move toward the living room, the phone rang. Carlyle reached over to the end table and picked up the receiver.

As before, he heard faint singing in the wire and knew that it was Eileen. 'Yes,' he said. 'What is it?'

'Carlyle,' his wife said, 'I know, don't ask me how, that things are not going so well right now. You're sick, aren't you? Richard's been sick, too. It's something going around. He can't keep anything on his stomach. He's already missed a week of rehearsal for this play he's doing. I've had to go down myself and help block out scenes with his assistant. But I didn't call to tell you that. Tell me how things are out there.'

'Nothing to tell,' Carlyle said. 'I'm sick, that's all. A touch of the flu. But I'm getting better.'

'Are you still writing in your journal?' she asked. It caught him by surprise. Several years before, he'd told her that he was keeping a journal. Not a diary, he'd said, a journal – as if that explained something. But he'd never shown it to her, and he hadn't written in it for over a year. He'd forgotten about it.

'Because,' she said, 'you ought to write something in the journal during this period. How you feel and what you're thinking. You know, where your head is at during this period of sickness. Remember, sickness is a message about your health and your well-being. It's telling you things. Keep a record. You know what I mean? When you're well, you can look back and see what the message was. You can read it later, after the fact. Colette did that,' Eileen said. 'When she had a fever this one time.'

'Who?' Carlyle said. 'What did you say?'

'Colette,' Eileen answered. 'The French writer. You know who I'm talking about. We had a book of hers around the house. *Gigi* or something. I didn't read *that* book, but I've been reading her since I've been out here. Richard turned me on to her. She wrote a little book about what it was like, about what she was thinking and feeling the whole time she had this fever. Sometimes her temperature was a hundred and two. Sometimes it was lower. Maybe it went higher than a hundred and two. But a hundred and two was the highest she ever took her temperature and wrote, too, when she had the fever. Anyway, she wrote about it. That's what I'm saying. Try writing about what it's like. Something might come of it,' Eileen said and, inexplicably, it seemed to Carlyle, she laughed. 'At least later on you'd have an hour-by-hour account of your sickness. To look back at. At least you'd have that to show for it. Right now you've just got this discomfort. You've got to translate that into something usable.'

He pressed his fingertips against his temple and shut his eyes. But she was still on the line, waiting for him to say something. What could he say? It was clear to him that she was insane.

'Jesus,' he said. 'Jesus, Eileen. I don't know what to say to that. I really don't. I have to go now. Thanks for calling,' he said.

'It's all right,' she said. 'We have to be able to communicate. Kiss the kids for me. Tell them I love them. And Richard sends his hellos to you. Even though he's flat on his back.'

'Goodbye,' Carlyle said and hung up. Then he brought his hands to his face. He remembered, for some reason, seeing the fat girl make the same gesture that time as she moved toward the car. He lowered his hands and looked at Mrs Webster, who was watching him.

'Not bad news, I hope,' she said. The old woman had moved a chair near to where he sat on the sofa.

Carlyle shook his head.

'Good,' Mrs Webster said. 'That's good. Now, Mr Carlyle, this may not be the best time in the world to talk about this.' She glanced out to the dining room. At the table, the children had their heads bent over the clay. 'But since it has to be talked about sometime soon, and since it concerns you and the children, and you're up now, I have something to tell you. Jim and I, we're getting on. The thing is, we need something more than we have at the present. Do you know what I'm saying? This is hard for me,' she said and shook her head. Carlyle nodded slowly. He knew that she was going to tell him she had to leave. He wiped his face on his sleeve. 'Jim's son by a former marriage, Bob – the man is forty years old – called yesterday to invite us to go out to Oregon and help him with his mink ranch. Jim would be doing whatever they do with minks, and I'd cook, buy the groceries, clean house, and do anything else that needed doing. It's a chance for both of us. And it's board and room and then some. Jim and I won't have to worry anymore about what's going to happen to us. You know what I'm saying. Right now, Jim doesn't have anything,' she said. 'He was sixty-two last week. He hasn't had anything for some time. He came in this morning to tell you about it himself, because I was going to have to give notice, you see. We thought – *I* thought – it would help if Jim was here when I told you.' She waited for Carlyle to say something. When he didn't, she went on. 'I'll finish out the week, and I could stay on a couple of days next week, if need be. But then, you know, for sure, we really have to leave, and you'll have to wish us luck. I mean, can you imagine – all the way out there to Oregon in that old rattletrap of ours? But I'm going to miss these little kids. They're so precious.'

After a time, when he still hadn't moved to answer her, she got up from her chair and went to sit on the cushion next to his. She touched the sleeve of his robe. 'Mr Carlyle?'

'I understand,' he said. 'I want you to know your being here has made a big difference to me and the children.' His head ached so much that he had to squint his eyes. 'This headache,' he said. 'This headache is killing me.'

Mrs Webster reached over and laid the back of her hand against his forehead. 'You still have some fever,' she told him. 'I'll get more aspirin. That'll help bring it down. I'm still on the case here,' she said. 'I'm still the doctor.'

'My wife thinks I should write down what this feels like,' Carlyle said. 'She thinks it might be a good idea to describe what the fever is like. So I can look back later and get the message.' He laughed. Some tears came to his eyes. He wiped them away with the heel of his hand.

'I think I'll get your aspirin and juice and then go out there with the kids,' Mrs Webster said. 'Looks to me like they've about worn out their interest with that clay.'

Carlyle was afraid she'd move into the other room and leave him alone. He wanted to talk to her. He cleared his throat. 'Mrs Webster, there's something I want you to know. For a long time, my wife and I loved each other more than anything or anybody in the world. And that includes those children. We thought, well, we *knew* that we'd grow old together. And we knew we'd do all the things in the world that we wanted to do, and do them together.' He shook his head. That seemed the saddest thing of all to him now – that whatever they did from now on, each would do it without the other.

'There, it's all right,' Mrs Webster said. She patted his hand. He sat forward and began to talk again. After a time, the children came out to the living room. Mrs Webster caught their attention and held a finger to her lips. Carlyle looked at them and went on talking. Let them listen, he thought. It concerns them, too. The children seemed to understand they had to remain quiet, even pretend some interest, so they sat down next to Mrs Webster's legs. Then they got down on their stomachs on the carpet and started to giggle. But Mrs Webster looked sternly in their direction, and that stopped it.

Carlyle went on talking. At first, his head still ached, and he felt awkward to be in his pajamas on the sofa with this old woman beside him, waiting patiently for him to go on to the next thing. But then his headache went away. And soon he stopped feeling awkward and forgot how he was supposed to feel. He had begun his story some-where in the middle, after the children were born. But then he backed up and started at the beginning, back when Eileen was eighteen and he was nineteen, a boy and girl in love, burning with it.

He stopped to wipe his forehead. He moistened his lips.

'Go on,' Mrs Webster said. 'I know what you're saying. You just keep talking, Mr Carlyle. Sometimes it's good to talk about it. Some-times it has to be talked about. Besides, I want to hear it. And you're going to feel better afterwards. Something just like it happened to me once, something like what you're describing. Love. That's what it is.'

The children fell asleep on the carpet. Keith had this thumb in his mouth. Carlyle was still talking when Mr Webster came to the door, knocked, and then stepped inside to collect Mrs Webster.

'Sit down, Jim,' Mrs Webster said. 'There's no hurry. Go on with what you were saying, Mr Carlyle.'

Carlyle nodded at the old man, and the old man nodded back, then got himself one of the dining-room chairs and carried it into the living room. He brought the chair close to the sofa and sat down on it with a sigh. Then he took off his cap and wearily lifted one leg over the other. When Carlyle began talking again, the old man put both feet on the floor. The children woke up. They sat up on the carpet and rolled their heads back and forth. But by then Carlyle had said all he knew to say, so he stopped talking.

'Good. Good for you,' Mrs Webster said when she saw he had finished. 'You're made out of good stuff. And so is she – so is Mrs Carlyle. And don't you forget it. You're both going to be okay after this is over.' She got up and took off the apron she'd been wearing. Mr

Webster got up, too, and put his cap back on.

At the door, Carlyle shook hands with both of the Websters.

'So long,' Jim Webster said. He touched the bill of his cap.

'Good luck to you,' Carlyle said.

Mrs Webster said she'd see him in the morning then, bright and early as always.

As if something important had been settled, Carlyle said, 'Right!'

The old couple went carefully along the walk and got into their truck. Jim Webster bent down under the dashboard. Mrs Webster looked at Carlyle and waved. It was then, as he stood at the window, that he felt something come to an end. It had to do with Eileen and the life before this. Had he ever waved at her? He must have, of course, he knew he had, yet he could not remember just now. But he understood it was over, and he felt able to let her go. He was sure their life together had happened in the way he said it had. But it was something that had passed. And that passing – though it had seemed impossible and he'd fought against it – would become a part of him now, too, as surely as anything else he'd left behind.

As the pickup lurched forward, he lifted his arm once more. He saw the old couple lean toward him briefly as they drove away. Then he brought his arm down and turned to his children.

The bridle

This old station wagon with Minnesota plates pulls into a parking space in front of the window. There's a man and woman in the front seat, two boys in the back. It's July, temperature's one hundred plus. These people looked whipped. There are clothes hanging inside; suitcases, boxes, and such piled in back. From what Harley and I put together later, that's all they had left after the bank in Minnesota took their house, their pickup, their tractor, the farm implements, and a few cows.

The people inside sit for a minute, as if collecting themselves. The air-conditioner in our apartment is going full blast. Harley's around in back cutting grass. There's some discussion in the front seat, and then she and him get out and start for the front door. I pat my hair to make sure that it's in place and wait till they push the doorbell for the second time. Then I go to let them in. 'You're looking for an apartment?' I say. 'Come on in here where it's cool.' I show them into the living room. The living room is where I do business. It's where I collect the rents, write the receipts, and talk to interested parties. I also do hair. I call myself a *stylist*. That's what my cards say. I don't like the word *beautician*. It's an old-time word. I have the chair in a corner of the living room, and a dryer I can pull up to the back of the chair. And there's a sink that Harley put in a few years ago. Alongside the chair, I have a table with some magazines. The magazines are old. The covers are gone from some of them. But people will look at anything while they're under the dryer.

The man says his name.

'My name is Holits.'

He tells me she's his wife. But she won't look at me. She looks at her nails instead. She and Holits won't sit down, either. He says they're interested in one of the furnished units.

'How many of you?' But I'm just saying what I always say. I know how many. I saw the two boys in the back seat. Two and two is four.

'Me and her and the boys. The boys are thirteen and fourteen, and they'll share a room, like always.'

She has her arms crossed and is holding the sleeves of her blouse.

She takes in the chair and the sink as if she's never seen their like before. Maybe she hasn't.

'I do hair,' I say.

She nods. Then she gives my prayer plant the once-over. It has exactly five leaves to it.

'That needs watering,' I say. I go over and touch one of its leaves. 'Everything around here needs water. There's not enough water in the air. It rains three times a year if we're lucky. But you'll get used to it. We had to get used to it. But everything here is air-conditioned.'

'How much is the place?' Holits wants to know.

I tell him and he turns to her to see what she thinks. But he may as well have been looking at the wall. She won't give him back his look. 'I guess we'll have you show us,' he says. So I move to get the key for 17, and we go outside.

I hear Harley before I see him.

Then he comes into sight between the buildings. He's moving along behind the power mower in his Bermudas and T-shirt, wearing the straw hat he bought in Nogales. He spends his time cutting grass and doing the small maintenance work. We work for a corporation, Fulton Terrace, Inc. They own the place. If anything major goes wrong, like air-conditioning trouble or something serious in the plumbing department, we have a list of phone numbers.

I wave. I have to. Harley takes a hand off the mower handle and signals. Then he pulls the hat down over his forehead and gives his attention back to what he's doing. He comes to the end of his cut, makes his turn, and starts back toward the street.

'That's Harley.' I have to shout it. We go in at the side of the building and up some stairs. 'What kind of work are you in, Mr Holits?' I ask him.

'He's a farmer,' she says.

'No more.'

'Not much to farm around here.' I say it without thinking.

'We had us a farm in Minnesota. Raised wheat. A few cattle. And Holits knows horses. He knows everything there is about horses.'

'That's all right, Betty.'

I get a piece of the picture then. Holits is unemployed. It's not my affair, and I feel sorry if that's the case — it is, it turns out — but as we stop in front of the unit, I have to say something. 'If you decide, it's first month, last month, and one-fifty as security deposit.' I look down at the pool as I say it. Some people are sitting in deck chairs, and there's somebody in the water.

Holits wipes his face with the back of his hand. Harley's mower is clacking away. Farther off, cars speed by on Calle Verde. The two boys have got out of the station wagon. One of them is standing at military attention, legs together, arms at his sides. But as I watch, I see him begin to flap his arms up and down and jump, like he intends to take off and fly. The other one is squatting down on the driver's side of the station wagon, doing knee bends.

I turn to Holits.

'Let's have a look,' he says.

I turn the key and the door opens. It's just a little two-bedroom furnished apartment. Everybody has seen dozens. Holits stops in the bathroom long enough to flush the toilet. He watches till the tank fills. Later, he says, 'This could be our room.' He's talking about the bedroom that looks out over the pool. In the kitchen, the woman takes hold of the edge of the drainboard and stares out the window.

'That's the swimming pool,' I say.

She nods. 'We stayed in some motels that had swimming pools. But in one pool they had too much chlorine in the water.'

I wait for her to go on. But that's all she says. I can't think of anything else, either.

'I guess we won't waste any more time. I guess we'll take it.' Holits looks at her as he says it. This time she meets his eyes. She nods. He lets out breath through his teeth. Then she does something. She begins snapping her fingers. One hand is still holding the edge of the drainboard, but with her other hand she begins snapping her fingers. Snap, snap, snap, like she was calling her dog, or else trying to get somebody's attention. Then she stops and runs her nails across the counter.

I don't know what to make of it. Holits doesn't either. He moves his feet.

'We'll walk back to the office and make things official,' I say. 'I'm glad.'

I *was* glad. We had a lot of empty units for this time of year. And these people seemed like dependable people. Down on their luck, that's all. No disgrace can be attached to that.

Holits pays in cash – first, last, and the one-fifty deposit. He counts out bills of fifty-dollar denomination while I watch. U.S. Grants,

Harley calls them, though he's never seen many. I write out the receipt and give him two keys. 'You're all set.'

He looks at the keys. He hands her one. 'So, we're in Arizona. Never thought you'd see Arizona, did you?'

She shakes her head. She's touching one of the prayer-plant leaves. 'Needs water,' I say.

She lets go of the leaf and turns to the window. I go over next to her. Harley is still cutting grass. But he's around in front now. There's been this talk of farming, so for a minute I think of Harley moving along behind a plow instead of behind his Black and Decker power mower.

I watch them unload their boxes, suitcases, and clothes. Holits carries in something that has straps hanging from it. It takes a minute, but then I figure out it's a bridle. I don't know what to do next. I don't feel like doing anything. So I take the Grants out of the cashbox. I just put them in there, but I take them out again. The bills have come from Minnesota. Who knows where they'll be this time next week? They could be in Las Vegas. All I know about Las Vegas is what I see on TV – about enough to put into a thimble. I can imagine one of the Grants finding its way out to Waikiki Beach, or else some other place. Miami or New York City. New Orleans. I think about one of those bills changing hands during Mardi Gras. They could go anyplace, and anything could happen because of them. I write my name in ink across Grant's broad old forehead: MARGE. I print it. I do it on every one. Right over his thick brows. People will stop in the middle of their spending and wonder. Who's this Marge? That's what they'll ask themselves. Who's this Marge?

Harley comes in from outside and washes his hands in my sink. He knows it's something I don't like him to do. But he goes ahead and does it anyway.

'Those people from Minnesota,' he says. 'The Swedes. They're a long way from home.' He dries his hands on a paper towel. He wants me to tell him what I know. But I don't know anything. They don't look like Swedes and they don't talk like Swedes.

'They're not Swedes,' I tell him. But he acts like he doesn't hear me.

'So what's he do?'

'He's a farmer.'

'What do you know about that?'

Harley takes his hat off and puts it on my chair. He runs a hand through his hair. Then he looks at the hat and puts it on again. He may as well be glued to it. 'There's not much to farm around here. Did you tell him that?' He gets a can of soda pop from the fridge and goes to sit in his recliner. He picks up the remote-control, pushes something, and the TV sizzles on. He pushes some more buttons until he finds what he's looking for. It's a hospital show. 'What else does the Swede do? Besides farm?'

I don't know, so I don't say anything. But Harley's already taken up with his program. He's probably forgotten he asked me the question. A siren goes off. I hear the screech of tires. On the screen, an ambulance has come to a stop in front of an emergency-room entrance, its red lights flashing. A man jumps out and runs around to open up the back.

The next afternoon the boys borrow the hose and wash the station wagon. They clean the outside and the inside. A little later I notice her drive away. She's wearing high heels and a nice dress. Hunting up a job, I'd say. After a while, I see the boys messing around the pool in their bathing suits. One of them springs off the board and swims all the way to the other end underwater. He comes up blowing water and shaking his head. The other boy, the one who'd been doing knee bends the day before, lies on his stomach on a towel at the far side of the pool. But this one boy keeps swimming back and forth from one end of the pool to the other, touching the wall and turning back with a little kick.

There are two other people out there. They're in lounge chairs, one on either side of the pool. One of them is Irving Cobb, a cook at Denny's. He calls himself Spuds. People have taken to calling him that, Spuds, instead of Irv or some other nickname. Spuds is fifty-five and bald. He already looks like beef jerky, but he wants more sun. Right now, his new wife, Linda Cobb, is at work at the K Mart. Spuds works nights. But him and Linda Cobb have it arranged so they take their Saturdays and Sundays off. Connie Nova is in the other chair. She's sitting up and rubbing lotion on her legs. She's nearly naked — just this little two-piece suit covering her. Connie Nova is a cocktail waitress. She moved in here six months ago with her so-called fiancé, an alcoholic lawyer. But she got rid of him. Now she lives with a long-haired student from the college whose name is Rick. I happen to know he's away right now, visiting his folks. Spuds and Connie are wearing dark glasses. Connie's portable radio is going.

Spuds was a recent widower when he moved in, a year or so back.
But after a few months of being a bachelor again, he got married to
Linda. She's a red-haired woman in her thirties. I don't know how
they met. But one night a couple of months ago Spuds and the new
Mrs Cobb had Harley and me over to a nice dinner that Spuds fixed.
After dinner, we sat in their living room drinking sweet drinks out of
big glasses. Spuds asked if we wanted to see home movies. We said
sure. So Spuds set up his screen and his projector. Linda Cobb poured
us more of that sweet drink. Where's the harm? I asked myself. Spuds
began to show films of a trip he and his dead wife had made to Alaska.
It began with her getting on the plane in Seattle. Spuds talked as he
ran the projector. The deceased was in her fifties, good-looking,
though maybe a little heavy. Her hair was nice.

'That's Spuds's first wife,' Linda Cobb said. 'That's the first Mrs
Cobb.'

'That's Evelyn,' Spuds said.

The first wife stayed on the screen for a long time. It was funny
seeing her and hearing them talk about her like that. Harley passed
me a look, so I know he was thinking something, too. Linda Cobb
asked if we wanted another drink or a macaroon. We didn't. Spuds
was saying something about the first Mrs Cobb again. She was still at
the entrance to the plane, smiling and moving her mouth even if all
you could hear was the film going through the projector. People had
to go around her to get on the plane. She kept waving at the camera,
waving at us there in Spuds's living room. She waved and waved.
'There's Evelyn again,' the new Mrs Cobb would say each time the
first Mrs Cobb appeared on the screen.

Spuds would have shown films all night, but we said we had to go.
Harley made the excuse.

I don't remember what he said.

Connie Nova is lying on her back in the chair, dark glasses covering
half of her face. Her legs and stomach shine with oil. One night, not
long after she moved in, she had a party. This was before she kicked
the lawyer out and took up with the long-hair. She called her party a
housewarming. Harley and I were invited, along with a bunch of
other people. We went, but we didn't care for the company. We found
a place to sit close to the door, and that's where we stayed till we left.
It wasn't all that long, either. Connie's boyfriend was giving a door
prize. It was the offer of his legal services, without charge, for the

handling of a divorce. Anybody's divorce. Anybody who wanted to could draw a card out of the bowl he was passing around. When the bowl came our way, everybody began to laugh. Harley and I swapped glances. I didn't draw. Harley didn't draw, either. But I saw him look in the bowl at the pile of cards. Then he shook his head and handed the bowl to the person next to him. Even Spuds and the new Mrs Cobb drew cards. The winning card had something written across the back. 'Entitles bearer to one free uncontested divorce,' and the lawyer's signature and the date. The lawyer was a drunk, but I say this is no way to conduct your life. Everybody but us had put his hand into the bowl, like it was a fun thing to do. The woman who drew the winning card clapped. It was like one of those game shows. 'Goddamn, this is the first time I ever won anything!' I was told she had a husband in the military. There's no way of knowing if she still has him, or if she got her divorce, because Connie Nova took up with a different set of friends after she and the lawyer went their separate ways.

We left the party right after the drawing. It made such an impression we couldn't say much, except one of us said, 'I don't believe I saw what I think I saw.'

Maybe I said it.

A week later Harley asks if the Swede – he means Holits – has found work yet. We've just had lunch, and Harley's in his chair with his can of pop. But he hasn't turned his TV on. I say I don't know. And I don't. I wait to see what else he has to say. But he doesn't say anything else. He shakes his head. He seems to think about something. Then he pushes a button and the TV comes to life.

She finds a job. She starts working as a waitresss in an Italian restaurant a few blocks from here. She works a split shift, doing lunches and then going home, then back to work again in time for the dinner shift. She's meeting herself coming and going. The boys swim all day, while Holits stays inside the apartment. I don't know what he does in there. Once, I did her hair and she told me a few things. She told me she did waitressing when she was just out of high school and that's where she met Holits. She served him some pancakes in a place back in Minnesota.

She'd walked down that morning and asked me could I do her a favor. She wanted me to fix her hair after her lunch shift and have her out in time for her dinner shift. Could I do it? I told her I'd check the book. I asked her to step inside. It must have been a hundred degrees already.

'I know it's short notice,' she said. 'But when I came in from work last night, I looked in the mirror and saw my roots showing. I said to myself, "I need a treatment." I don't know where else to go.'

I find Friday, August 14. There's nothing on the page.

'I could work you in at two-thirty, or else at three o'clock,' I say.

'Three would be better,' she says. 'I have to run for it now before I'm late. I work for a real bastard. See you later.'

At two-thirty, I tell Harley I have a customer, so he'll have to take his baseball game into the bedroom. He grumps, but he winds up the cord and wheels the set out back. He closes the door. I make sure everything I need is ready. I fix up the magazines so they're easy to get to. Then I sit next to the dryer and file my nails. I'm wearing the rose-colored uniform that I put on when I do hair. I go on filing my nails and looking up at the window from time to time.

She walks by the window and then pushes the doorbell. 'Come on in,' I call. 'It's unlocked.'

She's wearing the black-and-white uniform from her job. I can see how we're both wearing uniforms. 'Sit down, honey, and we'll get started.' She looks at the nail file. 'I give manicures, too,' I say.

She settles into the chair and draws a breath.

I say, 'Put your head back. That's it. Close your eyes now, why don't you? Just relax. First I'll shampoo you and touch up these roots here. Then we'll go from there. How much time do you have?'

'I have to be back there at five-thirty.'

'We'll get you fixed up.'

'I can eat at work. But I don't know what Holits and the boys will do for their supper.'

'They'll get along fine without you.'

I start the warm water and then notice Harley's left me some dirt and grass. I wipe up his mess and start over.

I say, 'If they want, they can just walk down the street to the hamburger place. It won't hurt them.'

'They won't do that. Anyway, I don't want them to have to go there.'

It's none of my business, so I don't say any more. I make up a nice lather and go to work. After I've done the shampoo, rinse, and set, I put her under the dryer. Her eyes have closed. I think she could be asleep. So I take one of her hands and begin.

'No manicure.' She opens her eyes and pulls away her hand.

'It's all right, honey. The first manicure is always no charge.'

She gives me back her hand and picks up one of the magazines and rests it in her lap. 'They're his boys,' she says. 'From his first marriage. He was divorced when we met. But I love them like they were my own. I couldn't love them any more if I tried. Not even if I was their natural mother.'

I turn the dryer down a notch so that it's making a low, quiet sound. I keep on with her nails. Her hand starts to relax.

'She lit out on them, on Holits and the boys, on New Year's Day ten years ago. They never heard from her again.' I can see she wants to tell me about it. And that's fine with me. They like to talk when they're in the chair. I go on using the file. 'Holits got the divorce. Then he and I started going out. Then we got married. For a long time, we had us a life. It had its ups and downs. But we thought we were working toward something.' She shakes her head. 'But something happened. Something happened to Holits, I mean. One thing happened was he got interested in horses. This one particular race horse, he bought it, you know – something down, something each month. He took it around to the tracks. He was still up before daylight, like always, still doing the chores and such. I thought everything was all right. But I don't know anything. If you want the truth, I'm not so good at waiting tables. I think those wops would fire me at the drop of a hat, if I gave them a reason. Or for no reason. What if I got fired? Then what?'

I say, 'Don't worry, honey. They're not going to fire you.'

Pretty soon she picks up another magazine. But she doesn't open it. She just holds it and goes on talking. 'Anyway, there's this horse of his. Fast Betty. The Betty part is a joke. But he says it can't help but be a winner if he names it after me. A big winner, all right. The fact is, wherever it ran, it lost. Every race. Betty Longshot – that's what it should have been called. In the beginning, I went to a few races. But the horse always ran ninety-nine to one. Odds like that. But Holits is stubborn if he's anything. He wouldn't give up. He'd bet on the horse and bet on the horse. Twenty dollars to win. Fifty dollars to win. Plus all the other things it costs for keeping a horse. I know it don't sound like a large amount. But it adds up. And when the odds were like that – ninety-nine to one, you know – sometimes he'd buy a combination ticket. He'd ask me if I realized how much money we'd make if the horse came in. But it didn't, and I quit going.'

I keep on with what I'm doing. I concentrate on her nails. 'You have nice cuticles,' I say. 'Look here at your cuticles. See these little half-moons? Means your blood's good.'

She brings her hand up close and looks. 'What do you know about that?' She shrugs. She lets me take her hand again. She's still got things to tell. 'Once, when I was in high school, a counselor asked me to come to her office. She did it with all the girls, one of us at a time. 'What dreams do you have?' this woman asked me. 'What do you see yourself doing in ten years? Twenty years?' I was sixteen or seventeen. I was just a kid. I couldn't think what to answer. I just sat there like a lump. This counselor was about the age I am now. I thought she was *old*. She's old, I said to myself. I knew *her* life was half over. And I felt like I knew something she didn't. Something she'd never know. A secret. Something nobody's supposed to know, or ever talk about. So I stayed quiet. I just shook my head. She must've written me off as a dope. But I couldn't say anything. You know what I mean? I thought I knew things she couldn't guess at. Now, if anybody asked me that question again, about my dreams and all, I'd tell them.'

'What would you tell them, honey?' I have her other hand now. But I'm not doing her nails. I'm just holding it, waiting to hear.

She moves forward in the chair. She tries to take her hand back.

'What would you tell them?'

She sighs and leans back. She lets me keep the hand. 'I'd say, "Dreams, you know, are what you wake up from." That's what I'd say.' She smooths the lap of her skirt. 'If anybody asked, that's what I'd say. But they won't ask.' She lets out her breath again. 'So how much longer?' she says.

'Not long,' I say.

'You don't know what it's like.'

'Yes, I do,' I say. I pull the stool right up next to her legs. I'm starting to tell how it was before we moved here, and how it's still like that. But Harley picks right then to come out of the bedroom. He doesn't look at us. I hear the TV jabbering away in the bedroom. He goes to the sink and draws a glass of water. He tips his head back to drink. His Adam's apple moves up and down in his throat.

I move the dryer away and touch the hair at both sides of her head. I lift one of the curls just a little.

I say, 'You look brand-new, honey.'

'Don't I wish.'

*

The boys keep on swimming all day, every day, till their school starts. Betty keeps on at her job. But for some reason she doesn't come back to get her hair done. I don't know why this is. Maybe she doesn't think I did a good job. Sometimes I lie awake, Harley sleeping like a grindstone beside me, and try to picture myself in Betty's shoes. I wonder what I'd do then.

Holits sends one of his sons with the rent on the first of September, and on the first of October, too. He still pays in cash. I take the money from the boy, count the bills right there in front of him, and then write out the receipt. Holits has found work of some sort. I think so, anyway. He drives off every day with the station wagon. I see him leave early in the morning and drive back late in the afternoon. She goes past the window at ten-thirty and comes back at three. If she sees me, she gives me a little wave. But she's not smiling. Then I see Betty again at five, walking back to the restaurant. Holits drives in a little later. This goes on till the middle of October.

Meanwhile, the Holits couple acquainted themselves with Connie Nova and her long-hair friend, Rick. And they also met up with Spuds and the new Mrs Cobb. Sometimes, on a Sunday afternoon, I'd see all of them sitting around the pool, drinks in their hands, listening to Connie's portable radio. One time Harley said he saw them all behind the building, in the barbecue area. They were in their bathing suits then, too. Harley said the Swede had a chest like a bull. Harley said they were eating hot dogs and drinking whiskey. He said they were drunk.

It was Saturday, and it was after eleven at night. Harley was asleep in his chair. Pretty soon I'd have to get up and turn off the set. When I did that, I knew he'd wake up. 'Why'd you turn off? I was watching that show.' That's what he'd say. That's what he always said. Anyway, the TV was going, I had the curlers in, and there's a magazine on my lap. Now and then I'd look up. But I couldn't get settled on the show. They were all out there in the pool area – Spuds and Linda Cobb, Connie Nova and the long-hair, Holits and Betty. We have a rule against anyone being out there after ten. But this night they didn't care about rules. If Harley woke up, he'd go out and say something. I felt it was all right for them to have their fun, but it was time for it to stop. I kept getting up and going over to the window. All of them except Betty had on bathing suits. She was still in her uniform. But she had her shoes off, a glass in her hand, and she was drinking right along with the rest of them. I kept putting off having to turn off the set. Then one of them shouted something, and another one took it up and began to laugh. I looked and saw Holits finish off his drink. He put the glass down on the deck. Then he walked over to the cabana. He dragged up one of the tables and climbed onto that. Then — he seemed to do it without any effort at all — he lifted up onto the roof of the cabana. It's true, I thought; he's strong. The long-hair claps his hands, like he's all for this. The rest of them are hooting Holits on, too. I know I'm going to have to go out there and put a stop to it.

Harley's slumped in his chair. The TV's still going. I ease the door open, step out, and then push it shut behind me. Holits is up on the roof of the cabana. They're egging him on. They're saying, 'Go on, you can do it.' 'Don't belly-flop, now.' 'I double-dare you.' Things like that.

Then I hear Betty's voice. 'Holits, think what you're doing.' But Holits just stands there at the edge. He looks down at the water. He seems to be figuring how much of a run he's going to have to make to get out there. He backs up to the far side. He spits in his palm and rubs his hands together. Spuds calls out, 'That's it, boy! You'll do it now.'

I see him hit the deck. I hear him, too.

'Holits!' Betty cries.

They all hurry over to him. By the time I get there, he's sitting up. Rick is holding him by the shoulders and yelling into his face. 'Hollits! Hey, man!'

Holits has this gash on his forehead, and his eyes are glassy. Spuds and Rick help him into a chair. Somebody gives him a towel. But Holits holds the towel like he doesn't know what he's supposed to do with it. Somebody else hands him a drink. But Holits doesn't know what to do with that, either. People keep saying things to him. Holits brings the towel up to his face. Then he takes it away and looks at the blood. But he just looks at it. He can't seem to understand anything.

'Let me see him.' I get around in front of him. It's bad. 'Holits, are you all right?' But Holits just looks at me, and then his eyes drift off. 'I think he'd best go to the emergency room.' Betty looks at me when I say this and begins to shake her head. She looks back at Holits. She gives him another towel. I think she's sober. But the rest of them are drunk. Drunk is the best that can be said for them.

Spuds picks up what I said. 'Let's take him to the emergency room.'

Rick says, 'I'll go, too.'

'We'll all go,' Connie Nova says.

'We better stick together,' Linda Cobb says.

'Holits.' I say his name again.

'I can't go it,' Holits says.

'What'd he say?' Connie Nova asks me.

'He said he can't go it,' I tell her.

'Go what? What's he talking about?' Rick wants to know.

'Say again?' Spuds says. 'I didn't hear.'

'He says he can't go it. I don't think he knows what he's talking about. You'd best take him to the hospital,' I say. Then I remember Harley and the rules. 'You shouldn't have been out here. Any of you. We have rules. Now go on and take him to the hospital.'

'Let's take him to the hospital,' Spuds says like it's something he's just thought of. He might be farther gone than any of them. For one thing, he can't stand still. He weaves. And he keeps picking up his feet and putting them down again. The hair on his chest is snow white under the overhead pool lights.

'I'll get the car.' That's what the long-hair says. 'Connie, let me have the keys.'

'I can't go it,' Holits says. The towel has moved down to his chin. But the cut is on his forehead.

'Get him that terry-cloth robe. He can't go to the hospital that way,' Linda Cobb says that. 'Holits! Holits, it's us.' She waits and then she takes the glass of whiskey from Holits's fingers and drinks from it.

I can see people at some of the windows, looking down on the commotion. Lights are going on. 'Go to bed!' someone yells.

Finally, the long-hair brings Connie's Datsun from behind the building and drives it up close to the pool. The headlights are on bright. He races the engine.

'For Christ's sake, go to bed!' the same person yells. More people come to their windows. I expect to see Harley come out any minute, wearing his hat, steaming. Then I think, No, he'll sleep through it. Just forget Harley.

Spuds and Connie Nova get on either side of Holits. Holits can't walk straight. He's wobbly. Part of it's because he's drunk. But there's no question he's hurt himself. They get him into the car, and they all crowd inside, too. Betty is the last to get in. She has to sit on somebody's lap. Then they drive off. Whoever it was that has been yelling slams the window shut.

The whole next week Holits doesn't leave the place. And I think Betty must have quit her job, because I don't see her pass the window anymore. When I see the boys go by, I step outside and ask them, point-blank: 'How's your dad?'

'He hurt his head,' one of them says.

I wait in hopes they'll say some more. But they don't. They shrug and go on to school with their lunch sacks and binders. Later, I was sorry I hadn't asked after their step-mom.

When I see Holits outside, wearing a bandage and standing on his balcony, he doesn't even nod. He acts like I'm a stranger. It's like he doesn't know me or doesn't want to know me. Harley says he's getting the same treatment. He doesn't like it. 'What's with him?' Harley wants to know. 'Damn Swede. What happened to his head? Somebody belt him or what?' I don't tell Harley anything when he says that. I don't go into it at all.

Then that Sunday afternoon I see one of the boys carry out a box and put it in the station wagon. He goes back upstairs. But pretty soon he comes back down with another box, and he puts that in, too. It's then I know they're making ready to leave. But I don't say what I know to Harley. He'll know everything soon enough.

Next morning, Betty sends one of the boys down. He's got a note that says she's sorry but they have to move. She gives me her sister's address in Indio where she says we can send the deposit to. She points out they're leaving eight days before their rent is up. She hopes there might be something in the way of a refund there, even though they haven't given the thirty days' notice. She says, 'Thanks for everything. Thanks for doing my hair that time.' She signs the note, 'Sincerely, Betty Holits.'

'What's your name?' I ask the boy.

'Billy.'

'Billy, tell her I said I'm real sorry.'

'Harley reads what she's written, and he says it will be a cold day in hell before they see any money back from Fulton Terrace. He says he can't understand these people. 'People who sail through life like the world owes them a living.' He asks me where they're going. But I don't have any idea where they're going. Maybe they're going back to Minnesota. How do I know where they're going? But I don't think they're going back to Minnesota. I think they're going someplace else to try their luck.

Connie Nova and Spuds have their chairs in the usual places, one on either side of the pool. From time to time, they look over at the

Holits boys carrying things out to the station wagon. Then Holits himself comes out with some clothes over his arm. Connie Nova and Spuds holler and wave. Holits looks at them like he doesn't know them. But then he raises up his free hand. Just raises it, that's all. They wave. Then Holits is waving. He keeps waving at them, even after they've stopped. Betty comes downstairs and touches his arm. She doesn't wave. She won't even look at these people. She says something to Holits, and he goes on to the car. Connie Nova lies back in her chair and reaches over to turn up her portable radio. Spuds holds his sunglasses and watches Holits and Betty for a while. Then he fixes the glasses over his ears. He settles himself in the lounge chair and goes back to tanning his leathery old self.

Finally, they're all loaded and ready to move on. The boys are in the back, Holits behind the wheel, Betty in the seat right up next to him. It's just like it was when they drove in here.

'What are you looking at?' Harley says.

He's taking a break. He's in his chair, watching the TV. But he gets up and comes over to the window.

'Well, there they go. They don't know where they're going or what they're going to do. Crazy Swede.'

I watch them drive out of the lot and turn onto the road that's going to take them to the freeway. Then I look at Harley again. He's settling into his chair. He has his can of pop, and he's wearing his straw hat. He acts like nothing has happened or ever will happen.

'Harley?'

But, of course, he can't hear me. I go over and stand in front of his chair. He's surprised. He doesn't know what to make of it. He leans back, just sits there looking at me.

The phone starts ringing.

'Get that, will you?' he says.

I don't answer him. Why should I?

'Then let it ring,' he says.

I go find the mop, some rags, S.O.S. pads, and a bucket. The phone stops ringing. He's still sitting in his chair. But he's turned off the TV. I take the passkey, go outside and up the stairs to 17. I let myself in and walk through the living room to their kitchen — what used to be their kitchen.

The counters have been wiped down, the sink and cupboards are clean. It's not so bad. I leave the cleaning things on the stove and go take a look at the bathroom. Nothing there a little steel wool won't take care of. Then I open the door to the bedroom that looks out over the pool. The blinds are raised, the bed is stripped. The floor shines. 'Thanks,' I say out loud. Wherever she's going, I wish her luck. 'Good luck, Betty.' One of the bureau drawers is open and I go to close it. Back in a corner of the drawer I see the bridle he was carrying in when he first came. It must have been passed over in their hurry. But maybe it wasn't. Maybe the man left it on purpose.

'Bridle,' I say. I hold it up to the window and look at it in the light. It's not fancy, it's just an old dark leather bridle. I don't know much about them. But I know that one part of it fits in the mouth. That part's called the bit. It's made of steel. Reins go over the head and up to where they're held on the neck between the fingers. The rider pulls the reins this way and that, and the horse turns. It's simple. The bit's heavy and cold. If you had to wear this thing between your teeth, I guess you'd catch on in a hurry. When you felt it pull, you'd know it was time. You'd know you were going somewhere.

Cathedral

This blind man, an old friend of my wife's, he was on his way to spend the night. His wife had died. So he was visiting the dead wife's relatives in Connecticut: He called my wife from his in-laws'. Arrangements were made. He would come by train, a five-hour trip, and my wife would meet him at the station. She hadn't seen him since she worked for him one summer in Seattle ten years ago. But she and the blind man had kept in touch. They made tapes and mailed them back and forth. I wasn't enthusiastic about his visit. He was no one I knew. And his being blind bothered me. My idea of blindness came from the movies. In the movies, the blind moved slowly and never laughed. Sometimes they were led by seeing-eye dogs. A blind man in my house was not something I looked forward to.

That summer in Seattle she had needed a job. She didn't have any money. The man she was going to marry at the end of the summer was in officers' training school. He didn't have any money, either. But she was in love with the guy, and he was in love with her, etc. She'd seen something in the paper: HELP WANTED — *Reading to Blind Man*, and a telephone number. She phoned and went over, was hired on the spot. She'd worked with this blind man all summer. She read stuff to him, case studies, reports, that sort of thing. She helped him organize his little office in the county social-service department. They'd become good friends, my wife and the blind man. How do I know these things? She told me. And she told me something else. On her last day in the office, the blind man asked if he could touch her face. She agreed to this. She told me he touched his fingers to every part of her face, her nose — even her neck! She never forgot it. She even tried to write a poem about it. She was always trying to write a poem. She wrote a poem or two every year, usually after something really important had happened to her.

When we first started going out together, she showed me the poem. In the poem, she recalled his fingers and the way they had moved around over her face. In the poem, she talked about what she had felt at the time, about what went through her mind when the blind man touched her nose and lips. I can remember I didn't think much of the poem. Of course, I didn't tell her that. Maybe I just don't understand poetry. I admit it's not the first thing I reach for when I pick up something to read.

Anyway, this man who'd first enjoyed her favors, the officer-to-be, he'd been her childhood sweetheart. So okay. I'm saying that at the end of the summer she let the blind man run his hands over her face, said goodbye to him, married her childhood etc., who was now a commissioned officer, and she moved away from Seattle. But they'd kept in touch, she and the blind man. She made the first contact after a year or so. She called him up one night from an Air Force base in Alabama. She wanted to talk. They talked. He asked her to send him a tape and tell him about her life. She did this. She sent the tape. On the tape, she told the blind man about her husband and about their life together in the military. She told the blind man she loved her husband but she didn't like it where they lived and she didn't like it that he was a part of the military-industrial thing. She told the blind man she'd written a poem and he was in it. She told him that she was writing a poem about what it was like to be an Air Force officer's wife. The poem wasn't finished yet. She was still writing it. The blind man made a tape. He sent her the tape. She made a tape. This went on for years. My wife's officer was posted to one base and then another. She sent tapes from Moody AFB, McGuire, McConnell, and finally Travis, near Sacramento, where one night she got to feeling lonely and cut off from people she kept losing in that moving-around life. She got to feeling she couldn't go it another step. She went in and swallowed all the pills and capsules in the medicine chest and washed them down with a bottle of gin. Then she got into a hot bath and passed out.

But instead of dying, she got sick. She threw up. Her officer – why should he have a name? he was the childhood sweetheart, and what more does he want? – came home from somewhere, found her, and called the ambulance. In time, she put it all on a tape and sent the tape to the blind man. Over the years, she put all kinds of stuff on tapes and sent the tapes off lickety-split. Next to writing a poem every year, I think it was her chief means of recreation. On one tape, she told the blind man she'd decided to live away from her officer for a time. On another tape, she told him about her divorce. She and I began going out, and of course she told her blind man about it. She told him everything, or so it seemed to me. Once she asked me if I'd like to hear the latest tape from the blind man. This was a year ago. I was on the tape, she said. So I said okay, I'd listen to it. I got us drinks and we settled down in the living room. We made ready to listen. First she inserted the tape into the player and adjusted a couple of dials. Then she pushed a lever. The tape squeaked and someone began to talk in this loud voice. She lowered the volume. After a few minutes of harmless chitchat, I heard my own name in the mouth of this stranger, this blind man I didn't even know! And then this: 'From all you've said about him, I can only conclude –' But we were interrupted, a knock at the door, something, and we didn't ever get back to the tape. Maybe it was just as well. I'd heard all I wanted to.

Now this same blind man was coming to sleep in my house.

'Maybe I could take him bowling,' I said to my wife. She was at the draining board doing scalloped potatoes. She put down the knife she was using and turned around.

'If you love me,' she said, 'you can do this for me. If you don't love me, okay. But if you had a friend, any friend, and the friend came to visit, I'd make him feel comfortable.' She wiped her hands with the dish towel.

'I don't have any blind friends,' I said.

'You don't have *any* friends,' she said. 'Period. Besides,' she said, 'goddamn it, his wife's just died! Don't you understand that? The man's lost his wife!'

I didn't answer. She'd told me a little about the blind man's wife. Her name was Beulah. Beulah! That's a name for a colored woman.

'Was his wife a Negro?' I asked.

'Are you crazy?' my wife said. 'Have you just flipped or something?' She picked up a potato. I saw it hit the floor, then roll under the stove. 'What's wrong with you?' she said. 'Are you drunk?'

'I'm just asking,' I said.

Right then my wife filled me in with more detail than I cared to know. I made a drink and sat at the kitchen table to listen. Pieces of the story began to fall into place.

Beulah had gone to work for the blind man the summer after my wife had stopped working for him. Pretty soon Beulah and the blind man had themselves a church wedding. It was a little wedding – who'd want to go to such a wedding in the first place? – just the two of them, plus the minister and the minister's wife. But it was a church wedding just the same. It was what Beulah had wanted, he'd said. But even then Beulah must have been carrying the cancer in her glands. After they had been inseparable for eight years – my wife's word, *inseparable* – Beulah's health went into a rapid decline. She died in a Seattle hospital room, the blind man sitting beside the bed and holding on to her hand. They'd married, lived and worked together, slept together – had sex, sure – and then the blind man had to bury her. All this without his having ever seen what the goddamned woman looked like. It was beyond my understanding. Hearing this, I felt sorry for the blind man for a little bit. And then I found myself thinking what a pitiful life this woman must have led. Imagine a woman who could never see herself as she was seen in the eyes of her loved one. A woman who could go on day after day and never receive the smallest compliment from her beloved. A woman whose husband could never read the expression on her face, be it misery or something better. Someone who could wear makeup or not – what difference to him? She could, if she wanted, wear green eye-shadow around one eye, a straight pin in her nostril, yellow slacks and purple shoes, no matter. And then to slip off into death, the blind man's hand on her hand, his blind eyes streaming tears – I'm imagining now – her last thought maybe this: that he never even knew what she looked like, and she on an express to the grave. Robert was left with a small insurance policy and half of a twenty-peso Mexican coin. The other half of the coin went into the box with her. Pathetic.

So when the time rolled around, my wife went to the depot to pick him up. With nothing to do but wait – sure, I blamed him for that – I was having a drink and watching the TV when I heard the car pull into the drive. I got up from the sofa with my drink and went to the window to have a look.

I saw my wife laughing as she parked the car. I saw her get out of the car and shut the door. She was still wearing a smile. Just amazing. She went around to the other side of the car to where the blind man was already starting to get out. This blind man, feature this, he was wearing a full beard! A beard on a blind man! Too much, I say. The blind man reached into the back seat and dragged out a suitcase. My wife took his arm, shut the car door, and, talking all the way, moved him down the drive and then up the steps to the front porch. I turned off the TV. I finished my drink, rinsed the glass, dried my hands. Then I went to the door.

My wife said, 'I want you to meet Robert. Robert, this is my husband. I've told you all about him.' She was beaming. She had this blind man by his coat sleeve.

The blind man let go of his suitcase and up came his hand.

I took it. He squeezed hard, held my hand, and then he let it go.

'I feel like we've already met,' he boomed.

'Likewise,' I said. I didn't know what else to say. Then I said, 'Welcome, I've heard a lot about you.' We began to move then, a little group, from the porch into the living room, my wife guiding him by the arm. The blind man was carrying his suitcase in his other hand. My wife said things like, 'To your left here, Robert. That's right. Now watch it, there's a chair. That's it. Sit down right here. This is the sofa. We just bought this sofa two weeks ago.'

I started to say something about the old sofa. I'd liked that old sofa. But I didn't say anything. Then I wanted to say something else, small-talk, about the scenic ride along the Hudson. How going *to* New York, you should sit on the right-hand side of the train, and coming *from* New York, the left-hand side.

'Did you have a good train ride?' I said. 'Which side of the train did you sit on, by the way?'

'What a question, which side!' my wife said. 'What's it matter which side?' she said.

'I just asked,' I said.

'Right side,' the blind man said. 'I hadn't been on a train in nearly forty years. Not since I was a kid. With my folks. That's been a long time. I'd nearly forgotten the sensation. I have winter in my beard now,' he said. 'So I've been told, anyway. Do I look distinguished, my dear?' the blind man said to my wife.

'You look distinguished, Robert,' she said. 'Robert,' she said. 'Robert, it's just so good to see you.'

My wife finally took her eyes off the blind man and looked at me. I had the feeling she didn't like what she saw. I shrugged.

I've never met, or personally known, anyone who was blind. This blind man was late forties, a heavy-set, balding man with stooped shoulders, as if he carried a great weight there. He wore brown slacks, brown shoes, a light-brown shirt, a tie, a sports coat. Spiffy. He also had this full beard. But he didn't use a cane and he didn't wear dark glasses. I'd always thought dark glasses were a must for the blind. Fact was, I wished he had a pair. At first glance, his eyes looked like anyone else's eyes. But if you looked close, there was something different about them. Too much white in the iris, for one thing, and the pupils seemed to move around in the sockets without his knowing it or being able to stop it. Creepy. As I stared at his face, I saw the left pupil turn in toward his nose while the other made an effort to keep in one place. But it was only an effort, for that eye was on the roam without his knowing it or wanting it to be.

I said, 'Let me get you a drink. What's your pleasure? We have a little of everything. It's one of our pastimes.'

'Bub, I'm a Scotch man myself,' he said fast enough in this big voice.

'Right,' I said. Bub! 'Sure you are. I knew it.'

He let his fingers touch his suitcase, which was sitting alongside the sofa. He was taking his bearings. I didn't blame him for that.

'I'll move that up to your room,' my wife said.

'No, that's fine,' the blind man said loudly. 'It can go up when I go up.'

'A little water with the Scotch?' I said.

'Very little,' he said.

'I knew it,' I said.

He said, 'Just a tad. The Irish actor, Barry Fitzgerald? I'm like that fellow. When I drink water, Fitzgerald said, I drink water. When I drink whiskey, I drink whiskey.' My wife laughed. The blind man brought his hand up under his beard. He lifted his beard slowly and let it drop.

I did the drinks, three big glasses of Scotch with a splash of water in each. Then we made ourselves comfortable and talked about Robert's travels. First the long flight from the West Coast to Connecticut, we covered that. Then from Connecticut up here by train. We had another drink concerning that leg of the trip.

I remembered having read somewhere that the blind didn't smoke because, as speculation had it, they couldn't see the smoke they exhaled. I thought I knew that much and that much only about blind people. But this blind man smoked his cigarette down to the nubbin and then lit another one. This blind man filled his ashtray and my wife emptied it.

When we sat down at the table for dinner, we had another drink. My wife heaped Robert's plate with cube steak, scalloped potatoes, green beans. I buttered him up two slices of bread. I said, 'Here's bread and butter for you.' I swallowed some of my drink. 'Now let us pray,' I said, and the blind man lowered his head. My wife looked at me, her mouth agape. 'Pray the phone won't ring and the food doesn't get cold,' I said.

We dug in. We ate everything there was to eat on the table. We ate like there was no tomorrow. We didn't talk. We ate. We scarfed. We grazed that table. We were into serious eating. The blind man had right away located his foods, he knew just where everything was on his plate. I watched with admiration as he used his knife and fork on the meat. He'd cut two pieces of meat, fork the meat into his mouth, and then go all out for the scalloped potatoes, the beans next, and then he'd tear off a hunk of buttered bread and eat that. He'd follow this up with a big drink of milk. It didn't seem to bother him to use his fingers once in a while, either.

We finished everything, including half a strawberry pie. For a few moments, we sat as if stunned. Sweat beaded on our faces. Finally, we got up from the table and left the dirty plates. We didn't look back. We took ourselves into the living room and sank into our places again. Robert and my wife sat on the sofa. I took the big chair. We had us two or three more drinks while they talked about the major things that had come to pass for them in the past ten years. For the most part, I just listened. Now and then I joined in. I didn't want him to think I'd left the room, and I didn't want her to think I was feeling left out. They talked of things that had happened to them — to them! — these past ten years. I waited in vain to hear my name on my wife's sweet lips: 'And then my dear husband came into my life' — something like that. But I heard nothing of the sort. More talk of Robert. Robert had done a little of everything, it seemed, a regular blind jack-of-all-trades. But most recently he and his wife had had an Amway distributorship, from which, I gathered, they'd earned their living, such as it was. The blind man was also a ham radio operator. He talked in his loud voice about conversations he'd had with fellow operators in Guam, in the Philippines, in Alaska, and even in Tahiti. He said he'd have a lot of friends there if he ever wanted to go visit those places. From time to time, he'd turn his blind face toward me, put his hand under his beard, ask me something. How long had I been in my present position? (Three years.) Did I like my work? (I didn't.) Was I going to stay with it? (What were the options?) Finally, when I thought he was beginning to run down, I got up and turned on the TV.

My wife looked at me with irritation. She was heading toward a boil. Then she looked at the blind man and said, 'Robert, do you have a TV?'

The blind man said, 'My dear, I have two TVs. I have a color set and a black-and-white thing, an old relic. It's funny, but if I turn the TV on, and I'm always turning it on, I turn on the color set. It's funny, don't you think?'

I didn't know what to say to that. I had absolutely nothing to say to that. No opinion. So I watched the news program and tried to listen to what the announcer was saying.

'This is a color TV,' the blind man said. 'Don't ask me how, but I can tell.'

'We traded up a while ago,' I said.

The blind man had another taste of his drink. He lifted his beard, sniffed it, and let it fall. He leaned forward on the sofa. He positioned his ashtray on the coffee table, then put the lighter to his cigarette. He leaned back on the sofa and crossed his legs at the ankles.

My wife covered her mouth, and then she yawned. She stretched. She said, 'I think I'll go upstairs and put on my robe. I think I'll change into something else. Robert, you make yourself comfortable,' she said.

'I'm comfortable,' the blind man said.

'I want you to feel comfortable in this house,' she said.

'I am comfortable,' the blind man said.

After she'd left the room, he and I listened to the weather report and then to the sports roundup. By that time, she'd been gone so long I didn't know if she was going to come back. I thought she might have gone to bed. I wished she'd come back downstairs. I didn't want to be left alone with a blind man. I asked him if he wanted another drink, and he said sure. Then I asked if he wanted to smoke some dope with me. I said I'd just rolled a number. I hadn't, but I planned to do so in about two shakes.

'I'll try some with you,' he said.

'Damn right,' I said. 'That's the stuff.'

I got our drinks and sat down on the sofa with him. Then I rolled us two fat numbers. I lit one and passed it. I brought it to his fingers. He took it and inhaled.

'Hold it as long as you can,' I said. I could tell he didn't know the first thing.

My wife came back downstairs wearing her pink robe and her pink slippers.

'What do I smell?' she said.

'We thought we'd have us some cannabis,' I said.

My wife gave me a savage look. Then she looked at the blind man and said, 'Robert, I didn't know you smoked.'

He said, 'I do now, my dear. There's a first time for everything. But

I don't feel anything yet.'

'This stuff is pretty mellow,' I said. 'This stuff is mild. It's dope you can reason with,' I said. 'It doesn't mess you up.'

'Not much it doesn't, bub,' he said, and laughed.

My wife sat on the sofa between the blind man and me. I passed her the number. She took it and toked and then passed it back to me. 'Which way is this going?' she said. Then she said, 'I shouldn't be smoking this. I can hardly keep my eyes open as it is. That dinner did me in. I shouldn't have eaten so much.'

'It was the strawberry pie,' the blind man said. 'That's what did it,' he said, and he laughed his big laugh. Then he shook his head.

'There's more strawberry pie,' I said.

'Do you want some more, Robert?' my wife said.

'Maybe in a little while,' he said.

We gave our attention to the TV. My wife yawned again. She said, 'Your bed is made up when you feel like going to bed, Robert. I know you must have had a long day. When you're ready to go to bed, say so.' She pulled his arm. 'Robert?'

He came to and said, 'I've had a real nice time. This beats tapes, doesn't it?'

I said, 'Coming at you,' and I put the number between his fingers. He inhaled, held the smoke, and then let it go. It was like he'd been doing it since he was nine years old.

'Thanks, bub,' he said. 'But I think this is all for me. I think I'm beginning to feel it,' he said. He held the burning roach out for my wife.

'Same here,' she said. 'Ditto. Me, too.' She took the roach and passed it to me. 'I may just sit here for a while between you two guys with my eyes closed. But don't let me bother you, okay? Either one of you. If it bothers you, say so. Otherwise, I may just sit here with my eyes closed until you're ready to go to bed,' she said. 'Your bed's made up, Robert, when you're ready. It's right next to our room at the top of the stairs. We'll show you up when you're ready. You wake me up now, you guys, if I fall asleep.' She said that and then she closed her eyes and went to sleep.

The news program ended. I got up and changed the channel. I sat back down on the sofa. I wished my wife hadn't pooped out. Her head lay across the back of the sofa, her mouth open. She'd turned so that her robe had slipped away from her legs, exposing a juicy thigh. I reached to draw her robe back over her, and it was then that I glanced at the blind man. What the hell! I flipped the robe open again.

'You say when you want some strawberry pie,' I said.

'I will,' he said.

I said, 'Are you tired? Do you want me to take you up to your bed? Are you ready to hit the hay?'

'Not yet,' he said. 'No, I'll stay up with you, bub. If that's all right. I'll stay up until you're ready to turn in. We haven't had a chance to talk. Know what I mean? I feel like me and her monopolized the evening.' He lifted his beard and he let it fall. He picked up his cigarettes and his lighter.

'That's all right,' I said. Then I said, 'I'm glad for the company.'

And I guess I was. Every night I smoked dope and stayed up as long as I could before I fell asleep. My wife and I hardly ever went to bed at the same time. When I did go to sleep, I had these dreams. Sometimes I'd wake up from one of them, my heart going crazy.

Something about the church and the Middle Ages was on the TV. Not your run-of-the-mill TV fare. I wanted to watch something else. I turned to the other channels. But there was nothing on them, either. So I turned back to the first channel and apologized.

'Bub, it's all right,' the blind man said. 'It's fine with me. Whatever you want to watch is okay. I'm always learning something. Learning never ends. It won't hurt me to learn something tonight. I got ears,' he said.

We didn't say anything for a time. He was leaning forward with his head turned at me, his right ear aimed in the direction of the set. Very disconcerting. Now and then his eyelids drooped and then they snapped open again. Now and then he put his fingers into his beard and tugged, like he was thinking about something he was hearing on the television.

On the screen, a group of men wearing cowls was being set upon and tormented by men dressed in skeleton costumes and men dressed as devils. The men dressed as devils wore devil masks, horns, and long tails. This pageant was part of a procession. The Englishman who was narrating the thing said it took place in Spain once a year. I tried to explain to the blind man what was happening.

'Skeletons,' he said. 'I know about skeletons,' he said, and he nodded.

The TV showed this one cathedral. Then there was a long, slow look at another one. Finally, the picture switched to the famous one in

Paris, with its flying buttresses and its spires reaching up to the clouds. The camera pulled away to show the whole of the cathedral rising above the skyline.

There were times when the Englishman who was telling the thing would shut up, would simply let the camera move around over the cathedrals. Or else the camera would tour the countryside, men in fields walking behind oxen. I waited as long as I could. Then I felt I had to say something. I said, 'They're showing the outside of this cathedral now. Gargoyles. Little statues carved to look like monsters. Now I guess they're in Italy. Yeah, they're in Italy. There's paintings on the walls of this one church.'

'Are those fresco paintings, bub?' he asked, and he sipped from his drink.

I reached for my glass. But it was empty. I tried to remember what I could remember. 'You're asking me are those frescoes?' I said. 'That's a good question. I don't know.'

The camera moved to a cathedral outside Lisbon. The differences in the Portuguese cathedral compared with the French and Italian were not that great. But they were there. Mostly the interior stuff. Then something occurred to me, and I said, 'Something has occurred to me. Do you have any idea what a cathedral is? What they look like, that is? Do you follow me? If somebody says cathedral to you, do you have any notion what they're talking about? Do you know the difference between that and a Baptist church, say?'

He let the smoke dribble from his mouth. 'I know they took hundreds of workers fifty or a hundred years to build,' he said. 'I just heard the man say that, of course. I know generations of the same families worked on a cathedral. I heard him say that, too. The men who began their life's work on them, they never lived to see the completion of their work. In that wise, bub, they're no different from the rest of us, right?' He laughed. Then his eyelids drooped again. His head nodded. He seemed to be snoozing. Maybe he was imagining himself in Portugal. The TV was showing another cathedral now. This one was in Germany. The Englishman's voice droned on. 'Cathedrals,' the blind man said. He sat up and rolled his head back and forth. 'If you want the truth, bub, that's about all I know. What I just said. What I heard him say. But maybe you could describe one to me? I wish you'd do it. I'd like that. If you want to know, I really don't have a good idea.'

I stared hard at the shot of the cathedral on the TV. How could I even begin to describe it? But say my life depended on it. Say my life was being threatened by an insane guy who said I had to do it or else.

I stared some more at the cathedral before the picture flipped off into the countryside. There was no use. I turned to the blind man and said, 'To begin with, they're very tall.' I was looking around the room for clues. 'They reach way up. Up and up. Toward the sky. They're so big, some of them, they have to have these supports. To help hold them up, so to speak. These supports are called buttresses. They remind me of viaducts, for some reason. But maybe you don't know viaducts, either? Sometimes the cathedrals have devils and such carved into the front. Sometimes lords and ladies. Don't ask me why this is,' I said.

He was nodding. The whole upper part of his body seemed to be moving back and forth.

'I'm not doing so good, am I?' I said.

He stopped nodding and leaned forward on the edge of the sofa. As he listened to me, he was running his fingers through his beard. I wasn't getting through to him, I could see that. But he waited for me to go on just the same. He nodded, like he was trying to encourage me. I tried to think what else to say. 'They're really big,' I said. 'They're massive. They're built of stone. Marble, too, sometimes. In those olden days, when they built cathedrals, men wanted to be close to God. In those olden days, God was an important part of everyone's life. You could tell this from their cathedral-building. I'm sorry,' I said, 'but it looks like that's the best I can do for you. I'm just no good at it.'

'That's all right, bub,' the blind man said. 'Hey, listen. I hope you don't mind my asking you. Can I ask you something? Let me ask you a simple question, yes or no. I'm just curious and there's no offense. You're my host. But let me ask if you are in any way religious? You don't mind my asking?'

I shook my head. He couldn't see that, though. A wink is the same as a nod to a blind man. 'I guess I don't believe in it. In anything. Sometimes it's hard. You know what I'm saying?'

'Sure, I do,' he said.

'Right,' I said.

The Englishman was still holding forth. My wife sighed in her sleep. She drew a long breath and went on with her sleeping.

'You'll have to forgive me,' I said. 'But I can't tell you what a cathedral looks like. It just isn't in me to do it. I can't do any more than I've done.'

The blind man sat very still, his head down, as he listened to me.

I said, 'The truth is, cathedrals don't mean anything special to me. Nothing. Cathedrals. They're something to look at on late-night TV. That's all they are.'

It was then that the blind man cleared his throat. He brought something up. He took a handkerchief from his back pocket. Then he said, 'I get it, bub. It's okay. It happens. Don't worry about it,' he said. 'Hey, listen to me. Will you do me a favor? I got an idea. Why don't you find us some heavy paper? And a pen. We'll do something. We'll draw one together. Get us a pen and some heavy paper. Go on, bub, get the stuff,' he said.

So I went upstairs. My legs felt like they didn't have any strength in them. They felt like they did after I'd done some running. In my wife's room, I looked around. I found some ballpoints in a little basket on her table. And then I tried to think where to look for the kind of paper he was talking about.

Downstairs, in the kitchen, I found a shopping bag with onion skins in the bottom of the bag. I emptied the bag and shook it. I brought it into the living room and sat down with it near his legs. I moved some things, smoothed the wrinkles from the bag, spread it out on the coffee table.

The blind man got down from the sofa and sat next to me on the carpet.

He ran his fingers over the paper. He went up and down the sides of the paper. The edges, even the edges. He fingered the corners.

'All right,' he said. 'All right, let's do her.'

He found my hand, the hand with the pen. He closed his hand over my hand. 'Go ahead, bub, draw,' he said. 'Draw. You'll see. I'll follow along with you. It'll be okay. Just begin now like I'm telling you. You'll see. Draw,' the blind man said.

So I began. First I drew a box that looked like a house. It could have been the house I lived in. Then I put a roof on it. At either end of the roof, I drew spires. Crazy.

'Swell,' he said. 'Terrific. You're doing fine,' he said. 'Never thought anything like this could happen in your lifetime, did you, bub? Well, it's a strange life, we all know that. Go on now. Keep it up.'

I put in windows with arches. I drew flying buttresses. I hung great doors. I couldn't stop. The TV station went off the air. I put down the pen and closed and opened my fingers. The blind man felt around over the paper. He moved the tips of his fingers over the paper, all over what I had drawn, and he nodded.

'Doing fine,' the blind man said.

I took up the pen again, and he found my hand. I kept at it. I'm no artist. But I kept drawing just the same.

My wife opened up her eyes and gazed at us. She sat up on the sofa, her robe hanging open. She said, 'What are you doing? Tell me, I want to know.'

I didn't answer her.

The blind man said, 'We're drawing a cathedral. Me and him are working on it. Press hard,' he said to me. 'That's right. That's good,' he said. 'Sure. You got it, bub. I can tell. You didn't think you could. But you can, can't you? You're cooking with gas now. You know what I'm saying? We're going to really have us something here in a minute. How's the old arm?' he said. 'Put some people in there now. What's a cathedral without people?'

My wife said, 'What's going on? Robert, what are you doing? What's going on?'

'It's all right,' he said to her. 'Close your eyes now,' the blind man said to me.

I did it. I closed them just like he said.

'Are they closed?' he said. 'Don't fudge.'

'They're closed,' I said.

'Keep them that way,' he said. He said, 'Don't stop now. Draw.'

So we kept on with it. His fingers rode my fingers as my hand went over the paper. It was like nothing else in my life up to now.

Then he said, 'I think that's it. I think you got it,' he said. 'Take a look. What do you think?'

But I had my eyes closed. I thought I'd keep them that way for a little longer. I thought it was something I ought to do.

'Well?' he said. 'Are you looking?'

My eyes were still closed. I was in my house. I knew that. But I didn't feel like I was inside anything.

'It's really something,' I said.